the strange side of the tracks

“So we beat on, boats against the current,
borne back ceaselessly into the past.”
F. Scott Fitzgerald, *The Great Gatsby*

“I’m a victim of coicumstance!”
Curly Howard, *The Three Stooges*

the strange side of the tracks

a novel

George Avant

Parkhurst Brothers Publishers
MARION, MICHIGAN

www.parkhurstbrothers.com

Parkhurst Brothers books are distributed to the trade through the Chicago Distribution Center, and may be ordered through Ingram Book Company, Baker & Taylor, Follett Library Resources and other book industry wholesalers. To order from Chicago Distribution Center, phone 1-800-621-2736 or send a fax to 800-621-8476. Copies of this and other Parkhurst Brothers Publishers titles are available to organizations and corporations for purchase in quantity by contacting Special Sales Department at our home office location, listed on our web site. Manuscript submission guidelines for this publishing company are available at our web site.

Printed in the United States of America

First Edition, 2015

2015 2016 2017 2018 12 11 10 9 8 7 6 5 4 3 2 1

Library of Congress Cataloging-in-Publication Data

Avant, George, 1950 - 2012
The strange side of the tracks : a novel / George Avant. — 1st ed.
p. cm.
ISBN 978-1-935166-95-5 (tpb : alk. paper) — ISBN 978-1-935166-96-2 (e-book)
1. Single mothers—Fiction. 2. Abusive parents—Fiction. 3. City and town life—Fiction. I. Title.
PS3601.V36S77 2013
813'.6—dc23
2015034352

ISBN: Trade Paperback 978-1-935166-95-5 [10 digit: 1-935166-95-6]
ISBN: e-book 978-1-935166-96-2 [10-digit: 1-935166-96-4]

This book is printed on archival-quality paper that meets requirements of the American National Standard for Information Sciences, Permanence of Paper, Printed Library Materials, ANSI Z39.48-1984.

Cover Design:	Matthew Avant
Page design:	Linda D. Parkhurst, Ph.D.
Acquired for Parkhurst Brothers Inc., Publishers by:	Ted Parkhurst
Editor:	Hayes Taylor
Proofreader:	Bill and Barbara Paddack

062015

Contents

GEORGE LARRY AVANT

December 22, 1950 - November 8, 2012

George Avant passed away just months after signing the publication contract for this, his first and only novel. George traveled all over the country with his family as a radio broadcaster for thirty years, often serving in gospel ministry. For many years, he was half of The Light Brothers, a comedy duo. A writer, humorist, painter, and avid reader, Avant returned late in life to rural Arkansas, to a small town rich with history and personal memories, where he was inspired to write this novel. He left behind a daughter and two sons, all of who helped George bring his work to completion, and assisted editors in preparing the text for publication.

Chapter One

Son of the Most Popular Grocery Checker

I slipped a hollow-point bullet into my Remington single shot, .22 rifle and took a deep breath.

My mother had just left for her ten-hour shift as the most popular cashier at Bailey's grocery store. That gave me plenty of time to carry out the plan I had spent my sleepless night putting together, but I had to act quickly before I lost my resolve.

I tried to be stealthy, but the warped, old floor shrieked with every tiptoed step. I made a mental note of the calendar as I crept through the kitchen. It was June 2, 1960—the day my life would change forever. Still six months away from my fifteenth birthday, I slowly made my way into the tiny back bedroom where my father—Goliath in boxer shorts—lay snoring off his drunk. A little oscillating fan strained valiantly to cool the room but only stirred the warm, gumbo-thick air reeking of booze and cigarettes, stale perfume, and those little cakes they put in urinals. It was my father's smell.

A trembling in the pit of my stomach was working its way out through my limbs. I fought to control my emotions. I had to focus on my anger and the threat that he represented to my mother in order to accomplish my mission. I picked up his rumpled pack of Lucky Strikes and stuck them in my pocket. He wouldn't need them. Plus, I had wanted to take up the habit ever since I saw a picture of Joe DiMaggio smoking in the dugout. And here I was about to smoke my old man.

I had begged my mother to leave him. There was no reasoning with her or arguing. I resorted to weeping and wailing and would have gone into gnashing of teeth, whatever that means, except it sounded painful. Yet nothing had moved her. Nevertheless, after what I saw last night, the tiny little bit of peace I had left in my life was blown to hell. It was now up to me.

I tried to put the fact that he was my *father* out of my mind, which didn't take much effort since he wasn't much of a *father*. He had never shown me any real love or affection. It appeared that I was nothing more to him than the result of his seed spilled in a moment of passion, the wages of his sin. I had become accustomed to his drunken rages at three o'clock in the morning when he would stagger in, break our dime-store dishes and jelly-jar drinking glasses, and punch holes in the walls. My mother would yell at him, and he would yell back, for an hour or two. A routine that had been a part of my life since I could remember was about to be forever changed.

My mother had launched her typical verbal attack as soon as he came in, which was usual. But he wasn't in the mood for a fight, which was highly *unusual*. From my cramped, little bedroom, I could see his broad back as he towered over her, swaying like a skyscraper in an earthquake. He was as drunk as I had ever seen him, and I thought for sure that he would just topple over, which occurred often enough that we had learned to live around his prone body. He was too big to pick up, so we just left him where he fell. Watching roaches scurry all over him was one of the few amusements of my boyhood.

This time, however, instead of passing out, he raised a huge right arm and screamed that he would knock her head off. I couldn't breathe as I waited for the blow to fall. I had never seen him threaten her like that before, and it scared the stuffing out of me. He finally dropped his arm, shoved her hard against the sink, and squeezed through the bedroom door. I could see the pain in her face as she followed and continued to fire salvos of acrimony long after he passed out. She eventually ran out of invectives and went to sleep on the sad, old sofa that had supported thousands of butts before ours.

She would never admit it, but I knew she was in serious *danger*. He may not have hit her *last night*, but his drinking was getting worse. Her daily life was becoming a never-ending gamble with his anger.

I had to remove that danger. I felt the weight of the gun in my hands and realized that the only things I had ever shot were bottles and snakes. I tried to convince myself that he was just another serpent.

The sweat was shrink-wrapping the Mickey Mouse Club T-shirt to my body, and I wondered if Annette could love a murderer. I was in love with Annette Funicello, the dark-eyed Mouseketeer on the show. Only baseball could keep me from being in front of our little black and white television every afternoon at four o'clock to drool and dream. I was aware that millions of other fools were goofy about her too, but I didn't care. I knew that if I could somehow get to Disneyland I could win her heart. I lived for the days when she introduced the cartoon or appeared in a *Spin and Marty* episode.

But this wasn't television. This was much too real. I had just thumbed the safety off and moved the tip of the barrel to within an inch or two of his left temple when a horrible thought struck me.

What if it didn't kill him?

Such a small caliber weapon may only serve to piss him off. The puny .22 slug could flatten against his massive skull like a penny run over by a train. On the other hand, it might just wound and enrage him. I had a vision of all six-foot-six, two hundred and eighty pounds of him leaping out of the bed and force-feeding me the little rifle without condiments or even an RC Cola to wash it down.

It was during that moment of "oh crap" hesitation that I was grabbed by the collar, snatched backward, and dragged like a sack of crawfish out into the pitiful little front yard where the Louisiana sun was scorching the last eight remaining blades of grass. Once released, I turned and looked into the freckle-sprinkled face of my mother. Her brown eyes were brimming with wet panic. She grabbed the rifle from my grasp, ejected the shell, and flung it about thirty feet. I braced myself for the conniption fit that was about to hit the oscillating fan.

"Have you lost your mind, Lonnie?" she whisper-screamed through clenched teeth. "Have you gone stark ravin' insane? Are you crazy? Are you walkin' in your sleep? Did a zombie eat your brain? Lord have mercy on us all! I cannot believe this, son! What in the world were you thinkin'?"

I could see right off that she found the situation a tad unsettling.

"Calm down, mama. Everything will be all right."

"All right? You try to shoot your daddy, that's all right?"

"Well, to be honest with you, I was thinking that I could arrange it to look like he shot himself."

"Arrange it to look like he … he …," she sputtered, dug around in her anger for words, and then paused as if giving the suicide scenario some thought.

"What are you doing home anyway?" I interjected as if I was the one who should be upset. "I thought you went to work."

"I did. I got halfway to the store and realized that I forgot my purse! *I forgot my purse!* I have *never* in my *life* forgot my purse, and it made me feel real *strange*, like somethin' was bad wrong. I tell you, Lonnie, I couldn't get back here fast enough. Now, I know it was the Good Lord Himself who made me forget it, so I would keep you from *ruinin'* your life! Thank you, Lord, thank you!"

I hadn't figured the God factor into my plan, but she seemed mighty pleased that He had used her as an instrument to thwart my ill-conceived solution to our domestic drama.

"Did you stop and think for one minute about what they would do to you? What they do to boys who kill their daddies? Did you, Lonnie? I'll tell you what they would do! They would come and take you away from me and throw you in jail with the scum of the earth!"

"I'm only fourteen, mama. They couldn't try me as an adult. The worse they could do is put me into a juvenile detention center."

"All right, smartass, so they would come and take you away from me and throw you in with the scum of the earth *in-trainin'*. Either way … it would just kill me."

"I wasn't trying to hurt you, mama, you know that. I just can't take it anymore. I can't take *him* anymore. I'm fed up, mama."

"Do you think killin' your father will make things better? That life will just go right along, la-dee-dah, and we'll be happy? That all our problems would just *disappear*?"

"That's what I was hoping for."

"Well, that's just stupid. Even if they didn't throw you in prison, killin' your own father … well, it just ain't right. *And*, it's somethin' you'd have to live with for the rest of your life. I just can't believe you would do such an ignorant thing!"

"I didn't do anything!"

"Only because I got here in time to stop you! Lord knows what would have happened if I hadn't been here."

"Hey, I know what! Let's find the humor in all this!" This was an attempt on my part to diffuse the tension by referring to a game she and I called "Man, that's funny" where we tried to find kernels of comedy embedded in the turds of life. My mother had a great sense of humor.

"This ain't funny, Lonnie. I just can't believe this. I would never in my wildest dreams ever thought that my only baby son would just … up and act a dang fool. Worse than a fool, more like a complete moron. A fool would have better sense. Just get up one mornin', have a bowl of corn flakes, and shoot your own father. Just throw your life away before your testicles have even dropped. Lord have mercy on us all."

She was giving me that look of pity she usually reserved for the elderly, epileptic lady who once had a grand mal seizure at the cash register. I wanted to inform her that my testicles had indeed dropped but was too embarrassed.

"I didn't have any corn flakes."

"What in heaven's name am I supposed to do now?" she said. "I sure can't leave you here alone. You know I can't miss work if we want to eat. Tell me what I'm supposed to do?"

“Let’s get out of here, mama! Right now! Let’s just pack up and go while he’s unconscious.”

“We can’t do that, Lonnie.”

“Why not? What’s stopping us? I can’t stand it anymore. I hate his guts, and I’m scared to death that he’s going to hurt you.”

“He ain’t gonna hurt me.”

“Have you forgotten that last night he said he was gonna knock your fuckin’ head off?”

“Lonnie Ray Tobin! Watch your mouth!”

“I’m just repeating what *he* said. See, he’s threatening you and corrupting me.”

“Just don’t talk like that. Besides, he knows better than to touch me.”

“When he’s drunk, he don’t know what he’s doing, mama. One punch from him *could* knock your head off. I don’t know about you, but I can’t live with that kind of risk.”

“There ain’t no risk. He talks big, but he won’t do anything.”

“I wish I could believe that, but after what he did last night … he almost *hit* you, mama! I’m done with living this way. That’s it. I’ve made up my mind. If you won’t go with me, I’m going by myself. Or I swear to God, *I will kill him*!”

I had her full attention.

“But,” I added, with visions of a Winchester .30-.30 dancing in my head, “I may need a bigger gun.”

“Quit talkin’ about guns and shootin’ your father for heaven’s sake. Where would we go, son? What in the world would we do?”

“I don’t care. Anywhere would be better than here with him. We could go to hell and do Satan’s laundry and I would be content.”

“Lonnie! Don’t say things like that!”

“I’m just saying that I will do anything, mama! I mean it! I’ll shovel cow crap till the cows come home and crap some more. Then, I’ll shovel *that* crap. I’ll shovel the accumulated crap of every bovine on earth. I’ll live in a lean-to and eat tree bark and berries. I’ll wear flea infested flour sacks. I’ll …”

"Okay, okay, okay, I get the picture," she interrupted. "I know things have been rough, Lonnie, but I didn't know you were this upset. I never dreamed that you would *shoot* him for cryin' out loud. Lord, have mercy. You're pretty serious about this, ain't you?"

"As a bullet in the brain."

We stood looking at each other as we tried to make some sense of the universe we found ourselves in. I wondered how many other boys were discussing murder with their mothers in the front yard.

"You know that just up and leaving is a big step, don't you?" she said. "We won't have a place to live. Are you ready for that?"

"I know it's a huge step, mama, but I'm really afraid of what might happen if we stay. He's going to lose his job with all the work he misses. He probably drinks on the job, too. Either way, he could lose his job at any time. What then? Could it get worse? Yes, it certainly could. He could take it out on you … or me."

Her eyes searched mine and saw that I wasn't trying to be the class clown this time. There was no punch line coming.

"Well," she said, "I uh … I … *shit fire and save matches* … give me a minute to think."

"Sure, mama, go ahead. But please don't think for long. He could get up to pee."

As she deliberated on our limited options, I looked down at my mutt, Sawbuck. Being a Civil War buff, I had named him after the famous black and white bird-dog that became the mascot of the Fourth Louisiana Brigade who always went into battle with the men and would run up and down the lines in order to watch the fight. My brown and black mixed-breed buddy wasn't quite that brave. Any loud noise would send him off like a minnie-ball from a rebel musket. Sawbuck was mine, and he was looking at me with an expression that said, "I'm behind you one hundred percent! Let's do lunch."

Even with that canine reassurance to bolster me, my guts were squirming like a bucket of night crawlers. I suddenly knew how Fay Wray felt lashed to the posts outside the gates of that island village, waiting for the appearance of King Kong. Finally, after enough time for the siege of Vicksburg, mama returned with a verdict.

"Well, I guess we can go to Moro and stay with mama till we figure out what to do."

Yes! She was referring to my Grandmother Birdie's house in Moro, Arkansas. That was exactly what I had hoped she would say. I couldn't have been more thrilled if Miss Funicello herself had stepped up and kissed me full on the lips.

"Besides," she added with an implication of a smile, "the insurance company won't pay off on somebody who kills himself."

Now that we had settled on a course of action, we quickly and as silently as possible, gathered up our meager belongings. I loaded the rifle, pulled the five school shirts off hangers, emptied my underwear drawer into a paper grocery bag, topped it off with my baseball glove and cleats, transistor radio, and my paperback editions of the complete works of Mark Twain, Edgar Allen Poe, and Sir Arthur Conan Doyle, who in my mind were the Holy Trinity of literature, and tossed it all into the cavernous trunk of her 1949 Dodge. The tired old heap was once bright green but had aged into the more subdued color of snot. It burned oil like a furnace, and the tires were as slick as a frozen pond; but with faith in the infinite mercy of Almighty God, who had already foiled my attempt to take matters into my own hands, I trusted that it would get us to Grandma Birdie's.

"Do you think I should pull the distributor cap off his truck so he can't follow us?"

"Lonnie, if our leavin' don't set him off, messin' up his truck certainly would."

She was right. He loved that truck more than he loved both of us put together. With Sawbuck hanging his head out the back window, trailing ribbons of slobber in the wind, we drove off without a note or a kiss my ass.

We stopped at Bailey's Grocery so my mother could explain the situation, delicately omitting the attempted patricide part of course, collect her final check, and call grandma to let her know we were coming. She headed for the back, and I went to the soda machine. I dropped in a nickel, pushed the lever, and pulled out a sweating bottle. I stuck it in the opener, popped the top off, and drank half of it before coming up for air. It burned all the way down but gave me a burst of energy. After the drain of no sleep and the eventful morning, that cold sugar rush was just what I needed.

I moved over to the front window and watched a morbidly obese woman at the register get her change and head for the front door. It took great effort to get her mountain of flesh to cooperate, and she could only shuffle slowly under the burden. I wondered how anyone could get *that* fat. I held the door open for her, and she smiled and said thank you. As she stepped over the threshold, something fell from under her dress and hit the top cement step with a *smack*.

She looked down and then at me. I thought at first that she had given birth. A wave of nausea spun my stomach. She suddenly turned, bounded down the remaining steps, and took off like a charging elephant. She was around the corner and gone in a matter of seconds. The object that had fallen from her was a six-pound Hormel smoked ham. That was why she could barely walk. The cashier did not see what happened, so I went looking for my mother. She and Mr. Bailey were leaning on opposite sides of the refrigerated meat counter sharing a good laugh.

They stopped talking when I walked up, and I told them about what I had witnessed.

"I ain't surprised," Mr. Bailey said. "People come up with all kinds of ways to shoplift. Lonnie, would you go get the ham for me?"

"*No, sir*! After knowing where it's been, I'm not going to touch it."

My mother laughed, but Mr. Bailey just looked annoyed. I returned his stare until he looked away.

"The house is right over here on Gassen Street, and it's furnished, Ruby Jo," Mr. Bailey said. "Y'all could move in right now. And I'll give Lonnie a job as a stockboy. And you can get all your groceries wholesale."

She turned to me. "Lonnie, Mr. Bailey don't want me to leave. He's offerin' to rent a house for us if I'll stay. And a job for you. You'll be gettin' your driver's license soon, maybe we could get you a car. What do you think? Wouldn't that be great? We would have a place of our own. We'd be free of him, and we won't have to drive all the way to mama's."

"It's not that far."

"I have a job here, Lonnie. I won't have anything in Moro."

"We'll survive, mama. It'll be okay. We'll do whatever it takes. Besides, I know the house he's talking about. It ain't much better than where we are now."

"But it'll be just you and me. It'll be fun."

"Daddy would find us and torment us day and night. It wouldn't be fun."

"I think you should show respect for your mother, Lonnie," Mr. Bailey said. "If she wants to stay, you should just say okay."

I had never cared much for Donald Bailey. He treated my mother well, and I appreciated that greatly. But, there was just something repellent about him.

"With all due respect, Mr. Bailey," I said, "It's none of your business. You can stay if you want to, mama. I'll hitchhike to grandma's. Just pray that I don't get picked up by some perverted psychopath."

"*Well,*" my mother said after quite a few awkward moments, "I guess that settles *that*. Thanks anyway, Mr. Bailey, but we'll be leavin'."

We stocked up on candy, cookies, chips, Vienna sausages, and other nutritious snacks for the eight-hour trip, and when we hit the road, I felt *unchained*. I was soaring with the eagles. It was the most sublime moment of my dysfunctional, latchkey life. Then, right in the middle of the elation, I felt a sharp twinge of apprehension, an uncomfortable sense of dread about what lay ahead. Somehow, I knew it would involve more than just my father.

Chapter Two

The Relief of It All

We headed north, following the old Mississippi River Road that twists and turns like asphalt intestines, past chemical plants spewing brown smoke, and rich farmland filled with enough sugarcane to put every diabetic in the country into a coma. We passed antebellum homes dozing in the shade of ancient, gnarled live oaks, dreaming of the days when they were belles of the bayou. As we crossed the bridge in Baton Rouge, I could see the State Capitol Building rising like a huge erection from the flat landscape. It was a monument to the late Governor Huey P. Long, who in his day was the biggest dick in the state.

Up to this point in our trip, I had been constantly looking behind us—my butt taking a bite out of the seat every time I saw a red pick-up truck, afraid that it was my father catching up. I feared that if he did, we might join the ranks of the luckless possums and other road kill littering the highway. But I began to relax with each click of the ancient odometer and every bug that splattered into the windshield like cream-filled bonbons. Even the baked air that blew through my mother's red hair began to take on the sweet smell of freedom. We laughed with the relief of it all. We even made up limericks using the names of the little towns we were driving through— Iota, Vienna, Quitman, and Bunkie.

There was an old man from Bunkie,
Who was considered to be quite spunky,
He ate lots of fruits,
And cut lots of poots,
And generally behaved like a monkey.

I never said they were good limericks. Still, even Sawbuck seemed to approve, sitting on his haunches with his long, pink tongue hanging out like a wet novelty tie. The twinkle in his eyes seemed to say, "This is wonderful! Got any more beef jerky?"

We rode in silence as I mused about how we had come to this point. My father worked in one of the chemical plants that had sprung up along the river, which was a well-paying enough job, but he would often get smashed and call in with brilliant excuses as to why he wouldn't be able to fill his shift: "The wheel came off my car," "My pants caught on fire," etc. He was so deep into the pink-elephant graveyard that whiskey had become the love of his life and acquiring it his mission. Every week, he took his paycheck, liquefied the assets in the dank bowels of some bar, then literally pissed it away in a 90-proof, yellow stream down a skid-marked toilet.

This proclivity to support the local tavern keepers rather than his wife and child had forced us to live like white-trash refugees, in one wretched sharecropper shack after another— decrepit little dumps with ripped and rotted screens that allowed hoards of undernourished mosquitoes to enter and find succor. Mold was the only thing holding the places together, and pieces of plywood haphazardly covered the holes in the floor. I walked long distances to and from school so none of my friends could see where I lived. Somehow, I had managed to deal with all of that like an infected boil on my ass and may have gone on tolerating it, but now the specter of domestic violence had reared its intoxicated head.

My father was a large and powerful man, capable of awesome feats of strength, with a hair-trigger temper. As a young, oversized boy on the Arkansas farm where he grew up, he once got mad at an uncooperative mule and knocked the huge animal to his knees with one blow to the ear.

He joined the Navy, started lifting weights and boxing, and became the undefeated heavyweight champion of his ship. He was good enough to turn pro when he got out, but alcohol already had him in its grasp.

I had heard of his feats all my life from people who knew him—everything from taking on three guys at once to knocking a man's eyeball completely out of the socket. Everybody was afraid of him and cut him a wide berth. I didn't care if he beat every barfly's and wino's ass in that little Louisiana town into a bloody rum pudding, but hurting my mother was crossing the Mason-Dixon Line. I would not let *anybody* hurt my mother.

"How did you meet dad?" I asked after failing to pick up any signal on the radio.

"Well, I met him the first time at a basketball game. Moro was playin' at home against Rocky Branch, where he went to school. I was working at the concession stand, and he came up and ordered a hot dog. I hate to admit it, but your father has always been good lookin', with that dark, curly hair and them blue eyes," she recounted as she looked in the rearview mirror and primped herself absentmindedly.

"We got to talkin' and just kinda hit it off. He asked me to go out with him that night after the game. I was shocked. Every girl in the county had her cap set for Harley Tobin, and he asked *me* out."

"You were cute, mama. I've seen pictures."

"Well, thank you. Does that mean I'm not cute anymore?"

"You know what I mean. You're a very pretty woman."

"You're just sayin' that because you love me, but it's sweet for you to say. Some of my friends told me I shouldn't go out with him, but I figured they were just jealous. I knew he was bad, but it was kind of a thrill to be with the guy that everybody was afraid of, you know? The allure of danger, I guess. Anyway, we went out that night and the next night, and I set my cap for him and I got him."

"Lucky you."

"All the girls hated me."

"They don't know what they missed out on, mama. He was a real catch."

"He had a lot of potential. Still does, but you can't tell it. He just won't quit drinkin' long enough for his good side to show through. Your dad could be anything he wanted to be."

"It appears that he wants to be a butthole."

"Lonnie, you shouldn't talk like that. He's still your father."

"Biologically speaking, but that's where it ends. How long did you know him before you got married?"

"We were both seniors in high school when we met, and we both got jobs at the bag plant over in Camden when we got out of school."

"Bag plant? What was that?"

"We made paper bags."

"Makes sense."

"We went out all that year, and then his daddy died, your grandfather … well, I swear, I forgot his name … Noah! Noah Tobin. Then, the next thing you know, his mama, Miss Sybil, died. I wish you could have known her, Lonnie. She was the godliest woman I ever met. Anyway, we were datin' off and on. He wouldn't call me for a couple of weeks, so I'd go out with somebody else. When he heard that I went out, it would make him jealous, and he'd show up at my door. That went on for a couple of years."

"You dated other guys?"

"Why sure. I had several guys who were tryin' to court me. I almost married Morris Benson. If I had, you would be Lonnie Benson."

"No, I wouldn't."

"Yes, you would. If I had married a Benson, you would be a Benson."

"I wouldn't exist, mama. I'm here *because* of my father. If he hadn't been in the picture, neither would I."

"Yeah, I reckon so. Anyway, he wanted to join the Navy but said we'd have to get married first. He said havin' me here, waitin' for him, would inspire him. I fell for it, like a fool. So, we got married when he came home from boot camp. Two weeks later, he went overseas."

The steering wheel of the old Dodge looked as big as a hula-hoop as she gripped it and stared at the rear end of the slow-moving farm tractor in front of us. A mile-long caravan had accumulated behind us. She watched oncoming traffic, waiting for a break so she could pass on the narrow two-lane road.

"We had a great marriage … until he got out of the Navy and come home," she laughed. She had a great laugh. "You were born in Camden while he was in Guam."

"Wow, I didn't know he was in Guam."

"The war was over by the time he got there. From the few letters I got from him, about all he did was box and get drunk. I gotta tell you this story, hold on." She steered the car to the left and accelerated past Farmer Brown.

"It ought to be against the law for tractors to be on the highway. Anyway, your daddy was in the medical corps in Guam, and him and some of his buddies used to meet in the back room of the morgue to drink and play cards. Nobody ever went in there at night if they didn't have to."

I could understand that completely.

"One night, they were playin' cards and got drunk, and one of them remembered that a colonel or a general or some kinda officer had died that afternoon, and the body was in the morgue. Well, they went and got the body out of the cooler and decided to have some fun with it, if you can call that *fun*."

"What did they do?"

"Well, at first, they just slapped his face for a while. Then, they got tired of that and came up with a game. There was four of them, so they split into two teams. One of them grabbed the guy under the arms, and the other one grabbed the legs, and they swung him back and forth and tried to throw the body across the room and land it on a table. You got so many points if it stayed on the table. Which it never did."

"You're kidding."

"No, I'm not. But that's not the worst thing they did to that poor man. Your daddy got a needle and sutures and sewed the man's lips together. He pushed the lips together like he was making a kiss and stitched them up."

I felt bad about it, but I laughed out loud at the thought of the indignities inflicted on that helpless corpse.

"Then, they went back to playin' cards," she went on, "and just before the sun came up, they remembered that they hadn't removed the stitches from the guy's lips. So, they go in and pull 'em out, and guess what?"

"What?"

"Rigor mortis had set in. His lips were froze in that position."

"Oh no … what did they do?"

"Your daddy said he got up on top of the body and punched him in the mouth till they were back in the normal position."

By this point, I was laughing so hard I fell into the floorboard.

"Then, they noticed that the stitches left holes in the lips, so they got makeup that the undertaker uses and filled them up. They were scared to death and hung over all day."

We laughed until we both had to pee, so we stopped at a little restaurant called The Blue Plate Special. After relieving ourselves, we talked about our predicament over cheeseburgers, fries, and a couple of milk shakes.

"We're not gonna be able to stay with mama forever, Lonnie. I'll have to look for work in Fordyce or Camden. They both have several big stores. With my experience, I shouldn't have any trouble landin' a job."

"I'll get a job too, mama. I'll work instead of playing baseball. We'll make it just fine."

"I want you to play ball. You're too good. Who knows, you could end up makin' a lot of money someday just by doin' what you love to do."

"Well, I promise I'll help any way I can. I can bag groceries or stock shelves. Maybe, I can get a paper route. We'll be all right, mama."

"I know. It's just all so … new. It feels strange to be makin' my own decisions about things. I hope I'm makin' the *right* decision."

When we resumed our journey, I looked at the houses we passed and wondered what went on inside them. Did normal families live there? Was it a happy home or a prison? Here I was about to become a high school freshman, and I didn't know what a *normal* family was like. Even so, my life wasn't completely void of positives. I had been blessed with an IQ of 140 and some talent on the baseball diamond. Baseball was my passion, and I intended to replace Mickey Mantle in the Yankee outfield one day. I also had literary aspirations and a desire to do standup comedy. In fact, I often pictured myself winning the World Series with a blast to the upper deck of Yankee Stadium, attending a gala banquet with Annette on my arm to pick up my Pulitzer, and taking a limousine over to *The Ed Sullivan Show* to trade ad-libs with Bob Hope. However, at that point in time, as we headed away from the past, I had trouble seeing the future.

"So, you have no love for your father at all?"

"At this moment … no. What is there to love? Every time he comes home, he lets us know how unhappy he is that he had to come home."

"I know, Lonnie. I'm sorry you've had to live in this kind of situation."

"I have pleaded with you to take me out of it many times."

"I know, baby, I'm sorry."

"Why in the world do you stay with him? Is it the furs and diamonds that he lavishes on you?"

"Yeah, that's it. What girl wouldn't be swept off her feet by a full-length sable? I don't know. Even with all the hell he's put me through, I just wasn't able to leave him for some reason. I can't explain it."

"Like the kidnap victim falling in love with her captor," I said.

"Maybe so. I guess I kept waiting for his good side to pop through. I know it's there somewhere, down deep in him. If it ain't already pickled." She stared down the road lost in thought. "Too bad the doctors can't give you a shot for stupidity."

The bald tires rolling down the sun-softened asphalt sounded sticky, like pulling tape."Would you really have shot him?"

"You'll never know," I said, laughing maniacally like a B-movie villain.

"I'm serious. If I hadn't shown up … would you have pulled the trigger?"

I had to think about the answer. Even though I hated him enough to do it, could I have pulled the trigger?

"I don't know, mama. It was certainly my intention at the time."

"I don't think you would have done it."

"Can't prove that now."

"And thank God for that," she said, raising her hand to the sky. The day was fading as we rolled through El Dorado. We had crossed not only a state boundary but also a line of demarcation, and I knew there would be no going back. At least not in the same condition we left in.

"Do you think he will come after us?"

"I don't know, Lonnie. I wouldn't put anything past him."

Just before dark, we turned off the highway onto the potholed, washboard gravel road that would take us the last ten rough miles to Moro. There were thriving farms encircled by acres of tall green corn, cattle of various hues grazing in open fields, and hogs wallowing in their own filth. Scattered along the way were long abandoned houses and barns, slowly collapsing into the weeds that would someday swallow them whole. We could hear the bang of rocks being thrown up against the bottom of the car. The acrid dust that boiled up in our wake seeped in and burned our nostrils. Darkness had overtaken us, so when the one good headlight illuminated the green and white road sign that said "MORO, POP. 110," I was so happy I nearly shat in my blue jeans.

The first white settlers had arrived in Moro around 1840. The number of families increased slowly over the years until a boom began shortly before the turn of the century. That was when the now-defunct Rock Island Railroad ran its tracks through town. Soon, passenger trains were stopping at the spacious new depot so that travelers to Little Rock, Memphis, and other destinations could make connections. It was at that very depot that my grandfather was killed under mysterious circumstances. Several restaurants and hotels sprang up near the tracks to accommodate the drummers, revenue agents, and others as they passed through.

The residents experienced a bit of fame one bracing autumn afternoon in 1926 when none other than Wyatt Earp stepped off the train. He was wearing a new Stetson hat, white shirt with a black string tie, and hand-tooled leather boots. He was seventy-eight at the time but still had a fearless look in his blue eyes. The ticket agent almost wet himself when he realized who it was. Wyatt commented on what a fine town they had as news of his presence spread quicker than a juicy rumor. A small crowd of locals soon gathered, all a'twitter about meeting the famous law man and gunslinger, and he graciously talked with them until his train steamed in. The *Moro Gazette* carried banner headlines and fanciful front-page accounts about the encounter for weeks: "LEGENDARY MARSHAL WYATT EARP COMPLIMENTS TOWN!"

Another surge of growth came when Guy Hanson built a large sawmill to take advantage of the vast forests of yellow pine, cypress, oak, red gum, and hickory that had grown untouched for centuries. It employed not only workers in the mill but scores of loggers who cut, trimmed, and hauled the trees out of the woods with teams of horses. Then, a broom factory opened and created many more jobs. The downtown area grew rapidly and soon boasted general stores, barbershops, banks, drug stores, and, in 1938, a movie theater.

All of the little one-room schools, strewn over a wide area, were consolidated in 1921, and a large new schoolhouse was built in the center of town, where the basketball team became a perennial powerhouse. The town's fortunes continued to increase through World War II so much so that local leaders had drawn up elaborate plans for streets and housing developments that would make them all wealthy. Then, just after the war ended, it all collapsed.

Mr. Hanson, citing financial problems, closed down the paper mill and had it dismantled and moved, lock, stock, and saw-blade, to Texas. The broom factory collapsed with the loss of the mill. Three months later, with the residents still staggering from that economic blow, Rock Island, blaming the lack of paved roads, diverted its passenger service forty miles north through Camden. That was the fatal blow. The town that had been so vibrant and full of hope died in its sleep.

In a matter of a few short years, nearly everything was gone. Buildings like the sawmill were moved to greener pastures or sold for the lumber. What was left burned to the ground; some said to collect on the insurance—for those who had the foresight to insure their business. The only residents that remained were men who had retired from the railroad, some of the farmers that had nowhere else to go, the elderly who had lived there all their lives, and the insane.

By that summer of 1960, the only thing left "uptown," as it was still referred to, were two stores and a post office. My great aunt, Kate, grandma's sister, and her husband, Willie Pierce, owned one of the stores. Everybody called it a "beer joint" because that was the main thing they sold. Wallace and Velma Summers ran the other store where "respectable" folks traded. Next door to Willie's was the Post Office where Doc Parker was the postmaster.

There also seemed to be something else in the nearly deserted town. Maybe it had been there all along but had gone unnoticed in its heyday. It was a vibration, for lack of a better term, that seemed to hum in the air and create perfect conditions for the unexplainable.

We drove past the rambling old wooden schoolhouse, where I would be attending in the fall, and turned right at the first street. About a quarter of a mile down the road, we pulled into the tree-shaded front yard of Grandma Birdie's white frame house. It was a modest home but had the welcoming patina of comfort. The porch light came on, and she stepped out wiping her hands on the flowered apron tied around her thick waist. She looked like an older version of my mother. My step-grandfather, Gideon Woods, had already gone to bed, since he always retired at sunset.

"Y'all get out and come on in!"

That was her standard greeting every time we arrived for a visit. I often wondered what she would do if we had replied, "No, thanks, we'll just stay in the car." But, we got out and stretched the trip out of our joints. Sawbuck policed the perimeter, sniffing and snorting and stopping at strategic locations to fling up a hind-leg to claim the territory for himself.

"Did y'all have a good trip, Ruby Jo?"

"Yeah, mama, just kinda tirin'."

"I'm sure proud your old car made the trip. I was worried sick you'd break down on the road."

"It ran great. I could probably drive it to California."

"Y'all could go to Hollywood and be in the movies," grandma

laughed. "Well, look at you, Lonnie! Lord a'mercy, you have grown! Y'all come on in the house and eat some supper. You can unload the car later."

Grandma Birdie had been the head cook in the high school lunchroom for years, the only cook now, and she equated love with slaving over a stove. We made our way into the kitchen where the table sat groaning under the weight of fried chicken, pork chops, mashed potatoes and gravy, black-eye peas and butter beans, smothered squash, a choice of biscuits or cornbread, and two homemade apple pies. When grandma prepared a meal at home, she had trouble adjusting the amount.

Grabbing a plate and utensils, I listened to the discussion about various relatives and their respective health problems, who was getting married and who was divorcing, and whose kids were "running wild." Hearing about other peoples' problems made me realize, with great satisfaction, that the only concern I had at that moment was saving enough room for a humongous slab of pie. Overcome by the pure pleasure of the moment, I proceeded to eat with abandon.

Once stuffed, we waddled out to the porch with steaming mugs of freshly brewed coffee and settled into the eclectic collection of chairs that had been there as long as I could remember. The night was dark as only a rural night can be. The breeze raised the hairs on my arms, and fireflies flashed like tiny green farts of electricity as we sat and digested. I quickly introduced the subject of the supernatural, which I found much more compelling than updates on family members.

"Hey, grandma, tell us about the ghost you saw when you were a little girl."

"Oh, Lonnie," she chuckled, "I've told you that story a thousand times."

"Come on, please?" I begged, my blood bubbling with sweet anticipation. "I never get tired of hearing it."

"Yeah, mama, tell it," my mother said, "but let me scootch over closer to Lonnie first."

Though I strained to appear brave, I certainly didn't mind my mother pulling her chair closer to me at all.

"Please, grandma?" I gave her my most baleful look.

"Well, all right. Just one more time," she began, "I reckon I was only eight or nine years old when it happened. We was livin' at Big Mama and Papa's old home place way out yonder in the woods, past where the gravel pit is now."

"Where exactly" I interrupted. "I would like to go out there sometime."

"Oh, honey, I'm sure it's all growed up by now. They tore down the house fifty years ago. You'd never find it."

"And I don't want you wanderin' around in the woods," my mother said. "Now, go on with the story, mama."

"Well, one evenin' in the fall of the year, we was sittin' on the porch after supper. It was near dark, and the sky had been gray and cloudy all day, and you could feel that the real cold weather was comin' pretty soon. Daddy and my brothers had already got the cotton picked, and it was a purty good crop that year. We was wrapped in shawls and blankets against the chill wind, each of us kinda thinkin' our own thoughts. I was thinkin' that maybe I might get a new dress, maybe some shoes ... and I remember hearin' the crickets just stop, all at the same time. Everything got still and quiet. Even the wind died. Then, I looked down the little wagon trail that led up from the main road and saw a man comin'. He was wearin' a long black coat with a hat pulled down low on his face, so I couldn't make out his features."

At this point in the story, my mother moved even closer.

"Now, we had this big ol' brindle hound named Samson that wasn't scared of nothin'. He once run off a whole pack of coyotes that was killin' Papa's chickens, all by hisself. Well, he come runnin' out from under the house barkin' like crazy, headin' straight for that man. He wasn't used to folks comin' up to our place. All of a sudden, he stopped in his tracks, tucked his tail 'tween his legs, whipped around and ran back under the house, yelpin' like he'd been scalded, and draggin' the ground so low he plowed a furrow we could have planted cotton in. We didn't know what had got into him. It was about that time that the man passed in front of our gate, and … well … I swear his feet weren't touchin' earth. He was just floatin' along about a foot off the ground. He got down near the barn and … just disappeared. Later, Papa found Samson curled up in a ball under the house, dead as a hammer."

When she finished recounting the events of that day, the shadows of the night seemed to intensify and deepen. My internal organs were having a jitterbug contest.

"You saw him with your own eyes?"

"Yes, Lonnie, I saw him with my own eyes. We all did. It scared the fire out of us."

"Why won't Big Mama ever talk about it?" I asked.

"Oh, mama don't want people to think we're all crazy. She blames it on some bad pork. Papa never said much about it either. I don't like to talk about it myself."

I had total faith in my grandmother's veracity. If she said she saw a ghost, then that was good enough for me. Besides, other-worldly occurrences seemed to be commonplace in Moro.

"It was the strangest thing I've ever seen," she said, "but I ain't the only one that's seen such things around here. Ruby Jo, do you remember the Howard sisters? Mavis and Beulah Howard? You know, the old maids who lived on the other side of Spates' Creek?"

"Yeah, I remember 'em. That was a strange pair. Wearing those little bonnets everywhere they went. Like something out of *Gone with the Wind*."

"Well, they claimed that one time, before they got power run out to their place, they come home after dark, and when they lit the coal-oil lantern, they saw a man standin' in the kitchen. They said he was very pale, dressed in what they called old-fashioned clothes that was wore-out lookin' and dusty. When they spoke to him and asked him what he was doin' there, he just, *poof*, vanished. Folks said they might have had too much muscadine wine, but I talked to both sisters myself and they sure seemed to be tellin' the truth. They were very upset about seein' a 'haint in their own house."

"And being old maids, they were probably upset that another man got away," I said.

They both cackled over the thought of the Howard sisters being desperate enough to look for a husband among the dead. I loved to make them laugh, but the chill bumps were still goose-stepping up and down my arms. There is just something about sitting in the dark hearing talk of beings and spirits moving about, that is intensely rich in the nutrients that feed the imagination. The sense of an unseen presence lurking nearby can rapidly grow to the point where you dare not dangle your legs over the edge of the porch for fear of being snatched under the house and dragged to a horrible fate. Though I loved every delicious tale, I knew it was going to take a while for sleep to overtake me.

Then, grandma said something that caused my spinal cord to snap so tight you could almost hear a *twang*.

"Oh yeah, I almost forgot to tell you. The Booger came back."

~

"The Booger" made its debut on one of the coldest Christmas nights in memory. The temperature was hovering around nineteen degrees when Wallace and Velma Summers were violently awakened around two in the morning by someone, or something, beating on the walls of their tiny clapboard house in the woods just outside town.

The blows came rapidly and with enough force that pictures crashed to the floor and the windowpanes rattled. It switched from one side of the house to the other in what seemed like seconds. Wallace ran back and forth, bashing the hell out of his shins on the furniture, trying to catch a glimpse of whatever it was, but it was impossible to see anything in the stygian darkness outside. Then, it stopped. The silence that enveloped them was so complete they could hear the fear pounding in each other's hearts.

Suddenly, the front door knob began to jerk and twist as if it was about to be ripped right off. After a few seconds, it stopped and then began the same thing at the back door. Then, it was gone. The whole thing had lasted less than ten minutes. Wallace and Velma sat huddled together, shaking from more than the cold, until the sun came up.

After news of the night visitor got around town, most everyone agreed it was probably some demented hobo from a passing train or a bungled burglary since Wallace was a store owner and thought to have cash on hand. When nothing else happened for a year, it was pretty much forgotten.

The following Christmas, at about two in the morning, it returned. It repeated the same pattern of beating and knob-rattling and was gone. Then, it came back the next night and the one after that. Nothing happened for the next two months. Just as the Summers' hopes were high that the nightmare was over, it came back, hammering the walls in the stillness of the night and shaking the very foundations of their sanity.

Speculations quickly turned from a hobo to ghosts and other supernatural explanations. Some suggested that the couple were victims of a bizarre ritual, while others brought up the possibility that the house might have been built on what was once sacred Indian burial grounds and that the spirits who rested there had a royal case of the red-ass.

Whatever the culprit was, it was soon dubbed "the Booger," and it continued to show up randomly, with "no rhyme nor reason" as Grandma Birdie put it, for the last *forty* years. It became a local legend, and many a parent had told their kids that the Booger would get them if they didn't behave. Of course, this did not help them become better children but did reduce the chances of them getting a restful night's sleep.

When the Booger showed up, the sound of banging rolled through town, echoed into the woods, across the fields and farms for miles in the night air. Many traps have been set for it, all of which had netted absolutely nothing. Close examinations of the ground around the house yielded not a clue. Several people had come under suspicion over the years, but they all died or became feeble with age; the Booger kept going strong.

When asked why he didn't just move, Wallace would swell up with indignation and declare, "I ain't gonna let no man nor spook run me off." Though he tried to brush it off, it was easy to see that he and Velma, a former beauty now prematurely wrinkled, had suffered for years.

Everyone knew they didn't have the financial ability to move and had to endure the terror. The worst part was not knowing when it would show up. Night after miserable night, they lay awake while every nerve in their body crackled with dread, alternately cursing the unknown and pleading with God for deliverance.

"It's been quite a while since the last time the Booger showed up," Grandma Birdie continued. "More'n two years Wallace told me. Then, night before last, it was back big as you please. Poor old Velma is looking bad. Whatever's going on, it's gonna kill her if she don't get away from there."

"If it *is* a man and not some kind of … ghost, what do you think would make him do that for forty years?" I queried.

"Lonnie, sweetheart, there are things on this old earth that cause a body to doubt their own faculties. I reckon that if we ain't figured it out after all these years, then we never will. Maybe it's better we don't know."

"Maybe not, but I would still like to know what it is."

"Well, you're smart, maybe you can figure it out."

The thought of that sent chills dancing down my nerves.

"Yeah, Lonnie," my mother said, "maybe you could solve the mystery, like your boy Sherlock Holmes of Scotland Yard."

"He wasn't with Scotland Yard. He just solved cases that were brought to him."

"Excuse me. I just know that kind of thing interests you. It sure as heck is a mystery."

"What do you think it is, mama?"

"Lord, I don't have any idea. It's been goin' on all my life. It's hard to believe it's just a man doin' it. But what else could it be?"

"Well," grandma said, "I do know it's about time to get ready for bed."

Not wanting to break the mood, it took me a few minutes to get up. I went into the kitchen, jumping like a little girl at the slightest noise, opened a can of dog food for Sawbuck, dumped it in a plastic bowl, and set it in front of him. He looked at me as if to say, "After all the delicious aromas coming from that kitchen, you give me this slop?" I felt bad about it and promised him table scraps tomorrow.

After I unloaded the car, we ended up sitting in the kitchen and talking about the situation with my father until midnight before finally going to bed. I lay in the dark and recalled "The Year of my Father's Sobriety," when he had actually quit drinking. I was nine years old at the time, and though it was a brief twelve months in duration, it was the closest we had ever come to bonding. We fished a few times and even spent a week camping on a winter deer hunt. We never hugged or kissed or said I love you or anything unmanly like that, but at least he cut way back on the number of times he called me an idiot.

Then, on a beautiful, crisp New Year 's Day, our neighbor, Marvin Boulware, a man I will hate for eternity, invited my father over for a little celebratory drink to usher in the wonderful new year of 1955. He wanted to go be sociable, my father said. We knew he hated Marvin and would not set foot in his house without the lure of alcohol. My mother refused to let him go, and he went nuts. They argued, screamed, and cursed loud enough to be heard by the tourists on Bourbon Street. When it was all over, he was gone. We didn't see him again for three days. Five years later, I was holding a loaded rifle to his stupefied head. I was too young for all this. I finally put it out of my mind, lulled to sleep by the hypnotic chirp of the big belt-driven electric fan that filled the window by my bed.

Chapter Three

A Time and Place

Is there anything better than waking up to the smell of bacon frying? Even if you don't eat it, you have to admit it's one of the top odors in the world. Another smell that I always found comforting was soft cotton sheets and pillowcases dried on a clothesline in the open air and sunshine. I awoke to both fragrances, and pure joy zapped through me when I remembered where I was. I jumped out of bed, dressed quickly, and followed my nose to the kitchen where grandma had once again cooked enough for the entire Confederate army.

"Good morning, Lonnie," my mother greeted me.

"Good morning, mama. Grandma."

"Are you hungry? How do you want your eggs cooked?" grandma asked, already knowing what I would say.

"Fried, with the yellow runny, Grandma." I noticed that along with the bacon there was link sausage, deer sausage, left over chicken and pork chops, smoked ham, fried potatoes, homemade biscuits and fresh churned butter, white and red-eye gravy, Brer Rabbit molasses and jars of homemade peach, blackberry, and fig preserves. I felt unworthy of such abundance, but I didn't let it hinder me or my appetite.

"Did all the talk about ghosts and the Booger keep you awake last night?"

"No, mama. I ain't a little kid," I snapped, blowing out a few bits of bacon.

"Well, you don't have to be so touchy. I get kinda scared myself sometimes. It ain't nothing to be ashamed of. I kept waitin' for the Booger last night myself."

"Lord a'mercy," grandma said. "I'd be outta here the *first* time somethin' come bangin' on this house."

"I don't get scared," I lied, "just a little *concerned* every once in a while."

I used a butter knife to spread a large mound of blackberry preserves all over one of grandma's "cathead" biscuits. She called them "cathead" because that was the size of the piece of dough you pinch off for each one.

"These biscuits are great, grandma."

"Well, I'm glad you like 'em, Lonnie. Eat all you want."

I proceeded to take her up on the offer.

"Do you think Harley will come up here?" grandma asked.

"I don't know, mama. He may be glad we're gone."

"It doesn't matter whether he's glad or not," I said. "We're out of there forever."

"But what's next, Lonnie? What are we gonna do?"

"First, we need to just relax for a few days. Let this be our vacation. We'll enjoy the peace and quiet, and at the same time show daddy that we're serious and that we *ain't* coming back. Then, we can decide what we need to do."

"I just hope and pray we're doin' the right thing."

"We are, mama. I know it in my heart."

"Well, okay. I just wish I felt it in my heart." She stood and began picking up the dishes. "We're going over to Big Mama's later. You want to go with us?"

"I'll ride over after I bring that old bike grandma got me last year up to Wallace's and put some air in the tires."

"You be careful getting that bike out," grandma said, "that shed is plum fulla wasps and yellerjackets."

"I will," I called over my shoulder as the back screen door slammed behind me. Sawbuck relished the heaping plate of leftovers that grandma had fixed up, per my request, and he … well, let's just say that for a brief moment I knew what it felt like to be worshipped.

Risking whiplash from jerking my head back and forth dodging airborne assailants, I quickly extracted the bicycle from the spider-infested stacks of junk and boxes of mason jars in the ancient shed. It leaned precariously to the left and looked like it could crash at any minute. I hoped that the collapse would crush the guts out of every dive-bombing wasp bastard in it. I wiped off a year's worth of dust and dirt dobber nests from the bike, and with a liberal coat of rust and no kickstand, it looked pretty much ready to fall apart. Fortunately, the tires hadn't completely dry-rotted.

I headed out of the yard pushing the bike when it occurred to me to ask my mother for soda and candy bar money in case I dropped by Aunt Kate's store later. I went back to the house and propped the bike against the front porch, and there in a ladder-back chair, chain-smoking hand-rolled cigarettes, sat my step-grandfather, Gideon Woods.

Everybody said that Gideon was crazy. I had said it a few times myself. It was easy to say that he was "as twisted as a door knob" when you consider he claimed to speak with seven different "spirits" on a daily basis. He said that each spirit was an "expert in his field" and kept him informed on everything from world politics to future events.

He wasn't always that way. He had labored on the railroad for many years and worked his ass off trying to farm forty acres of anemic cotton at the same time. A veteran of WWI, he was considered a solid and substantial member of the community, right up to the day he was kicked senseless by a mule named Bolix.

He told grandma that while he was unconscious he went to the most beautiful place he had ever seen, where everything was so bright it hurt your eyes, and he felt loved and accepted like he had just come home from the war. Seven spirits became his counselors and constant companions there. He never wanted to leave, Gideon said, but the spirits told him there was a reason he had to go back. But they would not name it.

The doctors judged him to be totally disabled, and he hasn't hit a lick at a snake since. He slowly withdrew from family and friends and rarely spoke a word to anyone visible. He arose with the first orange streak of dawn and deposited his substantial butt into a chair on the front porch. He would remain there, except for trips to the kitchen to consume prodigious amounts of groceries or to the back porch for a different view, until he went off to bed as the sun slipped below the treetops. He was like a piece of furniture that moved and ate. I stood there by the steps and watched him for a minute. It felt peculiar being in such close proximity to someone who had been to Oz.

Gideon sat hunched forward with his elbows on his knees, and his ever-present cigarette clipped between his yellowed thumb and forefinger. His ensemble never changed: a faded blue work shirt with the sleeves rolled up on his forearms, worn bib overalls with several red cans of Prince Albert tobacco in the chest pocket, a pair of untied brown wing tips, and no socks.

His large, bald head jutted out on a surprisingly scrawny neck over a chest that had long ago dived into his gut. Gideon's glassy green eyes always seemed focused on something only he could see. His thin lips pumped as if in a deep conversation. Occasionally, a soft chuckle would rattle the nicotine-infused phlegm in his throat. This had been his life, day after monotonous day, for the last fifteen years.

Gideon had never spoken to me. I wondered if he knew I existed. It was impossible to tell. He gave no indication that he was even aware that I was here right now. I went in and bummed a quarter from my mother while grandma warned me not to spoil my dinner. I bounded out the front door and was halfway down the steps when I noticed that Gideon was looking straight at me. I froze like I was playing a game of one, two, three, red light.

"You are here for a reason," he said.

My neck hair stood up like a crop of corn, and I suddenly felt as weak as Yankee coffee. It was the first time I had ever heard him say more than a "yes" or "no." Then, our eyes met, and for a couple of seconds, he appeared to be completely lucid. There even seemed to be a hint of a smile.

"Are … are you talking to me?" I stammered.

Just that quickly, Gideon's eyes glazed over. A twitch made my left ear jump.

"Uh, were you just saying something to me?"

It was no use; he was gone. I was only slightly aware of my extremities. Just as I turned away, he spoke again.

"Gonna come up a shower 'bout four o'clock, but it won't last no more'n twenty minutes."

I turned to see if he was looking at me again. He wasn't. I couldn't tell if Gideon had given the forecast to me or Sawbuck or the oak tree in the front yard. I studied his face and wondered if he was just trying to scare the hell out of me. Did he actually speak to me? If so, what did he mean by "you are here for a reason?" I had an excellent reason for being there: getting as far away from my father as I could. I knew that he didn't have a clue about that, so he had to be referring to some other unnamed reason.

I remembered that the spirits he claimed to have met in La-La Land had supposedly told him there was a reason for *him* being there. Maybe he was referring to himself. Or maybe he was just trying to be like his spirit pals and give me some vague assurance that I had a purpose for being alive. I came up with several arguments to try and convince myself to simply treat it as the babbling of a mule-kicked wacko, but I couldn't explain the way it made me feel.

After a few minutes with no further news or weather reports, I regained some strength in my legs, grabbed the bike, and started down the road with the gravel crunching under my feet. Sawbuck trotted at my side giving me his "thank you, thank you, thank you" look.

I walked along, oblivious to my surroundings, thinking about what Gideon had said. Just hearing him speak was a shock. Moreover, what he said, "*I am here for a reason,*" struck some chord inside me. *Did* I have a reason for being in Moro at this particular time? I must admit the thought of it was a little exciting. Maybe I *was* here to unmask the Booger. Who better to reveal whatever the hell it was than someone who had read every

Sherlock Holmes story Sir Arthur ever wrote, many times over? You could call it coincidence, but just two days before we left Louisiana, I purchased a large, silver-handled magnifying glass at the Thrifty Cent drugstore.

But who was I kidding? How could a fourteen-year-old kid catch something that had evaded detection for forty years? It was foolish, but I decided to go out to the Summers' place sometime and take a look around for myself.

Still lost in thought, I arrived at Wallace and Velma's store. It was a tall, stately building, considered rather grand in its day, with "THOMPSON GROCERY AND DRYGOODS" in faded white letters on the facade. Elmer Thompson, Velma's father, had built it in 1899. Wallace had worked for him until Elmer passed away, when he and Velma assumed ownership.

The unpainted wood siding had blackened with years in the sun. The rusted tin roof was a quiltwork of patches, yet it gave the impression that it would be there forever. A big window in the front displayed an array of goods from shoes to shovels. The portico covered a cement slab that had replaced the original wooden planks. Two hand-cranked Texaco gas pumps, one Regular and one Ethyl, stood out front. A small addition, later built on the side of the store, housed an air compressor and other tools for resurrecting flat tires. I rolled the bike up to the open door of the shed where the village idiot savant, Orville "Tater" Davis, was busy patching a tractor tube. Wallace paid him a few dollars to fix flats for his customers.

"Hey, Lonnie Tobin."

Tater called everybody by their full name.

"Hey Tater. How ya been?"

"Almost perfect, Lonnie Tobin. Almost perfect."

He always declared himself in this near pristine condition. Tater was around thirty and obviously had mental problems, yet had the gift of an unnatural ability to compute numbers in his head. He loved it when people gave him difficult math problems, so he could see the look of amazement when he solved them almost instantly. He also loved to take the gas cap off a car and inhale the fumes from the tank until he passed out. Tater said he liked the dreams it gave him.

"This bike is ugly, Lonnie Tobin." He was also honest as a small child.

"Yeah, I know. But it's all I got."

"You wanta gimme some figgerin' to do, Lonnie Tobin?" he asked as he aired up my tires.

"Sure, Tater. Let's see, how about two thousand three hundred forty-one times nine hundred eighty-seven?"

"Two million, three hundred ten thousand, five hundred sixty-seven, Lonnie Tobin," he replied immediately.

"Wow, that's great," I said. I had no idea what the answer was, but I knew he was right. He was always right.

"I know who the Booger is Lonnie Tobin."

"Really? Who is it?"

"It's Lucifer Beelzebub, Lonnie Tobin."

More like "Beelzebubba" if you ask me.

"I seen him one time, Lonnie Tobin."

"You did? What did he look like?"

"Almost perfect, Lonnie Tobin. Almost perfect."

Really tired of hearing my name, I thanked Tater and moved on. The subject of the Booger was obviously the main topic in town. People usually showed up at Wallace's store to talk about it every time it reappeared. Folks also came to stare at Wallace and Velma as if they were some kind of an exhibit. I felt the urge to go in and do the same, but there would be plenty of time for gawking later. I lived here now.

Less than one hundred feet away, separated by a vacant lot, squatted the establishment of Kate and Willie Pierce. Everybody just called it Willie's. It was long and narrow, swayed in the middle, and was nowhere near as impressive as Wallace's. The front and side of the building were adorned with fading advertisements for Pepsi, Shlitz, and a Day's Work chewing tobacco. There were a couple of dilapidated sheds hunkered under giant twin pecan trees in the back, along with his and hers outhouses. Like the other store, there were two gas pumps under a smaller front porch that carried the Pegasus symbol of Mobile Oil. Right next to it, so close they almost touched, was the small post office.

The sidewalk that separated the stores was broken and jagged, but no one seemed to know exactly how it got that way. I negotiated the crossing without incident and leaned the bike against the corner of Willie's building. I told Sawbuck to wait for me, went up the two cement steps, and through the battered double screen doors.

The first thing you notice as you enter the long, low room was the bar. It ran the entire length of the room on the left, with an opening about halfway down to allow passage. On the immediate right against the wall was a brightly colored jukebox that, though mute at the moment, was loaded with plenty of cry-in-your-beer country songs, guaranteed to stimulate consumption. Next to that was a pinball machine covered in garish pictures of scantily clad women. That machine had taken many a nickel from me. Beyond the mechanical bandits was the "conversation pit," complete with coffee can spittoons, where the men-folk sat in chairs held together with baling wire around a large handmade wood stove, dormant now in the summer heat, to talk of crops and weather and politics and general bullshit.

On the wall above a wooden bench hung a huge painting of Custer's Last Stand that Willie had gotten from one of the beer distributors. I had examined it many times and was always impressed with the fact that, even with his men slaughtered, scalped, and lying naked all around him, Custer stood defiant with a raised sword in one hand and a pistol in the other as the Indians closed in on him. The back of the store held a few shelves with dust-covered canned goods and boxes of pre-war cereal that nobody ever bought. The storeroom in the rear was stacked to the ceiling with case after case of beer.

There were several huge jars of pickled eggs on the bar and a large glass case with buttons, thread, sewing needles, and cheap jewelry. An autographed picture of country singer, Webb Pierce, who Willie claimed was a distant cousin, hung from tired tape on the inside of the glass. Behind the bar against the wall were shelves with open boxes of candy, gum, and other treats. Above that were racks of cigarettes, cigars, snuff, and chew.

A large dented cooler with the Coca-Cola logo kept the beer and soda ice-cold. I had been here on many a lazy summer afternoon when it was so quiet you could hear the rats in the back room, and on Saturday nights when people from miles around gathered to drink, argue, and listen to Earnest Tubb and Patsy Cline on the jukebox.

Aunt Kate was perched in her usual position on the padded chair behind the bar next to the front window. She was clutching a much-used flyswatter like a queen with a frayed scepter. She bore a strong resemblance to Grandma Birdie except that she dyed her hair jet black. It was from this vantage point that she had witnessed the town's demise. It was her portal on local history, and she had peered through it, seven days a week, for the last forty years.

The store was all that remained for her, and she pinched the blood out of every penny. She had lost the desire for anything else in life after her only child, an eighteen-year-old son named Norman, ran off the Whitewater Bridge on his motorcycle and was killed. What made it even harder on her was the fact that he had gotten drunk right here at the store that Saturday night before he rode off. It happened nearly twenty years ago. Aunt Kate had never forgiven herself.

"Hello, Aunt Kate."

"Well, I swar, Lonnie Ray, you're growin' like a weed. When did y'all get in?"

"Late yesterday."

"Birdie told me y'all were comin'. I'm sorry to hear about everything with your father and all. I knew it would be just a matter of time before Ruby Jo left him. You doin' all right?"

"Yes, ma'am. I'm just glad to be here."

"Well, we're glad to have you. I reckon' you'll be goin' to school here come this fall. It's gonna be a lot different than what you're used to."

"I'll get used to it pretty quick. I'm looking forward to it."

"This may be the last year for the school. There ain't enough kids to keep it goin'. I heard they might send buses from the school in Fordyce."

"Boy, that would be a long bus ride every day. I hope that's not true."

"Hello, Scorpion!" someone yelled behind me.

I turned to see Cooper Logan sitting on the bench beneath the Custer painting. He was a longtime friend of my family and had always called me Scorpion for some unknown reason. Heavyset with long white hair, too long some said, wolf-like gray eyes, and a booming voice, Cooper had recently retired from the railroad. He was a regular at Willie's. Next to him was Horace Moore who raised cattle on a little farm just outside town. Horace never said much because he always had a softball-size wad of tobacco crammed in his cheek. The third member of the group was Charlie "Goddamn" Banks, a stooped and grizzled pig farmer who seemed to relish using the Lord's name in vain.

"You all up for the summer?" Cooper asked.

"Yeah," I answered, not wanting to go into detail.

"How's things down in coon-ass country?"

"About as well as can be expected."

"You ever eat any of them crawdads?"

"Yeah, I've had a mud-bug or two."

"That's fish-bait, boy! Might as well eat crickets and worms!"

"And goddamn shiners too," Charlie Banks said.

"I eat all those things."

"Lordy mercy, you're a coon-ass yourself, Scorpion," Cooper laughed. "How's Ruby Jo and Harley?"

"They're fine."

"I talk to Miss Birdie ever once in a while at the post office. 'Course, I don't ever see old Gideon. He still talking to them spirits of his?"

"Well, he was when I left the house a little while ago."

That brought laughter from the group.

"What you reckon they talk about?" Cooper said.

"This morning I think they were discussing the weather," I said.

They all laughed again, and after a few more comments on Gideon's idiosyncrasies, they went back to the topic under discussion. I sat on a stool at the bar and talked with Aunt Kate for a while then ordered a soda and a bag of salted peanuts. I dumped the peanuts into the bottle and soaked up the atmosphere. Even at the tender age of fourteen, I had a heightened sense of time and place. As I sat there inhaling the smells and listening to the hum of the cooler behind the bar, I knew that one day I would think back on this very moment. I tried to memorize every detail of the room and record the conversation going on behind me.

"Ain't no goddamn way this country will elect a goddamn Yankee Catholic like Kennedy," Charlie Banks postulated. The presidential elections were coming up in November.

"I don't know, old Joe Kennedy's got a shit-pot fulla money. And the kid is a war hero," Cooper Logan said.

"Richard Nixon is a bony fide goddamn *American* hero. He got rid of them goddamn commonists in Warshington, didn't he? You goddamn right he did. Hell, the only real goddamn president we ever had was Jefferson goddamn Davis."

I wanted to ask Charlie if he had ever heard the story of Jeff Davis dressing in women's clothes to escape capture as he fled Richmond at the end of the war, but I was afraid I might end up as chunks in a goddamn hog trough.

"Ain't neither one of 'em worth a shit," Horace Moore mumbled as he picked up the coffee can by his feet and sent a shot of tobacco juice into it, then wiped the dribble off his chin.

"Maybe so," Cooper said, "but that's all we got to vote for. Who would you like to see as president, Horace?"

"Aw hell, I don't know. Maybe Stan Musial."

"Stan Musial?" Coop laughed. "What the hell would a ballplayer know about runnin' the country?"

"Well, at least I could trust him. He would be honest. That's more than I can say for either one of them jackasses that are runnin'."

"You may have a point there, Horace. Why don't we write Stan a letter and ask him to throw his hat in the ring?"

At that moment, the screen door opened and in walked the Roark brothers: Matthew, Mark, Luke, and Waylon. They were about the sorriest examples of humanity that I had ever seen. Since they had been born about nine months and thirty seconds apart, they were all in their early twenties. They lived with their parents, Eli and Dorphy, in a shack with no electricity or indoor plumbing about three miles up the road, where they raised cotton and hogs. Eli helped make ends meet by doing a little preaching in backwoods holiness churches and brewing up skull-popping moonshine, which the brothers appeared to have sampled on the way to Willie's.

Matthew, Mark, and Luke were rail-thin like their father, but Waylon was as big and thick as a Brahma bull. It appeared that he had gotten the lion's share of the victuals. The difference in their size prompted the local gossips to speculate that Dorphy had been less than faithful to old Eli, but I didn't believe it because they all shared the same ugly.

To say they were filthy would do them an injustice. They were what grandma called "cankered." The overalls and shirts they wore looked like something taken from long-dead corpses, dug from shallow graves. The stench of manure, sour sweat, unwashed privates, and a couple of mystery odors thrown in, quickly filled the room. It didn't look as if they had ever bathed and probably still had dried placenta from the day they were born caked in the cracks and crevices of their bodies. Far beyond soap and water, the only way to get them clean would be by scraping. Like stripping paint from an old dresser.

In addition to their outward appearances, they were all mean as stepped-on copperheads.

"Give us four of yore coldest Budweisers, Miss Kate. We 'bout to die of thirst," Waylon said as he threw a wad of bills on the bar. "We just sold some hogs, and we gonna drink all the beer that there money'll buy."

Waylon was the town bully. He was even bigger than my father. His nose looked like it had been gnawed on by some creature with blunt teeth, leaving it bunched up like a gob of bubblegum. His tiny eyes were like two brown M&Ms pressed into his fat, doughy face.

"And after that runs out, we gonna warsh it down with some a daddy's shine, 'cause we aim to git skunk drunk, don't we boys?"

This brought forth hideous guffaws from the brothers, their black, snaggled teeth reminding me of headstones in a neglected cemetery.

"What the hell you lookin' at, boy?" Waylon said as I realized I was staring at him. I instantly looked away.

"I axed you a question, boy. Who the hell you lookin' at?"

I did not like being the one he focused on, and I froze up.

"Boy! I'm talkin' to you!"

"I'm sorry … I … didn't mean to stare."

"What's yore name, boy?"

"Lonnie Tobin."

"Tobin? You Harley Tobin's boy by any chance?"

I nodded my head without looking at him, wanting out of there very badly.

"Well, kiss my ass. Harley Tobin's kid. How's yore ol' man doin'?"

"Fine." I still avoided his gaze.

He turned up his beer, drained it in one long swallow, slammed it on the bar, and wiped his grimy mouth on the back of his grimier hand.

"That tasted just like another one, Miss Kate. Give my brothers one too. Well, Lonnie, tell me somethin', is yore ol' man still a badass?"

I just shrugged my shoulders and wondered where he was going with this.

"Why don't you leave the boy alone?" Cooper Logan said.

"Why don't you jus' shut the fuck up, old man?" he snarled. He fixed Cooper with a malevolent glare until it was evident that no further protest was forthcoming. Then, he set his sights back on me.

"I'm only axin the boy a question. It's just that I heared Harley Tobin was a badass. Ain't never been whupped in a fight, the way it was told to me. Thinks he's somethin'. You wanna know what I think? I think he's got all these pussies around here skeered of him. But, he ain't never tangled with no *real* man. Has he, boy? No, sir, he ain't. He ain't nothin' but a pussy his own self. I would wipe my ass with him."

I wanted to say that it would be the first time he ever wiped his ass with anything, but I was afraid it would be the equivalent of mooning a werewolf.

"How's that good lookin' mama of yore's. I bet she ain't never tangled with no real man neither. Once't I got a holt of her, she wouldn't even piss on Harley Tobin. No, sir, nary a drop. I might just pay yore fine little mama a visit one day. I'd make 'er squeal with dee-light."

This elicited retarded giggles from his beanpole brothers. I could taste the rage that came up in my throat.

"Fact of the matter is, the way I heared it, Harley Tobin might not even be yore daddy a'tall. You might just be a little bastard. What do you think about that, boy?"

I was furious. Never in my life had I felt such anger. I wanted to tell him to eat a giant helping of shit, but I had an aversion to critical injuries. Yet, I had to do *something*, I couldn't just let this insult to my mother pass. I was so pissed that I actually wished my father were there. The only weapon I had was words, so I decided to execute a flank attack on his ignorance.

"I think," I said, "that someone of such profoundly pronounced porcine ancestry, as attested to by your repugnant countenance, should be precluded from casting aspersions on another person's lineage. I think your inebriation only exacerbates your woeful lack of cognitive reasoning. And I think your propensity to harangue adolescents reveals a miserably inadequate reserve of true courage, which, ipso facto, makes you the most capacious vagina on the premises."

The brothers looked at me as if they had just witnessed their prize hog dancing an Irish jig while juggling several chickens. The rush of blood through my eardrums sounded like a commode running, and I couldn't jiggle the handle.

"Ipso facto? What the hell kinda talk is that?" Waylon bellowed, his putrid breath coming in snorts.

"Sounds like he was talkin' in tongues," one of the scarecrow-like siblings said.

"You makin' fun'a me, boy? I wouldn't take kindly to that. No, sir, none a'tall. Now, I'm gonna whup yore ass if you don't tell me what all that damn gibberish means."

I was thinking that I could shoot out of there and be on my bike before he knew I was gone, when I saw Uncle Willie walk out of the storeroom with a double-barrel shotgun in the crook of his arm. The Roarks didn't see him. Having an armed relative in the room refueled my bravery.

"It means," I said, "eat shit."

I knew it was a stupid thing to do, but I couldn't help myself. I actually saw the wildfire ignite in Waylon's beady eyes. He started coming toward me, like the Indians after Custer, when Willie's voice sliced through the air.

"Hold it right there, Waylon!"

He stopped and slowly turned to face Willie. I took a shaky breath.

"He ain't done you no harm, Waylon. He's just a boy for cryin' out loud. I don't know what you got against Harley Tobin but don't take it out on a kid. Besides, he's my wife's kin."

"Why, I gotta good mind to take that gun away from you and shove it up yore old ass."

"Try it, and I'll scatter your good mind all over the wall."

The shotgun remained draped over his arm, but everybody knew that Willie didn't make idle threats. So did Waylon. They stood staring at each other. It was a stalemate.

"Look, I don't want no trouble with you boys," Willie said to breach the impasse. "There ain't no call for this. Y'all are good customers. Let's all just simmer down. Kate, set everybody up with a beer on the house. And give Lonnie another cold drink. Then you better run on home, Lonnie."

Waylon, appeased by the offering, and not wanting to subject his head to a high velocity blast of double-ought buckshot, finally sat down on a stool. I started to make a comment on how there wasn't enough brains in his head to make much of a mess but quickly dismissed it as a monumental mistake. I said no thanks to the soda and turned to leave.

"You just tell Harley Tobin what I said, you hear me, boy! And don't let the door hit you in the butt on the way out." Waylon's bony brothers laughed like a pack of giddy hyenas.

I thought of a number of exquisite tortures that I would like to inflict on him, all involving a blowtorch and his crusted genitals. I hoped that somebody would kick his nasty ass one day, but I wasn't sure that even my father could handle such a behemoth.

Chapter Four

Like Tom and Huck

My anger cooled as I rode along the gravel road to Big Mama's with Sawbuck loping along ahead of me with his nose to the ground, going from one side to the other like he was sweeping for land mines. How could I stay mad when I was living in Paradise? I cherished this place. It was like something Twain would have created, a barefoot boy's version of Heaven. I tried going barefoot like Tom and Huck once, but I kept stepping on sharp objects that hurt like hell. But I loved riding my bike on the miles of dirt and gravel roads with no traffic, fishing for bream and small-mouth bass in Spates' Creek, and swimming in the cold blue water of the gravel pit.

Or just sitting by myself on the bleached trunk of a fallen tree, deep in the cool green richness of the woods where the sunlight touches the thick carpet of dead leaves only in scattered spots. It's a soothing world where change is slow and steady, and time itself seems to gather in the branches of the trees like ethereal moss. I never fail to be stirred to the marrow when a soft rush of wind rustles the leafy canopy overhead, and the brittle harmony of the cicadas joins in with the desolate cry of mourning doves and the distant call of the bob-white and whippoorwill. It's a symphony unmatched by mankind's grandest orchestras.

I even loved the winter here, when the trees thrust naked branches into cold blue skies, and your breath billows in the icy air. I felt connected to this piece of land in the rear of nowhere. I was a part of the generations that had gone before me, one link in a never-ending chain. Like Gideon's cigarettes, when one life burns out another one is lit. Although we don't toss the butts in the yard.

There was an odd loneliness here, too. A kind of déjà vu sense of the people and of ages past seemed to reflect in the bleak windows of deserted houses and sweep like dust devils along the silent streets. At times, I had the feeling that if I turned my head quickly enough, I might catch a glimpse of someone long dead rounding a corner—a sense that if I had been there just a few seconds earlier, I could have spoken to them. It was as if the town, having died before its time, was coming back to haunt itself. It was that *hint* of the paranormal that I had always found to be Moro's most appealing quality. That and the fact that you could take a leak outdoors just about anywhere without being seen by another human.

I pedaled up the driveway to Big Mama's house and stopped at the front gate. The house was tall, wide, and one of the largest around. Though well-constructed, it now bore a look of faded distinction. The original coat of white paint, applied just after the turn of the century, had long ago flaked off and peeled away, leaving a few specks of white on the dark brown planks like bits of snow on the ground. The high-peaked, rust-stained tin roof swept down to connect with the smaller roof over the roomy front porch, where a swing invited contemplative afternoons, and several rockers awaited occupancy. The tall, richly detailed front door, adorned with etched and beveled glass, opened into a wide hallway that ran the length of the house to the closed-in back porch. Immense rooms with high ceilings bracketed the hall on both sides, and the front parlor featured a triple bay window.

Big Mama's name was Hilda May Calaway, but everybody called her Hildy. She lived in the kitchen and adjoining bedroom in the back, leaving the other rooms furnished but unused. Chrysanthemum and jasmine grew in abundance along the porch, and pomegranate bushes and green apple trees flourished by the garden fence which was laced with honeysuckle vines. Papa had spent many an hour in that garden bent over a hoe, cultivating peas and beans, tomatoes, corn, peppers, squash, and the sweetest watermelons known to man. The bucolic scene, complete with butterflies and hummingbirds, appeared tranquil and inviting on the outside, but it was the inside that I refused to be alone in, day or night. There were two reasons why.

First, the house was built in 1901 for Harold Paine, the corpulent manager of the Moro Savings and Loan, who was to be married for the first time at the age of forty-eight. He sweated every detail of the construction, wanting everything to be perfect for his twenty-five-year-old bride-to-be, Miss Lula Jean Stringfellow. She was nearly as rotund as Harold, and people said that when they partook of a meal together it resembled a gastronomic competition.

One night, Harold was unable to sleep, so he got up and dressed in a three-piece suit, the only thing he ever wore, left the rooming house he was living in, and walked a quarter of a mile over to his new home. It was finished except for the interior paint. He heaved himself up the steps, mopping his brow in the warm muggy air, crossed the porch, pulled the large keychain from his pocket, and fumbled in the darkness for the lock. Once he gained entrance, he lit the candle he had brought along—for electricity had not yet made its way to Moro. He took a few steps down the hall holding the candle at arm's length when, without warning, he collapsed right outside the parlor, dead before his fat carcass hit the hardwood floor.

The painters found him the next morning. All work ceased, and the house was locked and abandoned. The interior was never painted. It wasn't long until neighbors and passersby began to report seeing a light floating and flickering past the windows and moving up and down the long hallway in the middle of the night. The place was put up for sale, but nobody would go near it.

It sat empty for the next twenty years until my great-grandfather, James Calaway, who we called Papa, bought the house and seven acres of land for a song. They moved in and never bothered to paint or fix up the place other than eventually having it wired for electricity and indoor plumbing installed. Even today, it was virtually in the same condition as the day Mr. Paine expired. Though Big Mama and Papa both claimed they personally never saw or heard anything unusual, people still said they occasionally saw candlelight refracting through the beveled glass in the front door.

That alone put the house at the top of my list of places to avoid after dark, but there was something else that, in my opinion, made the spectral light seem like nothing more than a charming quirk. It was the other reason I refused to be in the house by myself.

It began with an incident late one summer day in 1951 when I was five years old. We were living in Louisiana, but I was staying with Big Mama and Papa for a week. I was sitting at the table while Big Mama stood at the old butane-fueled stove, stirring supper. Fading sunlight filtered through the tall open window and caused shadows to grow in the corners of the room. The screen door slammed on the back porch, and a few seconds later Papa walked into the kitchen. He had retired from the railroad in 1945 and spent the bulk of his time in the garden. He turned and hung his old battered and stained felt hat on a nail in the wall.

Papa's cottony hair was plastered to his head, and his well-worn blue shirt was soaked with farmer sweat. His perpetually gray-stubbled cheeks sank into his face from the lack of teeth, causing his chin to come closer to his nose than it was meant to be. He owned a set of dentures but had only been able to wear them once because of improper fit. He wasn't about to go all the way back to El Dorado to get the problem taken care of, he said, so he learned to do without them. He could eat anything he wanted, even a T-bone steak. To a five-year-old, watching his jaws bang together and his lips push out like an obscene kiss with each bite was rather frightening, especially when a rivulet of gravy snaked down his chin, giving him the appearance of a toothless vampire after a messy gumming.

Papa walked over behind my chair, rubbed his hand through my hair, and said, "How ya doin', Lonnie? What's fer supper, Hildy?"

"I fried up that pullet I killed this morning," Big Mama said. "I got mashed potatoes and black-eye peas. Wash up, you're filthy."

"Ain't nothing filthy about a man with a little of his own soil under his finger nails," he said as he scrubbed his hands at the sink.

He moved to the head of the table to take his usual seat. He pulled the chair away, then stopped and stood there for a moment as if he was trying to remember something. He turned toward me with a look of terrified surprise gleaming in his eyes right before his face began to twist and distort into a hideous grin on one side of his mouth. A strangled moan escaped his frail chest; he staggered and fell with a thud.

I don't remember anything after that but found out later that I had sat there alone with his unconscious body for nearly an hour as night closed in, while Big Mama ran up the street frantically looking for help. She finally found Ben Calhoun coming in from work. Ben came and got Papa and drove him to the nearest hospital, twenty miles away in Fordyce.

The stroke Papa had suffered partially paralyzed the left side of his body, though the doctors said he was lucky to be alive. For the next two years, Papa could walk only with the use of a cane. I often heard the sad sound of him moving up and down the hallway, dragging his useless left foot behind him like Igor headed out to locate another body part for Dr. Frankenstein.

Then, another stroke left him totally immobilized for the last years of his life. When we visited them on my summer vacations, I would hear his thin voice call out feebly for "Hildy" when he needed something. I was nine years old when we got the news that he had passed away quietly in his big iron bed.

We drove up from Louisiana as soon as we could and arrived at Big Mama's just after dark. In those days, the body was "waked" in the home, which means the corpse is put on display right there in the house that people have to live in after the funeral is over. Relatives and friends bring casseroles and cakes and try to console the bereaved by commenting on how "natural" the deceased appeared. I had always felt the practice to be more than a bit repulsive. We went in through the back porch and into the kitchen where every flat surface was covered with compassion food.

Big Mama was sitting at the table surrounded by people I had never seen in my life, along with grandma and some of the neighbors. After hugging Big Mama's bony little shoulders, I walked down the hallway toward the parlor where the funeral director had placed Papa's coffin right in front of the bay windows. I felt a familiar chill as I passed the spot on the floor where someone had penciled an "X" to indicate the exact location the banker's body had come to rest. Now, *two* people had died in this house.

I stepped into the parlor where a handful of mourners were sitting and talking quietly in metal folding chairs that had "NEWTON FUNERAL HOME" stenciled across the back. I walked up to the open casket to view the body. I had never seen Papa in a suit before. Looking at his clean-shaven and heavily made-up face, that awful day in the kitchen flashed through my mind. As I stared at what used to be my great-grandfather, I thought I could see a gentle rising and falling of his chest, moving up and down almost imperceptibly.

Fear grappled for control of my reason, and I found myself unable to look away. Suddenly, a repressed memory of the day he collapsed came back to me. In it, I was looking at him lying on the floor in the dim light of sunset, seeing his eyes flutter—as they seemed to be doing *right then*. My heart was pumping at a rate somewhere in the neighborhood of eighty-nine gallons a minute as total terror grew like a tumor in my brain and spread its fibrous tentacles down my spine. Just as it penetrated my last vertebra, I could have sworn I saw the pinky finger on his right hand *twitch* ever so slightly. Panic squeezed my last breath out through the pores of my skin.

Through sheer will power, I turned and walked from the room, barely able to control the urge to run and scream like a banshee. I made it to the porch where, drained and dizzy, I dropped into a rocker and drew the night air deep into my lungs. The sky was moonless, and everything beyond the reach of the porch light lay in darkness. I sat there shaking and sweating, listening to the rise and fall of the cricket chorus and the papery rustle of insect wings as they swarmed around the naked bulb above my head, until around midnight, when I walked with Grandma Birdie back to her house. The next day, as they lowered Papa into the ground, I couldn't help feeling that they were burying him *alive*.

The recurring dreams started the night after the funeral. Not your ordinary, run-of-the-mill, namby-pamby childhood bad dreams, I'm talking vivid, terrifyingly real *nightmares* that drive the fear down into the subatomic level of your being. Every one of them involved some incarnation of Papa. In these dreams, I was always alone in the house and usually in the room where he died. I would see him in the mirror on the dresser, along with numerous ghostly figures wavering and shimmering behind him, or he would slowly rise up from behind the chest of drawers in the corner. They came without warning and showed no sign of stopping. In fact, the most recent instance of this nocturnal necromancy had occurred just the week before we arrived in Moro and had been the granddaddy of them all so far.

In this particular dream, I found myself in Papa's bed, in the darkened room where he had breathed his last. I was even aware of the liniment-laced old man smell. The light from the open kitchen door seemed overly bright as it fell across the foot of the bed. I could hear murmuring and the tinkle of ceramic cups and metal spoons.

Then, I felt movement behind me. I turned to find that someone was in the bed. Before I could react, the sheet-covered figure began to rise. The face was revealed slowly, and *surprise*, it was Papa. Not the kindly, gray-haired and bewhiskered, sunken-cheeked Papa that I remembered, this Papa had no eyeballs. A flickering orange glow danced in the empty sockets, as if reflecting a fire that burned somewhere deep down in his dead soul. His lips peeled back into a demonic grin that revealed long, yellow teeth with a lizard-like tongue darting rapidly between them. I nearly leaped inside out.

I ran into the kitchen, with that dream-style run that feels like you're slogging through quicksand, wherein I found my mother, Grandma Birdie, and Big Mama sitting motionless at the table, coffee cups poised in midair as if frozen in the act of sipping. I started telling them about waking up with Papa, but they just sat there. I grabbed my mother's arm and was horrified to discover that she was as hard as a rock. They were all stoned but not in the good way.

Just as I realized that they would be of absolutely no help to me, I heard the squeak of bedsprings. I looked into the murky darkness of the room I had so recently exited and saw that Papa had gotten out of bed. I could see his eyeholes shining like a hellish jack-o-lantern. Then, he came toward me snapping his foaming jaws together. I lost all power of mobility and was slowly petrifying. Just as he got close enough for us to slow dance, I awoke slathered in sweat and trembling. I had to check and make sure that I hadn't soaked the mattress. I hated these damn dreams with a passion, and they seemed to be getting worse.

The remnants of those images, along with dead banker thoughts, were still blowing around in my mind as I stepped up on Big Mama's porch. I made sure Grandma Birdie's fire-engine red '53 Chevy was parked in front, because I wouldn't think of going in the house if there was even a modicum of a chance that no one would be there.

I walked down the hallway that was always dark even in the middle of the day, stepping over the X on the floor, as everyone did, and made my way into the kitchen. My mother, Grandma Birdie, and Big Mama were sitting at the table just like in my dream, except they were fully animated and in the act of doing serious damage to a pan of peach cobbler.

"Hey, y'all," I brilliantly quipped.

They all greeted me in the same intelligent fashion.

"Lonnie Ray, you come here and give me some sugar," Big Mama commanded.

As I made my way over to obey, I noticed how much she was looking her eighty or so years. Her face was lined like cracked glass, and she was little more than skin-wrapped bones. Yet, her eyes were the color of hand-rubbed mahogany and still twinkled like a mischievous child.

"Lonnie, I reckon you gonna be big as your daddy afore long. Then, you can give him a whippin', cain't you?" she said, laughing her little bird laugh.

"I guess so, Big Mama, I said as I gave her a peck on the cheek. I suddenly realized that kicking my father's ass would be much more satisfying than killing him. For one thing, I could do it more than once.

They asked what I had been up to, and over a bowl of cobbler, I recounted the events of my day so far. I didn't mention the part about Gideon speaking to me, and I told them about the encounter with the Roark brothers but didn't include my response to Waylon. I didn't want to bore them with every little detail.

"Well, don't that beat all," Grandma Birdie said. "Them Roarks are all useless as a three-legged dog. They ain't nothin' but criminals and ought to be locked up in jail. Ain't no tellin' how many cows they stole from folks around here."

"I bet Waylon could eat a whole bull for breakfast," I said.

They laughed.

"Well, he's shore fulla bullshit," Big Mama said.

We all laughed. Coming from an octogenarian, any dirty words she said were funny.

"You stay away from the Roarks, Lonnie," my mother said. "I don't like the thought of them around you."

"They rarely come into town, mama, and I sure ain't gonna' go visit them. I probably won't ever talk to them again."

"Does Dorphy Roark still have all them cats, Big Mama?" my mother asked.

"Oh Lord, Ruby Jo, she's got more cats than you can shake a stick at. I don't see how she can feed 'em all. Maybe they give 'em the milk from the stolen cows afore they butcher 'em. 'Course, Lonnie don't like cats, do you, Lonnie?"

Big Mama was referring to an incident with a barn cat when I was a small child. She never failed to bring it up and always laughed heartily at the retelling. It happened one day when I was four years old and playing in Big Mama's backyard. I was curious even then and liked to explore new places. I walked down the path behind the garden that ran like a long brown scar in the grass, past the smokehouse where hams and slabs of bacon were hung to cure over hickory fires, down to the huge old barn. It was a long building with acres of rusted tin for a roof. The pine-board walls had aged to the color of coal, and termites had chewed out jagged chunks along the bottom, like bites out of a gingerbread cookie.

It rose up in front of me like some medieval castle, but the high exposed beams and the hordes of bats that swept out through the open ends at dusk gave it the ambiance of a cave. The pungent smell of hay and leather and long departed mules permeated the air as I entered the cool confines. Corn husks from some forgotten harvest, dried to a crackling crisp, were gathered in the back corners of the empty stalls. Streaks of sunlight from the gaps and cracks shot through the shadows like dust-laden lasers. But what fascinated me most was the cats.

Cats of every color and description sat and watched from the overhead beams and played around the old harnesses and gear that littered the dirt floor. I had no idea that they were used as "ratters" only and were completely wild. At the tender age of four, I thought all kitty cats were supposed to be cuddly and sweet, and I became highly agitated when they wouldn't respond to my repeated "here kitty, kitty" attempts to make contact.

Frustrated, I stalked and finally captured one of the smaller calicos. Clutching it in both hands, I held it out away from my body as it hissed and spit and tried desperately to claw its way to freedom. Totally enraged at this rejection of my affection, not to mention the shredding of my arms, I ran as fast as my young legs would carry me, still maintaining my death grip on the struggling feline, straight to the well that was just outside Big Mama's backdoor. Without a moment's hesitation, I sent the unfriendly cat squalling into the dark watery depths below.

Unfortunately for me, but a stroke of luck for the cat, my father was in the kitchen at the time. He heard the pitiful mewing of the drowning animal and came out to investigate. Once he realized what had happened, he lowered the bucket down the well, and the cat was able to crawl into it. He cranked it back up, and as soon as the bucket cleared the lip, the cat shot out of it in a liquid blur and was gone before I could blink. I had never seen anything move so fast.

I, on the other hand, wasn't as quick. I was grabbed by the arm and whisked into the house where my father made me drop my shorts and proceeded to administer a rather severe beating with what felt like a sopping wet cat o' nine tails.

"I ain't never laughed so hard in my life when I seen that cat take off," Big Mama continued, "but I quit laughin' when Harley took you in the house and whipped you like he did. He drawed blood from your lil' legs with that belt, and you all scratched and bleedin' already. If I hadn't been scared to mess with Papa's shotgun, I'd a'shot him dead."

Join the club.

"Well, we ain't gotta worry about that no more," Grandma Birdie said. "Lonnie's here with us now. Ain't nobody gonna be whippin' on him no more."

I had never felt so secure in my life. I knew that these three women truly loved me and would do anything in the world for me. I was awash in waves of peace, floating along Moon River in the arms of the Goddess of Well Being, when I heard thunder.

Chapter Five

That Night the Train Blowed Up

I glanced at the large clock above the tiny refrigerator, the one with the painting of a rooster crowing, and saw that it was 4:02—just as Gideon had predicted.

"Look how dark it's got outside. I didn't hear anything about rain today. I need to get home and start supper," grandma said as fat raindrops began tapping the tin roof.

"It's probably just a shower and won't last long," I said.

I felt flushed, warm, and slightly guilty, as if I was harboring secret knowledge that was somehow taboo. Had Gideon given me a prognostication straight from beings that, if they existed, were probably on a first name basis with the Weather Maker Himself? I could no longer hear the conversation around me as I watched the minute hand slide, ever so slowly, past the rooster's crotch.

The rain continued to come down in sheets, with a liberal dash of lightning tossed in, until twenty-two minutes after four o'clock. The shower had lasted exactly twenty minutes. The sun popped out as the clouds rolled on to the east, but a storm still brewed in my mind. I felt like I had just made a pass through grandma's old ringer-washer. All kinds of thoughts swirled and churned in my head. Did Gideon use the rain shower to show me that he wasn't as insane as everyone thought? Should it cause me to assign more credibility to the "you're here for a reason" statement? Would this help me reach my goal of someday marrying Annette Funicello?

"Lonnie, will you come and stay the night with me sometime?" Big Mama asked, breaking into my reverie. "I sure would enjoy your company."

"Uh, yeah, I guess," I said. Just as soon as flying pigs and penguins happily cavort on the icy glaciers of hell. Besides, how much company would a quivering puddle of terrified goo be anyway?

"You can stay with her tomorrow night, Lonnie," mother said.

"What! I mean, what are you talking about?"

"I have to take mama to Little Rock to see the doctor. We're gonna spend the night up there with Aunt Ivy, and I know you'd be bored out of your mind. Besides, the Hogskinners will be playing baseball tomorrow, and I know you don't want to miss that."

My mother knew my weakness was baseball. I was going to miss playing that summer. I had been the centerfielder and cleanup hitter for the St. Thomas Angels from Little League to American Legion and had made the all-star team every year. What she didn't know was that, since I was big for my age, I was going to try out for the Hogskinners.

The amateur team was made up of local guys of various ages and skills who, for the love of the game, had formed a team and joined a league. They spent their Saturday afternoons every summer doing battle with other ragtag rural teams on rough diamonds in little podunk towns in a four county area, and I wanted desperately to be a part of the glamour of it all. But spending the night at Big Mama's was a heavy admission price to pay. I would have to deal with that later, however; I wanted to get back to grandma's to see if Gideon had anything else to say.

"Sure, I'd love to stay with you tomorrow night, Big Mama," I said.

"That's wonderful, Lonnie. We can play cards or something. And *Gunsmoke* comes on at nine o'clock."

Big Mama had a crush on James Arness.

"Just don't play poker with her," my mother laughed. "She'll clean you out."

"You mean the whole thirty-seven cents I have put away for

emergencies?" I said.

"Don't listen to them, Lonnie," Big Mama said. "They're just upset 'cause they stink at poker, and that's why I was able to clean *them* out."

When we left, I sat on the bike, grabbed and held on to the passenger door handle of grandma's car as she slowly towed me for the few blocks back to her house. The rain-cleansed air had a wet-dirt smell and was thick as a vanilla malt. Sawbuck ran alongside with a concerned look as if to say, "That looks dangerous. You could get hurt. Who would feed me?" When we got home, grandma and my mother went into the kitchen to begin another blue-ribbon meal, and I plopped down in an overstuffed chair on the porch. Gideon was in the same spot I had left him in that morning.

"You were right about the rain," I said tentatively.

There was no response. I couldn't tell if he heard me or not.

"It lasted twenty minutes, just like you said."

Still nothing.

"You could be the weatherman on TV or something. Can you do that all the time?"

I sat in the fading daylight and waited for a reply that I knew would probably never come. I didn't know if his "forecast" had come from the spirit world or was just a good guess. Thundershowers are common in the heat of summer afternoons. After about half an hour, I got up to go inside.

"You can't sleep around here for the damn telephone," he said suddenly.

I didn't know why, but his words hit me like a coconut-creme pie in the face. It felt like millions of ants were scratching and scurrying up my body to dine on the meringue.

"What did you say?"

No reply.

Why in the hell was he doing this? What reason did he have to play with my mind? I wanted to shove him off the porch and watch him sprawl in the dirt.

"Did the telephone bother you? Did somebody call? Were you talking to me? Hello?"

I stood at the door a while longer before giving up and going into the kitchen. I didn't know whether to be angry or scared. I made a mental note to listen for the phone to ring.

"What's this about me staying at Big Mama's?" I asked.

"Do you want to go to Little Rock with us?" my mother responded.

"No, I don't. Can't I stay somewhere else?"

"You would be keeping Big Mama company, Lonnie. She loves you and don't get to spend much time with you. She won't be around forever, you know."

My mother was very adept at cracking the guilt whip.

"What's the matter? Are you afraid to stay there?" she asked, with that "mother already knows the answer" look.

"Well, maybe a little. It's a scary place."

"I reckon you could stay here with Gideon," grandma interjected.

"I'm sure me and Big Mama will have a lot of fun," I said quickly. Ghosts beat a freaky old man any day.

I watched grandma busily creating her magic, with worn pots and black iron skillets as her props, as the faint odor of a thousand suppers hung in the air. She had walked many a mile on the split and peeling linoleum rug, worn into paths between the stove and the sink and the table. Even when she didn't have visitors she would be baking pies to give to friends or canning vegetables or preserves for the cold winter days. She found solace in her kitchen. She was in control there, and the drudgery helped pass the time. Though she was quick to laugh, there was a deep sadness in her eyes. People said that when my grandfather, Thomas Jefferson Spates, was killed in a locomotive explosion, the light went out of her heart.

I knew virtually nothing about my grandfather. I had never even seen a picture of him. My mother was just a baby when he died, and she had no memory of him at all. I asked grandma to tell me about him once, and tears swelled in her eyes. She said, "He was the purtiest man I ever saw," and that was all she volunteered.

We never visited our Spates' relatives very much, for reasons I wasn't privy to, even though Thomas' mother and father, my great-grandmother and grandfather, lived just outside of town. I would occasionally go by and visit with Mammy and Paw, but we were not close at all. I assumed that after my grandfather's death and grandma's marriage to Gideon things had changed. I had never asked Mammy about my grandfather because I was afraid that talking about it might cause her pain, too.

I did know something about how he died, however.

He had just received a promotion of some sort the week before he died. He had been chosen over several others with more seniority, and it had raised some hackles. A few of the men, some of them lifelong friends, had turned on him. On the night he was killed in 1924, according to the accounts I had heard over the years, he left the depot around 8:30 to walk up the street to Suzy's Cafe for dinner, as he often did when he worked at night. On this particular occasion, however, he was not back when he should have been.

After he had been gone for over two hours, one of his coworkers went to Suzy's to look for him and was told that he hadn't been there that night. At just that moment, a blast rocked the building, shattering the windows and knocking out the power.

People began running to the depot before the echo died. What they found was horrifying. A steam locomotive, number 1550, had exploded with such force that the boiler had been thrown 235 feet in one direction and the cab 185 feet the opposite way. The depot itself had sustained some damage, but other than a near myocardial infarction or two, no one inside was seriously hurt. Many windows lay in shards, and chunks of the train had rained down like metal hail over a wide area, narrowly missing homes and businesses.

Among the debris, nearly 100 feet from the twisted and smoking steel wheels that remained in place on the track, they found the body of my grandfather. He was pronounced "blowed up" at the scene.

No one knew where he had been for the two hours that were unaccounted for, or exactly what caused the explosion, but it appeared that he had climbed aboard the train unseen, and for some unfathomable reason, injected cold water into a sizzling hot, bone-dry boiler. Everybody said that was so unlike Tom Spates that there had to be another explanation. He was too smart, they said, to ever do anything so dumb.

No real investigation took place, however, and it was ruled an accident. But the general consensus from the people who knew Tom was, it was either sabotage, or he was murdered and left there before the engine blew apart. Neither scenario was especially appealing to me. I made up my mind that I would find out more about it.

I grabbed my Sherlock Holmes anthology and went to the back porch, sat on the steps, and started reading *The Hound of the Baskervilles* for the umpteenth time. It always got my juices flowing. I tried to imagine how Sherlock would solve the case of "The Booger of Moro."

The first thing I thought he would do is to establish a profile of the Booger and eliminate the people that it couldn't be. The Booger had been showing up for the last forty years. If it was human, it had to be a lifelong resident, most likely male, sixty years or older. Gideon himself fell into that category, but there was no sane reason to waste my limited amount of suspicion on him. Whoever it was had to be in fairly good shape to get away quickly, and Gideon couldn't get away from anything quickly.

That narrowed the list of suspects down considerably. I could think of several off the top of my head. The three men I had just seen at Willie's: Charlie Banks, Horace Moore, and Cooper Logan, as well as Willie himself, all fit the bill. I could pay every one of them a visit in a matter of a few days. I imagined asking clever, probing questions designed to trip them up and cause them to spill their guts. I pictured myself pointing to the guilty party and hearing him scream, "Damn you, Lonnie Tobin!" as the police hauled him away.

I was trying to figure out how I could strike up a conversation without making them suspicious when it dawned on me that all of them would have known my grandfather. I could use the excuse that I was seeking knowledge about him, which I would be. It was the perfect cover. I would be killing two birds with one story. I could hardly wait to get started. Now, if only I had Annette to act as my Watson, life would be sweet!

But even without 'Nette—my intimate name for her in our imaginary relationship—life was still pretty sweet as grandma called me to supper. I knew that there were kids all over the country eating their meal from a can, and I felt graciously blessed as I viewed the bounty laid out before me. Gideon joined us at the table for the first time since our arrival. I had forgotten what it was like to break bread with him. He was a feast for the eye and ear, if you could stomach it.

With a knife clutched in one fist and a fork in the other, he crammed in as much as he could hold with each bite, as if he were eating for himself and all seven of his spirit guides. He ate without a word. But the air whistled and wheezed in his nostrils with every breath, and his lip-smacking sounded like soldiers marching through mud. He sat bent over his plate while cornbread crumbs gathered at the corners of his mouth as he chewed. His gaze remained fixed on his food as if he feared it might get up and run away at any minute. Fortunately, he ate with the speed of the starving, thereby limiting our suffering. As soon as he was done, he pushed himself up and went out on the back porch for an after-meal smoke, then went to bed with the chickens. Not literally, they just had the same bedtime.

After polishing off two hunks of chocolate cake and washing it down with a glass of cold milk, I brought Sawbuck his supper. His tail was a brown blur as he anticipated the treat that awaited him. I wondered if he ever thought of other dogs that had to dig in the garbage to find sustenance while he ate like royalty. Probably not. The only way another canine might cross his mind would be if it had the gall to approach his bowl.

I grabbed my transistor radio and went out to the front porch. Grandma had a little black and white TV, but the reception was so bad that, even with rolls of aluminum foil wrapped around the rabbit ears, it was like the picture was under a foot of new-fallen snow. Besides, I would rather listen to a ball game. I sat in the dark and tried to tune in a station that might be carrying a game. Then, I tried to tune in any damn station at all. It appeared that the television and radio signals had skipped over Moro just like the twentieth century had. Being cut off from the outside world was a major drawback to an otherwise idyllic location, but in that moment,

I wouldn't have traded places with Mickey Mantle. Okay, I might have traded with "The Mick" but hardly anybody else. Well, maybe Annette's neighbor.

I listened to the murmur of my mother and grandma discussing their trip to Little Rock, which reminded me that I had committed to spending the night at Big Mama's. What the hell was I thinking? I would rather have sixpenny nails driven into my head than stay all night in that House of Usher. Though I loved all three of them dearly, I thought it unfair to force me to choose between a tedious trip to Little Rock and a ride on Satan's roller-coaster. But I really did want to try out for the Hogskinners, so I made up my mind that I was just going to suck it up and stay awake all night with the lights on.

The sudden ear-piercing ring of the telephone caused Sawbuck and me to levitate for a moment. As my heart slid back into place, I thought of Gideon's comment earlier. I heard grandma pick it up on the second ring.

"Hello … hold on a minute." She put her hand over the mouthpiece and called to my mother, "Ruby Jo, it's Harley."

"Shit, what does *he* want?"

"He wants to talk to you. Do you want me to tell him you cain't come to the phone?"

"No, he'll just call back. I'll take it." Grandma handed her the phone and sat down on the sofa.

"Yeah," my mother said. "What do you want? … Is that a fact? … Uh huh … well scratch your ass and get glad … I don't care … well you can come all you want to but we ain't gonna be here. I'm goin' to Little Rock to look for work."

My heart sank like a cat dropped down a well. He was coming. I should have known he would, but I had tried to convince myself that we were truly free of him.

"I don't care what you say, we ain't comin' back down there," she continued. "He's asleep … No, I ain't gonna wake him up, and he don't want to talk to you anyway. I know he's your son, but you ain't worth a damn as a father … well … you can bring your ignorant ass up here if you want to, but we ain't gonna be here." She hung up with feeling.

"Bastard!"

"Is he comin' up here?" grandma asked.

"Said he was. I told him we wouldn't be here, but he said he was comin' anyway. Lonnie, baby, come in here a minute please."

I got up and went into the living room. As the screen door closed, I heard Gideon cough. The phone had obviously woken him.

"I guess you was listenin'?" she asked. I nodded in the affirmative. "I reckon you'll have to go to Little Rock with us, Lonnie. I'm sorry, but it looks like we don't have any choice."

"Why, mama?" Suddenly the thought of staying with Big Mama seemed almost appealing.

"I'm afraid that if your daddy finds you he'll try to take you back with him just to spite me."

"I'll stay out of sight, I promise."

"You know if he comes here and don't find us, he'll go to Big Mama's. What are you gonna to do, hide under the house?"

Staying *under* that house instead of *inside* it might be less frightening.

"I'll keep out of sight, I promise. I'll watch for him. He may not come up at all. Was he drunk?"

"Hell, he's always drunk."

"See. Tomorrow he might not even remember calling. I'll go stay with Aunt Kate and Willie if I have to. Please, mama, I'm not a child anymore. I'm almost fifteen. I can take care of myself. I want to stay. Please?"

"Lord, help us," she said. "Why do we have to put up with this? I guess it's my fault for ever marryin' him in the first place."

"But if you hadn't, you wouldn't have Lonnie," grandma said.

My mother looked at me for a long moment.

"All right, Lonnie, you can stay, but you got to promise me that you'll be careful, and if you see that sorry thing, you'll run and hide."

"I promise, mama. Don't worry about anything. I'll be fine," I said with more confidence than I felt.

At that point, I heard a match strike from behind the bedroom door as Gideon lit a cigarette. I went back out on the porch. I realized that he had done it again. Gideon was communicating with me through little cryptic messages. It had to be. He was right about the rain, and now he had predicted that the phone would wake him. What other rational explanation could there be? If that was true, it could mean that I might indeed have a reason for being there. Maybe something was going on beneath the surface of everyday events. I went to sleep that night shadowboxing with the implications of that possibility.

Chapter Six

Wreathed in Smoke

My mother woke me up early the next morning to have breakfast before they left for Little Rock. I joined them at the table. Gideon had already eaten and was manning his battle station on the porch.

"Are you sure you'll be all right if I leave you here?" my mother asked.

"Yes, mama. I'll be okay, I promise. I really don't believe daddy will come up here. I think he was just bluffing. He's probably glad we're gone."

"Well, I hope so, but I'll be worried sick 'til we get back. Here's five dollars, so you'll have some money in your pocket."

To me, five dollars was a king's ransom. I did not intend to allow it to remain in my pocket for long.

"Now, don't make yourself sick buyin' candy and sodas with that," she warned.

"Don't worry. I'll stop before I become ill."

"We'll call Big Mama when we get there to check on you."

"I'll be fine, mama. Don't concern your pretty little head about it."

"Yeah, well, if you give Big Mama any trouble. I'll whip your pretty little butt."

After breakfast, I helped them load grandma's car with enough gear for an African safari. My mother had left her car at a friend's house so my father wouldn't see it if he came up. I stood by the road waving as they disappeared in the dust. As the sound of the tires in the gravel faded, I felt very grown up. I turned and walked back to the house. Gideon was at his post on the porch, wreathed in smoke as he conferred with his unseen entities. He had known my grandfather well. They were good friends from what I had heard. However, even *thinking* of getting any information from him was like expecting Sawbuck to author my term paper.

I retrieved a shovel handle that I had sawed off to the perfect length for indulging in my favorite activity, batting rocks. Over the years, I had worn out thousands of broom and mop handles doing this. It had really helped to strengthen my wrists and develop my eye and swing. After hitting a few million marble-sized stones with a thin piece of wood, a baseball coming in to the plate seemed as big as a pumpkin to me. Last year, I batted over .700 and was the only kid on my team that could clear the fence. I planned to get a good warm up before trying out for the Hogskinners that afternoon.

I was going to walk up the road a little ways where there was an open field that I could hit the rocks into, but I stopped by the porch first.

"You were right about the phone waking you up," I said to Gideon, "and I just wondered if you had anything else to tell me before I leave."

I felt foolish as I stood there in the silence.

"Any weather forecasts?"

Nothing.

I gave up, called Sawbuck, and was on the way out of the yard when he spoke.

"Miss Spicy."

"What?" I asked. "Did you say Miss Spicy?"

There was no answer. Obviously, this was his pronouncement for the day. I waited until I was pretty sure he wasn't going to reveal anything else then walked up the road. Miss Spicy Spates, if that was whom he was referring to, was my oldest living relative. The last time I had seen her was at Papa's funeral when I was eight and she was 100. I didn't know if she was still alive, but if she was, she would be 106. Was Gideon predicting her imminent demise? Hell, at her age, Sawbuck could predict her imminent demise. That couldn't be it.

As I tossed rocks up in the air and sent them rocketing into the field, wielding the shovel handle like a Louisville slugger, I mulled over the question of why Gideon would mention Miss Spicy. I knew she had been a teacher, was never married, and was my great, great, great, great aunt, but that was about it. I would have to ask Big Mama about her. I continued sending rocks sailing for the next hour, both right and left-handed, while Sawbuck dozed in a nest of pine needles.

Once I felt good and warmed up, I went back to the house. I stashed my now heavily chewed up shovel handle and checked in with Gideon for messages. I was becoming more comfortable with our curious relationship, but being all alone with him was still like trying to relax and watch a ballgame in Dracula's den.

I hooked my glove and cleats on the handlebar, jumped on my bike, and headed for Big Mama's with Sawbuck loping alongside. I always felt safer with Sawbuck near. I knew he would defend me to the death. He was like a brother and father-protector and friend all rolled into a dog hide. And damn it, I was convinced he practiced mental telepathy—at least on occasion.

I rolled up to Big Mama's back gate and felt the same old rush of apprehension. It was a cross between the heebie-jeebies and the creeps. I called it the "Heebie J. Creeps." I was a clever lad, but I had to look at everything from a somewhat humorous angle just to keep my wits about me. And lately my wits had been threatening to resign.

The backyard was dotted with chickens that were busy scratching and pecking the ground. I watched one snow-white hen for a moment as she stood on one leg and raked up a little dirt with the other foot. Then, she would turn her head from side to side to check for any uncovered treasure. She repeated the process until she found something worth consuming. She did this all of her waking life. Chickens aren't members of the bird world's intelligentsia; but being near to them and having to avoid their copious droppings brought to mind a traumatic incident from my early childhood.

One day when I was about six, I watched Uncle Willie and Grandma

Birdie slaughter a few fryers. Willie would stretch the chicken's neck over a stump and chop the head off with a small axe. It was grandma's job to throw a washtub over the body as it flapped around in its death throes. I could hear the thuds and bumps from beneath the tin tub as she held it down.

Everything went like clockwork until the third victim. After the blade fell, grandma missed, and I saw the headless body of that chicken haul ass across the yard and crash full-speed into the fence. It continued to pump its legs furiously until it suddenly stiffened and keeled over. I couldn't eat a drumstick for months. The first time I heard someone say, "running around like a chicken with its head cut off," I said, "Oh, did you see one too?"

Up the back steps I leapt, calling for Big Mama. I wasn't going to set foot inside the door until I knew she was home. She answered, and I entered the porch and went into the kitchen.

"Good mornin', Lonnie. How are you, sweetheart?"

"I'm fine, Big Mama. How are you doing?"

"Well, I ain't going to a barn dance anytime soon. Other than that I'm fair to middlin', I reckon. Are you hungry?"

"No, I ate before mama and grandma left. Did they tell you that daddy might come up here?"

"Yeah, Birdie told me. I ain't gonna let on about anything if he comes around here. I'm gonna tell him that y'all went to Little Rock, and I don't know when you're comin' back. It's been a long time since I had a chance to lie to somebody. Makes me feel a little naughty."

We both laughed at the idea of her wickedness. I could see the likeness of my grandma and my mother under the age-lines on her face. The same rich brown eyes, the full lips, and finely shaped nose, all perfectly placed. I had gotten my blue eyes and black hair from my father. I also hoped I would inherit his sheer bulk so that one day I could slap the crap out of him.

"Is Miss Spicy Spates still alive?" I asked.

"She sure is. Still lives on the old Spates' home place. Got a colored woman that stays there and takes care of her. Now, why in the world would you ask about her?"

"Oh, no reason, really. It's just that she would know a lot about our genealogy."

"Now, Lonnie, you got to keep in mind that I'm a poor old woman with hardly no schoolin'. What did you just say, sweetheart?"

"I mean she would know a lot about our family tree. I'd like to ask her some questions about the Spates' family. Is she really a hundred and six years old?"

"Well, I'm eighty three, and she was a full growed woman when I was just a sprig of a girl. She must be well past a hundred."

"Just think about it. It's 1960 now, so she was born seven years *before* the first cannon ball landed in Fort Sumter!"

"Well, what is it you was wantin' to know about the Spates? I ain't as old as Spicy, but maybe I could help you."

"I'm mostly interested in my grandfather, Thomas Spates. Mama don't remember him at all, and when I asked grandma about him, she got real teary and didn't really tell me anything."

"Well, I can tell you what I know about Tom. But, you might not like everything I might say."

"I don't care, Big Mama. I want to find out what kind of person he was. Good and bad."

She took a sip of tea. "Do you want some tea, Lonnie?"

"I'll get it," I said. "You can go on with what you were going to tell me."

I pried four ice cubes out of the only tray in the tiny freezer compartment of the ancient refrigerator, dropped them into a thick glass, poured the sweetened tea, added a liberal squeeze of lemon juice and sat down. She still hadn't said a word.

"Well?" I asked with upraised eyebrows.

She took a deep breath.

"Tom Spates was a real nice looking feller," she began. "Trouble was, he knowed it. He'd go with five or six women at the same time. And every one of 'em knowed about the others, and it didn't seem to bother 'em a bit. I wasn't happy at all when he come a'courtin' Birdie. Neither was Papa. He worked with Tom on the railroad, and he hated him."

"Why did Papa hate him?" I asked.

"Well, he said Tom was a smart-aleck and rubbed him the wrong way. And Papa knew about all the women, some of them married, that Tom fooled around with before he courted Birdie. We did everything we could to discourage her, but it was too late, she had already fell for him. She'd sit around the house all moony and frettin' knowing he was out with another woman and swear on the Bible that she'd never speak to him agin. Then, he'd come riding up on his horse and smile at her and she'd melt like lard in a skillet. Would you pour me some more tea, sweetheart?"

I jumped up, grabbed the pitcher, and refilled her glass.

"I hate to admit it, but I was real happy when Tom left to go overseas during the first war. He was gone for more'n two years. She wrote him a whole buncha letters, but she never heard one word back from him. She said he probably didn't get 'em, and that's why he didn't answer. I thought he had just lost interest, and I was awful proud he did. Birdie was a pretty girl and had a pack of suitors courtin' her, all of 'em better'n Tom Spates, in my opinion. I hope I'm not upsettin' you talkin' this way about your grandpaw, Lonnie."

"Not at all, Big Mama. Like I said, I want to know everything."

"Well, he come back from the Army and showed up on our porch one day. And it was just like he never left. Birdie was still in love with him. But he was kinda changed. He always seemed like somethin' was troublin' him. We kinda figgered the war had done it to him. Anyway, we begged her not to marry him, but she did anyway. Papa didn't go to the weddin' and never said a word to Tom after they was married, and Tom never come to the house. It just tore Birdie up that they didn't get along. Papa always swore that Tom run around on her."

"Do you think he did?"

"I don't have any idear. I mean, I wouldn't be surprised if he did, but I don't have no way of knowin'."

"What do you remember about when he was killed?"

"Oh Lord, Lonnie, it was awful. When that train went off that night it nearly knocked me outta bed. I thought the world was comin' to an end. Papa was workin' that night at the depot, fillin' in for Richard Hannagan, who was out sick. It was a terrible night, sittin' there by myself not knowin' what had happened. I didn't have no phone nor nothin'. I didn't find out 'til that next mornin' when Papa come home that Tom had been killed."

She paused and took another deep breath.

"His head was plum gone, they said. They searched for it with dogs and everything, but they never found it. They buried him without it. It perty near killed Birdie. She ain't never been the same since."

"Man, I didn't know that." I said, as the gravity of her words sank in. I had assumed that the body was somewhat mutilated due the force of the blast, but no one had told me that his head had been *lost*.

"I've heard that some people think that there was foul play involved. Do you know anything at all about that?" I asked.

"Yeah, some of the menfolk that worked with him said they thought somebody rigged it up to kill him. And the truth is, there was some that might'a done it. A lot of people thought he was too uppity. And some men didn't like the way he flirted with their women. But I think it was just one of those things that happen. Just a unlucky accident."

We sat quiet for a few minutes. I couldn't shake the vision of my decapitated grandfather lying in the weeds beside the railroad tracks while some shadowy figure made his escape. I changed the subject in hopes that it would go away.

"What about the Booger?" I asked. "Do you know anything about that?"

"Not really. A lotta people have said they've heard it bangin' on Wallace and Velmer's house. I never did, but I reckon' there's somethin' to it. It's been around a mighty long time."

"Do you know of anybody that might have something against Wallace or Velma?"

"Not that I know about. Everybody seems to like 'em both as far as

I can tell. Velmer is kinda unfriendly-like sometimes, but I don't reckon that'd be a reason to go beatin' on her house."

"No, I guess not. Well, thanks for talking to me, Big Mama. I'm gonna run uptown and practice with the Hogskinners before the game, if you don't mind."

"You be careful, Lonnie. Will you be back for supper?"

"Yeah, I'll be here."

"All right, I'll have us a bite cooked. I'll leave the porch light on if it's after dark."

Oh God, I will be in this house after dark. Suddenly, I didn't feel so grown up anymore. I finished my tea, kissed Big Mama on the cheek, and left. I pedaled past the ball field and Wallace's and Willie's stores all the way up to the railroad crossing where multiple tracks bisected the road. There were a dozen or more cars on the side rails waiting to be connected to some diesel engine and pulled to points unknown. I had often crawled into the empty boxcars and imagined what it would be like to ride the rails and see America up close. Watching the fruited plains and the purple mountain majesties slowly pass the open door all sounded adventurous and exciting, but I knew the first time I had to wipe myself with leaves I would want to go home.

I got off my bike and pushed it up the tracks to the right, all the way to where the old depot once stood. It was on this now barren spot that my grandfather had been blown into eternity. Every time I visited this lonely place, I could almost hear the blast of a steam whistle and a shout of "All aboard." I always had the feeling that I wasn't alone, and that day was no exception. Icy fingers started working on my spine, and it wasn't a Swedish massage.

I tried to imagine what it was like on that night long ago. The lights of the depot would have illuminated engine 1550 as it sat on the tracks, chuffing and hissing, building pressure in the boiler like air filling a balloon. I could picture my grandfather walking up out of the darkness, coming from who knows where. He climbs aboard the engine and doesn't notice that something is amiss. Then, he reaches for the water lever and pulls. Boom.

I didn't know where the various parts of the train had ended up, or where the body was found, but the fact that his head was never located caused my stomach to twist into knots. I suddenly wished that Big Mama hadn't shared that tidbit of information with me. The area around the weed-covered old foundation was open and clear, but just up the rails a short distance, the woods on both sides of the track became nearly impenetrable. Maybe that's where his head ended up. I thought for a moment about using Sawbuck to conduct a search myself but quickly dismissed it as the ravings of a lunatic.

"I'm going to find out who was responsible for this, Grandpa," I said out loud.

As soon as the words were out of my mouth, I realized how silly they sounded. The explosion had occurred thirty-six years ago for heaven's sake. Most of the people who were here when it happened have moved away or died. I had a much better chance of catching the Booger, and that was about as likely as Grandma Birdie screwing up a pot roast. Even though the sun was beating down, a sudden coldness brushed my face. I decided to mosey on down the road.

I moseyed up to Willie's in a cloud of dust. It's amazing how fast you can mosey when you're properly motivated. People were already gathering for the ballgame. The "Skinners," as they were called, were scheduled to take on the Star City Cowboys, the best team in the league. Willie always did a brisk business on home games. So much that he had bought new shirts for the team with "Hogskinners" printed on the front and "Willie's Beer Haven" on the back. It was rumored that Aunt Kate had a major hissy-fit over the expenditure.

I walked into the already crowded store and saw the man I was looking for sitting on a stool drinking a Pepsi. It was Ben Oliver, the coach of the Skinners. His nickname was "Two-By," which had been shortened from "two-by-four." He had acquired this peculiar sobriquet because his flat nose looked like someone had smashed him in the face with a two-by-four. As I approached him, I realized that he would fit the Booger profile also, along with half the men in the room.

"Hi, Mr. Oliver." I said, too uncomfortable to call him Two-By. "I'm Lonnie Tobin."

"Well hello, Lonnie. How are ya, son?"

"I'm fine, sir."

"I know your daddy real well. How's he doing?"

"He's okay, I guess."

"One time, I seen him knock a man out, cold as the grave, with an open hand slap. Damndest thing I ever saw. I sure as hell wouldn't want that man mad at me."

Everybody who knew my father seemed compelled to relate his exploits to me.

"Yes, sir, uh, I wanted to ask you if it was all right if I shagged some flies with you guys during practice?"

"I don't see why not. Besides, if I said no, it might make your daddy mad," he said with a chuckle. "I'm headed over to the field right now. Come on."

We walked across the street to where the guys were gathered around the single bench behind third base that served as the dugout, taking out the bats and balls and catcher's gear. The Skinners weren't the worst team in the league, but they were close. The best player they had was a pitcher named Buddy Kilgore. His claim to fame was that he pitched one year for the Arkansas Razorbacks. He went 7 and 0 with an ERA of 1.50.

He pitched only one season because, even though he had a fair fastball and a wicked country curve, he couldn't strike out his love of the bottle. It was the age-old story of squandered opportunities. When Buddy was on the mound, the Skinners usually won, but Two-By wasn't able to schedule him until he showed up at the field. If he was sober, he started.

And speak of the devil, just then a green '57 Chevy pulled up and out stepped Buddy Kilgore, sober as a judge, his black hair slicked back in the style of a fifties rock and roll singer. His appearance was a huge morale booster to the rest of the team because now they felt they had a chance to knock off the mighty Cowboys. The team seemed to play above its head when Buddy was pitching.

I laced up my cleats, grabbed my glove, and jogged to the outfield as Two-By started throwing batting practice. The railroad tracks served as the right field wall, and a long fence that curved around to meet the tracks and enclosed a patch of weeds and a small pond was both the left and centerfield boundaries. I stood smelling the freshly cut grass trying to shake the thought that my grandfather's head was still somewhere in the vicinity. Thanks, Big Mama.

Cars were parking along the gravel road as the rickety bleachers behind home plate filled up. Lawn chairs sprouted behind the dugouts and along the foul lines as children romped and played. Hogskinner home games were big events in Moro. People came in from miles around, with baskets full of fried chicken and biscuits, to cheer on the team, visit with friends, and drink a lot of Willie's beer.

I made what I thought were some pretty spectacular over the shoulder and shoestring catches, scooped up every grounder sent my way, and fired it into the appropriate base. I was trying hard to impress Two-By in hopes he might put me in the game at some point. I knew I was just a kid, but I was good, dammit.

Then, I saw Nelda Graves sitting in a folding chair behind the Skinner's bench, and my heart skipped a beat. She was the daughter of Homer Graves, the pastor of Moro Baptist Church, and his wife, Deborah. If there was any girl in the world that could steal my heart from Annette Funicello, it would be the lovely Nelda. We were going to be in the same class that fall at Moro High. The sight of her made me chew my tongue. I now had someone else to impress.

By this time, Buddy had taken the mound to throw some batting practice to warm up. With the power of his arm, the hits in my direction soon dried up. I jogged in to the bench in hopes of being able to take a couple of swings myself. I picked up three bats at once, something Ty Cobb had always done, and swung them several times while glancing over to see if Nelda was watching. I waited until the last man had taken his cuts then stepped into the batter's box and dug in.

"I ain't pitchin' to no kid," Buddy pronounced as he started off the mound. I was embarrassed at first, but when I saw Nelda sitting there with what I interpreted as a disappointed frown on her fetching face, I got angry.

"What's the matter?" I yelled. "Afraid a kid can hit you?"

He stopped, looked at me for a few seconds, turned, and walked back to the mound. Oh shit, he was going to throw to me. I must learn to keep my stupid mouth shut.

"Well, let's just see if a kid can hit me," he drawled as he shifted his chew to the other cheek. "Step up to the plate, *kid*."

Once again, I dug in. Though I could hit from both sides of the plate, I went right-handed because I was stronger from that side. I hoped Nelda couldn't hear my heart pounding. I stared at Buddy as he went into his windup. He kicked his leg high and came overhand with a blistering fastball aimed directly at my left ear. I hit the dirt rather unceremoniously. I lay there as the laughter washed over me.

"What's the matter, kid? I thought you could hit me," Buddy taunted.

I got up and brushed the dirt off. I looked at Nelda. She averted her eyes.

"Put one over the plate, and I'll show you," I said with a whole lot more boldness than I felt at the moment.

Buddy stared at me from atop the mound. "Well, you got guts, kid. I'll give you that. I'm gonna throw one right past you, just to shut you up."

I stepped to the plate and assumed my stance. I knew he was coming with the fastball, his best pitch. I knew he wanted to humiliate me. I knew the chances that he would succeed were astronomical.

I focused on his lanky form as he wound up, kicked, and fired. In the split second that I had to react, I saw that it was indeed the fastball coming right down the center of the plate. I stepped forward with my left foot and swung from the heels.

To me, there is no greater feeling in life than connecting with a baseball on the sweet spot of the bat. I drove a screaming line drive over the mound, causing Buddy to hit the dirt much as I had earlier. The ball ended up rolling to the fence in centerfield. It was like something out of a movie. I stood there with the bat in my hands knowing that I could never do that again if my life depended on it. Buddy got up amidst the laughter that was now directed at him. From the look on his face, I knew I had made an enemy. He stormed off the mound.

"Good hit, Lonnie!" Two-By said as I walked to the bench. Buddy was suffering the jibes from his teammates and wouldn't look at me.

"Thanks. Do you think I might be able to join the team?"

"How old are you?"

"I'm fourteen."

"Fourteen? Damn. If you can hit like that at fourteen, you gonna be a heck of a ball player someday. But you gotta be sixteen to play in this league. Sorry, kid."

"I'll be fifteen in December."

"Sorry. The rule is sixteen."

I was as deflated as a popped blister. I walked away not intending to even stay for the game, when I heard Nelda's voice.

"That was a good hit, Lonnie," she said. "Would you like to sit with me during the ball game?"

Did I want to sit with her? What an asinine question from such a cutie-pie. I would sit on a bed of hot coals to be next to her. My blister was full again.

"Sure. It would be my pleasure," I said, trying to sound as mature as my newly arrived pubescence would allow. "I'm about to go to Willie's for a soft drink. May I get you one?"

"Yes, please. May I have a root beer?"

I floated over to Willie's. "Yes, please, may I have a root beer?" she had asked with her soft, honey-dripping drawl. She wanted me, Lonnie Tobin, to sit with her. This was turning out to be a wonderful day. People were congratulating me on my hit and for putting Buddy Kilgore in his place, and now the prettiest girl this side of Disneyland had requested my presence for the game. If I had won the lottery, I couldn't have felt luckier.

I rejoined Nelda with the sodas and a bag of gingersnaps I had found on Willie's shelf that I hoped weren't *too* stale. She offered a lawn chair. I gratefully accepted and sat down beside her. I got lost in her lavender eyes and blonde hair as we made uncomfortable small talk before the game, all under the watchful eye of the Reverend Graves. I suddenly couldn't remember Annette, uh, what's her name.

The Star City Cowboys had arrived in their clean white uniforms with the word "Cowboy" written across the chest in rope-cursive. They looked good as they whipped the ball around the infield during pre-game practice. They had a couple of good pitchers, but their best player was the leftfielder, Clyde Nutt. He could "jack a ball a half a mile" someone once said. I had seen him send two rockets over the parked boxcars in right field in one game last summer when the Cowboys had branded the Skinners twelve to three. Buddy Kilgore just happened to be drunk and not on the mound that day.

Buddy mowed down the three batters he faced in the top of the first. In the Skinners' half of the inning, the Cowboys' pitcher struck out the first two swinging. Then Buddy himself parked a curve in the pond over the leftfield fence. The Skinners picked up another run in the fifth on a base hit and a triple and held on to the lead until the Cowboys started getting to Buddy. They got four runs in the eighth on a towering grand slam from Clyde Nutt and two more in the ninth. It was over.

I was only vaguely aware of the activities on the field, however. I was keeping one eye peeled for my father, but most of my attention was focused on the fair Nelda seated next to me. Over the course of the afternoon, I had plied her with several root beers and a fresh moon-pie I bought at Wallace's store after the gingersnaps from Willie's turned out to be leftover rations from a confederate knapsack. I was beginning to think of her as my girlfriend. I knew it was early in our relationship, but it seemed that she returned my affections. I walked with her to her parents' car, and we agreed to sit together at the next game. I was so smitten I even thought about becoming a member of her father's flock.

Things were getting rowdy at Willie's as Sawbuck and I headed back to Big Mama's. Saturday nights were always their busiest time, and on game days, he and Aunt Kate made a killing. I decided to go back after supper and check it out. Besides, if my father did show up, the first thing he would do, even before looking for us, is have a few cold ones at Willie's.

I told Big Mama of my feats on the field, with only minor embellishments, while we ate a supper of venison and fresh vegetables. I could see where Grandma Bertie got her culinary skills. She told me that my mother had called to let me know they had made it and to check on me. We talked for a while about various subjects as I wallowed in the afterglow of the day.

"Big Mama, would you mind if I went up to Willie's for a little while?" I asked as night settled in. "I can keep an eye out for daddy, because you know that's where he'll go if he shows up."

After some thought, she said, "I reckon it'll be all right. Just don't stay late, and if you do see your daddy, you get on home as fast as you can, hear me?"

"Yes, ma'am," I said as I bolted out the door. The thought struck me that leaving this house in the dark was going to be a whole lot easier than coming back to it.

I pedaled around the corner of Wallace's store, and my heart splashed into my stomach when I saw my father's red Ford pickup parked among the others in front of Willie's. Cursing under my breath, I stashed my bike behind the store then sneaked back up to the front. Johnny Cash was blaring from the jukebox about falling into a burning ring of fire as I looked through the window. I felt like I was dangling above the flames myself.

The room was full of men drinking, laughing, and talking loud to be heard above the commotion. I searched the faces of the crowd and saw my father sitting on the bench beneath the Custer painting with a beer in his hand. Once again, I was struck by his resemblance to John Wayne. Some of the guys he worked with called him "The Duke." He was actually bigger than Wayne, and I always thought he could whip the real Duke any day of the week. My brief moment of pride in him was over in the time it took to remember how he had threatened my mother.

I had been spying on things for about half an hour when I heard the unmistakable sound of the Roark brothers' mufflerless old truck coming up the road. I slipped around the corner as they roared to a stop near the gas pumps. They climbed out of the cab and the bed and lumbered inside.. I went back to the window.

The brothers ordered beers from Kate and stood at the bar drinking, scroungy as ever, while they surveyed the room. Had my father heard of my little run in with Waylon? More than likely he had, since gossip was the life-blood of this town. I was sure that if he did know he would say something. Hank Williams finished singing about melting a cold, cold heart, and the room fell silent for a moment.

"What in the hell is that stink?" a loud voice said. It was my father. He knew. "Smells like shit. Oh, it's Waylon and the boys. Hello there, Waylon. You too, boys."

Waylon looked over to where my father sat.

"Well, I'll be damn. If it ain't Harley fuckin' Tobin hisself."

"That's me. Hey, Waylon, tell me something, have you bullied any little boys lately?"

"What the hell you talkin' about?"

"Well, the way I hear it, you like to pick on children. Like my son, Lonnie. Is that true?"

Waylon turned to the bar, ordered another beer from Aunt Kate, and killed half of it. Everyone in the room held their breath as they waited for the impending confrontation.

"I shore nuff did speak with yore boy, now that you mention it. What about it?"

"From what I've heard, you was giving my son a pretty rough time. Even threatened to whip him, I understand. Did that make you feel like a big man, Waylon? Pickin' on my fourteen-year old son? What kinda low-life scumbag would pick on a kid?"

"You callin' me a scumbag, Tobin?"

I did a quick mental comparison of the two of them. My father was taller but about forty pounds lighter.

"Well, you know what, Waylon? There's several things I could call you besides a scumbag. Let's see, there's lard-butt, dip-shit, or dumb-ass. Which would you prefer?"

Laughter rolled around the room. Waylon stood like a grizzly bear, glaring at my father who was still calmly sitting on the bench. My heart was redlining and on the verge of throwing a rod.

"But I do feel sorry for you boys," my father continued. "If it weren't for them hogs of yours and your pitiful ugly-ass sisters, y'all wouldn't get no lovin' at all."

Waylon looked at his brothers as a rotten smile spread over his uncomely features.

"What do y'all think, boys? Y'all think I ort to teach this sonuvabitch to have some respect for his betters?"

"I reckon it to be yore duty, Waylon," one of the brothers said.

"You gotta get approval from a committee, Waylon?" my father called across the tension in the room. "Or am I gonna have to whip all four of you?"

"I won't need no help takin' care a yore pussy ass, Tobin."

"Bring it on, you hog-humper."

Waylon snorted and started moving toward my father as his huge hands folded into fists. I could almost see steam erupting from his ears. The crowd parted and backed out of the way.

"Y'all need to take this outside," Willie called out.

"This won't take no time a'tall," Waylon roared. "And I promise I won't make much of a mess."

He got closer, and my father hadn't yet moved a muscle. I thought he was waiting to see if Waylon was going to throw the first punch. But just as he got within a step, my father came off the bench in a blur with a crushing right hand to Waylon's jaw, then a left hook to the side of his head, followed by another shattering overhand right that connected with the point of his chin. All three blows had landed in the blink of an eye. Waylon stood for a millisecond before dropping like a pole-axed steer. A dust cloud rose when he hit the floor.

All eyes were on my father as he stood over the vanquished Waylon.

"That didn't take long," somebody in the crowd said. Nervous laughter replaced the silence.

"Now, you boys pick him up and get him out of here," my father said to the remaining Roarks, "before I cram all three of you up his sorry ass and set the whole stinkin' bunch of you on fire. Then, go take a goddamn bath."

I jumped on my bike and pumped hard for Big Mama's. I ran inside without giving a thought to ghosts or other such nonsense. Reality was much scarier. I told Big Mama what had happened and that I was sure my father would come to the house at some point.

"You don't worry yourself none, sweetheart," she said. "I can handle Harley Tobin."

"He'll be drunk, Big Mama. He might hurt you."

"Your daddy might be a lotta things, Lonnie, but I don't think he's the kind that would hurt an old lady."

I hoped she was right, but I couldn't shake the sight of him dismantling that huge ox without working up a sweat. It was a frightening and thrilling thing to see.

"Your mama called. They'll be home about lunch time tomorrow."

"How's grandma?"

"The doctor said she was fine."

"Why did she go in the first place?"

"She was having some female problems."

"Oh."

I didn't want her to expound on just exactly what "female problems" meant. We went into her bedroom where she had several chairs arranged around her little TV set. We were able to tune in *Gunsmoke*, but the picture was so snowy it looked like Marshal Dillon and Miss Kitty were battling a blizzard inside the Long Branch. But at least it took my mind off my father for a little while. That and a large bowl of hand-cranked vanilla ice cream with a chopped up banana mixed in. Just as the show ended, I had my face buried in the bowl trying to lick out the last cold drop when we heard the knock on the front door. I didn't need Gideon's spirits to tell me who it was.

"You stay here," Big Mama said as she rose and headed for the hall.

"Don't answer it. Pretend you're not home."

"Don't be silly, Lonnie."

I stood by the door ready to slip under the bed if necessary.

"Hello, Big Mama." It was my father's voice.

"Hello, Harley. How're you?"

"I'm a little drunk right now. Is Lonnie here?"

I went under the bed with the dust bunnies at the mention of my name. A man's gotta do what a man's gotta do.

"He went to Little Rock with his mama and Birdie."

"Well, I was told he was at the ballgame today. You wouldn't tell me no story now would you, Big Mama?"

"I don't 'preciate you calling me a liar, Harley."

"I'm sorry, but that was what I was told. Would you mind if I sleep here tonight?"

"Well, I'd say you're big enough to sleep about anywhere you want, but I would prefer you go somewhere's else."

I lay in near suspended animation under the bed that Papa had died in, praying fervently that my father would just leave. The seconds dragged as I waited in silence.

"I reckon I'll go to my brother's. Tell Ruby Jo I'll be back in a few days."

"I'll let her know you come by when I see her. Goodnight." She locked the door, turned off the porch light, and came back into the bedroom. I crawled out from under the bed feeling like a cobweb-covered coward. We listened as his truck started and drove away.

"He knows I'm here."

"He ain't gonna bother you tonight, sweetheart. Let's just go to bed and get some rest."

It took a few minutes for the statement "let's go to bed" to marinate in my brain before the realization hit me that I was indeed going to be in Big Mama's house all night. My picture-perfect day was over. The clawing, all-too-familiar fear once again took up residence in my soul.

Chapter Seven

Haints & Heart Attacks

"You can sleep in the front room," she said.

She was referring to the parlor where Papa's body had lain in state after he died and outside the door of where the banker had dropped dead. I felt as if I had been bound up in Mr. Poe's pit, and the pendulum had started its slow, deadly swing.

"How about if we play a few hands before we go to bed?" I asked. "We can play poker. I've got almost two dollars."

"Oh, Lonnie, sweetheart, I wouldn't take your money. And I'm just too tired anyways. We can play tomorrow if you want. Let's go to bed."

Though I struggled and strained, I couldn't think of anything else to delay the inevitable.

"Would you mind if I left the light on tonight, Big Mama?" I asked, trying hard not to sound like a baby.

"The light switch in that room is broke, sweetheart. Willie's been promisin' to come fix it, but he ain't never got the time. You can have my flashlight."

Oh joy! A flashlight! That will help if it's a magical flashlight that has the power to ward off haints and heart attacks. If not, what damn good would it do me? How could I sleep in this house when it was dark as a crypt? I wanted the light to flood every square inch of that funeral parlor, and a flashlight just wouldn't do the trick. But the only option I had was to sleep with Big Mama, and that was even more frightening.

"I'll be right here in the next room, so you needn't be scared," she said.

Was my fear that evident? Maybe the chattering teeth gave me away.

"I'm not scared, Big Mama," I lied.

"You can gather the eggs for me in the mornin', and I'll fix us a good breakfast."

I wondered if the hens would mind me bunking with them.

"I'll leave the door between our rooms open, so you just holler if you need anything," she said.

Oh, I'll holler, don't worry about that.

"And there's clean sheets and pillow cases on the bed."

I can't promise how long the sheets will stay clean.

"You do what you need to get ready, I'm gonna put on my nightgown."

As I washed up and brushed my teeth at the sink in the kitchen, the house seemed to get bigger and darker by the second. I kept hearing noises, and I wasn't sure if it was Big Mama or the gathering of ghouls. Oh Lord, I prayed, if you help me make it through this night, I'll start going to church … and not just because Nelda will be there either.

Big Mama went with me into the front room, with the light from her open door providing the only illumination. I crawled into the bed clutching the flashlight like a lifeline. She said goodnight and went back to her room. I heard her moving around for a few minutes, and then she turned the light off and everything was inky blackness. It was as if I had suddenly gone blind. It was so dark I could actually feel it on my skin. The hard cylinder of the flashlight in my death grip was my only comfort, but I didn't want to use it because the beam would only make things more surreal.

My wide-open eyes finally adjusted a little to the almost total lack of light. I could make out the vague shape of the chest of drawers against one wall and the immense dresser near the bay windows where Papa's coffin had sat. I felt like I was in a Boris Karloff movie. Every ghost story I had ever read came flooding back to me in photographic detail. I remembered each tale of apparitions that floated into darkened rooms and laughed maniacally through slashed and gaping throats, and every poor fool found stone cold dead from fright the next morning.

I lay there with the sheet pulled up to my chin for hours, quaking at every little creak of the house as it settled. At least I was hoping that the noise I was hearing was the house settling. Big Mama's gentle snoring coming from the next room made me want to slap her. How could she just go to sleep, damn it? I felt like I was alone in the world.

Then, I heard something.

It came from the back porch. A bump and a rustle. Then, another bump. Then, quiet. Not normal quiet but that stillness that magnifies the pounding in your chest until it rings in your ears like the Tell-Tale Heart.

I'm just imagining things, I told myself. I am fully awake and suffering from an overactive imagination. That's all. I just need to concentrate on something else. I tried thinking of Nelda Graves and Annette Funicello engaged in a hair-pulling catfight over my affections, but it didn't help. Then, I heard it again.

A *clump* then a dragging sound. Another *clump* and drag. It seemed to be moving up the hallway. *Clump* … drag … *clump* … drag.

My nerves went off like a Chinese New Year when I remembered that unique sound from my early childhood. It was *Papa*, walking up the hallway on his cane, dragging his stroke-paralyzed leg behind him. My whole body was as rigid as a corpse.

The *clump*-and-drag continued, getting louder as it got closer. It stopped right outside the door to the hallway. I cannot describe the total mind-numbing terror that gripped me at that point. I couldn't breathe as I sat bolt upright in the bed staring at the door. Time stood still, trapping me in a waking nightmare. I wondered if this was what dying felt like. Then, I jumped like a startled toad when Big Mama's voice cut through the darkness.

"Don't be scared, Lonnie. It's just Papa."

What! I silently screamed at the top of my lungs.

"What?" I squeaked out loud.

She didn't answer me. It would be physically and mentally impossible for a human being to be any more scared shitless than I was at that moment.

"Did you say something, Big Mama?" I called in a voice teetering on the edge of hysteria.

Still no answer.

Oh my God, is she dead? Did she inform me that it was Papa because she was about to join him? I turned on the flashlight only to find, to my further horror, that the batteries were nearly dead. The light it threw out was no brighter than the candle Harold Paine had been holding when he stepped out of this world right outside the door, where Papa was waiting at that very moment. I mentally kicked my ass for not checking it before. But it was enough light for me to jump out of the bed and fly into Big Mama's room. She was lying on her side facing away from me.

"Big Mama," I called as I gently shook her shoulder.

"What's the matter, Lonnie?" she said sleepily as she turned over.

Relief that she wasn't dead surged through me.

"Did you hear it?" I asked, as I fought the urge to crawl into bed with her like a toddler.

"Hear what, sweetheart?"

NO! NO! That was *not* the answer I wanted to hear.

"You didn't hear the noise in the hallway?"

"I was sound asleep, Lonnie. I didn't hear a thing. You must've been dreamin', sweetheart."

"But … but you spoke to me. You said for me not to be scared because it was only …" I couldn't bring myself to say his name.

"Oh, I was probably talkin' in my sleep. Papa used to tell me that some nights I carried on whole conversations while I was asleep. That's all it was. Why don't you go on back to bed and get you some rest, sweetheart."

Oh sure, I'll just stroll on back in the tomb and lie down amongst the remains. What better place to rest one's own bones. I couldn't move.

"Would you like to sleep in here with me?"

What? In the bed where Papa died? In the bed of my nightmares?

Are you insane? Then, I thought of going back into the parlor alone, armed only with a feeble flashlight. What a choice! After a few minutes of trying to choose between fear and loathing, I got in the bed. At least Big Mama was alive.

"Big Mama?"

"Yes, Lonnie."

"Don't tell anybody about this, okay?"

"I won't, sweetheart."

"And Big Mama?"

"Yes?"

"Please, don't die in your sleep."

~

I woke up the next morning back in the front parlor. I sat up and looked around in disbelief. I felt dizzy as questions began to hammer my brain. How did I get back in this bed? What the hell was going on? How could this be? The last thing I remembered was clutching the flashlight and lying as far away from Big Mama as I could get.

The hellish terror I had felt last night came back and clamped its talons around my neck. I heard Big Mama moving around, and I vaulted out of bed and was dressed before my feet hit the floor. I flew into the kitchen where she was pouring a cup of coffee.

"Good mornin', Lonnie," she greeted me. "Did you sleep well?"

What in the hell was she talking about? She must be getting senile.

"Well, I must have finally fallen asleep sometime after I got in bed with you. But how did I end up back in my bed? You couldn't pick me up."

"What do you mean, sweetheart? You didn't get in the bed with me. If you did, I sure don't remember it."

"You don't remember talking to me?" I asked as my throat constricted.

"Not after I said goodnight. Are you all right, Lonnie? You look kinda pale."

That was because every drop of blood in my body was pooled in my feet.

"I'm okay," I mumbled, far from okay.

"You musta been dreamin', Lonnie. You'll feel better after a good breakfast. I'll start fryin' up the bacon if you'll run gather the eggs for me."

"You don't remember talking to me at all?"

"No, sweetheart. I don't. What did you say to me?"

I found it hard to speak. "Uh … nothing. I was dreaming."

I walked out the back door in a daze. I felt the way I did the first time I went outdoors after recovering from days of fever delirium the winter I had pneumonia. It was like entering a whole new world. My legs were liquid. The birds were singing, and the sun was resplendent in the cloudless blue sky, but I beheld it all from another planet.

I moved robotically, gathering the mostly brown eggs from the straw-filled boxes lining the walls of the feather-strewn hen house. There was no way to avoid stepping in chicken crap, so I just pretended it wasn't there. I was wrestling with the question of whether I had truly experienced the paranormal or just an excruciatingly realistic nightmare. Could it have occurred only in my head while I slept? I didn't even remember getting drowsy. Fear has a way of keeping one fully awake.

The noise in the hallway that froze every fluid in my body was still echoing in my ears. Talking with Big Mama and getting in the bed with her were as real to me as the warm eggs I plucked from the nests. What was happening to me? Did I need to seek professional help? Was Big Mama a sorceress who had cast a spell on me? I knew it was stupid to think she had anything to do with the disturbing events of the previous night, but whatever happened, living in Moro wasn't quite as much fun as it had been only yesterday.

I felt strange all day and couldn't stop thinking about it. My mother and grandma came back around noon, and I wanted to tell them what happened, but I knew they would just say it was a dream. And maybe it was, I just didn't know anymore. I kept it to myself. My father went back to Louisiana without making contact with us, and for the next two days, all I did was bat rocks and try to sort things out in my head. Even Sawbuck sensed that I wasn't myself. I avoided all close contact with Gideon for fear he might say something that would add to my already overloaded circuits.

I couldn't help remembering two great aunts on my father's side, Millie and Tillie Tobin, who had spent their last ten years in an insane asylum. They were identical twins who never married and lived their entire lives together. They passed away before I was born, but I had heard stories of their eccentricities.

Before they were tucked away in the "loony lodge," they would often wander out at night completely nude, their full figures creating a rather disturbing sight as they walked the darkened streets. They insisted that they understood what the animals were trying to communicate to mankind, which was pretty much "please don't kill us." On Sunday afternoons, dressed in their finest gowns for tea parties in the parlor, Millie and Tillie were certain they were entertaining such notable guests as Julius Caesar, Thomas Jefferson, and Jesse James.

Millie died suddenly one Saturday. Tillie screeched and screamed until she also expired within the hour. I wondered if that strain of insanity had found its way to me. Even though I felt no impulse to disrobe in public, I did want to ask Jesse James what in the hell he was thinking when he turned his back on that weasel Bob Ford.

Even after regaining some sense of balance, the emotional charge of that night left me feeling almost born again, in an eerie sort of way. As life began to flow back into my mind and body, I made a solemn promise to myself that, come hell or high water, wars or rumors of wars, earthquakes, hurricanes, pestilences, or an attack from outer freaking space, I would never again spend the night at Big Mama's house. Upon reaching that firm, set-in-stone commitment, I was ready to rejoin the world.

Chapter Eight

Following the Path of My Ancestors

After breakfast one morning, I headed out from grandma's to pay Miss Spicy Spates a visit, because of Gideon's mention of her a few days earlier. I didn't know what I would learn, but if her mind was still sound, she could be a fountain of information. I hoped for at least a dribble.

I couldn't help being a little excited at the thought of finding out about family members who had once lived and loved, plowed and planted, swore and sweated on this land. People whose blood I carried in my veins, who struggled to pry a life from the hard fist of nature and were now resting from their earthly toils in the Spates' cemetery.

I rode through the glorious morning along the broad gravel road toward Fordyce. Right outside town, I passed one of the county's tall, yellow road-graders, with the driver ensconced in a glass cab on top. A wide blade under its belly was scraping and smoothing out the rough surfaces of the road like a giant metal insect tending its nest. The thick forest of trees that hugged both shoulders and towered straight up like verdant skyscrapers was a reminder of a time when this well-kept roadway did not exist.

It probably began eons ago as an Indian or animal trail, or both, slowly carved across miles of wilderness by a river of feet, hooves, and paws. An increasingly popular route that offered ease of passage and ample water and forage for the ancestors of both man and beast, it became permanent. The mode of travel had gone from moccasin to horseback to automobile, and the road, like a living thing, had grown and changed accordingly.

Now, I was following the path of my ancestors on a wobbly bicycle with flimsy fenders that rattled with each bump and alerted any wildlife within ten miles of my approach. Startled sparrows fluttered from their perch with shrill warnings, and squirrels scampered to the topmost branches as I clanked by. A group of five wild turkeys were flushed out and ran into the road about fifty yards ahead of me, then took flight when Sawbuck charged as if his very survival depended on catching one of them.

The wind in my face was ripe with pungent aromas of pine needles, rich dark soil, and decay. The sun warmed my shoulders and enveloped me with a peculiar sense of time, of going both forward and backward in the same motion. I experienced a curiously comfortable feeling, a gentle assurance that life continues unabated and unaffected by the planning and scheming of men. That God was in control and nothing happened without His approval. I soaked up the beauty and peace of the moment as an ache of pleasure pierced my chest.

Crossing the short wooden bridge that spanned Spates' Creek, I took the small dirt lane to the right. It was hardly wide enough for a car, and there was grass growing tall down the center. The trees on either side grew so close together that the limbs intertwined overhead to form a long shade-cooled tunnel, alive with enough adorable little forest creatures and bluebirds to film an Uncle Remus movie. I rode slowly through the shadowed green tube, thinking of the generations of Spates that had traversed this very ground. I had a sudden pang of regret that I never had the chance to know them. That sense of loss grew when the big, broad-shouldered, two-story log house came into view.

It was nestled in a grove of magnificent oaks that stood guard around it like powerful sentries. The deep front porch was filled with potted plants and hanging baskets of every description, as if someone had transplanted a part of the woods onto the house. The irregular size of the logs in the walls was evident by the differing amounts of caulk between them. On the top floor, two windows were slightly askew, giving the facade a cross-eyed look. The pale green moss that covered the wooden shingles on the roof added to the feeling of restful isolation. The house looked like it had been there since the sixth day of creation.

A badly rusted Plymouth sat leaking vital fluids in the scrub-grass-and-dirt front yard near the porch steps. I leaned my bike against a tree and told Sawbuck to stay. Stepping up onto the porch, I held my breath and knocked firmly on the hand-hewn door. Surely, she was home. Where would a one hundred and six year old woman go? Well, the hospital was a possibility.

While waiting for a response, I surveyed the unused and forgotten sheds and barn that sat off near the wood's edge. Pieces of farm equipment lay scattered throughout the tall brown grass like rusted debris from the crash of a small plane. Years of neglect were painfully obvious. There hadn't been a man's hand here in many a season. The whole place had the appearance of an under-manned frontier fort, locked in a losing war with hostile and aggressive vegetation that surrounded it on all sides. It was only a matter of time before it would be completely over-run. But for now it stood bravely in the face of the enemy. *Remember the Alamo*!

I heard the shuffle of feet inside the house. The door opened, and I found myself facing a plump, elderly black woman with a bandanna wrapped around her gray head. Her round face looked stern, as if she wouldn't put up with any crap, but there was tenderness in her large expressive brown eyes.

"Can I hep you?" she asked.

"Yes, ma'am. My name is Lonnie Tobin. I'm related to Miss Spicy, and I was wondering if I could visit with her for a few minutes."

"I never seen you before. How you related?"

"She's my great, great … several greats, aunt."

"Well, I don't know. I would haf to ast Miz Spicy if she feels up to it. Stay here, I'll be rat back."

She left the door open, and I could see down the hallway. There were small tables with flower-filled vases lining the walls beneath large framed pictures whose subjects I couldn't quite make out. At the far end of the hallway, a narrow staircase rose to the second floor. The smell of age wafted past me. In a few minutes, I heard her returning with that distinctive shuffling walk, like she was unwilling or unable to lift her feet.

"Come on in, Miz Spicy's in the back parlor."

I followed her down the hall as the creak of the plank floors and the drag of her feet broke the thick silence. She led me into a large room filled with furniture from another era, with even more plants and flowers plugging up the bare spots. A large ceiling fan was spinning slowly overhead. The one tall window was propped open with a stick to take advantage of any breezes, and it provided the only light in the semi-darkness.

"Here he is, Miz Spicy. This here's Lonnie Tobin. Says he's kin to you," Beulah said in a raised voice. Then, she turned to me. "You'll have to speak up, Miz Spicy's a little hard a'hearin'."

Seated in a chair in the corner shadows, she was tiny and incredibly pale. Dressed in a long blue dress, with only her head and hands exposed, she looked for all the world like a little China doll. On closer inspection, she appeared to be older than China. Her bird-like skull was sparsely covered with thin white hair, and a milky film dulled her brown eyes, giving the misleading impression that she was blind. Her hollow cheeks had been hastily swabbed with rouge, and her severely wrinkled lips were painted dark red, which gave her mouth the appearance of a fresh wound.

"Hello, Lonnie," she said in a surprisingly strong voice. "Are you Ruby Jo's boy?"

"Yes, ma'am."

"How's she and your grandmaw Birdie doin'?"

"They're fine, Miss Spicy. How are you?"

"Oh, honey, at my age I'm just grateful when I wake up. I've learned to live within my limits, and it just ain't no use to complain. I'm sure proud you come to visit me. I don't get much company now a'days. Please, have a seat. Would you like some lemonade?"

"Yes, thank you," I said as I settled into a musty wingback chair.

"Beulah," she called. "Would you bring Lonnie a glass of lemonade, and I'll have a cup of tea, please."

She was alert and clear-headed, I thought, but she seemed so fragile and delicate that I didn't want to breathe too heavily in her direction for fear of blowing her away like denture powder.

"Are y'all visiting for the summer, Lonnie?"

"We're living here now. My mother and me."

"Did something happen to your father?"

"No, ma'am. We're ... My mother and father are separated. He's still in Louisiana."

"Well, I'm sorry to hear that, Lonnie. Folks just don't seem to stay together like they used to. 'Course I ain't the right one to comment on such things, since I never married myself."

Beulah brought in a large silver tray with a cold glass of lemonade and a hot cup of tea.

"Did you have a purpose in coming to see me?" she asked as she sipped. "I'm too far off the beaten path for you to be just passin' by."

"Well, yes, ma'am. I wanted to talk with you about the Spates family. I really don't know much about them, and I was hoping you could tell me everything you remember."

"Lordy me, honey, I don't have enough time left on this earth to tell you *everything* I remember. One of the curses of old age, or blessin's depending on how you look at it, is the rememberin'. 'Specially when you try to sleep, and your head's fulla old memories."

She fell silent and hung her diminutive head for a moment. I could see her bone-white and blue-veined scalp. The liver spots on the back of her trembling hand looked like deep bruises as she brought the cup to her small gash of a mouth.

"Well, maybe not everything," I said. "I would appreciate anything you could tell me."

"I'll tell you as much as I can, Lonnie, but I warn you, I may give out in the middle of it."

"That's okay, I can always come back."

"Sure you can. Come back anytime. But I can get it started anyway."

She began by relating the story of the patriarch of the entire family, her own father, Abraham Isaac Spates, who was born in Virginia in 1820. He married Abigail Green, a fifteen year old Quaker girl from Kentucky, in 1839, and along with Abigail's two brothers and their families, they headed south in 1840 to look for a homestead of their own.

They stopped in Holly Springs, Mississippi, where Abraham had relatives, and debated for several days on settling there, before the lure of something better just over the next hill drove them on. They traveled through meadows, fields, and dense, unmapped forests until reaching the Ouachita River, deep in the heart of the Arkansas territory. They set up camp under an oak tree on the bank of the river while they constructed a pair of rafts large enough to support their families and gear.

Two weeks later, they launched the sturdy crafts on an overcast spring morning and for the next month floated downriver, stopping only to cook and hunt the abundant game on shore. By this time, Abigail was near delivery of their first child and was ready to settle down in one spot, so they struck out inland. After several days of laborious travel, they decided to take up residence on the very spot where we were now sitting. Living in tents while they cleared the land and cut the trees, they were soon able to build three small log cabins.

Abraham gave thanks to God that Abigail had a warm and safe structure in which to bring forth their firstborn child into the world. It was a girl they named Samantha, in honor of Abigail's mother. Working together with the other families, they cleared more land and planted a vegetable garden to supply the table and cotton for a cash crop.

Then, the rest of the children came, nine in all, five boys and four girls, eight of which lived to adulthood. Miss Spicy, whose real name was Sarah Elisabeth, was the seventh child and was born on April 5, 1854. She was nicknamed "Spicy" after a childhood incident when she bit into a hot pepper, after being repeatedly warned, and nearly burned the taste buds off her tongue. She said that for weeks after that she could have been eating cow manure and wouldn't have known the difference.

The oldest child, Samantha, who was the first to be born on this property, was also the first to die, at the age of ten from scarlet fever. Spicy told the story of how their father had denied Samantha after repeated requests for hair ribbons, claiming them to be a frivolous waste of hard-earned money. After her death, he was overcome with guilt and rode all day to and from the settlement at Fordyce to buy colorful ribbons to adorn her with before they laid her to rest. But Abigail refused to allow him to put them on her, saying, "You wouldn't let her have 'em while she was alive, you ain't gonna give 'em to her now."

Despite the heartbreak of losing a child, they prospered over the years and became respected members of the growing community, until the Civil War came along and the trouble started. Abraham was solidly against secession and refused to recognize what he called a renegade government. He tried to keep his views to himself, but people began to talk when he didn't seem to share their enthusiasm for the Confederate cause.

By 1863, it was obvious that the war wasn't going to end anytime soon, and Abraham was feeling increasingly threatened by former friends who were beginning to shun him. He felt it was too risky to stay any longer and decided to make his move. Along with his two brothers-in-law, Robert and Russell Green, and their families, they set off in wagons for Holly Springs. Their plan was to leave the women and children with relatives there and then continue on north to join the Union forces.

Tears filled her eyes as she told me what happened next.

They had gone about a hundred miles or so when a large group of heavily armed men on horseback overtook them. Miss Spicy, who had just turned nine, recognized neighbors she had seen in church the Sunday before. She still remembered the hard looks fixed on their faces.

The leader of the posse was Jonah Kane, whose property was just north of Abraham's cotton patch. He informed the three fugitives that they were under arrest and were to be taken back to Moro to stand trial for the crime of treason. He said their families were free to continue their exodus or could return for the proceedings. At this pronouncement, Russell Green bolted for the woods. A volley of shots cut him down before he had gone thirty yards.

They bound the hands of Abraham and Robert, placed them both on one horse, and headed out. The women buried Russell in a clearing, amidst tears and fervent prayers that they would be able to find the spot later. They began the long trip back home with much beseeching of God for the safety of the other two men.

Three days later, the women rolled into town, where their worst fears were confirmed. They were too late. Robert Green had been shot in the head shortly after being taken prisoner, and his body dumped somewhere along the trail. But they had brought Abraham, who they considered the worst offender, back for trial. Found guilty, he had been promptly hanged.

At this point in her story, Miss Spicy sent Beulah into another room to fetch a shoebox from her closet. She brought it back, and Spicy took the lid off, pulled a folded piece of paper from inside, and handed it to me. It was brown with age and made a crinkling sound as I opened it up. I noticed that it was uneven, as if it had been ripped from a bigger sheet. Inside was a short letter written in a clear, legible hand. It read:

May 11th 1863
Moro, Ark.

My dear wife and children,

It is now 7 o'clock at night and in two hours my soul will be in eternity, tried and condemned by a jury of 21 citizens to death by hanging for the unfortunate cause I have pursued.

My dying request is that my boys will live an upright, honorable and industrious life and never rebel against the country that gave them birth. And I want you to come back to our place in Moro, and if you, my wife and children live such a life as is honorable and virtuous, you will ever have friends and protection.

And my little girls, obey your mother and render her all the assistance you can.

Adieu, adieu and try to meet me in the other world.

Yours affectionately,
Abraham I. Spates

P.S. My remains will be buried where I am hung. If you come back remove them and rebury next to Samantha.

On the back of the letter was a scribbled note that said:
Delivered to Abigail Spates by Homer Grisham, May 13, 1863.

~

I sat there holding the crumbling paper that he had written on and folded with his own hands. When Spicy told me that his body had been buried in a secret location, and that his killers wouldn't tell them where it was, I nearly wept. Now, I had one grandfather with a missing head and one who was missing entirely.

Spicy went on to describe the hardships of living in what they called "The Big Woods" without her father. Ostracized from the neighbors and townspeople, they struggled to survive. They depended on the little garden and the game they could kill to keep them alive. The fields lay fallow. They saw more wildlife than they did human beings.

She told me of going to the creek by herself late one chilly evening to fetch water and coming face to face with a full-grown black panther. She dropped the buckets she was carrying and ran for the house as the panther sprang after her. She looked back and noticed that the big cat had stopped to sniff the buckets before resuming the chase. She ripped off her apron and threw it down as she ran. Sure enough, the panther stopped momentarily to smell the discarded cloth before coming after her again. Without breaking stride, she skinned out of her hand-knitted sweater and flung it over her shoulder. Again the beast halted, this time allowing her the chance to reach safety.

"If the cabin had been any further away," she said, "I'd a'been buck nekkid by the time I got there. Lordy mercy, I never was so scared in my life. 'Course one of my brothers said if I had throwed down my drawers first, it would have kilt the panther right off. Everybody thought that was funny, but I whopped his head for sayin' it."

I laughed out loud at the image of her running bare-ass through the woods, leaving behind a dead panther with soiled panties on its head.

"When was this house built, Miss Spicy?" I asked after getting over the giggles.

"Well, a few years after the war some of our relatives from up at Holly Springs come down and helped my brothers build this house. I reckon it was around 1870. They made it big enough for all of us, and we lived here 'til each one of my brothers and sisters got married and moved off to start families of their own. I stayed here with mama and taught school 'til she passed on. I took in boarders for a few years 'til I got tired of beggin' for rent money and just kicked the whole bunch of 'em out. I been livin' here by myself ever since. Some of my grandnephews come out here one year and rigged the place for electricity and indoor plumbin'. But, like me, the house is old and has the miseries."

"Did you know my grandfather, Thomas Spates?" I asked.

"Yes, I sure did know Tom. He was always one of my favorite people. I'd run into him uptown, and he'd say, 'Why, Miss Spicy, you get prettier every time I see you,' and I'd say, 'Why, Tom Spates, your eyesight gets worse every time I see you.' We always laughed and carried on when we was together. I must tell you, Lonnie, you remind me of him a lot."

"Do you have any pictures of him?"

"No, I don't. I'm sorry. We never was much on takin' pictures. But as soon as I saw you, I knew you was Tom's grandson. Ain't no disputin' it."

That was the first time anyone had ever mentioned my resemblance to him, and it made me more determined to find a photograph. What other family on earth didn't take pictures?

"I would be more than happy to tell you what I know of Tom," she said, as she pulled a shawl tightly around her emaciated body in spite of the mid-day heat, "but I'm afraid you'll have to come back 'cause I'm plum tuckered out. Old ladies like me need a soft lunch and a long nap every day just to keep goin'. Besides, that'll guarantee at least one more visit from you, won't it? Maybe I could spread this out for a whole summer of visits."

"I would love to come back, Miss Spicy," I said as I realized I had been there almost three hours. "I really learned a lot, and I'm looking forward to hearing more."

"You can come tomorrow about the same time if you want," she said with a tired smile. "I ain't going nowhere, unless the sweet chariot swings low enough to tote me off to Glory Land. But I'm beginnin' to think that the Lord don't want me."

I left with the feeling of having eaten a rich meal. I suddenly felt close to people that I had never given a thought to prior. They had become real to me. I had been a student of the Civil War since I learned to read but hadn't really considered my own family's involvement. I suddenly felt like I truly was a part of history. Of course, I really would have preferred that old Abe Spates had met his end while wreaking havoc with Stonewall in the Shenandoah Valley. Or had died riddled with bullets as he charged with a rebel yell into the teeth of the enemy at Gettysburg, or even succumbing to a self-inflicted wound when his rifle went off while he was cleaning it. Anything would have been better than being lynched as a Yankee sympathizer.

Now, I understand why I had never heard the story from my family before. They were all ashamed. I'm sure it took many years for the Spates to overcome the stigma, if they ever really did. But I felt good about the knowledge I now possessed, even if it wasn't something I wanted written up in the history books. I could hardly wait to hear what Miss Spicy had to say about my grandfather.

Stopping at the Spates' Creek Bridge on my way back, I laid my bike in the weeds by the side of the road and slid down the grassy embankment to a shallow spot in the creek where the water rushed and tumbled over speckled rocks. It was a spot, I realized, where the creek could easily be crossed. However, on either side of these miniature rapids, the creek widened, with deep pools where fat catfish waited for the right bait. The temperature was at least ten degrees lower by the water. It felt even cooler beneath the bridge itself. I could smell the creosote in the timbers used to construct it many years ago.

On the supporting beams that criss-crossed above my head was the graffiti record of succeeding generations. Names and dates, hearts with initials inside, short messages like "Go Hogs," even a misspelled "FUK YOU" were cut or spray-painted in random places, each one a testimony to the march of time. The earliest inscription I had found on my first visit was "G.T.S.-1908." Leaving one's mark on the Spates' Creek Bridge was sort of a rite of passage in this neck of the woods. I searched for and found my own initials. I remembered the day I climbed up to that precarious spot and hung by one arm, carving with a pocketknife that Big Mama had given me that very morning. I had snapped the tip off the blade on the last numeral in the date.

I had to walk out near the creek to see it clearly. The block letters about three inches high read:

L. TOBIN

6 21 55

I couldn't believe it had been five years since I climbed down from there all pissed off about breaking my knife. I was nine years old at the time. Then, it hit me. The date was June 21, 1955. *Today* was June 21, 1960, five years ago *to the day* that I had scratched my name and date into the wood. Today was also the summer solstice according to grandma's copy of the *Old Farmers' Almanac*. Did this have any significance, I wondered? Normally, I would have just considered it a coincidence, but at the time I could no longer define "normally."

After a few minutes of staring at the chiseled letters while the high noon sun warmed my scalp, a reassuring calm began to descend on me. It was a deep, soul-good feeling that everything was right with the world, and there was nothing of importance to be concerned about. I took off my high-top sneakers and stuffed the socks into them, rolled up my pant legs, and waded into the creek. The icy cold water tickled as it splashed and played around my feet.

I looked downstream and saw green turtles of all sizes lined up nose to tail, basking in the sun on half-submerged logs, and a brilliantly colored kingfisher keeping a sharp eye out for a tasty minnow from his perch on a limb stretched low over the water. The summer air was alive with the calls of blue jays and mockingbirds, and a murder of crows had gathered for a meeting in the top of a tall pine tree. I stood there relishing the moment as the soothing burble of the stream washed out the troubling thoughts that had been robbing me of peace. I wanted to stay in that spot forever.

Just downstream, a little eddy that was swirling near the bank and a familiar shape caught my eye. Stepping gingerly over the rocks toward it, I damned these tender feet. I reached down into the water and felt the rush of the current. My fist closed around the object as excitement mounted. I was overjoyed to find the most perfect arrowhead in the world.

I held it in my wet fingers and did a little happy dance until my heel came down on a pointy rock. But the pain in my foot was nothing compared to the thrill of my discovery. I turned the artifact over and over and examined every facet of it. It was large, probably intended for bigger animals like deer. Or man.

I walked over and sat down on a fallen tree near the edge of the deep water and tried to imagine what the Indian looked like who had held this same piece of flint in his hands, maybe a thousand years ago, chipping away until the edges were razor sharp. Many tribes had roamed these woods over the centuries, and it could have been any one of them.

Of course, I wanted this *particular* arrowhead to be shot from the bow of the great Shawnee chief Tecumseh himself. One that he personally launched and lost in the early part of the 19th century as he traveled from tribe to tribe in an effort to forge an alliance to defeat the hated paleface. If not him, then at least from the quiver of a brave that had gained *some* level of respect among his own fellow tribesmen.

I wondered how it got there. Was it from an errant arrow that missed its mark? Or had it been buried deep in the flesh of a strong buck that had escaped the hunter and died on this spot, then slowly decomposed, leaving the arrowhead like a jewel among the polished gravel in the creek bed?

However the arrowhead came to be here, it felt like a major discovery. I pictured a press conference with cameras flashing as I donated it to the Smithsonian and received the key to the city of Washington from the President himself. But since it gave me such a sense of wealth, I thought that maybe I should pass it on to my children, after I marry Nelda, of course.

After a prolonged reverie, I looked across the creek and noticed a cane pole, complete with line, bobber, and hook, leaning against a pine tree. Well, I thought, if I can dig up a few worms, I could do a little fishing. Maybe catch supper. The day was perfect for fishing, and I was feeling lucky.

Instead of going back to the shallows to cross, I decided to take a shortcut. A large rock jutted up about halfway across the creek, and I knew I could easily jump to it and then with another bound, land on the other side. I had jumped much greater distances in the past, so I was brimming with confidence. What I didn't take into account was the fact that since the rock was in the water, it offered the ideal conditions for colonies of fuzzy fungus to grow on the surface, causing it to become as slick as slug snot.

I leaped toward the waiting stone with the grace of a white-tailed deer clearing a garden fence, but when my right foot touched down, it shot forward like a flat rock skipping on the surface of a pond. I saw treetops and a patch of white clouds in a blue sky just before splashing into the frigid creek.

Even though I was an excellent swimmer, I experienced a moment of panic as the wet darkness closed over me. Quickly resurfacing, I realized that I couldn't touch the bottom. Humbled by my foolishness, I backstroked to the bank and pulled myself out. Standing there drenched and dripping, my T-shirt plastered to my ribs and my blue jeans feeling like they weighed fifty pounds, I rubbed the water out of my eyes. It dawned on me that my hands were empty. I had lost the arrowhead.

I peeled off my jeans and dived back in without hesitation. Kicking angrily, I swam deeper and deeper until the fire in my lungs forced me to return to the surface. How deep was this hole? I sucked in more air and dove again into the murky depths. My fingers finally touched the bottom, and I quickly grabbed handfuls before heading for the surface. The arrowhead wasn't in the mud and pea gravel I had scooped up. I was treading water and contemplating another dive when I spotted the undulating body of a moccasin swimming straight for my bobbing head.

The next thing I knew I was standing on the bank with no recollection of how I had arrived. I didn't know if I swam or shot straight up out of the water and landed there. The snake was nowhere in sight.

"SHIT!" I yelled from the bottom of my gut. The sound bounced down the creek and echoed back mockingly … shit … shit … shit.

My yell startled Sawbuck. He approached warily and licked my hand, looking up as if to say "I promise I won't tell anybody about this. You think lunch is ready?"

I tried to wring as much water as I could out of my Levis, but they still felt cold and clammy as I pulled them up my legs.

What kind of a damn omen was this? It just so happens that I return to the same spot exactly five years to the day and find a piece of history then attempt a stupid stunt and lose it. What the hell did it all mean? Was I doomed to find riches, only to have them slip through my fingers? Would the truth I was seeking elude me? Was I just a clumsy idiot?

I opted for the latter as I pedaled back to Grandma Birdie's, sick at heart over the loss of the once-in-a-lifetime find. I was still soaked when I walked in the kitchen.

"Lord, have mercy," my mother exclaimed. "What happened to you, Lonnie?"

"I fell in the creek."

"What caused you to fall in the creek?"

"I think it was gravity."

I wasn't trying to be a smartass, but I didn't want to go into detail. Besides, there was no use crying over lost arrowheads.

"Are you *all right*, smartass?"

"I'm sorry, mama. I just slipped on a rock. I'm not hurt or anything.

Just embarrassed."

"Well, go get out of them wet clothes and put on some dry ones," grandma said, "then come eat some lunch. We're just having sandwiches today."

I took a bath and put on clean jeans and my St. Thomas Angels' team T-shirt with the number seven on the back. Same number as Mantle. I had washed the coach's car all summer for that number.

By the time I sat down at the table, I was absolutely famished. I assembled one of grandma's "just sandwiches," which consisted of a thick slab of smoked ham, a large slice of juicy vine-ripened tomato, a crisp leaf of lettuce, onion, and a generous smear of mayonnaise, all on fresh baked sourdough bread. A honkin' wedge of cheddar cheese and a dill pickle the size of my arm were the sides.

"Which creek did you fall into, Lonnie?" my mother asked as I ate.

"Spates' Creek. I went to see Miss Spicy, and I stopped there on the way back."

"Did Spicy talk to you?"

"Yeah, for about three hours. Do you know about Abraham Spates who was hung during the Civil War?"

"No, I guess not. Have you heard of him, mama?"

"I ain't never heared of it," grandma said. "'Course Tom never told me much about his family."

"Does anybody have any pictures of my grandfather?" I asked. "Miss Spicy said I reminded her of him."

"I reckon there is some resemblance," grandma said after studying me for several moments. "But I don't have a single picture. I had a few, but they just got lost over the years. Mammy and Paw might have some, but I doubt they would give you one."

"They don't have to *give* me one, I just want to see one. I think I'll ride over and visit them after I eat, if it's all right with you, mama," I said.

"That's fine, just don't fall into any more bodies of water, okay?"

Chapter Nine

The Little Matchbox House of Cooper Logan

I walked out the back door and gave a slobberingly grateful Sawbuck his lunch then to the front yard to wait for him to eat. It had been a while since I had been this near to Gideon. He sat in his usual spot near the edge of the porch.

"Hey, Gideon," I said.

No response. I really didn't expect one. Minutes later, Sawbuck trotted up sucking his teeth in satisfaction. I climbed aboard the old bike and started out of the yard when I heard Gideon laugh out loud.

"A finger forever pointin' at nothin'," he said, a crooked smile on his face.

I wasn't sure if I had heard right, but I knew it would be useless to ask for a clarification. I would just have to figure it out for myself. I rode along turning it over in my mind. It sounded like he said a "finger forever pointin' at nothin'." What in heaven's name could that mean? I beat that question nearly to death before I finally gave it up.

I rode in the opposite direction from Miss Spicy's. As I headed to Mammy's, I fervently hoped she would have some pictures of my grandfather. It would be nice to finally be able to look into his face.

It was about two o'clock when I came upon the little matchbox house of Cooper Logan. I had known him all my life. He used to drop by Grandma Birdie's when we came up to visit, sitting and talking for a couple of hours. Then, he just stopped coming. I had always liked him, and he seemed to be genuinely fond of me. Just as I was passing his front gate, he stepped out on the porch.

"Hello, Scorpion!" he bellowed, his long white hair falling across his face.

I braked and slid to a stop in the gravel.

"Hi, Coop."

"Where ya headed?" he asked as he used both hands to tuck his hair behind his child-sized ears.

"I'm going to see Mammy and Paw."

"Would you mind bringin' them some stuff outta my garden? I got some okra and summer squash I want to send 'em."

"Sure," I said as I swung my leg over the bike and pushed it up to the fence.

"I'll be right back," he said, disappearing inside.

Looking around while I waited, I saw an old rusted push mower nearly hidden in the weed-choked little front yard. It was sitting there as if Coop had been in the middle of cutting the grass one day and just said, "to hell with this," and went inside never to come back.

The little shack had no indoor plumbing, which meant having to use the stinking little outhouse in all types of weather, and no electricity, which meant no television or radio or refrigerator. How could anybody live like that? I guessed some people were just worse off than me. At least in the dumps we were forced to live in we could shit indoors and watch *Bonanza.*

"I really 'preciate this, Scorpion. Tell Miss Effie that I'll have some peas for her soon," he said as he handed me a lumpy and rather heavy bag. He found a length of strong twine and helped me lash it to the handlebars.

"You shoulda been up at Willie's the other night, Scorpion. Your daddy cold-cocked Waylon Roark. Dropped him like a sack a'taters. I ain't never seen nobody hit that hard and fast. It was something else."

"Yeah, I heard about it."

He lit a cigarette and wiped his forehead with the sleeve of his tattered shirt.

"Waylon claims he was sucker-punched and swore to stomp your daddy's ass in the ground when he runs into him agin. But if you ask me, I don't think he really wants any more of Harley Tobin."

It was obvious that he was fixated on the fight as he blew out a cloud of smoke. I changed the subject.

"You were friends with my grandfather, weren't you, Coop?"

"Yes, I was."

"What was he like?"

"Tom Spates was a good man, an honest man. If Tom gave you his word on something, by God, you could count on him honoring it. I thought highly of him. His time was cut way too short. He would love to know you, Scorpion."

"Do you know anything about how he was killed? You think it was an accident?"

His eyes misted, and he cleared his throat. "I try real hard not to think about that awful night. I'm the one that … found him … and I just cain't talk about it. I'm sorry, Scorpion."

He turned his face in embarrassment over the display of emotions. It was obvious the trauma of discovering the body still haunted him.

"Hey, Coop, somebody told me you had a pet raccoon one time. Do you still have him?"

"You mean ol' Rastus?" he said, as he brightened up and wiped his eyes with the heels of his hands. "Best 'coon that ever lived. Yeah, I still got him. You wanna see him?"

"Sure," I said.

He went back in the house and returned with a board, upon which sat a thoroughly dead and poorly stuffed raccoon. It was ragged and misshapen and looked as if it had been clubbed repeatedly, either before or after it was mounted.

"This here is Rastus. Or what's left of him. I had him for nearly twelve years. He used to eat at the table and sleep in the bed with me. When he died, I just couldn't bear to part with him, so I skinned him and stuffed his hide with straw. Can you tell I did it myself?" he asked with the bright-eyed enthusiasm of a child showing off his crayon artwork. The fact that it was thicker in some places than others, was badly stitched together, had straw coming out of the ass, and different colored marbles for eyes did kind of give it away as a homemade job.

"No, I can't tell. It looks real professional," I said straight-faced.

He went on to tell me about all the cute and intelligent things Rastus had done, like the way he would grab food in his little black hands and dip it in a bowl of water before he ate it or crawl up in his lap and go to sleep. And how, without assistance, the coon developed the skills to piss in a slop jar without getting any on the floor. He said he came in from work one evening and found that his beloved pet had expired under the sink. He described the body as being "stiff as a board and hard as a brick." He unashamedly admitted that he cried for days. Obviously, I thought, one lonely man. Sawbuck came over, sniffed the remains of Rastus, and looked at Coop with eyes that said, "Damn, where did you drag this up from. May I have it?"

"Nothin' ever stays the same, Scorpion. One day everything you give a shit about is gone … just gone. You try to keep goin', but it gits harder every day. You feel like everything is all wrong, and the only thing you can do right anymore is just git older and die."

"You've got a lot of years left in you, Coop. I'll be bringing my grandkids to meet you."

"Maybe so, but if I don't make it, would you make sure somebody stuffs my hide?"

"Sure, Coop. Then, we'll put you and Rastus on display up at Willie's."

"And everybody could drink toasts to us on Saturday nights."

"That's right."

"I think I would like that," he said with a far off look. "And Rastus would too."

We laughed, and I said goodbye and continued up the road to

Mammy's. I coasted into the front yard and stopped next to the pin oak that shaded the front porch. The house looked like a smaller version of Big Mama's, without the bay windows. And like every other house around here, it was well-seasoned. There hadn't been any new construction in Moro since the thirties.

I untied the vegetables and went up on the porch. These were my great-grandparents, but I always felt uncomfortable around them. Their names were Jack and Effie Spates, and I had been there only a handful of times in my life. I could smell something sweet baking as I knocked.

"Who is it?" a voice called through the open door.

"It's Lonnie Tobin, Mammy."

"Come on in, Lonnie. I'm back here in the kitchen."

I walked through the sparsely furnished living room and into the kitchen. Mammy was standing at the counter amid bowls and spoons, covered in a dusting of flour. She was a stout woman with iron gray hair pulled into a tight bun on top of her head and a perpetual scowl on her face. She was the same age as Big Mama but looked ten years younger. A full-length apron covered her pillow-sized breasts and ample stomach.

"Well, hello there, Lonnie Ray."

"Hi, Mammy. This is some stuff from Cooper Logan," I said, indicating the bag in my arms.

"Just set it down on the table and come gimme a hug."

I could smell vanilla on her as we briefly embraced.

"My, my, you about full growed, ain't you? How old er you now?"

"I'm fourteen. I'll be fifteen in December."

"Lawd sake, you awful big to be fourteen. I reckon you take after your daddy. I got some fresh made teacakes, would you like some?"

Mammy's teacakes were like large thick sugar cookies, and I always tried to let at least a half a dozen melt in my mouth when I visited her.

"Yes, ma'am, thank you."

"If you'll wait just a minute, I'll get you some right out of the oven and a cold glass of sweet-milk."

I wondered if we would have treats like this in Heaven.

"How's your folks doing?" she asked.

"They're all fine, Mammy."

"I need to give Birdie a call, I reckon. It's been quite a spell since I talked to her."

Yeah, about twenty-five years. That was a month of Sundays and a coon's age longer than a spell.

"Where's Paw?" I inquired.

"Oh, he rode over to Camden with Clive Strickland to look at a horse Clive wants to buy fer his boy Nathan. They won't be back for a while. He'll be sorry he missed you. So, what have you been up to, Lonnie?"

"Not much, just kinda hanging around. I talked with Miss Spicy this morning and thought I would come visit you, too."

Mammy's scowl seemed to deepen at the mention of Miss Spicy. She leaned over, opened the door on the old oven, slipped on a mitt, took out a pan of steaming pancake-size tea cakes, and put them on the counter to cool.

"What did y'all talk about?" she asked as she reached in the cabinet for a saucer and drinking glass.

"She told me about Abraham and Abigail Spates and how Abraham was hung during the Civil War. I had never heard anything about that in my life."

"It ain't something that the Spates likes to talk about. Did she say anything about your grandpaw, Tom Spates?"

"No, she got tired and asked me to come back tomorrow."

"Well, just take anything she says with a pinch a'salt. She's old, and her memory ain't what it used to be. Here's some teacakes. Eat 'em before they get cold, and I'll get you some milk."

She placed the saucer with the warm teacakes on the table as I took a seat. I bit into one and thought that we could make a fortune if we packaged and sold them. They were addicting. I watched as Mammy took a thick crockery pitcher out of a brand new refrigerator, poured a tall glass of milk, and set it in front of me.

"I'll tell you about Tom, if you like," she said as she sat down on the other side of the table. "He was my son after all."

"That would be great. Do you have any pictures of him?"

"I had a whole box of family pictures and a buncha letters Tom wrote me when he was overseas, but they burned up in our old house. We lost everything. It broke my heart."

Well, crap, I thought. If *she* didn't have any pictures, there probably weren't any in existence.

"When was he born?" I asked as I began my second teacake.

"Let's see, it was in 1896. June 21, 1896."

I nearly choked.

"Today is June 21," I said chokingly.

"Well, it sure is," she said, checking the Fordyce Bank calendar that was hanging on the wall. "He'd a been sixty-four years old today."

This could not be just a coincidence.

"I tell you, Lonnie, Tom was a fine boy. He always showed me and his Paw respect. He was real helpful around the house, too. He would do whatever we asked him to do without a word or gripe. He was right mindful when he was small, but he got a mite fulla hisself when he got on up a little older. You might hear that some folks didn't like him, but it was 'cause they was jealous."

Her cheeks flushed, and it was clear that the thought of people being unkind to her little boy was still getting her dander up after all these years.

"Why were they jealous?" I asked.

"He was smarter'n everybody around here, and some of 'em didn't like that. And he was always so fulla fun when he was growing up. He always broke everybody up. We used to have the dangdest Christmas parties ever' year, and Tom would just be a clown and make us laugh 'til we had to beg him to stop. But he did drink some. But no more'n the other boys his age. And he got in to a fight er two, but nobody ever got bad hurt."

She sat looking out the window, and I could almost see the Ghost of Christmas Past reflecting in her eyes.

"That was all before the war. Tom was different after he came back from that damn war, pardon my language, and got married. He never liked

Christmas parties anymore or eatin' with the family after that. Him and Birdie just quit comin'. People said he was stuck-up, but he weren't. He was just … to hisself."

"What do you think changed him?"

"I believe somethin' happened to him in the war, while he was overseas. I cain't say what exactly happened 'cause he never would talk about it, but I know he went through a lot. But he served his country, which is more'n I can say about some of the men around here. I want to show you somethin', Lonnie."

She rose slowly and went into an adjoining room. I heard dresser drawers being opened, dug around in, and shut. She called out, "Here it is!" and came back in the kitchen, breathing a little harder, with what looked like a jewelry box in her hand. She gave it to me just as I finished washing down my third teacake. Inside, resting on black velvet, was a beautiful gold-edged, heart-shaped medal with a cameo of George Washington on it.

"That's Tom's Purple Heart. He got it for bein' shot in the leg."

I was flabbergasted. The Purple Heart! Why had I not heard about this before? I lifted it out of the box to get a closer look. It felt heavy with military history.

"I … I had no idea he … got the Purple Heart."

"He never talked about it much, but I know he was mighty proud of it. Ain't nobody else around here got a Purple Heart. Let 'em put that in their pipe and smoke it."

I could see her getting all fluffed up with pride.

"And," she added, "let me show you this."

She walked over to the pantry and retrieved a Mason jar. As she brought it to the table, I could see that the top had rusted to the point that it would never be opened again. As I took it from her, I noticed that it was about three-quarters full of a cloudy, greenish liquid. I held it up to the light and saw something floating around inside. It looked like some kind of a little prehistoric pickle that was mushily decomposing.

"That's the index finger from Tom's left hand. He accidentally shot it off when he was about your age. I put it in that vinegar so's he'd have it."

My stomach lurched, and the teacake I was chewing suddenly became a mouthful of maggots. I put the jar on the table with a little too much force, which jostled the liquid and caused the putrefied bit of meat to turn slowly in a circle. It was the "finger forever pointin' at nothin'."

"Some folks think it's strange for me to keep Tom's finger in a jar, but it is a piece of him after all," she said.

My mind was spinning as a little rhyme played over and over in my head: *with a piece of grandpa here ... and a piece of grandpa there ... here a piece ... there a piece ... everywhere a piece, piece.*

She went on to tell me tales of when he was a boy growing up and some of the things he did and all the boo-boos he got, but I barely heard a word she said. I couldn't take my eyes off the hideous dead digit. It was sickening.

"Well, Lonnie, you sure seem to be taken with that finger," she said as I sat staring at it in morbid curiosity. "I tell you what, why don't you take it home with you?"

Oh, God, no. I didn't want to be near it. I searched my mind for a reason to decline her generous offer without hurting her feelings.

"I ... uh ... I would love to Mammy, but I ... I'm afraid I'll drop it and break the jar while I'm riding my bike. I don't have a basket or anything. Maybe I should leave it here where it'll be safe."

"Well, all right. But I want you to have it after I'm gone."

How sweet. She was going to give me the finger when she died.

"Do you want anymore tea cakes, Lonnie?" she asked.

"No, thanks. I'm full."

"You usually eat twice as many as that. Is there anything wrong with 'em?"

"No, ma'am, they're real good. I just had a big lunch."

Now that I knew the kind of things she kept in there, I would never again be able to eat a teacake that came from that kitchen.

After talking for a while longer, I hugged her goodbye and rode away with the vision of what I had seen in that jar burned into my brain.

I couldn't shake it. I didn't remember what the Purple Heart looked like, but I could picture every nauseating little flap of fetid flesh that had split away from the bone.

I was now convinced that Gideon had made a connection to a power beyond mortal man. Predicting the rain shower could have been a lucky guess, and the phone waking him up might have been calculated because he figured that my father would call at some point, but the "finger forever pointin' at nothin'" was just too specific. I fought a shiver that threatened to loosen my teeth.

When I got back home, my mother and Grandma Birdie said they didn't know about the Purple Heart or the pickled finger. If they had, I would have been highly upset that they hadn't shared it with me. I could understand not telling anyone about your mother doing something so strange as keeping your finger as a memento of your carelessness, but I found it hard to accept that a man could be awarded such a prestigious medal without even mentioning it to his own wife. What else had he kept to himself? Gideon didn't say anything to me before he lumbered off to bed that night. I was rather relieved. I needed a break from spooky shit for a while.

I started reading the book, *Wild Horse Mesa* by Zane Grey, that I found in grandma's closet. My love of reading had started early. Once I had mastered a few words in the first grade, I tackled my first book, *The Cat in the Hat*, and was hooked. Books had always been friends to me, companions that came and snatched me out of the misery and took me to other places, far from my screwed up life.

I would often cross the levee and sit on a rock by the broad, brown Mississippi and read away an afternoon. I could journey from the teeming streets of London to the vast, uninhabited wilderness of Alaska from that spot. Twain's stories of life on that very river could transport me to the wheel of a ribbon-bedecked paddle-wheeler docking at the foot of Canal Street, while calliopes played and the passengers applauded my skill. Reading accounts of the Civil War caused me to imagine that the debris floating by was the wreckage of a Yankee frigate, blasted apart by Rebel cannons somewhere upriver.

But, I couldn't concentrate on Mr. Grey's western prose, so I dog-eared the page and went out to the front porch. The moon was nearly full and gave the landscape that washed out, black-and-white look. Sawbuck jumped down from the chair he had been occupying as if he was embarrassed to be discovered in the forbidden seat.

"Boy, grandma will kick your hairy butt if she catches you in her chair," I said to him as I sat down.

He looked at me as his eyes said, "I guess this means a snack is out of the question?"

I mulled over the recent unsettling events as Sawbuck settled at my feet. Oh, to be an animal, I thought, with not a care or concern in the world. Just a few days ago, I was a regular fourteen-year old boy, but after arriving at what I thought was paradise, I had been sucked into some weird, time-bending vortex that seemed to be aging me beyond my years.

I went inside and turned on the TV. It was a nineteen-inch model with multiple scars on the cabinet, as if someone might have lost his grip on it at the top of a flight of stairs. The round plastic dial turned with a clack as I went from station to station. On some channels, I could make out vague human-like outlines, but even with twisting the foil-wrapped antenna into every configuration possible, it appeared that all the networks had been destroyed in massive snow slides. The static coming from the button-size speaker provided the sound effect of the avalanche.

Now I knew why country people went to bed so early. There ain't a damn thing else to do. I tried reading again but kept drifting off and having to reread whole pages. Finally, around nine-thirty, I gave it up and went to bed. My mother and grandma had already retired, and I could hear Gideon in the next room snoring like a chainsaw with a serious miss. After what seemed like enough time to grow a crop of kumquats, I finally fell asleep. And as if I didn't have enough to deal with, I had another Papa dream.

In this one, Papa was sitting at Big Mama's table in the kitchen, with fire still burning in his eye sockets and yellow fangs exposed. He had a large pocketknife with a broken blade in his hand and was systematically chopping his fingers off and dropping them into individual jars of bubbling, foaming green liquid. After he completed the self-butchering, he slowly rose and floated toward me as gore spewed from his wounds and splashed on my bare feet. I was unable to move a muscle. Just as he came close enough for me to smell the Ben-Gay, hundreds of arrows began to thunk into his body from every direction. He reached up, pulled his own head off, and thrust it toward me. His mouth snapped open wide enough that I could see the back of his stringy, rotted throat as he let loose a gut-wrenching scream that came from the depths of Hell.

I jerked awake with a kick. Damp with sweat, I felt chilled in the warm night air. I lay there repeating every curse word I had ever heard, and some I made up, until I finally went back to sleep sometime in the foggy, early morning hours.

Chapter Ten

Like Paint on Parchment

I slept later than I wanted to the next day and only had time enough for five of grandma's buttermilk biscuits with sopping gravy, two more with fig preserves, nine strips of bacon, and a couple of mugs of coffee. Then, two more just plain biscuits. But that was all because Miss Spicy had asked me to come back at the same time I did yesterday. I had to hurry.

While Sawbuck ate, I shuffled around the front porch to see if Gideon might say something. Besides, overeating had slowed my legs. After waiting for what I thought was an adequate amount of time for him to do his Nostradamus routine, and for my breakfast to settle, I pedaled off.

As I crossed the Spates' Creek Bridge, I thought that one day, maybe another thousand years from now, the creek will dry up and some future fourteen year old boy will experience the same thrill I did in finding the arrowhead. I just hoped he had enough sense to immediately put it in his damn pocket.

Beulah greeted me at the door and after a few pleasantries, ushered me into the parlor. Miss Spicy sat in the same chair as before, wearing a rose-colored, long-sleeved dress. She had taken more care in applying her makeup and looked a little better, though cosmetics on her was like paint on parchment.

"Good mornin', Lonnie," she greeted cheerily.

"Good morning, Miss Spicy."

"Did you sleep well?"

"Yes, ma'am. How about you?"

"I think I had the best hour's sleep I've had since Ulysses S. Grant was president," she laughed.

I was amazed at how clear her mental faculties were for a woman who was born when Franklin Pierce was in the White House and who had lived through twenty-one presidential administrations.

"Lonnie, would you like some more lemonade, or would you rather have a soda?"

"A soft drink will be fine, Miss Spicy."

"All I have is ginger ale. Is that all right?"

"Yes, ma'am. That'll do. Thank you."

"I think I'll have one, too."

Beulah shuffled off to get the drinks, and I thought it was a good thing there was no carpet on the floor or she might fry herself, or Miss Spicy, with stored up static electricity.

"Well, now, you wanted me to tell you about your grandfather, Tom Spates, didn't you?" she asked.

"Yes, ma'am. Did you know that he won a Purple Heart during World War I?"

"Oh, yeah. I had forgot about that. There's a story behind that. Tom used to come out to see me right often back then, and one day he told me that he give that Purple Heart to a girl he was in love with. He wouldn't tell me who she was 'cause she had given it back to him and said she weren't interested. He never mentioned it to me again. That was before he married your grandma. I always wondered who the girl was that turned him down. Most of the girls around here stood in line to go out with him."

So, that's why he had never mentioned the medal to grandma. There was another woman involved. Beulah returned with two tepid bottles of ginger ale with straws already inserted in the necks.

"Not everybody liked Tom, though I sure did," she said. "He was a lot of fun to be around sometimes. But he had a kinda mean streak in him, too. He could see a person's weakness and jump on it. If he thought somebody did him wrong, he wouldn't rest 'til he got revenge. I used to tell him that the Bible says, 'revenge is mine, saith the Lord.' He would just laugh and say, 'there's enough revenge for the both of us.'"

"Do you think somebody could have disliked him enough to kill him, Miss Spicy?"

"I reckon you know how he was killed, don't you?"

"Yes, ma'am."

"Well, I have always thought that a certain man might have done somethin' to that train. I just cain't see Tom being that careless. It just wasn't like him at all. He was smart and might've been the head of the railroad one day if he'd a'lived."

"Who do you think it was?"

"Oh, I don't want to say 'cause I don't know nothin' for sure. The man died a number of years ago all eat up with cancer. I wouldn't want to bear false witness against the dead. That would be slanther."

"Slanther?" I blurted.

"Yes, tellin' somethin' about someone that ain't true. It's a lawyer word, slanther."

"Oh, yeah," I said. "Then what makes you think that this man would have reason to harm my grandfather?"

"If I tell you all the details, you might be able to find out who I'm talkin' about. I'll just tell you that the man hated Tom's guts and was heard makin' threats after Tom was promoted over him."

"Was the man seen around the depot the night the engine blew up?"

"Well, as a matter of fact, he was. Or so I was told. But there weren't enough proof that he did anything. Folks just suspected that he might a done somethin'."

I was aggravated that she wouldn't give me the man's name, but I thought that by doing a little detective work I could learn his identity.

"Tom was a free spirit you might say," she said. "He liked to have a good time. But he'd get a little crazy sometimes when he was drinkin'. One time he got drunk at Willie's, and a man insulted him in some way. When

Tom went to hit him, the man run up the road and got on the train. Tom chased after him, dragged him off the train, and beat him senseless right there in front of the passengers waitin' to get on board."

Nothing wrong with that, I thought. A man has to defend his honor.

"Then, one night, him and some of his drinkin' buddies went out to a revival meetin' that a travelin' preacher was holdin' under a tent just outside town. I was there that night. They come staggerin' up the aisle shoutin' hallelujah and praise the Lord and taking big swallers from a jug of moonshine. The preacher told them to leave, and Tom said, 'Don't you want to save my soul preacher?' When the preacher asked them to leave agin, Tom started yellin', 'You ain't nothin' but a damned ol' hypocrite. All you care about is how much money is put in the offerin' plate.'"

I had also felt that way about some of the evangelists that had visited our church.

"I sure was ashamed of Tom for actin' that way. And people tryin' to worship the Lord. Well, Tom and his friends wouldn't leave, and the sheriff come out and arrested 'em and locked 'em up for disturbin' a religious meetin'. But that's all bad stuff. I'd ruther talk about happy things," she said, daintily sucking soda through the straw. She proceeded to share more pleasant memories of my grandfather as the morning wore on. She was a storehouse of information. I was beginning to feel very close to her and regretted the lack of a relationship before this.

"Please, don't say I told you this," she said as she lowered her voice, "but the reason that your mammy don't like your grandmaw is 'cause Birdie buried Tom in the Moro cemetery instead of the Spates' cemetery. All the Spates was buried there back then. I know it sounds kinda silly now, since the family's been so scattered around that I 'spect we got people buried all over the country. But back then where you was buried was very important to the family. I mean, you cain't just change your mind once you're in the ground."

I didn't care where they were buried; I just wanted them to stay buried.

So, that was the reason that I had so little contact with Mammy and Paw growing up. I felt a shot of sadness as I realized that they had sacrificed a relationship with their great-grandson over the possession of a headless cadaver. And who was to say that it was my grandfather's body? Without the head, there was no way to know for sure. And he was a clever man, from what I had learned, and therefore could have staged his own death. He could be picking coffee beans in Brazil at that very moment for all they knew. Though I doubted that very seriously, I did see where my grandfather was the type of man that could have been a target for a little bodily harm.

"Do you know anything about the Booger that's been beating on Wallace and Velma's house all these years, Miss Spicy?" I asked after she seemed to have exhausted her supply of Tom Spates' stories.

"Well, their house ain't far from here as the crow flies. It's just across the woods over by Whitewater Creek. I have heard that devilish bangin' many times, and I have my suspicions of who's doin' it."

"Who?"

"I cain't tell you that," she laughed. "I ain't got no proof. Just like I ain't got no proof about somebody killin' Tom. It's just the imaginin' of an old woman."

"Aw, come on, Miss Spicy, you can tell me. I won't say anything."

"I just cain't, Lonnie. It wouldn't be proper. Besides, it's gotta stop soon 'cause whoever's doin' it has to be gettin' on up in years. In fact, whoever the fool is might just drop dead out in the woods one night. He could lay out there and rot like ol' man Hollis Dunn."

I remembered the story of eighty-three-year old Hollis Dunn very well. He and his ugly dog, Cicero, were fixtures in town. I had seen him walking the roads and drinking beer at Willie's many times. One day, someone remarked that they hadn't seen Hollis around for a while, so a couple of the men went out to his old shack. It was apparent that no one had been there in some time, and a search party went out and combed the woods but couldn't find a hair. About a month later, Cicero walked up to Willie's front door with a boot in his mouth. There was a foot still in it. He later led them to what was left of Hollis.

"And speakin' of gettin' up in years, it's about time for my nap. I have to keep up my strength."

I thanked her for allowing me to visit and for the room temperature ginger ale and left. I felt like I was getting to know my grandfather a little better. And I was intrigued by her mention of the mysterious man that she thought could have caused his death, as well as the one she suspected of being the Booger.

~

I meditated on what I had learned as I enjoyed the next couple of sweet summer days, batting rocks, roaming the woods with Sawbuck, and riding my bike all the way out to the gravel pit. Actually, there were several pits where gravel had been excavated over the years. Each of them had filled with water, but there was one in particular that was the gem of the bunch. It was the local "swimmin' hole" and was fed by a refreshingly cold underground spring. Stripped down to my underwear, I would get a running start and hurtle off into space from the high embankment and fall twenty feet, with legs kicking all the way down, into the deep, turquoise blue water below. Sawbuck followed right behind me. He showed no hesitation at all. He could have been a circus performer. I thought of the money I could make charging people to watch him dive.

We scrambled back up and repeated the process until we were too weak to continue. I jumped up and down on one leg, with my head cocked to the side in an attempt to dislodge the quart of water that had accumulated in my ear canal. I knew that my mother would have a whole herd of pissed-off cows if she found out I was here. I felt guilty about it, especially since several people had drowned there over the last few years. But I also felt scrubbed clean, inside and out. It was one of those rare pleasures in life that if you don't indulge in at least once, you'll regret it forever. And I didn't want to end up a cantankerous old man, bitching and moaning about all the things I had missed out on.

One day, I rode out to the Spates' cemetery and walked among the graves of my relatives on my grandfather's side. I saw the grave of Samantha, the first to be buried here. What a sad accomplishment that was, to personally start a cemetery. The weathered, nearly erased letters on her crumbling, hand-chiseled headstone read:

BORN 9 20 1841

DIED 3 27 1853

Next to her was her mother Abigail, with a newer monument that read:

BORN AUG. 8 1822

DIED APRIL 9 1914

She was almost ninety-two when she passed away, fifty-one years after her husband was hanged and buried somewhere in the woods around here. The unused plot next to her was a mute testimony to that tragedy. Another tragedy in the Spates' family's eyes was the fact that my grandfather's bones weren't interred there.

At the Moro cemetery, I read the markers of my Callaway ancestors on my Grandma Birdie's side of the family. I stood for a long chilling moment in front of Papa's plain piece of granite and read:

JAMES LEROY CALLAWAY

BORN FEB. 19, 1878

DIED JULY 11, 1953

A memory flashed in my mind of that broiling day seven years before when I watched two sweating, gray-haired Negro men lower the shiny blue casket into the dark, gaping hole in the ground, while I pictured Papa inside trying desperately to alert someone to the fact that he wasn't dead. I shook the thought from my mind for fear it might touch off another round of mind-twisting dreams. The grass needed cutting on the plot reserved for Big Mama. What a lonely-ass job that would be, mowing for the dead. But you wouldn't need a complaint department.

Then, just a few feet down was the tombstone of my grandfather. I had been here many times over the years, but now that I knew more about him, I felt a cloying sense of regret in not having had an opportunity to know him in person. His marker had a small scene of a mountain lake etched into the marble above the inscription, which read:

THOMAS JEFFERSON SPATES

BORN SEPT. 18 1894

DIED DEC. 22 1924

LOVING HUSBAND AND FATHER

Standing there looking at the little piece of ground that held his headless body, I was suddenly smacked in the face by a glaring fact that I had overlooked for my entire life. My grandfather was killed on December 22, 1924, and I was born December 22, 1945. Was that just another coincidence? Tiny little fingers began playing my nerves like a harp.

And then the question arose in my mind about where Grandma Birdie would be buried. Here, next to the only man she ever loved? Or beside her current husband, Gideon Woods? But I quit thinking about it and hurried away because I wasn't ready for that choice to be made, and because I get creeped out easily in graveyards.

~

On Friday night, I rode up to Willie's in hopes of being entertained by the colorful, inebriated patrons, who never failed to put on a great show. The place was packed, and the jukebox was working overtime. I sat on a stool at the end of the bar near Aunt Kate, drinking my second root beer of the night, always on alert for my father. Marty Robbins' song "El Paso" ended, allowing me to pick up on an animated conversation taking place across the room.

"I'm just sayin' that I would have caught the son of a bitch by now," a farmer named Orville Turner said. "I wouldn't let nobody bang on my house for forty damn years."

"What if it ain't a man that's doin' it?" another man said.

"Aw hell, a'course it's a man. I don't believe in haints. I think Wallace is jus' scared to try and catch him," Orville said.

"Well, I think it's a goddamn spook of some kind," Charlie Banks interjected. "What the hell else could it be? Ain't no goddamn *man* gonna do somethin' so goddamn stupid for so goddamn long."

Charlie's outburst brought to my mind the line from Shakespeare: *Me thinks he doth protest too goddamn much.*

"You ever seen a spook, Charlie?" Orville asked.

"No, I hain't. But that don't mean they ain't real, goddamn it."

"I seen somethin' one time," Uncle Willie said. "I was about fifteen, I reckon, and me and Doyle Laws had been squirrel huntin' all day, and I was walkin' home after dark. I had to go by Moro cemetery on the way, and I seen what looked like a man come straight up outta the ground and then kinda disappear like smoke. I run like a deer."

The room was quiet, all eyes on Willie.

"Bullshit!" Orville said. Everybody laughed.

"You can laugh if you want, but I know what I seen."

"Are you tellin' me some damn *smoky ghost* could be bangin' on the side of a house?" Orville said.

"No, Orville. I ain't. I'm jus' sayin' there are things goin' on that we don't know about. Stuff you cain't explain. That's all I'm saying'."

Willie, also one of my suspects, seemed to be blaming the supernatural as well.

"Well, I am not calling' you a liar, Willie, but I bet it are just a man. I bet it's somebody we all know. Hell, he could be in this room right now."

Again, the room fell silent as everyone cast suspicious glances at each other. There were at least half a dozen men that would meet my requirements for the Booger.

"Well, it ain't my problem," Orville said. "Give me another beer, Kate. We need some more music in this place." He walked over and dropped a quarter in the jukebox.

Johnny Horton's "North to Alaska" came through the speakers, and the Booger was forgotten for the moment. It seemed a perfect time to relieve myself of the root beer I had consumed. I went out the front door and made my way around the post office. I had no intention of going all the way to the outhouse in the dark, especially after hearing of figures rising out of the ground, so I stopped where no one could see me, unzipped, and created a puddle. Just as I zipped back up, someone spoke from out of the dark, which caused me to rise up off the ground myself, and made me glad I had nothing left in my bladder.

"How you doin', young man?"

The voice came from a figure seated on the back steps of the post office. He stood up and walked toward me.

"I didn't mean to scare you. I waited till you finished your business." As he came closer, I saw that he was about three inches shorter than me and had a thick and powerful build. His white hair and beard made him look to be over sixty, and he was dressed in worn but clean clothes.

"I'm Garland Purifoy. You ever hear a me?"

Of course, I had heard of "Scrub" Purifoy. He was Moro's most infamous part-time resident. He was born and raised here but had started riding the rails thirty years ago. He would show up for a few days and then disappear for years at a time.

"Yes, sir, I have." I said as my nerves buzzed.

"I bet you have," he chuckled. "Folks tell all kinda tales about me. Hell, I ain't lived long enough to do half a what they say I did. You ever hear that I kilt a man?"

I had heard many times of him killing some guy in a knife fight, and that he took up the hobo lifestyle to avoid capture.

"Yes, sir, I did." I was poised for flight.

"Do I look like somebody that would kill a man to you?"

I didn't know what a killer might look like. I had almost become one myself.

"I … guess not."

"Well, I didn't kill nobody. But I let folks think I did, so they don't mess with me." He laughed, revealing a surprisingly perfect set of white teeth.

"I been here since yesterday visitin' my sister, Cora. Long enough to get some good meals and take my first bath in about six months. I'll be leavin' tonight on the freight they're makin' up right now."

I could hear the sound of a diesel locomotive hooking up cars over at the crossing.

"I need to ask you a favor, young man. Willie don't like me for some reason, and I ain't exactly welcome in his store. I need you to buy somethin' for me, if you don't mind."

"I don't have any money," I said, thinking I was just being panhandled.

"I'll give you the money," he said as he dug into his thin pants. He pulled out a crumpled bill and held it out. "Here, take this."

I took the bill and opened it up. It was a five.

"Get me a six-pack of any kind of beer, long as it's cold, and two packs a Camels. Make sure you get the ones without filters. If you gonna filter the damn smoke, you might as well not smoke. And for damn sure, don't tell 'em it's for me. I'd prefer that Willie didn't know I was here."

"I … I don't think they'll sell me beer. I'm too young."

"Tell 'em it's for a cripple ol' man who cain't walk to the store."

"They know everybody in town. They won't buy that."

"Okay, then, tell 'em it's for a cripple ol' hobo out at the train. Just *don't* tell 'em that I'm the hobo. Please, I ain't got nobody else to ask."

"I'll try," I said, even though I knew it wouldn't work.

"Thank you, son. I'll be settin' right over here on the steps. I tell you what, you keep whatever's left over. And 'cause you're doin' me a favor, when you come back, I'll tell you which woman in town will give you some pussy for a quarter."

He laughed and patted me on the back as I turned to go. The thought of what such a two-bit date would look like made me shudder. I was glad it was too dark for him to see my face redden. After rounding the corner of the post office, I stopped under the porch and leaned back against the wall. I took a few deep breaths to collect my thoughts. There was no way Aunt Kate would just hand over beer and cigarettes to her niece's underage son based on a wild tale of a thirsty but handicapped hobo.

While I pondered my next move, it came to me that I might have just come face to face with *the Booger*. He was about the right age, in fairly good shape, and he came and went at odd times over the years. That could be why he was never caught. He would just hop a freight and avoid capture.

Breaking out in a cold sweat, I wrote him in at the top of my mental list of prime suspects. I started back to ask him some questions but decided to put it off.

Back in the noise and smoke of Willie's, I called Aunt Kate over so we wouldn't be overheard.

"Aunt Kate, I don't suppose I could buy some beer … and some, uh, cigarettes … could I?"

"What are you talkin' about, Lonnie?"

"There's a hobo outside, and he gave me five dollars and asked me to buy him beer and cigarettes. I told him you'd say no, but he wanted me to ask anyway."

"A hobo! What are you doin' talkin' to hobos! You stay away from them filthy criminals, you hear me! I will tell your mother to stop lettin' you come up here at night."

I hadn't expected such a violent reaction.

"It's okay, Aunt Kate. He's here visiting his sister."

"Are you talkin' about Scrub Purifoy? Is that outlaw in town?"

"He didn't want me to tell you it was him. He said he's not welcome in here."

"No, he is *not* welcome in here. Lord, if Willie knew he was here … you stay away from that man, you hear me?"

"What about the money he gave me?"

"Put it in your pocket. He probably stole it anyway. You just go on home right now and stay away from him. I swear, I'll tell Ruby Jo if you don't."

"Okay … but I just don't feel right about keeping his money."

"Give it to me then," she said. "I have no problem keeping it."

I knew she would take it in a heartbeat. "Uh … I guess I'll keep it."

She came around from behind the bar and followed me outside.

"Lonnie, I'm gonna stand right here and watch you 'til you're out of sight. You go straight home, or I swear … just git on home."

I said goodnight and pedaled off with her eyes boring holes in my back. After I turned the corner headed for grandma's, I looked back and saw her go inside. I felt guilty for keeping Scrub's money, but I couldn't risk returning it with her on watch. I lay in bed listening to the train leave and wondered how long Scrub waited before giving up on me.

Chapter Eleven

He Was a St. Louis Cardinals Fan, but I Forgave Him for It

As I woke up Saturday morning, my pulse quickened when I remembered my date to sit with the ravishing Nelda Graves. The Hogskinner game was that afternoon, and I had five dollars to blow. The mere thought of her stirred things in me that I had never felt before. I wondered what I had ever seen in that homely Annette Funicello.

Out on the front porch, I heard Gideon sneeze and then say, "Thank you," as if someone had told him, "God bless you." I dressed, went to the kitchen, and dug into another belt-loosening country breakfast.

"We're gonna go by and pick up Big Mama and take her to the Skinners' game this afternoon," my mother said. "She likes to get out and talk to people every once in a while. Are you going to the game, Lonnie?"

"Yeah, Coach Two-By said I could warm up with the team."

I didn't feel that the time was right to mention my future wife, Nelda, to her yet.

"Will he let you play in the game?" grandma asked.

"No, I'm too young. He said I had to be sixteen."

"You're as good as any sixteen-year-old I've seen play," my mother said. "I've been to every one of your games, and I know you're good. Probably better than half of them ol' boys that are playin' right now."

"Well, thank you, mama. But that don't change the rules. And I enjoy shagging flies."

"What are you gonna do 'til the game?" she asked.

"Just go bat some rocks, I guess."

"Lordy mercy, I wish I had a nickel for every rock you've batted," she laughed.

"Heck, if I had a nickel for every broom handle you wore out, I could retire. Just be careful, and we'll see you at the game."

"I will," I said as I went out the back door to feed a now completely spoiled Sawbuck.

I rolled my bike up to the front porch where Gideon sat in his regular seat. He lifted his cigarette to his lips and brought his arm back down to his knee, then up and down again, and again, so rhythmically that he could have been used as a really ugly timepiece.

I stretched and said out loud, "Well, I guess I'll be going," to alert him of my presence in case he had any messages from the future for me. I coughed a few times and pretended to examine the rear axle of my bike until Sawbuck trotted up with the smug look of a pampered pooch. Just as I was about to throw my leg over the seat, Gideon spoke.

"Sometimes, the rules change," he said.

Goosebumps began square dancing all over my body.

Sometimes, the rules change. That's what he said, I was absolutely sure of it. I wondered if he had overheard our conversation about the age limit on the baseball team. If he had, he might be trying to tell me that Two-By would actually let me play. After the accuracy of Gideon's previous predictions, I took what he said very seriously. Excitement about the possibility of getting in the game had a calming effect on my crawling flesh.

I walked up the road with the fifth shovel handle that I was forced to locate, after wearing out the first four, and batted rocks while trying not to get my hopes up too high. Besides, everybody would be watching: my mother, Grandma Birdie, Big Mama, and most importantly, the charming Nelda. It might be too much pressure for one so young. Maybe that's why you had to be sixteen.

After about an hour of rock batting, I decided to ride up to the post office and visit with Doc Parker before the game. He had been in the little dollhouse of a building, sorting the mail and "shootin' the shit" with people since I could remember. I had often batted rocks out onto the ball field from the gravel driveway beside the post office as Doc leaned his elbows on the windowsill and talked baseball with me. He even made the remark one day that I was moving the driveway out to the field one rock at a time. He was a St. Louis Cardinals fan, but I forgave him for it.

I bounded up the steps and entered the front door. The entire left wall was filled with individually numbered mailboxes except for a small barred window in the center. The wall on the right was cluttered with wanted posters, some of which had been there since the first time grandma brought me in as a small child. The guys in the mug shots appeared to have gone out of their way to groom themselves to look like criminals. I remember thinking that either the posters hadn't been updated in years, or those were some really slippery crooks.

I walked over to the little window and could see Doc sitting with his back to me.

"Hey, Doc," I said.

"Well, hello, Lonnie," he said brightly as he turned around. "How in the world are you doin'?"

He was in his mid-fifties, short, bald, and slightly built. He kept a dip of snuff packed in his lower lip, which made it look perpetually swollen.

"I'm doing good. How about you?"

"Aw, you know me," he said. "Nothin' ever changes much for me. I heard you was in town. Everybody's been talkin' about how you nearly bounced the ball off Buddy Kilgore's skull last Saturday. I wished I had seen that. I usually stay for the game, but I had the shits all day long and just wanted to get home. I'm sorry as hell I missed it."

That was far more information than I needed. "It was just luck," I said with what I hoped sounded like modesty.

"I don't know about that. I've watched you bat many a rock. That's gotta help you at the plate. You got a real smooth swing and damned if you don't hit 'em a mile. And Miss Birdie tells me you're one of the best players on your team in Louisiana. I wouldn't necessarily call it luck."

"Well, thanks for the sweet talk, Doc. And did I ever tell you that I really admire the way you sort the mail? You're a natural."

"Hell, a trained monkey could do my job."

"Really? If I get a monkey, will you train him?"

"I'll train him to tear your ass up," he laughed. "So, you gonna warm up with the team?"

"Yeah, I guess. I wish I could actually play in a game, but I have to be sixteen."

"How old are you now?"

"I'm fourteen."

"You're big for your age. I bet you could pass for sixteen."

"It's too late. I already told Coach that I was fourteen. Unless you know of a way to get around that rule."

"No, I'm afraid I don't. I wish I could help you out. I'd put in a good word for you, but they wouldn't put any stock in what I said."

"That's because you're a Cardinals fan, Doc."

I thanked him for his support, and we speculated about who would win the pennants that year and make it to the World Series. We agreed that it would be the Yankees and the Cardinals but disagreed on the outcome of that match-up.

"Doc, did you know my grandfather, Thomas Spates?"

"No, not really. He was quite a bit older than me. I saw him a few times, but I never spoke to him or anything."

"What did you hear *about* him? What did people say?"

"I really don't know much, Lonnie. Some folks liked him, and some folks didn't. I guess both sides had their reasons. I didn't know him enough to pass any kinda judgment."

"What about the Booger? Do you know anything about that?"

I saw his cheeks blush as he quickly picked up a handful of letters and began shoving them into the boxes.

"I don't know anything about that. I live up near Fordyce and don't know what goes on around here at night."

He was hiding something from me.

"I'm sorry, Doc. I've known you since I was just a piglet, and I can tell that you know *something*. We're friends, right? Please, tell me. I can keep a secret."

He shuffled papers on his tiny desk then leaned close to the window bars.

"Come around to the back door," he whispered.

"Why? There's nobody else here."

"Somebody could walk in on us. If you want me to tell you, come to the back door."

I went out the front and around to the back of the building, tingling with anticipation. Doc was standing on the steps when I arrived.

"You gotta promise me that you won't tell a soul that you heard it from me," he said quietly, as if we were engaged in a deadly conspiracy, "but a lot of folks around here have told me who they think the Booger is."

He looked around to make sure there were no unauthorized people within earshot then fired a brown stream of snuff-infused saliva from between two fingers pressed to his lips.

"Well, who is it?"

"I ain't sayin' that it *is* him, I'm just sayin' that a lot folks think it *might* be him."

"For crying out loud, Doc. Who is it?" I fought the urge to bounce a rock off his forehead.

"Well, a lot of folks think it might be … now don't say I said this … a lot of folks think it might be your Uncle Willie."

Even though he was on my list, it was still a shock to hear it spoken out loud.

"Why Willie? What would he have to gain?"

"Well, keep in mind that this is just talk. I've heard say he's tryin' to run Wallace off so he'd have the only store in town."

I was a little taken aback. "Wait a minute. Let me get this straight. Willie is the *Booger* because he wants to run Wallace off and become the sole proprietor in downtown metropolitan Moro? You've got to be kidding. This has been going on for nearly forty years, Doc. Don't you think Willie would have given up on that plan by now?"

"Like I said, that's just what folks tell me."

"Willie is happy the way things are. He don't want to sell groceries and crap."

"Well, you asked, and I told you," he snapped.

"No need to get upset, Doc. Thanks for telling me. I appreciate it. I really do."

Willie was already on my list of possibilities, but he would have been the last one I considered. He just didn't seem the type to do something so off the wall. He was a stoic, hardworking, hard-nosed, slow-moving owner of a country beer joint who dabbled in real estate and timber on the side. According to Grandma Birdie, he and Aunt Kate were very well off. I would need to give it some thought.

I noticed that the team was gathering on the field so I said goodbye to Doc, after swearing on an imaginary stack of Bibles that I wouldn't divulge what he had shared with me, and jogged over to the third-base bench. I was disappointed to find that Nelda had not yet arrived.

The Skinners were taking on the Warren Wildcats, who had won the last meeting between them. But that was without Buddy on the mound. The two teams were about equal in talent with the exception of Buddy. The Wildcats had lost the last five times that they faced him. But as of that moment there was no sign of Mr. Kilgore.

I put on my cleats and ran out to centerfield for batting practice. I saw my mother, Grandma Birdie, and Big Mama take their seats in the bleachers behind home plate. About thirty minutes later, I saw Nelda and her family setting out lawn chairs behind the fence between the bleachers and third base. My heart beat heavy with first-love palpitations, and my feet felt winged as I chased down fly balls on the Elysian Fields of youth.

Coach Two-By gave me a turn at the plate after everyone else had batted. He wasn't bearing down too hard, and I managed to scatter a few well-tagged hits around the field. I turned around after each one to make sure that Nelda was watching. I felt myself grow in stature every time she clapped her hands and waved at me. I pictured her sitting in the players' wives' section of Yankee Stadium. The prettiest one there.

Batting practice ended and still no Buddy. The number two pitcher, Louis Avery, was warmed up and ready to start. I hung around the bench in hopes that Two-By might say I could actually play in the game. After all, Gideon had predicted it, hadn't he?

I felt foolish thinking that way, but I wanted to play so badly that I was willing to clutch any available straw. I watched the other pitcher closely as he warmed up. He was a tall, rangy country boy with a limited arsenal. Two actually: a fairly good fastball and a change-up. I really believed that I could hit him.

But my hopes of getting in the game sunk as Two-By called out the lineup. When he finished, he took his clipboard and walked over to talk to the other coach. It appeared that Gideon had missed the target this time. Unless he meant that the rules of *reality* sometimes change.

I was deeply disappointed, but at least I had the consolation of spending the afternoon with the angelic Nelda. What a vision she was. I sat down next to her in a folding chair with a ripped seat. I could swear that her hair was more golden, her eyes bluer, her smell more intense, and her girlish breasts bigger, than just last Saturday. My imagination ran wild with the thoughts of the first time experiences we could share. First date. First kiss. First pawing in the backseat of a car. Of course, I fully intended to do the honorable thing and marry her. I was not a cad.

"Hello, Lonnie," she said smiling.

"Hi, Nelda."

"You sure were hitting the ball well out there. You're very good. I think you should be playing for the Skinners."

"Thank you. I get lucky sometimes."

"Don't be so modest. It doesn't become you," she laughed.

"In that case, I'm the best player here."

"That's more like it. Have confidence. Why don't you ask Two-By if you can play?"

"Already did. I'm too young. I really don't mind though because that means I can sit here with you," I said sheepishly.

"Oh, that's sweet, Lonnie. I enjoy sitting with you, too. So, tell me, what have you been doing since I saw you last?"

I was so intoxicated with her dazzling teeth and richly tanned skin that I would have told her anything. I heard myself rambling on and on about what I had found out about my grandfathers, the preserved finger, the Purple Heart, my father decking Waylon Roark, finding and losing the arrowhead, swimming in the gravel pit, and batting rocks. I talked so much that I was afraid she would regret asking the question.

"I envy you," she said after I finally shut up.

"You envy me? Why would you envy me?"

"Because … you have such freedom. You go where you want to go, do what you want to do. I envy that. I can't leave the house unless it's with mama or daddy. They watch me like a hawk. Sometimes, I feel more like a prisoner than a daughter."

I instantly saw myself dressed in gleaming armor on the back of a thundering white stallion charging through the gates of a castle, slashing down the guards with my broadsword as, at full gallop, I lean over in the saddle and scoop up Princess Nelda. Effortlessly, I lift her up behind me and ride into the sunset, her arms tight around my waist.

"For once, I'd like to do something crazy," she said, breaking into my daydream of a damsel in distress.

"Like what?"

"Like … I don't know, like maybe sneaking out of the house in the middle of the night or something."

"I've done that a few times. What would you do if you sneaked out? Where would you go?"

"Well, to start with, I would have to have somebody with me. I'd be too scared to go anywhere by myself. It would have to be somebody who wasn't afraid of the dark, you know?"

She was looking at me with a peculiar expression. I felt a drop of sweat roll down between my shoulder blades.

"Yeah, I guess having somebody with you would be better."

"Yes, it would. Would you go with me, Lonnie?"

"I, uh, if you sneak out, you mean? You want me to go with you? In the middle of the night?"

"Yes to all the above." Her lashes fluttered ever so softly. "I've been thinking about this for a long time. It may sound silly to you, but I need *some* excitement in my life. I'd rather have the experience with you than anyone else. Would you go with me, Lonnie? For protection?"

I would attack a lion with my bare hands, throw myself under the wheels of a southbound freight, or even wander around in the preternatural night of Moro, Arkansas for her.

"Sure."

"How about tonight?"

I didn't expect my services as a covert escort to be called upon so soon.

"Sure, I guess."

"Be in the church parking lot at midnight tonight. I'll climb out my bedroom window and meet you there. We'll decide where to go and what to do then. Oh, I'm so excited that I can't stand it!" she squealed then looked around quickly to make sure Reverend Graves couldn't hear us.

"Are you sure you won't get caught?"

"Yeah, I'm sure. My parents sleep like the dead. They'll never know I was gone."

"Well, okay then. I'll see you tonight at midnight."

"This is so great. I really appreciate this, Lonnie. We'll have a lotta fun."

Dreams of fun with Nelda began to unfold in my head.

The Wildcats were finishing up their infield practice, and Buddy still hadn't shown up. The coaches were exchanging lineups when a beat up old Ford truck came to a brake-screeching stop near the Skinners' bench. A grime-covered man got out, walked over, and started talking to Two-By. Then, they summoned the whole team over to the third-base bag.

After a few minutes of discussion, they broke up, and some of the team members went to the bench and started taking off their cleats and picking up their gear. Two-By walked across the infield and began conferring with the Wildcat coach. I could hear people around me asking each other what was going on. Then, Two-By walked up to home plate and faced the crowd.

"I'm sorry to have to inform you that we'll have to forfeit today's game," he said in a loud voice.

A wave of groans swept the stands.

"There has been a major train derailment over near Smackover, and a lot of the guys have to go to work," he continued. "We don't have enough men to field a team."

"How many do you have?" someone in the stands yelled out.

"I only have seven players left," he said.

At that precise moment, Buddy Kilgore's Chevy rolled up.

"Make that eight."

"Why don't you let Lonnie Tobin play?" a large red-faced man I had never seen before said.

"Yeah, put the kid in," someone else said.

"The kid can handle it," another voice called. Suddenly, a chant started: "Put in the kid, Put in the kid, Put in the kid."

I couldn't believe my ears. This couldn't be happening. But Nelda's adoring look confirmed that it was. After a few minutes of the chant, Two-By walked over to the other team's bench and talked with the coach. He then retraced his steps back to the Skinners' bench.

"Lonnie! Come here please," he said, motioning me over.

With adrenaline squirting out of my ears, I jogged to the bench.

"You wanna play with us, son?"

"Yes, sir!" I answered. "But I thought I had to be sixteen."

"Sometimes, rules change."

Gideon had done it again. But I didn't have the time to dwell on that.

"Here," Two-By said as he pulled a jersey from the equipment bag. "Put this on."

As he tossed the shirt to me, I saw the number seven on the back.

And I didn't have to wash his car for it. I stripped off my T-shirt and slipped the jersey on. I waved at Nelda and hustled out to my assigned position in right field as Buddy took the mound.

I was on top of the world. Never in my most creative imagination could I have anticipated what was happening: people chanting for me, a beautiful girl was eager to do who knows what in the middle of a rural night, and I had a chance to shine on the field.

Of course, I also had the chance to make a fool of myself. But I didn't want to think about that. I was alternating between wishing a ball would be hit in my direction and praying that it wouldn't. I didn't have to worry much because Buddy fanned the three batters he faced in the top of the first. I felt like a major leaguer as I ran in after the last man went down swinging.

The opposing pitcher's fastball was working pretty well. It was three up and three down in our half of the inning. Two-By had penciled me in as the ninth batter, which meant that if no one got on base, I would come to the plate in the third inning. I was eager to bat but not in a hurry.

The first Wildcat up in the top of the second reached first on an error by the Skinners' shortstop. Buddy got the next batter to hit into a double play, struck out the next guy, and ended our defensive stretch.

The first Skinner up in the bottom of the second popped up behind the plate. The next man dribbled a weak grounder to first base for the second out. It looked like a repeat of the first inning. Then, the Wildcat pitcher seemed to lose some of his control and gave up back-to-back singles and walked the next batter. I felt lightheaded as I realized that the bases were full as I prepared to step to the plate.

The number of spectators was surprisingly large for a small-town ball game. Cheers assaulted my ears as I wiped my hands on my pants and hefted the bat. I felt like I was supporting the weight of the world. Nelda was sending her blinding smile my way, and I hoped she couldn't see the raging anxiety in my eyes. Then, Two-By called me over.

"Listen up, Lonnie. This guy is rattled and can't find the plate. He's gonna have an even harder time hittin' your strike zone, so I want you to take every pitch. He'll walk in a run, and that'll bring up the top of the lineup. If we play our cards right, we might get a couple runs out of this. Do you understand what I'm sayin', son?"

"Yes, sir."

I walked to the plate with mixed emotions. On the one hand, I wanted a chance to be a hero, but on the other, I didn't want to be the goat. But the coach had spoken, so I stepped into the box with the bat in my relaxed grip. If I was going to take every pitch, there was no reason to tense up. I dug in and looked out at the pitcher. He had a big grin on his face as he rolled his eyes and shook his head as if to say, "Now, I'm throwing to children."

Behind me, I could hear voices calling, "Come on, kid! You can do it! Knock one out of the park, kid!" But the voice that soared above them all in my ears belonged to Nelda.

"Come on, Lonnie! Get a hit for me!"

I wished the hell I could, but if I can't take the bat off my shoulder, it will be difficult. I glanced down at Two-By who was coaching third. He gave me the take sign. The pitcher went into his stretch, hesitated, and released the ball.

It was a fastball down the center of the plate, but he didn't put much smoke on it. He was just trying to get it over the plate because he knew I would be taking all the way. I was sure I could have hit it. The second pitch was a carbon copy with just a little more heat for strike two.

I stepped out of the box and tapped the dirt out of my cleats as I looked down at Two-By for the sign. Surely, he would let me swing away since there were two outs. He motioned by touching his hat and belt then back to the hat. Take again? Shit. To make me take with two strikes meant he didn't think I could hit this guy. I glanced at him again, and he repeated the take signal. This wasn't fair. I was going to strike out without taking a single cut and look like a fool. I dug in with fury and faced the pitcher. He checked the runners, went to the stretch, and threw.

I saw immediately that it was the changeup. He obviously figured I would be tight as a drum expecting a fastball and would fall all over myself on an off-speed pitch. The ball seemed to float like a balloon as it approached the plate. It appeared to be screaming at the top of its lungs, "Hit me, Lonnie. Hit me! You'll never get a pitch this fat again in your life! Hit me, damn it!"

I never was good at self-control and swung with every ounce of strength in my body. I heard the satisfying *thwack* of the bat and felt the solid connection all the way to my toes. My eyes followed the ball as it rose in a majestic arc into left field.

The leftfielder, who had moved in close when he saw me come to the plate, now wheeled around and took off at full speed. I headed for second and saw the ball bounce near the fence. As I rounded the bag at second, I saw Two-By frantically waving me on. I turned on the after-burners as I raced to third. From the corner of my eye, I could see the leftfielder fire the ball to the cut-off man, who pivoted and threw to third.

Two-By was signaling for me to slide with a palms-down motion as I neared the base. I flung myself headlong into the dirt and felt my fingers touch the bag a split second before the ball popped into the third baseman's outstretched glove.

"SAFE!"

I called time, stood up to brush myself off, and spit a cubic foot of dirt out of my mouth. The spectators were going nuts. I had just hit a triple! I drove in three runs on my very first at bat! I was having an out-of-body experience. Surely, I was home in bed, and God was giving me this great dream to make up for all the Papa nightmares I had suffered through. There was no way this could be happening to *me*.

I could see my mother's red hair in the crowd as she waved both arms. Calls of "Way to go kid!" rolled over me. Nelda's yellow tresses flew in the air as she jumped up and down and screamed. I felt like an all-American hero. Then, Two-By came over and rained all over my ticker-tape parade.

"What in the hell was that, boy!" he said through gritted teeth as he leaned his reddened face in close to my mine. "Didn't I tell you to take every pitch?!"

"He threw me a change-up coach, like he thought I was just a kid who couldn't hit. I'm sorry."

"I don't give a goddamn rat's ass in hell if he threw the ball *underhanded* 'cause he thought you was a split-tail girl! I told you to take every pitch! Every damn pitch! I did not say, 'oh, pick out one you like.' I said every damn pitch!"

I looked over Two-By's shoulder during this verbal assault and was relieved to see that nobody could hear what he was saying. As far as they knew, he was congratulating me.

"If I had somebody to replace you with," he continued unabated as two large throbbing purple veins formed a "V" on his forehead, "I would snatch your ass out of the game so fast your ears would bleed. If you want to be a ball player, the first thing you gotta learn is that the coach's word is above the damn ten commandments. You hear me, boy?"

"Yes, sir," I said, feeling like a dog that had been soundly chastised with a rolled up sports section.

He stood there for a few seconds throwing fiery fastballs at me with his eyes then turned and walked back to the coach's box. After a few deep breaths, he came back.

"As long as we understand one another," he said. "Good hit."

My hit opened the floodgates, and it turned into a rout. I went four for nine, drove in a total of five runs, and scored two more as we tamed the Wildcats twenty-one to three. After the game, I changed back into my T-shirt and handed the Hogskinners' jersey to Two-By.

"Keep the shirt," he said. "You played a helluva game today. I wish I could let you play every game, but I cain't."

"Thank you, Coach. Hey, I might get to play again. You never know. Sometimes, the rules change."

"Don't count on it, kid. This was a real fluke. If the other coach had said no, we'd have forfeited the game. I bet he wishes that he hadn't agreed to it now. But the game counts just the same, unless he tries to dispute it."

"You think he will?"

"Naw, he would be shamed like a dog by everybody if he did that.

He'll just have to take this ass whippin' like a man."

My mother and grandma and Big Mama hugged my neck and made a big fuss over me, saying I was the next Mickey Mantle. I was just thankful that I hadn't turned out to be the next Mickey Mouse. Strangers that I had never laid eyes on before in my life were slapping me on the back and calling me "The Kid." It appeared that I had just been bestowed with the honor of a nickname. I kind of liked it, even though it hadn't been too lucky for Billy the Kid. But he wasn't a ball player. And it was a hell of a lot better than Tater or Two-By.

Nelda ran over and, after looking over her shoulder to see if her father was watching, gave me a quick hug.

"Oh, Lonnie, that was great. I'm so proud of you. I could just kiss you!"

I wanted to say, "Go ahead, you beautiful thing. I'm too tired to fight you off."

"I'm *so* looking forward to tonight," she said as she lowered her voice. "You haven't forgotten, have you?"

I might forget my mother's name, where I live, or even to take the next breath, but I would never forget our rendezvous.

"I haven't forgotten. I'll be there."

"Oh, can you bring some cigarettes with you?" she asked in a whisper.

"Cigarettes? I didn't know you smoked."

"I don't really. I just want to try it. See what it's like, you know? But if you can't, that's okay."

"Yeah, sure, I can get some." I remembered the pack I had taken from the side of my father's bed the morning I almost shot him. I still had them hidden at the bottom of my gym bag. Maybe the old saying that the preacher's kids were always the wildest was true. I hoped it was.

"If my father wasn't looking, I *would* kiss you, Lonnie Tobin."

Oh, yes! Tonight, I would finally experience "face sucking."

"I'll see you later," Nelda said as she turned and left. She had just turned fifteen, and I watched her already shapely form walk over to join her mother and father. I wondered what kind of in-laws they were going to make.

I rode back to grandma's with Sawbuck running happily alongside. Good old Sawbuck would have been just as happy with me if I had made a total ass of myself. I knew that he would be forever loyal to me no matter what. At least as long as I kept giving him vittles from grandma's kitchen.

When I got home, my mother went on and on about my future in baseball and made me promise to buy her a house once I was rolling in all that major league dough. I said I would not only buy her a house but a Cadillac, too. After all, she would need a nice vehicle to come and see me and Nelda and the grandkids.

Then, the pep rally came to a sudden end.

"Your father called, Lonnie," she said with a hopeful look on her face.

"So?"

"So, he told me he hasn't had a drink in a while now, and he's gonna quit for good."

"Bullshit."

"Lonnie, you ain't too big to whip. Don't talk like that in front of your grandmother."

"I agree with, Lonnie," Grandma Birdie said. "How many times has he promised you he would quit drinkin'?"

"That's right, mama," I said. "It's the same old story. He comes home shit-faced, you get mad at him, and y'all fight and he swears he's going to quit. I've heard it a million times."

"You don't have to use that kinda language, Lonnie. I don't appreciate it," mama said.

"I'm sorry. I just don't want him to sucker you in with his empty promises."

"But I never left him before. I think he might just appreciate me now that I ain't there to wait on him hand and foot."

"Is that what you want, mama? To go back to being a slave? To be stuck with him again when he breaks his promise and comes home drunk? And you know he will. He's not gonna change. We're free of him now. Do you want that misery again?"

"But what are we gonna do, Lonnie? We can't stay here forever. Mama can't afford it."

"We'll make do, Ruby Jo. Don't worry 'bout that," grandma said. "I might can get you a job with me at the lunch room."

"He said he was gonna get us a nice house over in Mimosa Park," she went on, ignoring our protests. "You know, that real nice subdivision by the high school? You can play baseball for your team again. Wouldn't you like that?"

"Mama, listen to me. It won't last. It wouldn't be a week before he was right back to his old ways. You know I love you but *please* don't be gullible, mama."

"Well, would you just think about it? Will you do that much for me?"

"Yes, for you I'll think about it. Well, I thought about it. I'm not going."

"Lonnie Ray, I meant to think about it for a couple of days."

"All right, mama, I'll give it two days. But unless I receive a massive head wound that renders me incapable of intelligent thought, the answer will still be no."

There was no more mention of it while we ate supper. I found it a little difficult to swallow past the hard lump in my throat. The idea of going back to Louisiana with my alcoholic father severely curbed my appetite. Even grandma's to-die-for banana pudding seemed dead.

After we finished eating, I went out back to feed Sawbuck and discussed the situation with him. I told him what was going on with my father, and though he was noisily slurping up his dinner like he hadn't eaten in weeks, I knew he agreed with me that there was no way in hell that we would go back. We would take to the woods and live off the land first, no matter what hardships we had to endure. Of course, we'd sneak back to grandma's every once in a while for a home-cooked meal.

I summarily dismissed the thought from my mind. There were more important things to consider. Like my midnight meeting with Nelda, the temptress. How would I be able to make it through the next seven hours? In dog years, that was like three days. Good thing dogs have no concept of time. I went and took a long hot bath.

After dressing, I went to the front porch. Gideon was holding down his seat and dialoguing with his spiritual advisors while blowing out purple-gray clouds of cigarette smoke. I sat in the worn-out overstuffed chair and watched him for a while, wondering what was going on in his mind. He appeared to be completely free of the constraints of sanity, but he had proven that he had some kind of conduit into a world I couldn't understand.

I found myself hoping that he would say something that would give me an idea of what to expect on my date with Nelda. Like "Love is in the air" or "Lonnie's gonna lose his virginity." But he spoke not a word before rambling off to bed as the evening shadows deepened. Hell, the chickens were still awake and scratching, and I wondered how anyone could go to bed that early. But then, I guess it's easy for people who have less of a life than a chicken. I felt a pang of pity for his empty existence.

The minutes dragged by slower than the last hour of school. I found myself staring at Sawbuck and thinking about the differences between dogs and cats. Much has been written through the centuries of unswerving canine loyalty and fierce feline independence. To me, dogs give you the impression that everything is all right, while cats are the only animals that seem to always be "on the rag," as my father would say. Dogs are blue-collar workers that get the job done no matter how daunting the task, while cats sit in ivory towers, sip champagne, and look down with superior sneers. Dogs are the guy next to you in the foxhole watching your back, while cats are safe behind the lines at headquarters issuing orders and bitching about the quality of the caviar. It was clear to me that *all* cats should be thrown down a well.

I read, paced, fidgeted, then watched as a breathtaking full moon rose like an orange ball over the trees, so close I could see the shadows in the craters. It was perfect. A big lunar orb dripping romance all over the place was exactly what I would have ordered. The stars and the Good Lord seemed to be smiling down on me.

My mother and grandma went to bed. I eased into the deserted kitchen to see if the banana pudding tasted any better and to pick up my mother's wristwatch that she always left on the table. I needed it to keep up with the time while Nelda and I did whatever we were going to do. The pudding was delicious. Almost as good as the anticipation of seeing Nelda. I combed and re-combed my hair and splashed on some after-shave lotion from a dust-crusted bottle of dubious vintage that I found under the bathroom sink. I wanted to be irresistible.

Finally, the moment arrived, and I stuffed the pack of Lucky Strikes and a matchbook in my shirt pocket; quietly, I crept out the front door and grabbed my bike. I started to tie up Sawbuck but realized that he might be handy to have along. No telling what we may run into, and I could always send him for help like Lassie. I had to smile at that because, though I loved him dearly, Sawbuck was no Lassie. But then, neither was Lassie.

Chapter Twelve

The Play of Life

I rode over to the church, my heart doing a cymbal-crashing drum solo. The moon, now silver in color, made everything nearly as visible as daytime. My mind was fondling the thought of the luscious Nelda as I arrived for our clandestine meeting. I stopped under the streetlight, one of only two in the whole town, to wait for her. I pulled my mother's watch from my pocket and noted that it was exactly twelve midnight. I was prompt if nothing else. Nelda was nowhere in sight.

I watched as all manner of insects circled madly, flitting and crashing into the bulb of the streetlight above me like the fate of their entire species depended on getting inside. I could hear their stiff-winged buzz, and the *tink* their bodies made as they repeatedly hit the glass. Hundreds of their compatriots lay in heaps on the ground below where they had fallen after their fatal attempts at gaining entrance. They reminded me of my father. He was a barfly irresistibly drawn to neon liquor signs, and one day he too would drop into the pile of burned out dummies who wasted their short stay on earth searching for something that never even existed.

I heard an owl off in the distance to my right. I've always been amazed at how far sound travels in country air at night. The city seemed to just soak up sound waves, but out here they were unfettered and free to roam far and wide. I heard another owl hooting off to my left as it answered the first. They carried on an intermittent long distance conversation as the time slipped by.

I checked the watch again and saw that it was 12:20. Something must have happened. Maybe she just couldn't stay awake. I had almost dozed off a couple of times myself. But I thought I would wait a little longer. As 12:30 approached, I came to the conclusion that I had been stood up. I was scraping the disappointment off my heart and preparing to leave when I saw movement out of the corner of my eye.

Nelda slid out of the shadows pushing her bike at a rapid clip. She was wearing a T-shirt and a rather revealing pair of shorts. I couldn't help noticing how womanly her legs looked in the artificial light.

"I am so sorry, Lonnie," she said as she came up beside me. "I fell asleep. I was trying to read a book to stay awake, but it didn't work."

"Oh, you like to read?" I said, trying to hide my nervousness.

"Yes, I do. I read a lot. What else is there to do in this town?" "What were you reading?"

"*The House of the Seven Gables* by Hawthorne."

"That'll put anyone to sleep," I said.

She laughed, threw her arms around my neck, and kissed me hard on the lips, slipping her tongue in my mouth at the same moment. I had never kissed a girl before in my life, much less felt a tongue down my throat. I liked it very much.

"Where do you want to go?" I asked as if I was French-kissed every day of my life.

"I don't care. Let's just get outta here."

"I guess we can go wherever the roads lead us," I said, trying hard to sound like a character from a Kerouac novel.

"You lead; I'll follow."

"You sure your folks are asleep?"

"Positive. Did you bring some cigarettes?"

"Why, yes, I do believe I did."

After that assurance, we pedaled off as I led the way. We rode toward town and heard the jukebox at Willie's long before we stopped at the ballfield across the street. The soft glow of the lights was warm and inviting, and voices mingled in a friendly banter. Half a dozen worn out pickups were parked out front, and I noticed that all but one of them was missing the tailgate.

"Things are jumping at Willie's again," I said. "It's been this way for many years. The same people take their Saturday night baths and show up here to get smashed. It's so sad."

"They have to socialize somewhere. None of them go to church. In a way, this is their church. They sure attend religiously," she laughed.

We watched Aunt Kate rise from her chair at the window and move behind the bar.

"There goes Sister Kate to take up the offering," I said. "And the next hymn will be 'I Saw the Light,' sung by Brother Hank Williams."

We sat on our bikes and watched for a while, and I was suddenly aware of being *alive*, of existing on this planet, in this spot, at that very moment. People in other places were doing other things, but we were here right now. I was engulfed with euphoria.

"Hey, I just remembered something," Nelda said. "Follow me."

She took off, leaving me no choice but to follow. We rode hard and soon arrived at the rear of the high school.

"What are we doing here?" I asked.

"Marcy Miller told me about a window that won't lock," she said. "Do you want to go in and look around?"

"I don't know. What if we get caught?"

"We won't break anything. It'll be fun. I'll show you our classroom. Besides, we have to see if the window is open first. How about it, Lonnie?"

I looked around to make sure we couldn't be seen, trying not to look like a sissy. "Sure. Why not? Which window is it?"

"That one right there," she pointed to the window above our head. "Give me a boost, and I'll see if it's unlocked."

I laced my fingers together, put her foot in my hands, and lifted her up to the window. Even the feel of her foot gave me a slight hormonal jolt. She slid it open and scrambled in. I jumped, grabbed the sill, and pulled myself inside. The moonlight streaming in the large windows allowed us to see well enough to maneuver.

"Isn't this exciting, Lonnie?" she squealed as she grabbed my hand. "Come on."

She led as we weaved our way around the desks and through a door into a large room full of tables and chairs.

"This is the study hall. We'll have one hour a day in here to do homework or study for tests."

"No passing notes or goofing off?" I said.

"That too but don't get caught. Mr. Bowie is the principal, and he doesn't have a sense of humor."

We made our way across the room to a door on the right. Nelda opened it and led me inside.

"This is our class. Miss Dunn's room. She teaches seventh, eighth, and ninth grade in here. It will only be you, me, and Marcy Miller in the ninth grade this year. Of course, we'll sit together."

"Of course."

"I've been going to this dull, dead school for three years. I have hated every minute of it. But now that you're here, Lonnie, I'm looking forward to this year."

"So am I. We'll have a good time."

"More than you know," she said as she wrapped her arms around my neck and pulled me to her. "More than you know."

We stood fused together kissing for a while then ran around the desks laughing like we were losing our minds. A car driving by slowly spooked us. We slipped out the window we had come in and took off into the night.

We headed down the wide gravel road toward Fordyce. The pavement looked milky in the moonlight. Side by side, we glided through the magical night, drifting through time, talking and laughing, and puffing on stale cigarettes. We rolled into low-lying fog banks that rippled and twirled around us like smoky cotton candy as we passed. We were alone on the planet, out surveying our kingdom. I felt so good I thought I would die.

We found ourselves at the Spates' Creek Bridge, so we parked our bikes and stood looking over the waist high railing. Stars were scattered in the black sky, and reflections of the moon sparkled and danced in the water below. The vastness of the universe around us was palpable. Nelda was as radiant as a goddess, and I enjoyed the warmth of her standing next to me.

"Is this where you found the arrowhead, Lonnie?"

"Yeah. And where I lost the arrowhead. I'm such an idiot."

"You are not an idiot, Lonnie Tobin."

"Thanks, but I sure felt like one that day."

"We all make mistakes," she said. I was staring at her profile as she looked at the sky. "Lonnie, do you believe in fate? In destiny?"

"I guess so," I said after a moment of thought. "You mean, like, we're here for a reason?" I pictured Gideon telling me that exact thing.

"Yes. The Bible says that our days are numbered from the womb. That means that we all have a certain portion of time in this world." She turned to look at me. "God already knew what we would do in life before we were even born. There must be a plan for each of us, and we can't change it. We each have a role to play here on earth, and you just follow the script you're given."

"Oh, I don't know about that. I think we are able to make choices."

"But don't you see, even when we're facing choices, God already knows what choices we're going to make. We think we're choosing, but in reality we have no choice. Things are just meant to be. Like you and me being here on this bridge tonight. It was arranged long before we were even born, I just know it."

"Why do you think God, or fate, has brought us here tonight?"

"I don't know. But I know it was prearranged. We're supposed to be here."

"Have you ever thought that, maybe, we've been here before?" I asked. "That we were here, right here on this bridge in the middle of the night, in some other … life … or dimension, or whatever?"

"You've been watching *The Twilight Zone*, haven't you?"

"As a matter of fact, I have. It's my favorite show."

"Well, the Bible also says that it is appointed unto man once to die, so I don't believe in reincarnation or stuff like that, if that's what you mean."

"Do you believe in ghosts?"

"I don't know," she said as she nervously looked over her shoulder. "I guess it's possible that they exist. It's real easy to believe *anything* out here in the dark," she laughed.

"Well, if ghosts exist, doesn't that prove there are other dimensions that we don't know anything about?"

"I really don't want to think about that right now, Lonnie."

"What about someone being able to foretell the future? Do you think that's possible?"

"Yes, I do. I think that, if the play of life is already written, someone could get a glimpse of the script now and then, you know. There's probably only a few that can really *see* events in the future, but I think that we all have intuition, a kind of *knowing* about things. I can say that the first time I saw you, I knew that we would be close. Something in me knew you were going to play a part in my life."

"I felt the same way," I said, thinking it was more her beauty than kismet that drew me to her. "And I'm thankful for whatever forces brought us together."

She reached over and took my hand. "I think you're sweet. And cute."

"And I think you're … ravishing."

"Ravishing? No one has ever said I was *ravishing*."

"Well, it's about time someone did."

She moved in my direction and pressed herself against me as my arms encircled her tender young body. We stood there in pure bliss for the next million years as she introduced me to some of the ancient mysteries and pleasures of the female. I was completely love-drunk and giddy when she whispered in my ear, "Someday, we'll go all the way, Lonnie." The first thing I thought was, what better time than the present?

"It's getting late," Nelda said as she pushed me away. "We better head back."

"I don't want to go. Let's stay here and watch the sun come up."

"My father gets up before the sun. I don't want to worry you or anything, but if he caught me out here with you … well, we'd both be in a lot of trouble."

"In that case, if we get back to your house and all the lights are on, I suggest that we keep riding."

"That's not funny at all, Lonnie."

"Sorry. But what if we're destined to get caught? Why worry about it?"

"Because I don't want to tempt fate, that's why."

"Tempt fate? If your theory is correct, our fate is already sealed. How could you tempt it?"

"Shut up and kiss me."

We remounted our bikes after the exchange of more saliva and headed back in the direction of town. My lips were sore, and there was no doubt that the Love Bug and Cupid had conspired together to fashion an arrow that bit deep into my heart. I broke the shaft off at the chest and threw it end over end into the night. I was madly and hopelessly in love. There are few forces on earth more powerful than that of first love. I felt like I could slay dragons with a flick of my wrist. This had been a perfect night, and I didn't want it to ever end.

We rode into the sleeping town and were passing in front of Big Mama's house when Nelda slammed on her brakes. I stopped beside her.

"What is that?" she asked with a catch in her voice. She stood astride her bike and pointed.

I looked at the dark hulking form of Big Mama's house as the moon illuminated the roof. My eyes squinted as I strained to peer into the shadows that fell from the eaves and cloaked the front of the house. And then I saw it. In the middle bay window was a light. It was about the size of a candle flame but didn't flicker or give off a glow. It was more like someone had cut a small hole in a big sheet of black construction paper, and we were seeing through it into a world on the other side. Every hair on my body, including pubic, stood at rigid attention.

"Do you think it's your grandmother?' she asked.

"I don't think so. That don't look like a candle or flashlight, or any light I've ever seen before."

"Then what could it be?"

"You got me."

I quickly looked in all directions for something that might be reflecting on the glass, but there was nothing in sight. The question of a reflection became a moot point however when the light began to move. It drifted ever so slowly to the right. It didn't jump or shake, just a smooth steady slide across the blackness of the window for about six inches. And then it winked out like someone had put a hand over it.

"What *was* that, Lonnie?"

"I don't know. Probably just a reflection," I said with forced bravado.

"That wasn't a reflection, and you know it. What could it have been?"

"Do we really want to know?"

"No. I think it's time for me to go home."

We pedaled hard as we headed back, causing the muscles in my thighs to burn. But I was glad I had a witness to the mystery light so I didn't have to question my sanity once again.

"Thank you, Lonnie," Nelda said as we rolled to a stop back where we started and saw with relief that her house was still dark. "We'll have to do this again sometime. But without the ghost lights next time."

"How about tomorrow night? I'll get some fresh cigarettes."

"That's too soon. We don't want to press our luck, do we?"

"You just name the time, and I'll be there," I said, not wanting to part with her.

"Would you sit with me in church tomorrow?"

"Sure. What time does church start?"

"Ten o'clock. Sunday school starts at nine, but I wouldn't expect you to come that early."

"I might just surprise you," I said, staring at her like a lovesick puppy as we stood in the glare of the streetlight.

She leaned over and kissed me. "I'll see you in the morning, Lonnie."

Then, she was gone.

I pulled the watch from my pocket and saw that it was almost four a.m. I rode home and sneaked back into the house, also relieved that everyone there was still asleep. Realizing that I would never be able to wake up on time, I left a note on the table with the watch asking my mother to get me up for church. Then, I crawled into bed and fell into an exhausted slumber, relishing the taste of tobacco and Nelda's tongue in my mouth.

Chapter Thirteen

The Things of the Lord

I awoke the next morning with my mother sitting on the side of the bed shaking my shoulder. "Lonnie, time to go to church."

I stretched sleepily and found that every muscle in my body was sore. But it was the good kind of sore that makes you feel stronger because of it.

"Wake up, sleepy head," she said. "Time to rise and shine. You don't wanna miss Pastor Grave's sermon, do you? I'm sure proud to see that you are interested in the things of the Lord, Lonnie. Or is it that you're interested in the pretty little daughter of Brother Graves?"

"Oh, mama. She invited me to church, that's all."

"I saw the way she carried on over you at the ballgame. I think she likes you."

"Stop it, mama," I wasted my time saying.

"And I don't blame her. You're the best lookin' boy in town. She'll have to fight the other girls off you."

"Get outta here with that. We're just friends."

"Well, she is very cute, and I think y'all make a great couple. Now, get dressed and come to breakfast."

Although my mother's comments made me feel uncomfortable, I liked the sound of the word "couple" associated with me and Nelda. I got dressed in my best jeans and a short-sleeved white shirt. In the kitchen, a hearty breakfast was just the medicine I needed. The soreness in my body faded.

"Maybe I should go to church myself," my mother said as she sipped a cup of coffee. "Maybe that's why my life is so messed up."

"Well, I just don't care for Homer Graves. He ain't much of a preacher if you ask me," grandma said.

"You're not supposed to go to the church for the pastor's sake. You're supposed to go to worship the Lord," my mother laughed.

"That might be true, but I'd like to have somebody else leading the worship is all I'm saying."

"Don't you think Lonnie and Nelda Graves make a cute couple?" my mother teased.

"Come on, mama."

"Why, I reckon they do make a lovely couple," grandma laughed. "But I wouldn't let her daddy preach at the weddin'."

At about a quarter to ten, I set off on my bike for the church. Painfully sweet memories of last night with Nelda spiked through me as I rode into the now sun-drenched parking lot. The owls were probably sleeping, and there would be a whole new batch of doomed bugs to swarm and die under the streetlight tonight.

I leaned my bike against the light pole and went through the back doors into the cramped vestibule. There was no sign of Nelda. I walked into the small sanctuary and saw people milling around and talking before the start of the service, but no Nelda. She probably had trouble getting up this morning after being out all night. Then, I ran into Doc Parker.

"Good mornin', Lonnie. It's nice to see you in church for a change," he laughed. "I was afraid you was a heathen."

"Oh, it's you, Doc. I didn't recognize you without a dip of snuff."

"Yeah, well, these mossy-back old Baptists won't let me bring my spit-cup in. Are you here for the pastor's sermon or his daughter?"

"That's very funny, Doc," I said, trying to choke off the blush I felt rushing to my face.

"Hey, I don't blame you none. Nelda is a beautiful girl. I would ask you to sit with me, but I reckon you're lookin' for a more pleasant seatmate. I'll see ya later."

The choir assembled on the platform in their royal blue robes as the piano player played the first notes of "I'll Fly Away" to begin the service. I took a seat in the rear pew. Pastor Graves and his wife were not in the room. We sang "Farther Along" and "Will the Circle Be Unbroken" as I watched for Nelda to come in the back door. Then, as Mrs. Dottie Randall screeched out a solo that made me pray that the Lord would call her on home and put us all out of our misery, Nelda came in wearing a flowing yellow dress that complimented her hair and deepened the blue of her eyes.

She stood at the back of the room for a minute as she scanned the small crowd. Our eyes met, and she looked away as she strode quickly toward the front of the church. As she passed the pew I was sitting in, she tossed a piece of paper in my lap and continued walking. She took a seat in the very first pew, right in front of the pulpit.

I wondered what was going on as I unfolded the missile that she had flung at me. It took a while to open because it was a full sheet of lined notebook paper that had been repeatedly folded to the size of a matchbook. I saw the looping letters and the little circles dotting the i's that only a female would use. My heart shriveled up like an over-ripe tomato as I read:

Dear Lonnie,

I'm so sorry that I couldn't tell you before you came to church, but my father knows I sneaked out last night. He said the Lord told him, but it was my little sister Libby because she woke up when I came back in the window. He made me tell him that it was you I was with. I am so sorry, please, please, please, please, please forgive me.

Nelda

I couldn't believe what I was reading. This was the worst possible thing in the world that could have happened. And I had been so wrapped up in Nelda that I hadn't even noticed she had a bratty little sister. I looked up and saw that Pastor Graves was at the pulpit staring straight at me.

"Today, I want to speak for a few minutes on raising our children up in the nurture and admonition of the Lord," he began, his eyes boring into my neck. "It's a message that the Lord laid on my heart just this very morning. I had prepared a totally different message, but when the Lord speaks to me, I try to listen. Folks, the Bible says if you spare the rod, you hate—not spoil as a lotta people say—the Bible says you *hate* your child."

I looked at the back of Nelda's head as she sat close enough to her father to be sprayed with his spittle as he warmed to his topic.

"When the children that you love," he continued as he preached directly at me, "and care for, and sacrifice for, and do without so they won't have to, when that beloved child thumbs her nose at you and the teachings of the Lord, it just breaks your heart. *Don't it?* And what are you supposed to do about it? Well, brothers and sisters, we have to apply the loving rod of God!"

I was overcome with compassion for Nelda's plight. She wouldn't be able to leave the house until she was twenty-one. Reverend Graves continued to rant and rave while I squirmed in my seat, wanting desperately to flee but afraid that he would call me down in front of the whole congregation. Finally, it mercifully ended with the altar call. Nelda sat like a mannequin in her seat, and it was obvious that she wasn't going anywhere. Probably on orders from her father.

As I made my way out, I overheard people saying that that was the best sermon Brother Graves had ever preached. "One little boy even went forward for salvation," they said approvingly. But I knew there was no salvation for my relationship with Nelda. Like the arrowhead at Spates' Creek, she was lost to me. I was sure that things just couldn't get any worse. I was wrong.

I made my way through the parked cars over to my bike, mourning the loss of my love, when I heard a voice behind me.

"Well now, if it ain't Lonnie Tobin."

I turned around and saw three boys standing with their hands on their hips. I didn't know two of them, but the one in the middle was Mike

Kilgore, Buddy's fifteen-year-old brother.

"Hey, Mike," I said.

"Fellas, let me introduce you to the guy that got a lucky hit off Buddy, and now he thinks his shit don't stink," he said with a smug smile. "Ain't that right, Tobin?"

"I don't know what you're talking about."

"Sure, you do. My brother said he took it easy on you."

"Whatever you say, Mike."

"Then, you somehow pull some luck out of your ass and hit the ball and go struttin' around like you really done something. There's no way you could hit Buddy if he really used his heat."

"Whatever you say, Mike."

"Is that all you can say, dickhead?"

He was at least an inch taller and twenty pounds heavier than me, so I thought it wise to let it slide. I was reaching for my bike when he said, "What's the matter, Tobin? You gonna run away?"

"I don't want any trouble with you, Mike."

He laughed sarcastically. "No, you sure as hell don't want any trouble with me, Tobin. 'Cause I will kick your ass so hard you'll be crappin' out the top of your head. And another thing, you stay away from Nelda. I'm gonna ask her out myself. You hear me, you stupid bastard? I saw how you was droolin' all over her at the game. She's mine, you little turd."

"Fuck you," I said and started to leave.

Then, he hit me. Because I was in the act of turning, it was more of a glancing blow on my left temple but still hard enough to make me see sparkly little stars dance and bring a coppery taste to my mouth. I reflexively spun and smashed him in the face as hard as I could and felt his nose collapse under my fist. He stumbled back a few steps before falling hard on his butt on the pavement of the parking lot.

"My nose is broken!" he screamed, trying to stem the flow of blood as it ran through his fingers and down his arms. "And my ass hurts!" he cried out as he rolled over in agony.

People on the way to their cars had stopped to look at us. I saw Doc

Parker staring at me, and I felt a wave of shame. Mike continued rolling on the ground and was now weeping like a child.

"You son of a bitch!" one of the other boys yelled at me as Sawbuck growled at him.

"You want some too!" I yelled back, the fight or flight mechanism inside me running at full steam. He must have seen something in my face because he backed off. I got on my bike and rode off with Mike's pitiful cries of pain in my ears.

What in the hell had just happened? One minute I've got the world by the tail and the next, it turns around and bites the living shit out of me. My head was hurting, and I felt sick to my stomach. And I still had to face my mother. I *had* to tell her what happened because the way news traveled in this little burg she might have already heard about it. But I definitely decided that there was no need to share my adventure with Nelda. I looked at the front of my shirt and saw a smattering of Mike Kilgore's blood. When I got home, I told my mother and Grandma Birdie about the fracas.

"Are you hurt, Lonnie?" my mother asked with a worried look.

"I'm okay, mama. My head and hand hurts a little, that's all."

"Lord have mercy on us all. I can't believe this, Lonnie. Fightin' at church of all places."

"I told you, he hit me first, mama. I tried to walk away. What was I supposed to do, just let him beat on me?"

"I know that Mike Kilgore," Grandma Birdie said. "He's a bully. Always pickin' fights from what I hear. And he's older'n Lonnie. Bigger too."

"Why would he hit you? Did you do anything to him?"

"He was upset about me getting a hit off Buddy, and he told me to stay away from Nelda."

"Nelda? Fightin' over girls at your age. I declare. How's the Kilgore boy? Is he all right? You've got blood on your shirt."

"His nose was busted and bleeding pretty bad."

"Lord, Lord, Lord. Well, I'll call Mrs. Kilgore after while and make sure he's all right. Lonnie, I just don't know what to make of this."

"You can make whatever you want out of it; I didn't do anything wrong." As soon as I said that, a gust of guilt blew through my heart as I remembered my tryst with Nelda.

"I believe you, Lonnie. I know you wouldn't lie to me. I'm just upset. I don't like the idea of you fightin'."

"I'm not planning to make a habit of it, mama."

"Well, change out of your clothes and eat some lunch. I don't know if I'll ever get them blood spots out."

"I'm not hungry. I think I'll go lay down for a few minutes."

I washed my face, changed shirts, and fell across the bed. My body was completely drained of energy. I lay there with my knuckles throbbing and thought of how gorgeous Nelda had looked in that yellow dress until I fell asleep.

I was awakened sometime later by a knock on the door. I listened as grandma answered it.

"Hello, Miss Birdie," a male voice said. "Remember me? I'm George Kilgore."

George Kilgore? I wondered if he was related to the boy whose nose I had just altered.

"Yes, George, I remember you."

"How are you, Birdie?" a different but familiar male voice said.

"I'm fine, Brother Graves. How is your family?"

"They're doin' well, thank you."

Kilgore *and* Pastor Graves? I knew the dung storm had started.

"I was wonderin' if Ruby Jo was here," Mr. Kilgore said. "I need to speak with her about her son, Lonnie."

My mother must have been listening because she stepped out on the porch.

"Hello, Mr. Kilgore. Brother Graves. You wanted to see me about Lonnie?"

"I'm sorry to have to bother you, Ruby Jo," George Kilgore said, "but I'm sure Lonnie probably didn't tell you what happened at church this mornin', so I …"

"Yes, Lonnie told me what happened," she interrupted. "My son don't keep things from me."

"Well, he hit my boy unprovoked and broke his nose. And he's got a cracked tailbone to boot."

"Lonnie said that your boy hit him first."

"Of course, he would say that. But I've got two witnesses that say Lonnie hit Mike first without warnin'."

"I'll be right back," she said.

She came into the bedroom. "Lonnie, get up and come out to the porch please."

I laced up my shoes and went out to face my accusers. Gorillas on pogo sticks jumped up and down on my nerves. Both Mr. Kilgore and Reverend Graves looked at me as if I was something disagreeable that they had just stepped in. I saw Mike sitting in the passenger seat of his father's car with his nose bandaged and eyes swollen to purple slits. He was still in his blood-soaked shirt. Then, my heart leaped into my windpipe when I saw Nelda sitting in her father's car. She was still wearing the butter-colored dress and staring at the floorboard.

"Lonnie, Mr. Kilgore claims he has witnesses that says you hit his boy first. What about it?" my mother asked.

I looked at each one of them then glanced out at Mike and Nelda.

"I told you, mama, he hit me first. But I guess it's my word against theirs."

"I believe you, Lonnie," she said with finality. She turned to the two men. "My son says that Mike hit him first. He don't lie to me."

"Well, fightin' in the church parkin' lot is bad enough," Reverend Graves said, "but your son also enticed my daughter to sneak out of the house after we were asleep last night. Did he tell you about that?"

"What? What are you talkin' about?"

"Forgive me for being blunt, Ruby Jo," the pastor said, "but I'm afraid you're raising another Harley Tobin here. My daughter Nelda has been pretty sheltered all her life and … well, Lonnie's been raised different. He knows the ways of the world, and, well, she said he lured her out of the house in the middle of the night to do Lord knows what. She even had the smell of smoke on her clothes, and she said it was Lonnie that gave her the cigarettes."

"Is that true, Lonnie?"

I felt like I had been stabbed. I looked over at her, but she still had her head down, her shiny hair hiding her face. She must have been scared out of her mind, afraid of the consequences of telling him the truth. I could identify with that feeling.

"Yes, ma'am."

"Well, Lonnie, what in the world were you thinkin'? You know better than to do somethin' like that. What's got into you?" I saw the look of hurt in her eyes and felt like crying.

"I'm sorry."

"I'm afraid sorry ain't enough," Mr. Kilgore said with disdain. "I'm filing charges of assault against your boy, Ruby Jo. I'll be seekin' to get the doctor bills paid and for pain and sufferin'."

"You do what you have to do, Mr. Kilgore. You can't get blood from a turnip," she said.

"And I must ask you to keep your boy away from my daughter," Pastor Graves said.

"I'm afraid he's just too much of a bad influence on her. In fact, he ain't welcome at the church anymore."

"That's fine. I don't imagine he would want to go back after this."

"The boy is not bein' honest with you, Ruby Jo. You might look into some of the good military schools for him. He obviously needs discipline and a strong, moral, male influence in his life."

"I think that's none of your business, Pastor. And Lonnie don't lie to me," she snapped.

Suddenly, Nelda's voice rang out.

"Stop it! Just stop it!" she yelled as she got out of the car and walked a few steps toward the porch. "Lonnie didn't do anything. I saw Mike Kilgore hit him first. Lonnie was trying to get away from him, and Mike punched him when he wasn't looking. Lonnie just reacted."

You could hear a pin drop on the porch.

"And another thing, daddy, I lied. I asked Lonnie to come with me last night. I asked him, not the other way around. And I asked him to get the cigarettes. It was me. I'm the one to blame, not Lonnie!"

With that, she broke into sobs, turned, got back in the car, slammed the door, buried her face in her hands, and wept uncontrollably. God, I loved that woman.

We all stood speechless. Then, Mr. Kilgore and Pastor Graves mumbled something that sounded like, "Sorry," got back in their cars, and drove away. I saw Nelda lift a hand in a weak wave just before they went out of sight.

"I'm sorry, mama," I said after a few minutes of silence.

"It's my fault for lettin' you run loose without keepin' a better eye on you," she said with a note of despair. "Brother Graves was right, you need a father in your life."

"That has nothing to do with this situation. I might need a father, but I don't have one."

"Your father can be a good man when he ain't drinkin'."

"Yeah, he's all right when he's asleep."

"I wouldn't be a smartass right now if I was you, Lonnie."

"I'm sorry. I just don't think that forcing me back into the hell we just escaped from is in my best interests. I promise you that nothing like this will ever happen again."

"Well, we'll talk about this later. You need to come eat something before you get sick."

She went back inside. I couldn't decide which I felt worse about, punching out Mike Kilgore, or getting caught with my hand in Nelda's cookie jar. I came to the conclusion that upsetting my mother was the biggest sin of all.

It rained off and on for the next three days, trapping me inside with nothing to do. I went to Fordyce with my mother and grandma one day to buy groceries. They bought me a pair of jeans and a couple of shirts at a cut-rate clothing store, and we ate corn dogs at the Red Bug Drive-

In. Grandma Birdie got me a card at the little library, and I checked out biographies of Robert E. Lee and Davy Crockett so I would have something to read for the duration of the monsoon.

But finally, the sun returned and began drying up the puddles that had accumulated in all the usual low spots. Its warm rays also acted as a balm on my sore spirit. Slowly, I began to regain a desire to live. I went out and batted wet rocks until I was exhausted. The next day, I went fishing in Spates' Creek after informing my mother of where I was going and caught nine big, fat bluegill bream. I cleaned them, and grandma fried them up with potatoes and fresh baked bread. I slept free of Papa dreams and felt refreshed and somewhat restored.

Chapter Fourteen

Sherlockier by the Day

I woke up on Friday morning to the sound of Gideon's low laughter coming from the front porch. I hadn't really given much thought to him, or the Booger, or grandpa's killer in the last few days. In fact, the weird, prophetic messages from Gideon seemed like a dream to me. Like it never happened. But at the same time it troubled me, like there was unfinished business that needed tending to.

I yawned and stretched and pondered the eternal questions of mankind that Nelda and I had touched on. Are our steps really predestined and our days numbered, or do things happen by chance? Are things meant to be or just a random series of events that have no purpose? For example, a ragged peasant in some pathetic, little, humid country is dancing in a dirt road in celebration of a military coup and is killed when the top of his head is punctured by a spent bullet that had been fired into the air in jubilation. Is that just a case of being in the wrong place at the wrong time, or was it *supposed* to happen? Is God involved in the daily minutiae of man, or does he just kick back in his golden recliner and watch us like a soap opera?

All questions better pondered on a full stomach, I thought, entering the kitchen. I was halfway through a platter of both buttermilk and blueberry pancakes when grandma said something that chilled my coffee.

"The Booger came back last night. I got a call from Deanna Laws this mornin'. She talked to Wallace, and he told her about it."

My itinerary for the day was established. It was time I checked out the scene of the crime.

"I'm beginnin' to think that the Booger ain't human," my mother said. "I just can't believe that anybody would do such a crazy thing for so many years."

"Like a poltergeist?" I asked.

"A what?"

"A poltergeist. A ghost or spirit that manifests its presence by making noises or knocking on walls."

"Well, there's somethin' mighty strange going on. I don't know if it's a poltergeist or a poltergoose, but I would move out of that house so fast it would make that Booger's head spin."

She got up and refilled her cup.

"Your father called again, Lonnie."

"And?"

"He says he hasn't had a drink since the last time I talked to him."

"And you believe him?"

"He sounds good, Lonnie. Like he's clear-headed. I think he's telling me the truth."

"Well, I would advise you to avoid the guy that's selling swampland."

"Have you thought anymore about what we talked about?"

"About going back to Louisiana with dad? Yeah, I thought about it. But the debilitating headache that it brought on forced me to stop."

"He said he's gonna come up in a couple of weeks. I'm gonna talk to him, and I want you to, too. That is, if you love me."

"That's not fair, mama. Just because I don't want to talk to him doesn't mean I don't love you."

"Well, you've got two weeks to think about it. I just want to do the right thing for you, son."

"I know."

After breakfast, I fed Sawbuck. He was grateful, though pancakes weren't his favorite. I went and sat on the porch with Gideon to see if he had any insight on the most recent Booger attack. I waited about fifteen minutes then jumped on my bike with my magnifying glass in my back pocket. I wondered if Gideon would ever say anything again.

Wallace's store was my first stop; I had to make sure both he and Velma were there. I wanted to have complete freedom to snoop around their house and look for clues. Seeing them through the window, I knew I would have the place to myself until Velma went home to make lunch. I aired up my tires from Tater Davis and gave him a mind-boggling multiplication problem, which pleased him greatly.

Riding across the railroad tracks, I wondered if Scrub Purifoy was back in town. I pedaled past Myrtle Dawson's house and Charlie Banks' pig farm, where the odor nearly knocked me into the ditch. About a mile down the tree-shaded gravel road, I came to the little driveway that led to the Summers' house. The drive twisted to the left through the woods for about a hundred yards and led to a clearing where the little clapboard house sat.

It was evident that it had never seen a drop of paint. The sagging front porch gave the impression that it had been hastily built about a hundred years ago. Tall, slender sweet gum trees surrounding the house had littered the ground with their spiked seed-balls. The window shades were drawn, and a palpable feeling of sadness lay heavily over the place.

I tried to picture whatever or whoever it was that stood beside the house and pounded on the walls. My eye ran along the uneven boards looking for any sign of an indention or mark. But the wood was so warped and full of knotholes that the Booger could have pounded on it with a ball-peen hammer and you wouldn't be able to tell he had been there.

I wondered which direction he came from. The clearing was about a half-acre in size, and the surrounding tree line was thick with dense undergrowth. I walked slowly around the house while carefully examining the ground, still soft from the recent rain, for any sign of a footprint. After two circuits, I found myself at the back door without any discovery.

I was staring at the doorknob thinking about the hand that rattled and twisted it in the night when I noticed that Sawbuck was sniffing the ground like he was on the trail of something. I began to encourage him with, "Good boy; follow the scent boy," and he headed toward the woods directly behind the outhouse. Following him, I pondered why nobody ever thought of using a bloodhound to track the miscreant down.

Sawbuck didn't slow down when he reached the woods and disappeared into the trees. When I approached the spot where he entered the brush, I thought I could make out a faint path leading deeper into the forest. Sawbuck was ahead of me, yelping as I followed him into the unknown, ducking under limbs and pushing through knee-high weeds. The farther I went the more that it appeared to be a trail or path of some kind, though you would really have to be looking for it to make it out. I went on for what seemed like several hundred yards, keeping in mind the direction I had come from.

I came out at a tree-lined creek that twisted off in both directions. Sawbuck was lapping water as he walked down the stream to the left. I had no idea which creek this was. There were dozens of them in the vast forest, branching off like veins in a circulatory system that brought life to the plants and trees. It looked smaller than Spates' Creek, at least the section I knew.

Sawbuck was sniffing the ground as he trotted alongside the creek. I walked behind him searching for anything suspicious. Then, up ahead, I saw him stop and smell what looked like a wad of paper. As I neared it, I saw that it was a white cloth of some kind. Picking it up by the corner, I discovered that it was a well-used handkerchief. It was stuck together by what appeared to be a large amount of mucus. My stomach turned as I dropped the rag. To me, gathering snot in a rag and saving it was no different than wiping yourself and sticking the toilet paper in your pocket to be used again later. But, I thought, this handkerchief could very well belong to the Booger, seeing as it was full of them.

Then, I saw a footprint. I ran over and squatted to get a better look. It wasn't complete, but one side of the sole and the entire heel was clearly visible in the mud. Pulling out my magnifying glass, I studied it. It was a rather large shoe print. At least a size fourteen, I determined as I compared it to my own size tens. But there were no distinguishing patterns or designs that could identify the manufacturer. Damn cheap common footwear.

I stood up and walked a little farther down the creek, where another print caught my eye. A whole one. I began to get excited as I discovered that the same shoe had made both impressions! Could these be Booger tracks? I knew that hunters roamed these woods chasing after squirrels and rabbits and 'coons. These tracks could have been made by any one of them, but I liked the thought that it might be *him*. I continued down the creek for about a quarter of a mile and found several more prints from the same shoe, some trash, and a molded pile of potato sacks.

I felt uncomfortable going any farther in these unfamiliar wilds and decided to turn back. Once I found out which creek this was and where it went, I could come back and continue the search. Calling Sawbuck, we made our way back to my bike. I rode back to town and decided to stop and visit with Aunt Kate to see what I could find out about Uncle Willie's whereabouts last night. I hadn't forgotten what Doc Parker had said about people's suspicions that Willie was the Booger.

I walked into the store and found Aunt Kate lying on the bar with a Sears-Roebuck catalogue under her head as a pillow. She stirred and sat up as I stepped to the bar.

"Hello there, Lonnie. How are you?"

"I'm fine, Aunt Kate. Sorry to disturb your nap."

"Oh, I wasn't sleepin', just restin' my eyes. This old bar ain't very soft. Can I get you somethin'?"

"Yeah, a root beer, please." Nelda's favorite.

"I heard about your fight with Mike Kilgore," she said as she placed the mug in front of me. "Did he hurt you?"

"Not really. My hand was sore for a little while, but I'm okay."

"Well, I should be ashamed, but I was kinda tickled when I found out you broke his nose. He got what he deserved. He's always pickin' on and tormentin' other boys. He just picked on the wrong one this time. And I heard about you and Nelda, too. I think ol' man Graves is too hard on that girl. One day she's gonna just bust loose."

I felt a rush of aggravation that my entire life's story had been broadcast all over town, but it was too late to worry about that. I tried to come up with a way to broach the subject of the Booger.

"Do you know if Scrub Purifoy is in town?"

"Not that I know of. And I better not hear of you ever talkin' to him again. Why are you wantin' to know?"

"No reason, really. What size shoes does Uncle Willie wear?" There was no doubt about it, I needed to work on my interrogating skills.

"Well, Lord, what a question. He wears a size thirteen, I think. Why would you want to know that? You plannin' on buyin' him a pair?"

A thirteen could have made the footprints I saw. I looked at Aunt Kate's face as she waited for a reply, and I decided that honesty was the best approach.

"I'll just tell you right up front Aunt Kate, someone told me that they thought Uncle Willie might be the Booger."

"Yeah, a lot of folks have said that over the years."

"Oh, you know about it?"

"There ain't many secrets in this town."

"Well … Is he?"

She paused and stared out the window. I could hear a fly buzzing around somewhere in the back.

"I don't know," she finally said.

"What do you mean you don't know? You live with him."

"Willie and me have been sleepin' in separate rooms for a lotta years. I don't know what he does after I go to bed."

"Has he ever given you any reason to suspect him?"

Again there was a long silence as she stared out the window, her eyes squinted as if straining to catch a glimpse of someone coming up the road to take her out of this dump.

"Yes, just last night in fact. I got up to go the bathroom and noticed that his truck was gone. It was 3:30 in the mornin'. Then, today I hear the Booger come back."

"Has this happened before?"

"Yes, many times."

"Did you ever confront him about it?"

She leaned over the bar and lowered her voice. "Lonnie, I'm gonna tell you somethin' that a lot of folks already know, but I ask that you not repeat it. Your Uncle Willie has several moonshine stills in the woods around here, had 'em since before I knew him, and when I ask him where he goes at night, he tells me he's tendin' his stills. I used to think it was another woman, but I began to take notice of all the times he was gone when the Booger showed up."

"Does he have something against Wallace and Velma?"

"Him and Wallace has hated each other's guts for years. They even come to blows one day. Willie accused him of tellin' the sheriff about one of his stills and beat him up pretty bad. Wallace denied it. But they haven't spoken in forty years."

"So, this happened before the first time the Booger showed up?"

"One week before, to the day."

I couldn't believe my ears. Aunt Kate seemed to genuinely think that her husband could be the one that had been tormenting Wallace and Velma all this time. Still, I could imagine him sneaking around to see a woman a lot easier than banging on a guy's house that he doesn't like. Willie just seemed too laid back.

"'Course, some folks say it's Charlie Banks," she said.

"Really? Why do they say that?"

"'Cause Wallace bought that land he's livin' on from Charlie's father, and Charlie thought that Wallace cheated ol' man Banks on the deal. Believed he took advantage of the fact that he was sick and couldn't work and needed the money. Some say that Charlie is makin' sure that Wallace don't enjoy his ill-gotten gain. There's been bad blood between 'em all these years."

"But, did the land transaction take place before the appearance of the Booger?"

"I'm sure it did. Seems like it was a hundred years ago."

"But the land couldn't have been worth *that* much."

"It ain't about the money, Lonnie. To Charlie, it was a wrong done against his daddy. That kinda thing is hard to forgive."

I should have come to Aunt Kate earlier. For the first time, I felt like I was getting somewhere.

"Anybody else?" I asked.

"I don't know of anybody else that would have a reason."

"It seems like you've thought about this a lot, Aunt Kate."

"There ain't much else to do, just sittin' here on my butt all day. I've heard the bangin' in the middle of the night, and I know for certain that somebody's doin' it."

"But do you *really* think that Uncle Willie would do something like that for forty years?"

"Lord, I don't know. You think you know a person, but can you ever be sure? Him and me don't talk much. Haven't in a long time."

I thought I saw a tear sparkle as she turned her face back to the window. I didn't want to upset her, so I dropped the subject. "Do you know which creek that is that runs behind Wallace and Velma's house, Aunt Kate?"

"That's Whitewater Creek. Why do you ask? You ain't been back there, have you?"

"Yeah, once."

"You don't need to be back there, Lonnie. It ain't safe. There's bobcats and panthers in them woods. Not to mention snakes. Promise me you won't go back."

"I'm careful, Aunt Kate. And I've got my dog to protect me."

"You better be careful. If somethin' was to happen to you, it would kill us all."

I finished my root beer, bought a Clark Bar to go, and headed down the Fordyce road for Whitewater Creek. It was quite a distance, more than two miles past Spates' Creek, so I ate the candy to keep up my strength and because I really liked Clark Bars. When I got there, I laid my bike down and walked out onto the plank bridge that stretched over one hundred yards from end to end. Only one vehicle could cross it at a time. There were no protective railings to keep a car, or motorcycle, from plunging six stories to the rocks below. Probably a cost-cutting decision by some county bureaucrat. It was here that Aunt Kate's son, Norman, was found with his neck broken after that drunken night. I had the feeling of walking on a tightrope. Even Sawbuck acted jittery as we walked along looking over the side.

I knew that the creek wound around behind Wallace and Velma's to the right, but I had no idea where it went to the left. I needed to find out if there was any kind of a topographical map of this area available. Although that would only show where the creek went and wouldn't reveal the identity of the Booger, I felt it might be helpful in some way. Where I could find a topographical map was another question.

I went back to grandma's for lunch then spent the rest of the day batting rocks and trying to get into the mind of the Booger. Why would he feel compelled to keep up this insanity for all these years? Just because of a grudge against someone he thought ratted him out forty years ago? Or because he gypped your old man out of a few bucks? That didn't sit right with me. I felt like it had to be much deeper than that. I knew if I could come up with the *real* reason, a motive, it would lead to the guilty party. I was feeling Sherlockier by the day.

Chapter Fifteen

The Vanishing Man

Time flew by like a Whitey Ford fastball. My father was scheduled to show up in a few days, and I was dreading his arrival. His incessant phone calls and promises of a rose garden gradually eroded my mother's resistance. I feared she would completely cave in and drag me back into the eye of the storm.

"Are you gonna talk to your father when he gets here?" she asked as we ate breakfast.

"I guess," I said with a sigh. "It won't hurt to talk. But I'm not buying his baloney."

"Thank you, Lonnie. I really appreciate this. I think you're gonna be surprised when you talk to him."

"Why? Has he learned to speak French?"

"Spanish actually, funny-boy. Look, I know he hasn't shown it, but your father loves you."

"Yeah, sure, and Sawbuck invented a time machine."

"Okay, be a smartass. Just as long as you talk to him."

I went out the back door and fed Sawbuck. Too bad the mutt didn't really have a time machine. But he would probably just waste it by continually returning to his last meal.

I sat on the front porch and relaced my sneakers while Sawbuck dined. Gideon was in his place, present and accounted for. He was rarely absent. He hadn't said a word since he predicted that the rules would change when I got the chance to play with the Skinners. I had gotten to the point that I didn't expect him to say anything. Then, he spoke.

"Rabbits are good eatin', but they're hard to catch."

I couldn't help jumping just a tad at the unexpected sound of his voice. I sat there a moment and let his words sink in. *Rabbits are good eatin'*, he said. Was he putting in his order for supper? *But they're hard to catch*, he had added. Maybe he wanted me to build a rabbit trap. No, that was stupid. There was no telling what he meant.

I rode out to Miss Spicy's. I had grown very fond of her over the course of my visits. She regaled me with more family stories for a couple of hours, and then I rode back to town. As I came in sight of the store, I saw Willie walk around the back. Perfect, I'll follow him and check for footprints that I can compare to the ones I found at the creek.

I parked my bike and walked to the back. Willie was inside one of the little shacks. I walked up to the open door that was hanging by a single hinge and looked into the murky interior. It smelled of rotted wood and kerosene. I could see Willie leaning over in the back corner. He stood up and turned quickly when he heard me approach.

"Hey, Lonnie," he said as he hurriedly stepped out, closed the door, and snapped on a padlock as big as my head. He probably had some moonshine in there, but it was ludicrous to lock the splintered old door when anybody could walk right through it like it wasn't there.

"Hi, Uncle Willie," I said as I glanced at his shoes. They were pretty big.

"Whatcha up to today, Lonnie? Or should I call you 'The Kid?'" he laughed.

"I'm just going to the outhouse. I had too much coffee this morning."

"Well, don't fall in," he said as he turned to go into the store.

"Uncle Willie, can I ask you a question?"

"Sure. What is it?"

"You knew my grandfather, Tom Spates, didn't you?"

"Yes, I did. He was my brother-in-law. I was the best man at his weddin' when he married Birdie. Yeah, I knowed him real well."

"What kind of guy was he? Did you like him?"

"I liked Tom quite a bit. We hunted some together. Me and Kate used to go out to eat every once in a while with him and Birdie. I helped him build that house where Birdie's livin' now. But I cain't say we was *real* close. Tom kinda kept to himself."

"Did you notice a change in him after he came back from the war?"

"Yeah. Everybody did. He told me once that his best buddy was killed right beside him. Tom said he was holdin' him when he died. I reckon it's hard to be the same after somethin' like that. I remember one time, I saw Tom standin' at the railroad crossin' in a pourin' rain, just starin' down the rails. He musta stood there for an hour then walked over to the depot. I can still recall how sad he looked."

"Miss Spicy told me that there was a man that some people thought might have had something to do with his death. Do you know anything about that?" I asked.

"Oh, she's probably talkin' about ol' man Hannegan. Richard Hannegan. He had it in for Tom, that's for sure."

Richard Hannegan was the name that Big Mama had mentioned as the man that Papa had filled in for the night Tom Spates was killed. Yet, Miss Spicy said that the man she thought could have rigged the train, probably Hannegan, was seen the night of the explosion. Why was he there if he was off sick?

"Do you know why he had it in for Tom?" I asked.

He started to laugh, "Yeah, Tom rigged up some kinda trick to scare Richard one time, and it made him real mad."

"So, you think this guy Hannegan would kill a man over a little trick?"

"Well, the way I understand it, the trick scared Richard so much that he ... well, he pissed his pants. And Tom wouldn't let him live it down. Kept makin' fun of him, called him "leaky britches" after that. That didn't set well with Richard. But I really don't believe that he would'a gone so far as to kill him. But he's dead now, too, so I guess we'll never know for sure."

I asked Uncle Willie a few more questions about Hannegan, but he didn't know any more that might have been helpful. Willie went into the store, and I waited until he was out of sight to begin looking at the ground where he had been standing. Sure enough, I could see his footprint in the dirt near the door of the shed. I kneeled down and checked it out. I didn't have my magnifying glass, so I had to examine it with the naked eye. It looked very similar to the prints at the creek. The only way I could make a match would be to take casts of both sets and compare them. Then, I remembered that I was a fourteen-year-old boy in Moro, Arkansas, and where in the hell would I get the materials for making casts. Maybe at the same place that sells topographical maps.

The only thing I *could* do was to go back out to the creek and take another look at the prints there while Willie's prints were fresh in my mind. Not very scientific, but it was the best I could manage under the circumstances. I jumped on my bike and headed out for Wallace and Velma's place.

As I approached Charlie Banks' stink farm, I saw him at his mailbox by the side of the road. I slowed to a stop to check out his shoes.

"Hello, Mr. Banks."

"*Mister* Banks? That was my goddamn daddy's name, son. I'm just plain ol' Charlie. Just an ol' pig jockey who gits more goddamn bills in the mail than he can pay."

I was impressed that he could be a brilliant conversationalist without losing his affinity for the blasphemous. I also saw that he was wearing a mud-crusted pair of rubber boots. As Charlie sorted through envelopes and flyers, I thought that since he lived so close to the Summers' it would be very easy for him to slip through the woods and engage in acts of lunacy without being witnessed.

"Goddamn gover'ment takes money out of the goddamn paycheck afore we ever lay eyes on it. Then, ya gotta pay more goddamn taxes ever'time ya buy somethin'; it's just a goddamn shame."

I sat there on my bike wondering how in the name of profanity his family tolerated this man. How could they coexist with him on a daily basis? I had been in his presence less than thirty seconds, and I felt morally unclean. I wanted to ask him some questions about my grandfather but couldn't bear to listen to his goddamn answers. I said goodbye and rode away.

I had just reached the Summers' driveway when a large rabbit streaked across the road about thirty feet ahead of me. Sawbuck tore out after him like a Cheetah chasing down an antelope. The rabbit crashed into the brush on the left side of the road with Sawbuck hot on his little cottontail. So, here was Gideon's rabbit. I figured that Sawbuck would run it to ground pretty quick, and I pictured myself riding up at grandma's with the carcass slung over my handlebars. After I skinned it, grandma could smother it down and serve it to Gideon. But there wouldn't be enough for all seven of his spirits.

I could hear Sawbuck barking like a maniac, somewhere far out in the woods. Having never heard him carry on like that, I was worried. At the place where he and the rabbit had entered the treeline, I laid my bike on the side of the road and went in after him. Thoughts of *Alice in Wonderland* coursed through my head.

I ran toward the barking, dodging trees and skirting briar thickets. Occasionally, I paused to get a fix on what now sounded like howls from Sawbuck. I felt helpless to offer assistance to him as I ran blindly, zigzagging through the trees in what I thought was the direction the sounds were coming from. After about ten minutes, I stopped, out of breath, and heard only silence. I started calling Sawbuck at the top of my lungs then listening for any sound of him. I heard only the breeze in the branches overhead, and the warbles and twitters of the natural aviary around about were the only reply. *What a lonesome sound happily chirping birds can make!*

I was considering my next move when a sudden chest-crushing rush of panic hit me like a tidal wave and almost knocked me on my ass. *Where in the hell was I*? I had no earthly idea *which* direction I had come from, or how *far* I had come. My throat slammed shut, and I struggled to breathe. An almost hallucinatory panic seized me. It seemed like the thick, heavy forest was slowly closing in on me, inch by inch, menacing and malignant.

Any minute the branches and vines would reach out and encircle me and absorb my body, sneakers and all, leaving no trace of my having ever been there.

If you've never been totally lost in the middle of a primeval forest, there is no way to describe the absolute terror that attacks your senses. Complete hopelessness consumes your very soul, and the worst part is the inability to form a coherent thought. I sat on a stump and tried to regain my bearings, only to find that I didn't have a single bearing left. I had obviously blown them out somewhere back down the trail. If I hadn't been fourteen years old, I would've cried like a fat baby denied his bottle.

Why in the living hell didn't Gideon warn me about this? Instead of talking about how tasty a damn rabbit was, he should have said, "Stay the hell away from the *damn* rabbit, or you'll get your stupid ass lost!" And on top of that, something was wrong with Sawbuck. He had never failed to come when I called him. Horrible images of him being ripped apart by a panther and a bobcat wearing women's drawers working together as a tag-team invaded my disconnected thoughts. But there was nothing I could do for him now, so I forced myself to focus on finding my way out of this lush hell. I decided to walk a straight line in one direction, hoping that I would eventually hit a creek or road somewhere.

I walked. And prayed. And walked. I repented of every sin I could remember and for all the sins I would probably commit in the future if God would only let me live. Gnats by the teeming billions swarmed my sweaty face as I trudged through weeds, sticker bushes, and briar-laden vines that ripped and clawed at my jeans as if trying to drag me back to their lair. I stopped often to call for Sawbuck but saw and heard nothing.

On and on I went, while the sun made its way across the sky. Everything seemed to blur together. One tree looked exactly like the next. I had the feeling that no matter how hard I tried to stay on a straight course, I was ending up where I started. Thoughts of how Hollis Dunn's body laid out here and decomposed barraged my brain. Ravenous and nearly dehydrated, I had been stumbling around in this wilderness for hours and still hadn't come upon anything that even slightly resembled civilization.

Paranoia began playing "Taps" in my ear. I wondered how my mother would take it when Sawbuck showed up with a sneaker containing my blackened foot.

Just as I was about to abandon all hope and curl into a fetal position among the toadstools, I smelled the creek. My pace quickened as I sensed the water ahead. Through an exceptionally rough patch of downed trees and underbrush, I emerged at a bend in a meandering stream.

My knees nearly buckled with pure, precious, delicious, homogenized relief. I still didn't know where the hell I was, but at least I had found a landmark. Looking up and down the creek, I tried to determine which way to proceed. I was so turned around I didn't know where to go to find my ass. I got down on my hands and knees by the water. I'd never drunk from a stream before, but I had seen many a movie cowboy dip up a hat-full. Palming a few scoops, I gratefully sucked it up.

I closed my eyes, splashed my face repeatedly, and tried to calm down by taking deep breaths and repeating, "Let not your heart be troubled," over and over. When I opened them, I was startled to see a man on the other side of the creek. I jumped to my feet. He blended with the surroundings, and I hadn't noticed him. He was sitting on the ground with his back against a Cyprus tree. His chin was on his chest, and he appeared to be sound asleep. He was wearing what looked like a brand new khaki shirt and pants, heavily starched and well pressed, and a pair of lace-up work boots. He had a full head of dark brown hair, but I couldn't see his face. There was a cane pole on the ground beside him with a rock weighting down one end, while the other end rested in the notch of a forked stick in the ground, with a fishing line tied to the tip. The cork was slowly twisting in the gentle current at the end of the line.

It's amazing how transcendently beautiful the sight of another human being can be. I felt like the nightmare was over. I knew this guy could direct me out, but I didn't know if I should wait until he woke up naturally, or if I should assist him. I coughed loudly a couple of times, but he didn't stir. My desire to get home overcame the hesitancy to disturb his slumber.

"Excuse me, sir!" I yelled across the creek. "Sir! Excuse me!"

He woke up with a jerk and almost knocked the pole into the water. He looked to be about thirty. I had never seen him before.

"I'm sorry to wake you, sir, but I'm kind of lost, and I was wondering if you could tell me which way to go to get back to town?"

"Lost? You shouldn't be out in woods you're not familiar with young man. It's very dangerous. I've known good, well-experienced men who got so mixed up out in these ol' woods, they got lost and was never heard from agin'."

Well, thanks a lot, Mr. Safety Ranger, but I didn't need dire warnings. I needed to know the damn way out of here.

"What are you doin' out here anyways?" he asked. I didn't like his nosy manner, but his concern seemed heartfelt.

"I was just following my dog. He was chasing a rabbit and … I got lost. Can you tell me which way I go to get back to a road or something?"

"Well, this here is Whitewater Creek. And back to your right," he said as he pointed, "it winds through the woods and on into the swampy bottoms. If you go in that direction," he lifted his other arm, "right around that bend up there, you'll come to the Whitewater Bridge. But you're a long way from town to be afoot."

"That's okay, I'm so glad to be out of there I could skip all the way to town."

"Do you live around here, son?"

"I'm staying with my grandmother, Birdie Woods."

"Birdie? Yes, I know Miss Birdie well."

"Thank you very much for your help, sir. I need to get back home."

"You be careful."

As soon as I turned to head for the bridge, I saw footprints in the soggy ground. They were clear and distinct and followed hard by the creek. They looked very similar to the prints behind the Summers' house. Of course, they could have been made by anyone who came here to drop a hook in the water; it could have even been the guy I had just met. I realized I hadn't even asked his name.

I got to the bend in the creek and looked back. He was gone. *Where the hell did he go?* A herd of wildebeests went stampeding through my chest. He couldn't have left that quickly. He didn't have time to make it around the other bend in the creek. Was he hiding? Was he a pervert, slinking through the woods at this very moment seeking to ambush me? Was he an angel sent by God to rescue me from my own stupidity? Or had he just stepped behind a tree to relieve himself? I began to cover ground at full speed.

As the bridge came in sight, I was shocked at how high and unsafe it appeared from below. The footprints ended at the rock and boulder strewn shallows of the creek. Badly winded, I looked for a way up the steep embankment to the road, but there was no place to climb on this side. As I walked under the bridge to check the other side, I couldn't help thinking about Norman Pierce's crushed body that had lain here for hours, his blood smeared on the rocks, until a passing motorist happened to spot his mangled motorcycle. That thought and the vanishing man I had just encountered brought on a shudder that lasted a full five minutes.

Chapter Sixteen

How Could I Refuse Her?

A rough path had been gouged in the embankment on the other side of the bridge that offered a steep and strenuous but passable route to the top. Once my motor skills returned, I scrambled up, slipping and sliding and starting mini-rockslides as my feet fought to find purchase. Once back on the road, I saw the sun low in the west. Only a couple of hours of daylight left. I was soaking wet and layered with red dirt. It was four or five miles back to town and then another mile or so to where I left my bike. It wasn't that far as the crow flies, but unfortunately I didn't crap through feathers.

I began at a brisk pace and then jogged for a while. I had already missed lunch and knew my mother would be worried if I wasn't there in time for supper. After alternating between walking and jogging for about fifteen minutes, I heard a car coming behind me. I moved to the side of the road as a familiar blue Buick rolled to a stop as the dust billowed over me. When it cleared, I looked through the passenger window and saw the smiling face of Reverend Homer Graves. He leaned over the seat and opened the door.

"Hello, Lonnie."

"Hello, Pastor Graves."

"What are you doin' so far out of town?"

"Uh, just doing a little jogging."

"Well, that's good exercise. Do you want to jog back to town, or would you like a lift?"

"No, no. I've had enough. I appreciate the ride," I said, getting in. "I'm kinda dirty; I hope I don't mess up your car."

"Oh, don't worry none about that. It can't get much dirtier than it already is."

We rode for a few minutes in a clumsy silence. I hadn't really noticed how big he was, over six feet and at least two hundred pounds. He was average looking, and it was obvious that Nelda hadn't got her looks from him. The only thing they had in common was their blue eyes. I wanted to quiz him on "entertaining angels unawares" as mentioned in the Bible; however, I was concerned that he would ask why I wanted to know, and I didn't want to discuss the man at the creek.

"I'm sure glad I run into you, Lonnie. You've been on my heart since … since the other day. In fact, I feel like the Lord put you in my path today. I've been wantin' to apologize to you for my actions, and the things I said. I reacted in anger."

He fell silent. We weren't moving much faster than I had been jogging.

"That's all right," I said. "I understand."

"No, it ain't all right. I'm supposed to be a man of God, and I had already judged you and condemned you to hell. I thought you was a bad influence on my little girl, and the truth was she was a bad influence on you."

"No, she wasn't. Nelda is a sweet, decent girl, Pastor Graves. It was all innocent. You should be proud of her."

"I am. She's a beautiful and intelligent girl. Any father would be proud. And I'm proud of the way you was willing to take all the blame for her actions. It takes a certain kind of boy … young man to do that."

"I didn't want her to get in trouble."

"Well, I love my daughter very much, and she's pretty much got me wrapped around her finger. Once she told me the *truth* and promised not to do it anymore, I forgave her. She thinks highly of you. So do some other people. I've had several folks come to me and tell me that despite your ... well ... that you were a good kid. They were all members of the church that I have a great deal of respect for."

"I really appreciate them doing that," I said, not knowing what else to say.

"Nelda would be thrilled if you sat with her in church this Sunday. That is unless you don't feel like you want to come back to the church. I wouldn't much blame you if you didn't, after the way you was mistreated."

Was he kidding? I would gladly wallow around in vats of mistreatment for a chance to be near Nelda again.

"Thank you for the invitation, sir. I would love to."

What a turn of events. I felt like I was being jerked around like a rag doll in the jaws of some cosmic puppy. Things go great one minute ... then everything turns to shit ... then it goes great again.

"Don't get me wrong," he said. "I don't think Nelda is old enough for serious dating, but I have nothin' against a friendship. As long as it's a *daytime* friendship."

"Yes, sir. Sorry about the other night. I give you my word that it won't ever happen again."

"Thank you. I'll hold you to that. And I hate to say it but getting popped in the nose was the best thing that ever happened to Mike Kilgore," he continued. "He was always kinda rowdy and mean. But since that day, he's changed. He's gentle and polite and respectful."

Glad I could be of help. I directed Pastor Graves to my abandoned bike.

"Sometimes the Lord truly does work in mysterious ways," he said as we arrived. "Is that your dog?"

Sure enough, there sat Sawbuck beside my bike, looking slightly retarded with his tongue flopped out of the side of his mouth. I thanked Reverend Graves for the ride, promised to see him in church, and got out. He turned the car around and headed back toward town.

"Well, where the hell have you been?" I asked Sawbuck. "A lot of good you are, leaving me stranded in the jungle. I may not feed your sorry ass for that."

He looked at me as if to say, "It wasn't my fault; I was weak with hunger." I checked him for cuts or scratches, but he seemed to be fine. We headed back to grandma's while I tried to remember every detail of the man I had met at the creek. Maybe I'd see him around town. I walked in the kitchen just as Grandma Birdie was putting supper on the table.

"Where in the world have you been, Lonnie? You're filthy," my mother said.

"I was just out *chasing rabbits* with Sawbuck," I said with emphasis, looking for any kind of reaction on Gideon's passive face. He just shoveled mashed potatoes into his mouth, hunched over his plate, smacking away. I felt like hitting him with a rabbit punch. "I lost track of the time. I'm sorry."

Though I didn't tell her about being lost in the woods, I did mention talking with Pastor Graves. I was so ecstatic about the reprieve he had given me I wanted to declare it from the rooftops.

"Well, that was nice of him," she said. "Now, I think that ol' man Kilgore ought to apologize, too. Him and Mike and his two *witnesses*."

"Pastor Graves invited me back to church. I might go."

"I'm sure that seein' Nelda won't have any effect on whether you decide to go or not. Will it?" she asked with a knowing smile.

"Well, I do need a little more incentive than Brother Graves' soul-stirring sermons."

"Just don't go slippin' off in the middle of the night."

"We'll never do that again. We'll slip off much earlier next time."

"Okay, smartass, go wash up. Grandma won't let you sit at her table in that condition."

After we finished eating, I fed Sawbuck though I didn't think he deserved it. Then, I went to the front porch. I wondered if Gideon had any idea what I had just gone through, and if he did, why he didn't give me some kind of warning. But then, maybe the mention of the rabbit *was* a warning that I just didn't pick up on. That's what was stewing inside my brain when the phone rang. I listened as grandma answered it.

"Hello … well, hello there, Nelda. How are you, dear? … Yes, he's here, hold on a minute."

I was moving when I heard her say, "Nelda." I took the phone from grandma as she winked at me and grinned.

"Hello."

"Hi, Lonnie." Her voice sounded even sexier on the phone. "What are you doing?"

"Nothing really."

"My father told me about picking you up on the road. He said he invited you to come back to church. Are you coming?"

"Sure. I would like to see you again."

"Oh, me too, Lonnie. I'm so sorry for what happened. I wouldn't hurt you for the world."

"It's okay, Nelda. It's all water under the Spates' Creek Bridge."

"You're sweet. I'll save you a seat."

"You think your father will really be okay with that?"

"He wouldn't have said anything if he didn't mean it."

"In that case, the gates of Hell couldn't restrain me."

We talked for an hour. Blissfully unaware of my surroundings, I floated along on delicate memories: the touch of her hand, the smell of her hair, and the sensual feel of her lips on mine. We made a date to go bike riding the next day before hanging up.

I took a hot bath, but even though exhausted from my wanderings in the wilderness, I had trouble falling asleep. The question of what happened to the stranger in the woods still haunted me. There had to be a logical explanation. That's what I was trying to convince myself of as I finally slipped off to "Nappy's House."

~

I rushed through breakfast the next morning.

"What are you and Nelda gonna do today?" my mother asked as I was preparing to leave.

"I don't know. Just ride bikes and stuff, I guess."

"Well, don't do anything you're not supposed to."

"Like what?"

"Like … you know … smoochy-smoochy."

I laughed out loud. I wouldn't have described what Nelda and I participated in that night in the moonlight as "smoochy-smoochy." But, however you defined it, I was hankering for a return engagement. I promised we would behave and headed over to Nelda's.

I rode up to the back of the modest parsonage just behind the church and timidly knocked on the door. Mrs. Graves answered and ushered me into the kitchen.

"Nelda will be out in a minute, Lonnie. Would you like some milk and cookies?"

"No, thank you, Mrs. Graves. I just had breakfast."

"It sure is a pretty morning."

"It sure is."

We didn't know how to top that and fell into an uncomfortable silence. Everybody called her Miss Debbie, and I watched as she fussed around wiping counters and putting dishes in the cabinet. She was a very attractive woman, sun-yellow hair, liquid blue eyes, a perfect mouth, and quite a figure. That's where Nelda got her looks from, I thought, only Nelda had improved on them. She was the "New, Improved Formula."

"How's your mother and Miss Birdie?" she asked.

"They're fine."

"Tell them that I invited them to our ladies' social on the first Tuesday of every month. We eat together and play games and have a lot of fun."

"I'll tell them."

At that moment, Nelda came in wearing a pair of denim jeans and a pale-blue men's button-down short-sleeve shirt. The untucked tail nearly reached her knees, and the sleeves hung to her elbows, giving her the look of a little girl in her daddy's shirt. Her glistening blonde curls hung loose on her shoulders, giving her the look of a young woman.

"Hi, Lonnie," she said with a smile that melted the soles of my sneakers.

"Hello, Nelda. It's good to see you again."

"What do you two have planned?" Miss Debbie asked.

"We don't know, mama. Lonnie and I might go out to Spates' Creek Bridge and look for arrowheads, if that's all right with you."

Spates' Creek Bridge had just officially become "Our Place."

"Well, y'all just be real careful out there and watch for snakes."

We gave our solemn word that we would avoid poisonous reptiles with all due diligence. Nelda loaded a brown paper bag with her mother's cookies, and we were off. If only she had a girl dog for Sawbuck, it would have been a double date. I felt a little embarrassed to be riding in broad daylight on my pile of junk next to her shiny, chrome-encrusted new Schwinn, but that went away when I looked at her beside me. Who cared what I had to ride? At that moment, I could have sworn I was seated on a rainbow.

No mention was made of the earlier unfortunate incident. It was as if it had never occurred. We rode along in the balmy morning air, the woods on either side of us alive with sound and motion. When we got to the bridge, I helped her down to the refreshing wetness of the creek bed. We took off our shoes, waded in the water, and splashed each other, laughing like second graders. I was standing high on the cloud-covered pinnacle of love mountain, breathing the rarified air of unmitigated joy, yet at the same time feeling like it was all too good to be true and soon I'd be tumbling back down into the valley of fecal matter.

After searching for arrowheads, we rested on the same log I had sat on the day of my unexpected dip. We talked about books and music and what colleges we wanted to go to. Purely by coincidence, I wanted to attend the same school she did. Wherever it was.

Then, I told her everything about my Papa nightmares, hearing him in the hallway, Gideon's cryptic messages, what I had learned from Aunt Kate, getting lost in the woods, and meeting the man at the creek, everything. It felt good to have someone to unload on.

"I had no idea all this was going on, Lonnie. It's all kind of creepy but exciting. Do you think that the light we saw at Big Mama's house was the ghost of that banker?"

"I don't know. That was the strangest thing I've ever seen. Well, except for Gideon first thing in the morning."

"Who do *you* think the Booger is: your Uncle Willie, or Charlie Banks, or Scrub Purifoy?" she asked.

"If I had to bet money, I would say it's Charlie Banks. I think he has more of a motive, and he's real close by. It would be real easy for him."

"I don't like that man. I always feel an evil presence when I'm around him, though that's not very much since he's never stepped foot in the church. He seems like the kind of man that would do something that *mean.* Your Uncle Willie wouldn't, but I don't know anything about Scrub Purifoy."

"I wish there was a way to catch him in the act. Set some kind of foolproof trap or something. Unfortunately, I have neither the skills nor the ingredients to construct such a device," I joked.

"Lonnie, would you take me out to Wallace and Velma's house? And down to the creek to see the footprints?"

"Well, okay. You mean now?"

"Why not? I told mama not to expect me for lunch. That's why I brought the cookies. I've got plenty of time."

"Well, then, let's go," I said as I helped her up. We walked back to the bridge, and I was about to go up the embankment when she stopped me.

"Show me where your initials are, Lonnie."

"Okay, you need to walk out in the shallows a few steps," I said as I led her by the hand and pointed to a beam above us. "See, right up there next to the big 'T.S. + V.T.'"

I blushed when I realized it was also next to the spray painted "FUK YOU."

"That must have been hard to get to," she said as she craned her neck. "Uh, Lonnie?"

"Yes?"

"Can I ask you a … personal question?"

"Sure, I guess."

"What do you think of me? I'm sorry for being so forward, it's one of my many faults, I was just wondering ... how you felt."

"I ... uh ... I really like you a lot, Nelda. A whole lot."

"Really?"

"Yeah, it's like we talked about. I feel like we're supposed to be ... together, you know."

"Together enough to carve our initials in the bridge?"

"I would do it in a heartbeat, but I don't have a knife."

"I do."

She pulled it from her back pocket with a smile. She had been planning this. I took it from her hand, and she melted into my arms. Once again, centuries rolled past as we kissed in a clumsy but passionate neophyte dream world. When we finally came up for air and became aware that we were back on earth, I climbed up into the beams and carved "L.T.+N.G." I wanted to use the word "loves," but the wood was hard and would have taken forever.

"It's beautiful," she pronounced. "And it will be there for future generations to see."

"Yeah, but they won't have a clue who the letters stand for."

"It doesn't matter. They are supposed to be there. Let's go."

We pedaled back into town and took the road to Wallace and Velma's. As we passed Willie's store, Nelda stopped me.

"Can we go inside Willie's? I've always wanted to see what it looks like in there."

"I don't know if your folks would like that. What if somebody tells them they saw you in there?"

"Aw, I'll just tell them we stopped to get some drinks to have with our cookies. Please?"

How could I refuse her? We parked our bikes and went in. I felt like a tour guide while showing her around the store. We poured over the Custer painting, with me pointing out my favorite dead soldiers. I dropped a few nickels in the pinball machine and watched her excited blue eyes reflect the flashing lights as she pulled the plunger. I punched up Patsy Cline's "Walking After Midnight" on the jukebox, which was a song that had a special meaning for us now. There was no one else in the store, so we sat at the bar talking with Aunt Kate and sipping a couple of root beers.

"What was it like in Moro when the mill was here, Aunt Kate?" I asked.

"Well, it was a lot different, I can tell you that. When we opened this store in 1925, we couldn't hardly handle the business. This town was *hoppin'* back then. We had lots of stores and lots of people. Even a picture show. I saw my first movie there, but I can't remember what it was to save my life. There was stores right across the street where the ball field is now. In fact, the Moro Bank was at the corner of the Fordyce road. For years after they tore the bank down, we would find coins after a heavy rain."

"What about Scrub Purifoy?" I asked. "Why won't Uncle Willie let him come in the store?"

"That old bum? He ain't nothin' but a thief. He stole from us and probably everybody else in town."

"Did he really kill somebody?"

"That's what they say. Him and some man nobody knew was seen drinkin' together, and then they found the man stabbed to death and no sign of Scrub. I believe he did it."

"Do you think he could be the Booger?" Nelda asked.

"No, it couldn't be him. He was in jail in Indiana one time for five years. The Booger came back several times while he was locked up."

Then, the screen door opened. In walked Charlie Banks and Cooper Logan.

"Hello, Scorpion. Hello, Miss Nelda," Cooper boomed. "How are you young folks doin'?"

We both said "Fine" at the same time. I could see that Nelda was ready to go.

"What are y'all up to?" Cooper asked.

"Oh, we're just out riding bikes," I answered.

"Beautiful goddamn day for it," Charlie said.

"Yes, sir, it is."

That was the signal for us to hit the road. We said goodbyes, hopped on our bikes, and headed down the road, after making sure that Wallace and Velma were both still at the store.

"I can't stand that horrible Charlie Banks," Nelda said. "If Scrub Purifoy can't be the Booger, then Charlie's gotta be."

"Yeah, goddamn it."

Her laugh was cute and infectious. It made me weak in the knee joints to hear it. We stopped at the tracks, and I showed her where the train blew up. We sat cross-legged on the foundation of the old depot, talked, and ate cookies. I had a totally different feeling about this location with Nelda seated beside me.

"This is a lonely place," she said. "Kinda *strange* and … lonely. Oh, I can't describe the feeling I have."

"I know what you mean. It's like this area is, I don't know … separated from the rest of the world."

"I think the whole town of Moro feels separated from the rest of the world," she laughed.

"I can't argue with that. Well, are you ready for an even stranger place?"

"Ooh, yes! Thanks for doing this for me, Lonnie."

"Believe me, it's my pleasure. It's great to have somebody to share stuff with, you know."

We brushed off the crumbs and resumed our ride.

"Look at this place," Nelda said after we pedaled up to Wallace and Velma's secluded little shack. "This is *spooky*. How could anyone live out here?"

We stashed our bikes at the edge of the woods.

"Can you imagine how dark it must be out here at night? The Booger must have cat eyes," she said. "I bet you can't see your hand in front of your face."

Even in the light of day, the place had a dark aura about it, like a lost soul whose grief only deepens with the passage of time, an emptiness that you could almost touch. We walked around the house looking at the ground and speaking in hushed tones, as if someone inside might overhear us.

"Oh, Lonnie, look," she said after opening the door to the outhouse. "These poor people still actually use this. There's toilet paper in here. And some girlie magazines."

"Girlie magazines?" I asked, my curiosity piqued.

"Yeah, a whole stack of them."

"Let me see," I said as I stepped into the little odiferous hut while Nelda held the door.

The topmost magazine had a picture of a chubby topless woman reclining on a sofa. I reached to pick it up and noticed that it was severely wrinkled, like it had been very wet at some point; since I didn't know what type of liquid had soaked it, I decided to leave it be.

"I guess that's Wallace's *reading* material," I said.

"It must be hard to hold a magazine with one hand."

"Nelda! You … you, brazen hussy, you!" I said as we laughed at the thought of Wallace Summers as a dirty old man.

With Nelda's soft warm hand in mine, I led the way to a faint opening in the undergrowth. As we entered the woods, I was momentarily struck with a minor panic attack. A side effect of getting lost, I assumed, afraid that I would never be able to enjoy the wonders of God's creation the same way again.

We walked without saying much until we came out on the creek. Open space felt liberating after the crush of dense woods. There seemed to be a perpetual breeze flowing along with the water, like natural air conditioning. I saw something on the ground catch the sun for a split second and leaned over to pick it up. It was a Wrigley's spearmint gum wrapper.

"Did you find a clue, Lonnie?" Nelda asked, coming up behind me and wrapping her arms around my waist. She nestled her head on my shoulder and looked to see what was in my hand.

"Yeah. If you're looking for a litterbug. It's just trash. A gum wrapper and foil. But I didn't see it the last time I was here. I thought I had given this whole area a pretty good going over. I must have missed it." I tossed it aside.

"Show me the footprints."

"Right over here m'lady." I took her by the hand and led her to the spot where I had seen them before. There were fresh prints mixed in among the old ones.

"These weren't here last time," I said, pointing them out. "And look, the soles are ridged, just like what you find on your regular everyday pair of rubber boots."

"Like the ones you said Charlie Banks was wearing when you talked to him yesterday."

"Right. The plot thickens."

"Ooh, this is so exciting. Thank you again for bringing me, Lonnie."

"No problem. I'm having a blast."

"So, if we continue down this way, we'll come out at Whitewater Bridge, right?" she asked.

"Yeah. It's probably not far if you go by the creek, but going back out, and then around on the Fordyce road is a *long* way. I would have walked for hours if your father hadn't come along."

"In theory then, the Booger could have used the creek as a quick getaway to the vehicle he secreted on the Fordyce road."

My Nelda was not only fetching but smart.

"Right. Who would think to look for the Booger way over on the Fordyce road?" I said.

"The way I hear it, nobody ever looks *anywhere* for it anymore. Nobody really cares enough to make the effort. They all sit around and talk about it, but none of them want to do anything about it."

"Sounds like they've gotten comfortable with it. The Booger's been around so long it's just part of life."

"This could only happen in Moro."

We continued down the creek and saw that the bootprints went in both directions. They had been made since I was there the day before.

The thought that someone had been here so recently after I had left made me uneasy. Sawbuck didn't seem to feel well either. He had eaten some blades of grass earlier and was yakking up something in the weeds. Then, we heard noises downstream.

"Lonnie, do you hear that?" she whispered, clutching my arm.

"Somebody's coming. Quick, over here."

I grabbed her hand and pulled her behind the dirt-caked, upturned roots of a huge oak tree that appeared to have recently blown over. Sawbuck came immediately when I quietly called his name. We squatted at a point where we had a limited view of the creek but couldn't be seen and clung to each other. I could smell strawberry shampoo in her hair as the breeze lifted strands into my face and tickled my nose. If I had not been completely numb with anticipation, I would have thoroughly enjoyed the closeness of her body.

We heard the distinct sound of footsteps among the rocks coming in our direction, with an occasional splash as if he had stepped hard in the water. Because a noise can seem to come from every direction at once when you're in the middle of the woods, there was no way to determine how far away he was.

I felt her little heart knocking against me like it wanted to come in. She was trembling, or I was, or we both were, as we waited to see who, or what, was coming. The narrow gap that we were looking through afforded only a limited view of the creek. The way I figured it, he would be right on top of us before we could see him. The steps were steady and getting louder. Nelda was squeezing me tighter when they suddenly stopped. We sat holding our breath as the seconds beat past, hearing nothing but the natural woodland noises. I suddenly had to pee badly.

"Are they gone?" Nelda breathed as her lips brushed my ear.

"I don't know. He couldn't have passed here without us seeing him. Maybe he went back the other way. If we don't hear anything in a little while, I'll take a look."

"You mean *we'll* take a look. You ain't leaving me."

I noticed Sawbuck lift his nose and sample the air. His ears perked up, and he had a "what the hell is that" look in his eye. My blood was colder than creekwater.

"Hear something, boy?" I said as I placed a hand on his head. I could feel the tenseness in him.

"Lonnie, I'm scared."

"Don't be scared. It's okay. Me and Sawbuck are right here. We won't let anything happen to you." I pulled her even closer.

Every second was a thousand years as we hunkered down, arms wrapped around each other, melted and fused together. I had no idea how long we had been there when Sawbuck snorted softly, like he had gotten wind of something. I saw the fur on his neck rise, right along with my blood pressure. And suddenly, there he was.

It was my uncle, Willie Pierce. He came from the same direction we had and was only in our sight for a moment as he passed. It was a brief glimpse but long enough for me to see that he was wearing a pair of rubber boots. We sat like statuary as the sound of his footsteps receded. Then, we waited five minutes more.

We slowly stood up and looked over the trunk of the downed tree. There was no sign of him.

"What do you think he's doing out here, Lonnie?"

"I don't know. Maybe he's got one of his stills around here."

"Oh, really? Do you think we can find it? I've always wanted to taste moonshine."

"*You* are something else, Nelda. I don't think that's a good idea. Besides, it's probably well hidden."

We had just stepped back out to the creek when we heard what sounded like Willie coming back toward us. I told Nelda to follow me, and we took off running for the trail back to Wallace's. And just like every woman in every movie I had ever seen that had to run from any kind of danger, Nelda fell and twisted her ankle. I went back and helped her up, put her arm around my neck, and my arm around her waist, and supported her as she hopped along. We ran like contestants in a three-legged race, and I kept expecting to hear Willie's voice yell, "Hold it right there!" Not satisfied with our progress, I scooped her up in my arms and carried her to the opening in the brush that we had emerged from and then up the trail for another twenty yards before I stopped and put her down.

"Are you all right?" I asked between deep breaths.

"Yeah, I'm okay. Just turned my ankle a little. I'll be able to walk on it. I just feel like one of those stupid women in the movies that fall down at the worst possible time."

We were both struck at the same instant with the absurdity of the whole situation. We had been running for our lives from my *uncle,* a man I had known all my life. A gentle man. A moonshiner maybe but no killer. It wasn't as if he would have hacked us up and left the pieces to the fowl of the air. Nelda began to giggle, and we grabbed each other and collapsed to the ground in a paroxysm of deep, shuddering, uncontrollable, cathartic laughter. We rolled together among the pinecones and moldy leaves until we lay exhausted and emotionally sated. It was one of those rare, gossamer moments in life that tastes eternal but is gone way too soon.

"I feel like I've known you all my life, Lonnie," she said as we slowly came down from our adrenaline high.

"Yeah, me too. I remember when you first moved here. We came to grandma's for a visit that summer. That was three years ago, wasn't it?"

"Yes. I have to tell you, Lonnie, I *did not* want to come here. We were living in El Dorado, which is a pretty big town, and I had all my friends there. When daddy said he was going to be the pastor here in dull, dead Moro, I cried until I made myself sick."

"Well, I know it's kinda dead and everything, but I like it."

"I like it a whole lot more since you came here," she said, looking away self-consciously.

"I'm not planning to go anywhere."

"That's just it, Lonnie. I have this feeling … I don't know"

"What feeling? Something bad?"

"It's just … I just feel like you'll be leaving soon."

"Bite your tongue, woman! But not hard enough to put it out of commission."

"I'm serious, Lonnie. Like we talked about before, it's intuition. I have a *strong* feeling that things are going to change … for us."

"Well put it out of your mind and let's concentrate on the moment. That's all we have anyway, this moment, then the next. You never know when you're gonna run out. We can't all be as lucky as Miss Spicy so let's enjoy 'em one at a time," I said, trying to sound deep and wise.

"I'm sorry. I don't mean to sound so negative. I am enjoying our time together. But I do need to get home. We don't wanna mess things up with my mother right off the bat."

"Can you ride?"

"Yeah, I'm okay."

After making sure the coast was clear, I made a pit stop in the outhouse while Nelda stood outside telling me to put the magazine down and hurry up. We rode slowly, squeezing out every precious drop of togetherness that we possibly could.

"Tomorrow's Saturday. Got any plans?" I asked as we biked up to her back door.

"We're going to El Dorado to see my grandmother. She broke her hip and is in the hospital. But you're coming to church, right?"

"Yes dear, I'll be there in my 'Sunday go to meetin' clothes'."

Chapter Seventeen

Note the Time

As soon as I got back to grandma's, the grilling began. My mother wanted a moment by moment account of my day. I told her everything we did, with the exception of the jaunt out to the Summers' house.

"Did you … well …" my mother said with a silly look.

"Yeah, we smoochy-smooched a little."

"Now, Lonnie," she said laughing. "I told you not to do that. Are you sweet on her?"

"*Sweet* on her? What kind of question is that? Am I *sweet* on her?"

"You know what I mean. Do you like her?"

"Well … we were going to wait until we could get you and her parents together for this, but I'll just go ahead and announce our betrothal."

"Be a smartass if you want, but I can tell you like her."

"It does seem that we've hit it off."

"Oh, Lonnie," Grandma Birdie said. "Miss Spicy called and wants you to come out to her house tomorrow if you can. Said she had something she wants to give you."

"Did she say what it was?" I asked, concerned it might be another body part in a jar.

"No, she didn't."

After supper, I fed Sawbuck and retreated to my favorite front porch chair. A few minutes of daylight lingered, so Gideon's butt was straining the cane-bottom seat of his ladder-back chair. I began reading the memoirs of Ulysses S. Grant that grandma had picked up for me from the Fordyce library. I read it realizing that Miss Spicy was *alive* during the events that he was recounting. I thought of how Grant had hurried to complete his memoirs in a race against the cancer that was consuming him, and how Mark Twain, in a generous and selfless act, published the book posthumously giving the proceeds to the widow Grant and her children.

Usually when I read about the War Between the States, I am transported to the smoke and cannons, minnie-balls whistling around my ears, right in the heat of battle. Or standing in a tent during a torrential downpour as General Lee, his face glowing in the lamplight, pours over maps with his officers while plotting troop movements. But this time, I found myself riding in a wagon with my grandfather, Abraham Spates, as we are being stopped and arrested.

"Time machine," Gideon said.

The heavy book jumped in my hands at the suddenness of his voice. Time machine. What did he mean by that, I wondered? I didn't like these enigmatic messages anymore after my experience with the rabbit. I thought maybe he had overheard my silly comment to my mother about Sawbuck inventing a time machine and was just now getting the joke. But I knew that wasn't it. I went to sleep that night with dreams of Nelda's hair, rubber boots, and H.G. Wells.

~

I left for Miss Spicy's right after breakfast the next morning, riding the now-familiar roads wondering what it was she wanted to give me, keeping an eye out for Gideon's "time machine" to make its appearance. When I got to Spicy's, I leaned my bike against the porch and knocked on the door. I heard Beulah coming, her cross-country skiing gait was unmistakable.

"Mornin', Mr. Lonnie."

"Good morning, Miss Beulah."

"Come on in, Miz Spicy's waitin' in the parlor. Lordy me, Mr. Lonnie, that ol' lady mus' think the world of you."

"What do you mean?"

"Just come on in. You'll see."

I followed her into the parlor where Miss Spicy was sitting in her chair, nestled in pillows, wearing a plum-colored, ankle-length dress.

"Good mornin', Lonnie."

"Hi, Miss Spicy. Sorry I missed your call."

"That's all right. It gave me a chance to talk with Birdie. We had a good conversation. I need to call her more often. I remember the first telephone in this area. It was at the bank, and people come from miles away to talk on it, and when they got a chance, they didn't have nobody to call. So they'd all just stand around and wait for it to ring. I thought it was just a time wastin' contraption. Birdie told me that you was sweet on that little Nelda Graves. Is that true?"

Thank you, Grandma Birdie.

"I like her, if that's what you mean."

"You must bring her out here some time. I've met her mama and daddy, but I'd like to meet her. She must be nice if you like her. Well, set down, Lonnie. Beulah, would you bring Lonnie and me some of your fresh lemonade?"

I sat in my usual wingback chair as she asked a few "sweet old lady" questions about me and Nelda. Beulah brought the lemonade in and flashed a long-toothed smile at me for the first time since I had met her. It made me feel most peculiar.

"I wanted you to come down, Lonnie 'cause I got somethin' I want to give you. It may not be much to some people, but it's the most precious thing that I own."

She dabbed her weak eyes and wiped her veined nose with a tissue. It was plain that she was emotional. I was getting a little cranked up myself.

"I'm not gonna be around too much longer, Lonnie. I don't have no children, but I got a passel of grandnephews and nieces that will come lookin' through my piddlin' little belongings when I'm gone. I wouldn't care 'cept they don't never come to see me while I'm alive. And they're welcome to everything I got. Except one thing."

By this point, my curiosity was out murdering cats.

"I even prayed about who I should give it to. Then, it come to me. You are the only person who ever seemed to have an interest in the family history. The only one who just come out to see me 'cause you wanted to, not 'cause you had to. There ain't nobody else that I want to have it."

She lifted her frail arm toward me and in her palm laid a silver pocket watch.

"This is my father Abraham Spates' watch. I want you to have it, Lonnie."

I took it from her and turned it over in my hand. It was covered in small dents, indicating some rough times. I pushed the button on the side, and the cover flipped open to reveal the aged, ivory-colored face under a cracked crystal. It was ticking, and a glance at the grandfather clock in the corner showed it kept correct time.

"Daddy carried that watch with him most of his life. He had it with him when him and mama left Kentucky and on the raft down the Ouachita River. He used it to time the labor pains mama had for every one of her children. I cain't tell you how many times I seen him take it out of his pocket and open it. If he was outside, he would check the time and then look to see where the sun was in the sky. He did it every time. Then, he would wind it and put it back in his pocket."

She sat with her brittle hands in her lap as a tear made its way down her leathery cheek.

"Just before they took him away from us that day, he kissed me goodbye and slipped that watch in my hand. I never saw him again. I have cherished it all these years. It's the only thing I have from him. I take it out every day and wind it. It hasn't stopped since the minute he give it to me. The only thing I ask you, Lonnie, is to keep it wound up. Don't let it stop."

I was stunned. I had never been so honored. I held the watch in my hand and felt the presence of Abraham standing beside me.

"I promise I'll keep it running, Miss Spicy."

"I knew you would, that's why I want you to have it. You understand its value. The others would just want to know how much it was worth. You know, this sounds awful silly, but I got to where I thought that as long as I kept daddy's watch runnin', I wouldn't die. Ain't that crazy?"

"If it's true, you'll live forever."

"I'm countin' on it," she laughed.

I thanked her profusely and swore yet again to care for and guard the priceless heirloom with my life and someday pass it on to my own son or daughter. I kissed her rouged cheek and followed Beulah to the front door.

"You see what I mean 'bout Miz Spicy thinkin' so high of you," she said as I stepped out on the porch. "That watch mean the worl' to her. She been makin' hersef sick worryin' 'bout who she was gonna give that ol' watch to a'fore she died, but since she make up her mind to give it to you, she been jus' happy as the cat who et the canary."

I was pretty happy myself as I rode back toward town feeling the weight of the watch warm against my leg. As I pedaled along, I stuck my hand in my pocket and ran my fingers over its worn surface. *Suddenly, I am at the rear of a huge log raft that I had built with my own labor, my hand on the rudder, and my pregnant wife sitting before me, surrounded by everything we possess. We are headed into the unknown, armed only with a musket, a knife, an axe, and a determination to prosper in the freedom that this nation offered. I have no idea that one day my fellow countrymen will take that freedom, and my life, away from me. As we skim along the quiet river, I reach into my homespun breeches and take out my watch and note the time, then I check the position of the sun.*

It hit me in a flash of clarity. The reason Gideon had mentioned Miss Spicy in the first place was so I would get to know her and come into possession of this "time machine." It had marked the minutes and hours of my great, great, great, great-grandfather's life, and Miss Spicy's. With proper care and maintenance, it could keep on ticking through eternity. As I held it, I could almost feel it vibrate with all the years that had been stored in its battered case. I felt privileged to have it.

I stopped at the post office to show it off to Doc and to get updated on what the Yankees were doing and if Mantle was on track to break the

Babe's home-run record. I just knew that The Mick was the only man alive who could hit sixty-two homers in one year. Doc always saved the Sunday paper from Little Rock for me. I sat on his back steps and read every description of every game and all the statistics in the box scores while Doc worked just inside the open door listening to a Cardinals game on his static-plagued little radio.

I went into Willie's and showed the watch to Aunt Kate and the handful of old men that were in the middle of solving the world's problems over in the conversation pit. Willie came in wearing a pair of black, lace-up brogans. As I watched him go behind the bar and get a Pepsi out of the cooler—he never touched alcohol—I could not imagine Uncle Willie as the Booger. He was too mellow, solid, and frugal with his time to waste that amount of effort for no return. Charlie Banks, on the other hand, seemed to harbor a hardness in him that might allow him to torment someone and consider the pleasure of it to be reward enough. It had to be him, I thought. Plus, I didn't want my own uncle to be the damn Booger.

When I got home, I proudly showed my mother and grandma the watch, while telling them of its history.

"Now, you can keep up with the time while you're out gallavantin' around town," my mother said.

"Mama, this is an *antique* for crying out loud. It's a piece of our family history. I'm not gonna haul it around with me."

"Well, what good is it then?"

"Oh mama, mama, mama," was all I could say.

"Your father called again."

"Whoop-ti-doo."

"He'll be here next Saturday. He said he still hadn't took a drink."

"Of water maybe. He likes his whiskey straight."

"I can tell when he's been drinking. *And* when he's lying. I believe him, Lonnie."

"You know, mama, that would be great. It would be wonderful. I wish that we could have a father-and-son relationship, but I'm almost fifteen years old, and he ain't never made much of an effort before. Can you blame me for doubting him?"

"No, I can't. But he's changed. *He has.* I know that you'll see it over time."

"That remains to be seen. He may not even show up."

Nelda called, and we talked for an hour until her mother made her get off the phone. I told her about the watch and promised to sit with her in church tomorrow. She also invited me to join her family for lunch at the Catfish Shack in Fordyce after the services. I said that catfish was my all-time favorite food in the world. Of course, I would have said the same thing had she invited me to The House of Possum.

I put the watch inside a thick white sock and stuffed it in the web of my fielder's mitt and put them in the top drawer of the dresser. I wanted to know exactly where they were in case we had to evacuate in an emergency. Then, I read a few more chapters of Grant's memoirs, batted rocks till sundown, took a bath, and went to bed.

Chapter Eighteen

Spun Gold Drifting on the Wind

I woke up that Sunday morning with a feeling that something unwelcome was on the way, and it wasn't coming for a chat. I dressed in the new clothes that my mother had purchased on a trip to Fordyce and was pleased to find that the blue shirt and black dress pants fit as if my tailor had created them just for me. I should recommend him to Gideon.

"My, don't you look handsome," my mother said as I walked into the kitchen.

"Thanks for the new duds, mama. I really appreciate it. I know money's tight."

"I'm just glad that everything fit. I hate taking clothes back. So, you're going to lunch with the Graves bunch, huh?"

"Yeah. Do you mind if I invite Nelda over after we get back so I can show her the watch? I don't want to take it to church with me, in case I have to break somebody's nose."

"Lonnie, if you ever fight at church again, you better give your *heart* to the Lord, 'cause your *butt* will be mine."

"What would you do with two butts, mama?"

"Ain't you heard, smartass? Two butts are better than one."

"I bet Gideon wishes he had two butts. Surely, he's worn out the one he's got," grandma said.

After breakfast, I fed Sawbuck and went to wait on the porch with Gideon. I sat in a patch of sunshine as that uneasy feeling clung to the back of my mind. It troubled me as I ransacked my brain for some kind of clue as to what was bothering me. I didn't like it, and I couldn't shake it. I waited to see if Gideon might issue some convoluted message that would shed light on my dilemma until it was time to head off to church.

Nelda and I sat together in the middle pew, a compromise between the front and the rear, and I really didn't hear a word of the sermon. It was hard to concentrate on hearing *about* heaven when it was sitting right next to me. Or at least an angel fresh from the golden streets of that glorious city. It was the best service I had ever attended.

"Let's go to the fellowship hall for cookies and punch," Nelda said after the dismissal. "It'll be a while before my folks will be ready to go. Daddy has to shake everybody's hand, or they'll all be offended. I swear, I think most people come to church just to be acknowledged."

Boy, that sure in heck wasn't the reason I came, I thought, as I stared into the blue eyes of the real reason I came.

"Do you want to come over to my grandma's when we get back to see the watch Miss Spicy gave me?"

"I would love to, Lonnie. I'm looking forward to meeting your mother and grandmother. And especially Gideon."

"Well don't expect to engage him in any witty repartee."

"I just want to ask him one question," she said with a smile.

"What's that?"

"Will I ever meet my true love?"

"I can answer that, and I'm quite sane."

"Some would doubt the sanity part."

We went to the little fellowship hall that was connected to the main church by a covered walkway. There were a few tables and chairs in the middle of the floor, and a tiny kitchen in the back with a stove and refrigerator. The church used the facility for banquets and wedding receptions. I had just picked up a stale cookie and a cup of weak cherry punch when I turned and was met with the puffy, bruised eyes of Mike

Kilgore. I thought this might be what was troubling me. Maybe I had sensed that we would meet again.

"Hey, Lonnie."

"Hey, Mike. How are you?" I put the cookie and cup down so I would have my hands free for any contingency.

"I'm healing. My nose isn't so bad, but let me tell you, a cracked tailbone is some serious pain. But at least my daddy can't accuse me of sittin' on my butt."

"I'm sorry about all that, Mike."

"It wasn't your fault. I started it. Man, you hit hard."

It was obvious that the fight had been taken out of him. He couldn't be the impending sense of trouble I had been feeling. We talked for a few minutes about the fact that the Hogskinners were in second place and were going to play the number one team, The Star City Cowboys, at home next Saturday. Mike said he would see me there. Pastor Graves finished feeding his flock's egos, and we left.

Nelda and I sat in the backseat on the drive to Fordyce with her little tattletale sister, Libby, planted like poison ivy between us. Though I felt like yanking on her braided pigtails for being a stool pigeon, I had to admit that she was going to be a beauty like her older sister someday. At the restaurant, we consumed heaping platters of greasy, deep-fried catfish, tater tots, coleslaw, and rolls, with a square of carrot cake for dessert. We washed it all down with pitchers of iced tea.

The ride back was both exhilarating and miserable. I was overjoyed just to be breathing the same air as Nelda yet ached to reach over and touch her. But I was afraid that the Reverend didn't feel *that* guilt-ridden about falsely accusing me. I knew that sweet, little Libby would immediately report any move on my part.

As soon as we piled out of the car at the parsonage, Nelda and I took off for grandma's. She pushed her bike while I walked alongside and burped. Sawbuck met us, smelled the fish on our hands and gave us a look that said, "May I please lick you?" Gideon was on the porch, dependable as the four seasons. After we watched him for a few minutes, Nelda introduced herself to him with a look of apprehension.

"Hi, Mister Gideon. I'm Nelda Graves."

"He's not going to say anything," I said. "He doesn't know we're here. Look at his eyes."

"Lonnie, he can hear you. He's sitting right there."

"I'm telling you, he's not aware of us. He's off running around with his spirit friends."

"You shouldn't make fun of him. He can't help it."

"I don't mean anything by it. It's just that I wish he would talk to me like a normal person. He says things out of the blue that end up having some meaning, but I never know what it will be."

"Do you think he might say something while I'm here?"

"There's no way to know. I wish he would, so you could see that I didn't make it up."

"I believe you, Lonnie."

"Sometimes, I don't know if I believe myself."

We went in and had a great visit with my mother and Grandma Birdie. Nelda charmed and won their hearts. I was impressed at how comfortable she was around my family. I felt like the finger of fate had pushed us together, and it wasn't floating in some mason jar. We decided to go visit with Big Mama and were about to jump on our bikes when Gideon spoke.

"When one door shuts, another one opens."

We looked at each other and then at Gideon.

"That was him talking, wasn't it?" Nelda asked.

"Yeah, see what I mean. Look, his eyes have enough glaze on 'em to frost a cake."

"What do you think he meant?"

"Who knows. We'll just have to wait and see if it means anything at all."

We rode off as Nelda looked over her shoulder at the figure of Gideon on the porch. We discussed his enigmatic message all the way to Big Mama's. She had claimed that she wanted to see where the light had appeared at the window, but it took some coaxing to get her in the house once we got there. We talked with Big Mama for about thirty minutes, and I could tell that Nelda was getting antsy.

"Are you okay?" I asked.

"Yeah, I'm fine. Why don't you show me around the house, Lonnie? Give me the tour."

"Have you purchased a ticket, ma'am?"

"How much are they?"

"It's negotiable."

"Well, y'all just look around or whatever you want to do," Big Mama said. "I hope it won't offend you if I was to lay down for a few minutes. My ol' shoulder hurts me so bad sometimes, I just gotta take an aspirin and lay down 'til it passes. Y'all don't ever get old, you hear me."

We promised to halt our aging process, wished her a nice nap, and went out through the kitchen door to the back porch. At one time it had been open to the elements like the front porch. But at some point, what appeared to have been skilled carpenters had closed it in with rows of windows that kept it well-lit and inviting, and featured an awe-inspiring view of the chicken house. They walled off enough space at the other end to install a bathroom, complete with a huge enameled claw-foot tub.

"It was right there inside the kitchen that Papa had his stroke and fell. And it was right here," I said, pointing at the sill of the hall door, "that the noise started."

Nelda grabbed my arm with frighteningly strong fingers.

"I don't want to offend Big Mama," she whispered, "but this place gives me the creeps."

"I call it the Heebie J. Creeps."

"What?"

"I'll explain later. Come on."

I took her into the unoccupied rooms across the hall. Each one was furnished with a couple of ratty chairs, doilies on the dresser, and the beds were made up. They had been in this exact condition since my earliest memories. Cobwebs hung like hammocks from the corners of the ceiling, lending an air of desolation and wasted effort, as if everything had been prepared for someone who wasn't coming. We found an old trunk and dug through the out-of-style clothes, with Nelda holding dresses up to her neck and modeling until the mothball fumes and the dust we stirred up made it too hard to breathe.

We stepped back into the hallway, and the feeling of discomfort from that morning returned. A sense of foreboding, like something was going to happen if I didn't stop it. And the memory of the ghastly sounds I had heard in this very hall didn't help to perk me up.

"There it is. See it?" I said, indicating the "X" marked on the floor. "That's where the banker died."

"This is a lot spookier than the Summers' house. I'm all goose-pimply."

"And through this door … is the parlor." I said as I put my arm around her shoulders and pulled her tight. I turned the black ceramic doorknob and swung it open. A sweet, over-ripe fruit smell filled the room.

"Oh, Lonnie. I don't know if it's what you've told me about this place or not, but I just sense something here. A presence or something. I just feel strange."

"Do you want to leave?"

"Not on your life. We've got the place to ourselves."

God, I loved that woman.

We went in and shut the door behind us. We stood there in the gloom conjoined at the ribs. There *did* seem to be a feeling in the room, heavy yet not threatening. The door that opened into Big Mama's room was closed. We walked over to the bay windows and saw that the shades were pulled down. I pushed the middle one aside, and we looked out at the yard and the gravel road where we had stopped that night.

"This is the window where we saw the light," I said.

"Were the shades down when we saw it?"

"I don't know. It was too dark to tell."

"Lonnie, do you think what we saw in this window was, you know, something … supernatural?"

"Have you come up with any other explanation?"

"No."

"Me neither."

We turned and walked to the bed and Nelda sat on the edge.

"And this is where you were when you heard … your Papa … coming down the hall."

"Yep," I said as I flopped across the bed behind her. She pulled her legs up and turned to face me.

"And," I continued, "he ended up right outside *that* door. Probably stopped to chat with the banker. I can hear them now, 'So, how's death treatin' ya?' 'Oh, not too bad. I'm here to scare the crap outta my great-grandson.'"

She laughed and launched herself on top of me. We rolled around tickling each other and acting like two-year-olds until the inevitable happened. Our lips became sealed. Hormones that I had not yet been introduced to were making my acquaintance. I found them to be a great buncha guys as they kicked off their shoes and made themselves at home.

"Lonnie?" she said, her voice low and husky.

"What?"

"Remember when we were at the bridge, and I said that someday … we'd go all the way?"

"How could I forget?"

"Well … I think … it may be that time."

"Yeah, me too."

Things were getting hotter than Miss Spicy's forbidden pepper, and Nelda had become especially pliant in the heat. However, it was at this advanced stage in our amorous liaison that I realized that I had no idea of what to do. I had some vague notions, of course, mostly gleaned from the much-handled deck of pornographic playing cards my best friend Pee-Wee had copped from his older brother. But the cards only depicted scenes in progress, nothing about how to get started. Just as Nelda herself began to show some knowledge of the art of lovemaking, we heard a thud. We snapped upright.

"What was *that*?" she asked, digging her nails into my flesh.

"I have no idea. It sounded like something fell."

"You think it might be Big Mama?"

"I don't know, but I have a sudden craving to find out."

We leaped out of bed and high-stepped it as one body out the door, into the hallway, and down to Big Mama's room. Before I could call her name, the door to the parlor we had just left slammed shut with such force that it rattled the glass in the front door. Nelda and I grabbed each other while we were still airborne. Then, we heard the front door click and watched as it slowly swung open, as if pushed by a gentle breeze.

"Lonnie, is that you?" Big Mama called from behind her door.

We stared into each other's eyes, only inches apart, breathing heavily as if we *had* consummated our love.

"Yes, it's me, Big Mama. I'm sorry. Go back to sleep. We're leaving now."

We were standing in the back yard before she could say, "Y'all be sweet."

"That is the weirdest thing that ever happened to me," Nelda said as we stood staring at the back of the house. "One door closed, and another one opened. Just like Gideon said. How strange is that?"

"That was far, far beyond strange."

"What do you think caused it, Lonnie?"

"Probably the wind."

"You don't believe that. All the windows and outside doors were closed. Where did the wind come from?"

"Well, we did leave the room rather quickly. Maybe the suction pulled the door shut."

We both laughed with that "glad we're out of there" hysterical laugh you get after a narrow escape.

"First the light in the window," she said, "and now this. I think this house is possessed."

"You mean by evil spirits?"

"Well, maybe not *evil* spirits. Just some kind of … *something*."

"Then, you do believe in ghosts?"

"Oh, I don't know, Lonnie! Maybe there's a logical explanation for it. I just can't think of one right now, okay?"

"Maybe we should get your dad to perform an exorcism."

"Are you kidding? My father is scared of his own shadow."

"Really? What's the matter? He don't have enough faith?"

"It's not a matter of faith. He's just a big sissy."

I wondered how the Reverend would feel about his daughter's assessment of him as we rode back to the parsonage. We discussed Gideon's unusual gift, made a date for the next day, and I went home. I should have been as happy as Sawbuck with a full bowl, but the little prodding in the recesses of my mind that kept saying something's not right wouldn't let me.

~

I took Nelda out to meet Miss Spicy the following day, and it was love at first sight. Miss Spicy was wearing a western-style dress and looked like Howdy Doody's great-grandmother. I had brought the watch along, and the little puppet of a woman that I had come to love sat caressing it like a talisman throughout our visit. She told me that she was having Abraham's last letter laminated to preserve it and wanted me to have that also. I thanked her again for her generosity, and she hugged us both with arms no bigger than a broom handle. We then went to Mammy and Paw's, where Nelda was treated to a viewing of the "finger forever pointin' at nothin'." We begged off the tea cakes with the excuse of just having loaded up on pie.

I loved sharing my odd life with her. Compared to her staid family of "sissies," we were as wild and exotic as a traveling band of gypsies. After deciding that the time to "go all the way" wasn't right, we spent unforgettable hours just talking and bonding and touching and exploring. One day she packed a picnic lunch, and we ate chicken salad sandwiches and Clark Bars on the banks of Spates' Creek. We were lying on a blanket in a place where we could see our initials, now immortalized in the bridge. I made a mental note to do something about that "FUK YOU." Either blot it out completely or add a "C."

Our days together were like strands of spun gold that drifted on the wind and fell at our feet, making us feel rich with a wealth not of this world. We talked more of the cosmic forces and planetary alignments that had brought us together. How, if I had a normal, stable home life, I wouldn't have come to Moro to live in the first place. It made me wonder if Gideon's original message to me about being here "for a reason" was to meet Nelda. I knew that had to be part of it, but I felt there had to be much more.

Chapter Nineteen

Burned Too Many Times

I woke up Saturday morning to the always-welcome smell of bacon sizzling. From the porch I heard Gideon say, "Lordy mercy." It sent a chill through me as I dressed and went in for breakfast.

"What are your plans today, Lonnie?" my mother asked as I bit off more biscuit than I could chew. After I cleared my palate with a slug of coffee, I said, "I'll probably go talk with Doc, and then shag flies with the team during warm-ups, and then meet Nelda for the game."

"Well, sounds like you got your day all mapped out. Did you forget anything?"

"Well, mama, it stands to reason that if I *did* forget something, then I wouldn't remember what it was. Why don't *you* tell me what I forgot?"

"Your father is comin' up today. You promised to talk to him."

"Oh, yeah, I tried to forget. When will he be here?"

"I don't know. He said he had some things to take care of first thing this mornin', and then he would come on."

"Probably has to return the empty whiskey bottles for the refund to scrounge up gas money."

"Now, Lonnie, you have to at least give him a chance. If you talk to him, and you don't think he has really changed, I won't bother you about it again. Do we have a deal?"

"All right, mama. But I'm not gonna sit around and wait for him. I'll talk to him when I get back home."

"Thank you, son. I really do appreciate it. And you can introduce him to Nelda."

Maybe *that* was what had been bothering me. I didn't want Nelda to meet my father. Or maybe I just didn't want him fucking up my life again. I did not want to talk to him, other than to tell him to leave my mother and me alone. But I promised to give him a few minutes, and for her sake, I would.

After breakfast, I served his Majesty, Sawbuck the First, and went to the front yard and oiled the chain on my bike. It was a cloudless day with a strong wind blowing from the east. The weather forecast predicted afternoon thundershowers. I should confirm that with Gideon, I thought. I put the oil can back in the toolbox and went to retrieve my bike.

"Danger comin' out of the smoke," Gideon said as I came up to the porch.

Of all the little communiqués I had received from him so far, this one had the most immediate impact on me. I sensed something ominous as soon as the words were out of his mouth. Was there a chance of fire? Should I warn somebody? I never knew what these damn messages meant. I just knew something unpleasant lay ahead.

~

"Ehh, what's up, Doc?" I said as I walked in the post office.

"What do you want, you cwazy wabbit?"

"I knew I shoulda took a left toin in Albuquerque."

We were both Bugs Bunny fans.

"How are you, Doc?"

"Same ol', same ol'. The most exciting thing that happens around here is when I get new wanted posters."

"I've been meaning to ask you about that. I remember some of those posters from the first time I came in here on my mother's hip with a bottle in my mouth. What's the problem? Are you lazy?" I joked.

"You sure can remember a long way's back, Lonnie. I have trouble remembering the last time I took a dump. The *problem* with the posters is they send the new ones to me every month, but they don't tell me if the old ones have been captured. I don't feel right taking 'em down unless I get official word."

"Did you ever get a poster on Scrub Purifoy?"

"No, they only send posters on important criminals."

"Well, I've heard that he is a murderer. You know anything about that?"

"Yeah, I heard that, too. But he's mostly just a petty thief. He ain't worth a poster."

With that cleared up, we talked for a while about, what else, baseball. I was disappointed to discover that he was still a Cardinals fan.

"Have you ever heard the rumor that Charlie Banks is the Booger?" I asked.

"Yeah."

"Why didn't you mention that when you told me about Willie?"

"I really don't think it could be Charlie."

"But he's so close to the Summers' place that it would be easy for him to go over there and back without being seen."

"Well … I have my reasons for thinkin' it's Willie."

"What are they? Don't just leave me hanging here, Doc."

"Come around back."

I met him at our *secure* location on the back steps. He packed in a new pinch of snuff, which caused him to maintain a stiff lower lip.

"Now, you cain't ever tell any …"

"Swear to God," I interrupted, "on a stack of Bibles and my mother's grave. Just tell me, please."

"Well, about three years ago, I was comin' home from a party over in Harrell real late one night. I had been drinkin' a little, which I wasn't used to since I still lived with my mother, and that was the first party I had been to in, oh, I don't know, ever. So, I'm not *exactly* positive about what I saw."

He paused to go through his routine of putting two fingers to his mouth and ejecting a slimy, brown stream. He only spit like that when he was outdoors; indoors he collected it like sap in a bucket.

"I was comin' up the road from Harrell real slow 'cause my head was swimmin'. There was a full moon, and it was bright enough that I could have turned my headlights off. Then, just below Wallace and Velmer's place, I saw a man cross the road ahead of me, way down the road. It was just a shadow, but I could tell it was a man. I slowed down, but he had gone into the woods. I drove on real slow and saw a truck backed up in one of them old loggin' roads, kinda like it was hid. I stopped and tried to make it out. The moon was bright enough for me to clearly see that it was Willie's truck. I saw that big metal frame he's got welded to the bed. Ain't another one like it around here. Then, sure enough, the next day I hear the Booger came back."

"That doesn't *prove* anything. It might look suspicious, but it's all circumstantial evidence."

"Well, *Perry Mason*, what other reason would he have to be skulkin' through the woods at two o'clock in the mornin'?"

"I don't know," I said, not wanting to bring up the secret family moonshine business. "But I still say Charlie has more of a motive."

"Well, pardon the hell out of me. You want me to tell you what I know, then you make fun of what I tell you. I ain't gonna tell you anymore."

"I'm sorry, Doc. I didn't mean to hurt your feelings. Please, tell me anything more you know. Please?"

"Well, the other reason I don't think it could be Charlie is that he's too stupid to pour piss out of a boot."

Unable to argue against such sound logic, I said goodbye and went over to the ball field. Just as I got there, Nelda rode up on her bike with the wind in her hair and my heart in her pocket.

"Hi, Lonnie. Are you going to practice with the team?"

"Yeah, I want to be ready to play in case there's another train derailment somewhere."

"Is your father here yet?" she asked with a look of concern.

"No. I don't expect him anytime soon. It's hard to make good time when you're leapfrogging from one bar to another."

"But your mom thinks he's changed. Maybe she's right."

"I doubt it seriously. Besides, I don't want to leave Moro. Or you."

"Oh, Lonnie, don't you think it would be great for you and your dad to learn to love each other. We're young; we've got time. I would miss you and write you every day, and I could see you when you come to visit your grandmother."

"He's got to prove himself to me. I ain't seen nothin' yet."

"Did Gideon say anything before you left?"

"Yeah. He said, 'Danger coming out of the smoke.'"

"I guess you don't have an idea about what he …"

"Not a clue. Just keep an eye out for a fire."

"Will do."

The loyal Skinner fans had obviously grown tired of having just cold chicken to eat at the games, so several people had set up barbecue pits along the left-field line and were grilling up hot dogs and hamburgers and various other meats. The aromas rivaled Grandma Birdie's kitchen. There was almost a medieval fair atmosphere, with the peasants feasting on roast piglet while waiting for the jousting to begin as screaming urchins gamboled in the grass.

Nelda sat in the bleachers, and I laced on the cleats that my tender feet were rapidly outgrowing and sprinted out to center. The field had been newly mowed, and I thought that there was a fortune to be made if I could just bottle that fresh-cut grass smell. I'd call it "Outfield Afternoon." It would probably be even more popular than the other fragrance I wanted to bottle, "Morning Mitt."

I ran down balls and caught a few flies, but my mind was swarming with thoughts of my father, and Nelda, and Gideon's "Danger comin' out of the smoke" warning that had contributed greatly to my already prickly sense of unease. Two-By let me bat, and I caught a low ball and one-hopped it over the left field fence. In a game situation, that would only have been a ground-rule double, but to me, I had just broken Ruth's record before The Mick could do it. I went back to the bleachers with chants of "Put in the Kid" ringing in my ears, which caused me to execute several internal somersaults.

Nelda and I went together to Willie's to get our usual root beers and to Wallace's for moon-pies. We sat as close as we dared to watch the game. Buddy had shown up and was pitching brilliantly. He had held the league-leading Cowboys to only one hit through seven innings, and he had driven in all five Skinner runs himself. I had to admit that he was a damn good athlete. The eighth inning had just started when I sensed someone walking up beside me.

"Hello, Lonnie."

I turned to find the towering form of my father. He looked bigger than ever.

"Your mother told me you would be here."

"I … uh … I wasn't sure when you would get here. I … uh … this is Nelda Graves."

"Hello, Nelda," he said with his best movie star smile. "I'm pleased to meet you. You are lovely."

"Thank you, Mr. Tobin. It's nice meeting you, too."

I saw immediately that, just like that, Nelda was now in my father's camp.

"May I talk with you privately for a few minutes, Lonnie?" he asked.

"Yeah, I guess so."

"Will you pardon us, Nelda? We'll only be a minute."

"That's fine," she said in a dreamy voice. "Will you be coming back?"

He promised a quick return, and we walked down to a spot behind the Skinner's bench out of earshot. Several of the fat, sweaty men in "Kiss the Cook" aprons waved a respectful greeting to my father with long-handled, two-pronged forks and then used them to turn the meat over the coals.

"So, how've you been, Lonnie?"

"Fine."

"I heard about you getting a triple in the game the other day."

"Lucky hit."

"And I heard about your little run-in at the church house. I was told that you got the best of the situation."

"Lucky punch."

"Nelda sure is cute."

"Yes, she is," I said. Then, I caught a whiff of the familiar, sour-sweet smell of alcohol. Anger rose up in my throat. "I thought you told mom that you quit drinking?"

"I did. Uh, I have … I had a couple of snorts with Cooper Logan earlier, that's all. And that's the first I've had in weeks. I just had 'em to help me talk to you. I was shaking a little."

"Why were you shaking? Were you afraid to talk to me? Are you saying you had to drink before you could talk to me?"

"No, no, I'm not saying that. I'm not drunk. I just took a couple swigs off his bottle."

"That don't sound like you've quit," I said. "Does mom know about the swigs? She believes that you really stopped."

"I have, Lonnie. I swear. I've finally beat it. I know because of how guilty I felt about taking a nip. That's why I only had a couple. The old me would have kept goin' all night."

"But you still had drinks. This will be the last straw with mom."

"No, son, your mother doesn't have to know. This is between you and me. I swear to you that I haven't had a drink since I came up here the first time looking for you and your mother. I just happened to run into Coop, and we talked and had a few swallows, and that was it. I won't do it again."

"How am I supposed to know that? You've been calling mama and swearing to her that you've quit for good, then you come up here and …"

"I know, I know," he broke in. "I have quit. It was a stupid thing to do, and it won't happen again. Lonnie, I'm gonna to come to the point. I want to apologize to you from the bottom of my heart. I know that I haven't been much of a husband for your mother or a father to you. But since you and your mother have been gone, I realize how much I love you both."

He stood there looking at me like he expected a response. I didn't know what to say. I knew that I had the situation under control. Just letting my mother know that he had been drinking with Cooper Logan would kill any talk of going back with him.

"A man I work with just lost a son," he said. "Him and his wife and boy went to visit the State Capitol building, and when they went to the top, his son just suddenly climbed up on the rail and jumped. The guy had a breakdown and ain't been to work since. The boy was only fifteen. They said he did it because he was unhappy. I thought of you."

How touching. I wondered if he thought that would move me. Behind us the cheers meant that something favorable had happened for the home team.

"This ain't a good place to talk," I said.

"I know your mother told you that I want y'all to come back home, but I just want you to know that I'm not going to try and force you to go. I took a week of vacation, and I was hoping we could just spend some time together. Go out to eat, maybe see a movie, and just talk. At the end of the week, if you don't want to go, I'll drive on back and leave you alone. Okay?"

"I don't know. I've heard this story before."

"I know, I know. But I mean it this time. I want to prove it to you. I'm not gonna force myself on you. Just give me a week. Like I said, if you don't wanna go back, you don't have to. How about it? I'm footing the bill, you ain't got nothing to lose."

"You can't buy me. Or mama."

"That's not what I'm trying to do, Lonnie. I just want to spend some time with you. I'm gonna stay with my brother Ransom while I'm here. I'll come pick you and your mother up whenever you want me to. And you and me can go off by ourselves and talk. How about it?"

I wanted to hug him and cut his throat at the same time. My emotions were being shredded into confetti. Of course, I desperately hoped that he was telling the truth, but I feared I was being set up for a free fall into the abyss. I wanted to go home with him, while wishing he would be killed in a car wreck.

Then, over his shoulder, I saw Gideon's words of warning spring to life. Coming through the billowing smoke of the barbecue pits, like a battleship through the fog, was Waylon Roark. He was walking rapidly toward us with a three-foot piece of wood in his hand.

I yelled for my father to watch out behind him. When he saw Waylon, he pushed me out of the way and was able to raise his left arm and partially deflect the first blow. He staggered backward toward the bag at third base, holding his arm in pain. Waylon charged and struck again. This time it connected with my father's forehead, and he hit the ground face first.

"How you like that, motherfucker!" Waylon screamed at my father as he stood over him. "How does it feel to git hit when you ain't lookin', huh? You chickenshit sonuvabitch. I'm gonna make you wish yore ass was never born!"

His rage was out of control, and he was oblivious to everything around him. He kicked my father in the side with a sickening thud, flipping him over on his back. He raised the hunk of lumber and brought it down again and again. I was in a state of shock as I watched the drama unfold. It had an unreal look and feel, like a scene in a movie.

I suddenly came to myself and ran to the bench and grabbed the first bat I came to, turned and ran back as I saw Waylon preparing to strike again. I focused on the back of his head and swung for the fence. I caught him on the sweet spot and heard his skull crack like a rifle shot. He dropped like a three-hundred-fifty-pound sack of feed right on my father. I saw the mush that used to be the back of Waylon's head, and everything began spinning like a runaway carousel.

I was aware of movement around me but had no earthly idea of what was happening. I saw a flash of faces with mouths that were speaking to me in silent words, and colors that flew by and left traces in their wake. And then I found myself alone in the woods, where everything was calm and quiet and the dampness of the creek breeze caressed my face. I was debating the question of what is real and what is an illusion and had decided that everything was fantasy when I heard Nelda calling my name from far, far away. Like the distant hoot of an owl in the night.

"Lonnie! Lonnie! Come on! We gotta get your father to a hospital!

My dad's taking him in our car. I'm coming, too," she yelled in my ear as she shook me back to reality.

I looked at the bat in my hand and saw the long, greasy hairs plastered to the bloody barrel and dropped it on the ground. Charlie Banks and Cooper Logan and several other men were placing my father into the back of Reverend Graves' car. A few feet up the road the Roark brothers were grunting under the weight as they wrestled Waylon's body into what was left of the rusted-out bed of their truck. They were all covered in blood.

I pushed everybody out of the way and crawled into the backseat and cradled my father's unconscious head in my lap. There was a horrible open gash on his forehead just at the hairline and one on the top of his head, both of which were pumping out blood in gobs and soaking my new jeans. From somewhere, I was handed an armload of rags and towels and ripped up shirts and told to keep pressure on the wounds at all times. Pastor Graves took off slinging gravel with Nelda leaning over the front seat offering encouragement.

The trip to the hospital was a blur. Staring at my father's unconscious face while holding the compresses tight to the wounds, I realized that I didn't want him to die. Not in a car crash, or a bullet in the head, or at the hands of Waylon Roark. Way down deep in my heart, in a spot so far below the cockles that you have to go there to mine for cockles, there was a trapped pocket of air that still had a few particles of love for him still floating around. Had he really meant to quit drinking? Did he really love me? Or was it just another load of Harley Tobin's well-intentioned bullshit, designed to make himself feel better and sucker us in? Now, I might never know.

Surely this was what I had been dreading. That nagging something that had been buzzing around in my head like a hyperactive bumblebee. I was racked with guilt that I had not been able to alert my father quicker. If he would have had more time, he could have defended himself. Or had the whiskey he drank with Coop been enough to slow his reflexes? I noticed that I was crying as we arrived at the hospital emergency entrance.

Medical personnel scrambled to remove my father from the

backseat and put him on a stretcher. We followed them into admissions, and then they wheeled him through a set of double doors with a sign that said "Authorized Personnel Only." My mother arrived minutes later and answered all the medical questions about him.

As we were standing at the nurse's desk, I noticed for the first time that Nelda was holding my hand, right in front of the Reverend. She had blood on her shirt. Suddenly, the doors burst open, and medics came in with Waylon Roark on a stretcher. His head was wrapped in towels, and a nurse was running alongside holding an oxygen mask over his face. They disappeared behind the same doors that they had taken my father through. The remaining Roark brothers came in looking like they had just butchered a hog. They stopped cold when they saw us then disemboweled me with their eyes.

We moved into the waiting room. A nurse took me into the doctors' locker room, and I showered, changed into the scrubs that she had furnished, and threw my blood-soaked clothes in the trash. I moved without thinking. I went back to the waiting room to find the sheriff of Fordyce, whose jurisdiction included Moro, talking with my mother.

"Lonnie, I'm Sheriff Porter. I just need to ask you a few routine questions. I have a truckload of witnesses that say you were just protecting your father. That was a brave thing you did, young man."

"Am I in any kind of trouble?"

"No, not at all. If you hadn't stopped him, Waylon would have more than likely killed your father."

"How *is* my father?"

"I don't know, son."

"What about Waylon?"

"I'm not sure … but I don't think he's gonna make it. If he does, we'll put him in jail."

I couldn't even react to the news that I might have killed a man.

"I have the Roark family secluded in a back room. I'll keep one of my deputies here at all times for your safety."

He proceeded to ask me what I remembered about the events, and I told him everything I could recall. He said my account matched that of the other witnesses, and he would have no further questions. He left a burly, black officer standing with his arms crossed by the door of the waiting room.

"How are you holding up?" Nelda asked after we sat down.

"Okay, I guess. I feel kinda empty."

"You've been through a lot. Your father was almost killed."

"We don't know yet if he's gonna make it. Did you see his head?"

"Yes, but the doctors are working on him. I just know in my heart he'll be all right."

"Do you know in your heart if Waylon will be all right?"

"Oh, Lonnie. I wish I did. I'm sure praying that he will be. Even if he is a rotten human being."

"He's rotten all right," I said as hatred suddenly boiled up inside me. "A no good rotten piece of shit. He couldn't face my father like a man. He knew he would get his gigantic, fat ass kicked!"

"Calm down, Lonnie. We'll let the police handle it. When he heals up, they'll arrest him and put him in jail for attempted murder."

"*If* he heals up."

She leaned over and rubbed her hand up and down my back. "What did you and your father talk about before … the attack?"

"He was … making promises. Saying he missed us. That he was gonna quit drinking. Same thing he's said before."

"You didn't believe him?"

"I smelled booze on him. He had been drinking before he came to the ball field."

"Oh, Lonnie, no. Are you sure?"

"He admitted it. But he swore up and down that he hadn't had a drop for weeks."

"And you think he's lying?"

"I don't know. I want to think he's telling the truth, but I've been burned too many times. I believe he wants to quit but so far hasn't had the willpower to go for more than a few days or months at a time. And it's always worse when he's drawn back."

"Are you going to tell your mother that you smelled alcohol on him?"

"No. She's pretty upset right now, and I know it would break her heart if she knew. She still loves my father, that's obvious, and she really wants to go back with him."

"What about you? Do you want to go back?"

I leaned back, stretched out my legs, and crossed my ankles.

"There may not be anything to go back to. Anyway, I have no idea what I want right now. I'm just tired."

The afternoon wore on, and Nelda and I both passed out from nervous exhaustion in the hard plastic chairs. I was awakened by the doctor's voice.

"Mrs. Tobin?"

I jumped up and rubbed my eyes.

"Yes, sir. I'm Mrs. Tobin, and this is my son, Lonnie. How is he, doctor?"

"He caught a couple of wicked blows to the head that caused a concussion and took eighteen stitches to close up, and he lost a good bit of blood. He has a broken arm and collarbone, two cracked ribs, and some pretty nasty bruises. He hasn't regained consciousness yet, but I have no reason to think he won't. He took quite a beating, but he's strong and will heal quickly. I want to keep him for a few days to make sure there are no internal injuries. I'll have someone call you as soon as he's awake."

"Thank you, doctor. How's the other man? Mr. Roark?" my mother asked.

"I'm not certain. Dr. Hubbell is tending to him. He's in a deep coma. There's substantial brain swelling. The next twenty-four hours will be critical."

My mother had picked up my father's truck on the way to the hospital, and Nelda rode back to Moro between my mother and me. Even with her soft hand in mine, I felt drained of all emotion.

"Lonnie, are you all right, baby?" my mother asked.

"Yeah," I answered woodenly. "I'm okay."

"Did you and your father get a chance to talk before all this mess happened?"

"Yes. For a few minutes." I knew what she wanted to hear. "I think you're right, mama. I think he might have changed." Nelda smiled and slid a little closer to me.

"I'm awful glad to hear you say that, son."

When we got home, grandma cooked up what she called "breakfast for supper"—scrambled eggs, sausages, and pan-fried toast. I found that I was hungry with the first bite and ended up licking the plate. There were no leftovers, so I ignored Sawbuck's cold, accusing stares and gave him the last can of dog food. Doc Parker called to see how my father was and to tell me that Buddy Kilgore had hit a home run with the same bat I had used on Waylon. I found no comfort in that. Then, I went to bed and fell into a fitful sleep.

Chapter Twenty

The Real Gideon

The next morning the hospital called to let us know that my father had regained consciousness and that we could see him. When we got there, my mother said she wanted to give my father and me some time alone, so I went on ahead while she and Nelda parked the car. I walked into his antiseptic-smelling room and found him propped up on pillows, sipping orange juice from a straw stuck in a carton. His head was bandaged, left eye a swollen purple mass, left arm in a cast, and there was an IV drip feeding the needle taped to his massive arm. He seemed too large for the little bed.

"Hello, Lonnie," he said as tears sprang to his eyes. "Come here."

I walked over to the bed, and he took my hand and looked in my eyes.

"You saved my life, son. I would be dead right now if it weren't for you. I don't know what to say. I owe you my very life. I'm so proud of you; I don't know *what* to do. I tell you what, coming close to death makes you take stock. I have been laying here trying to figure out how I got to be such an ass. I was never there for you, Lonnie. Lord God, I'm sorry."

He pulled me to his chest, and we hugged as best we could.

"Did you tell your mother about me drinking with Coop?"

"No."

"Why not?"

"Because it would hurt her. She's had enough crap in her life. And she loves you."

"I love her, too. And I love you, too, son. I really do. My daddy always treated me like crap, and I swore I would never do that to my son. But when the time come, I didn't know how to be a father. I ended up being *worse* than my daddy."

Seeing him lying there bandaged and bruised made me realize, for the first time in my life, that he was indeed a mortal man. He wasn't invincible after all.

"Do you remember that time I quit drinking, Lonnie?"

"Yes."

"We had some good times then, didn't we?"

"Yeah."

"I've thought of those times a lot. You wouldn't believe how many times I've said to myself, 'Damn it, I'm gonna take Lonnie fishing this weekend.' Then, I'd stop at Boo's Bar, and before I knew it, the weekend was gone. The whole damn weekend. And the real sad thing is, I didn't ever remember what I did."

He winced in pain as he adjusted his position in the tiny bed.

"I see what a waste my life has been," he said. "I don't want to die with my son hating me. I haven't had a drop to drink in weeks before yesterday, and I found out that I like to be sober. I can't promise you I won't ever take a drink again. I've made and broken that one before. But I *can* promise you that I have never wanted to quit more than I do right now, and I will try harder than I've ever tried before. I know it's a lot to ask, but will you please forgive me, Lonnie? Give me a chance to prove it to you?"

I knew I was seeing him the way I *wanted* him to be, the way my mother wanted him to be. But something in his eyes and the way he was squeezing the juice told the recently mined cockles of my heart that he might really mean what he said. Even though it remained to be seen if he would follow through. But then, life is a gamble.

"Okay, dad."

He broke down and wept. I had never seen him cry. I joined in. After a few minutes, we were able to re-gather our manliness and straighten up.

"Thank you, son. I promise you'll never regret it. I've been looking at a house over in Mimosa Park. It's real nice. Got a big backyard for Sawbuck."

"The first time I smell alcohol on you, or hear a slurred word, it's all over. Mom and me will leave, and you'll never see us again. That's the bottom line."

"Agreed."

My mother and Nelda came in, and we spent the morning visiting with him. Then, Nelda and I went to eat what passed for lunch in the hospital cafeteria. I found it hard to put food in my mouth knowing that a man I had clubbed may be dying just a few feet away. I could still feel the bat in my hands and the way it felt when I connected with Waylon's head. It wasn't like hitting a baseball; it had a sick give to it, like whacking a cantaloupe. The thought that I may have killed him caused my guts to constrict.

"Are you okay, Lonnie?" Nelda asked.

"No, I'm not. I feel like crap."

"None of this is your fault. You came to your father's defense."

"I know, but that doesn't change the fact that if Waylon dies, I'll have to live with that for the rest of my life. I see his busted head every time I close my eyes. I hear that awful sound …" I was unable to continue as my stomach churned, and I pushed my plate away.

"Try not to think about it, Lonnie. It's all over. You did the right thing. You stopped a murder. And if Waylon dies, it's his own fault."

"Do you think this was meant to be? That maybe the reason I'm here was to save my father's life? That I was destined to bust Waylon's head?"

"Oh, I don't know, Lonnie. I just know you did the right thing. Come on, let's go back to the room."

The police officer from last night was nowhere in sight. I guess that the promise of having him here "at all times" meant just until the donuts were done. I was concerned about running into the Roark brothers in the hallway as we went back to the room, but we made it without incident. Just after we arrived, a nurse came in with some pain medication for my father.

"I don't want no drugs," he said. "I want to be clearheaded. I can handle the pain. Just a couple of aspirin will do me."

"Well, I'll leave the pills on your table, just in case."

"Do you know how Waylon Roark is doing?"

"I just heard that they think he might pull through. He's still critical, but the signs look good."

"Thank God," my mother said.

"Yeah, it was touch and go there for a while," the nurse said. "Whatever hit him in the head sure did a number on him."

Everyone but the nurse looked at me. I didn't care. The fact that he was going to live was all I cared about at the moment. I was weak from relief and felt like I had received a last minute pardon from the governor.

We spent the next couple of days shuttling back and forth to the hospital as my father, and Waylon, slowly improved. Nelda went with us each time, sitting close to me and making me forget that I would have to leave soon. We pledged ourselves to be faithful and to write at least one letter every day. And we swore that we would take turns calling each other on Saturday nights. We were both as sincere as could be, but I think we somehow knew that our affair would cool and wane with the separation of time and space. Life didn't always work out the way you wanted it to. But we would always have the Spates' Creek Bridge. Here's looking at you, kid.

~

The day before my father was to be released, I woke up with that familiar sense of unfinished business. I got out of bed, dressed, and went into the kitchen.

"The ol' fool ain't been behind the wheel of a car in a hundred years," Grandma Birdie was saying, visibly upset.

"What's going on?" I asked.

"Gideon drove off in the car sometime early this mornin', and just got back a little while ago. He won't say where he went," my mother said.

"Crazy ol' man will go out and get hisself killed," grandma ranted, "drivin' off the Whitewater Bridge or somethin'. I don't need this kind of worry. It might be time to see about puttin' him in a home somewhere. It's plain as your nose that he's loony as a bedbug."

I wondered if there was such a thing as a sane bedbug. I also wondered where Gideon could have gone. I couldn't picture him behind the wheel of a car. Maybe one of his spirits chauffeured him around.

"Well, just make sure you hide the keys from now on," my mother said. "Lonnie, are you and Nelda goin' to the hospital with me?"

"No, not this time. Nelda and her folks are going to visit relatives this afternoon, and we want to spend the morning together and then have lunch at her house."

"Well, me and your grandma are goin'. Just be careful, and we'll see you this evenin'."

Gideon was sitting on the porch as my mother left, and I headed to Nelda's. I felt anxious, and jumpy, and weary of feeling that way. I thought that the attack on my father would be the end of all that. It troubled me as Nelda and I rode our bikes over to the old depot foundation. We sat together in the sunshine on the cracked and broken slab of cement that the boots of Wyatt Earp had once walked on.

"Have you decided what you're gonna do?" she asked.

"Yeah, we're going back. For my mom's sake."

"I'm gonna miss you, Lonnie."

"Oh, you don't know how I'll miss you. I can't put it in words."

"We'll write to each other, won't we?" she asked.

"Sure we will."

"And we'll be true to each other?"

"As long as there's a perfect arrowhead at the bottom of Spates' Creek."

"I guess my intuition about you leaving soon was right," she said.

"Yeah, looks that way. Got any other intuitions?"

She was quiet for a moment. "Well, I know we were brought together for a reason, and I don't think we know what that reason is yet."

"What do you mean?"

"I don't know. I can't explain it. It's just a feeling that even though you're leaving, it's not over yet."

We talked for a while longer and went back to the parsonage for lunch. After we ate our tuna fish sandwiches and potato chips, they left for El Dorado, and I headed back to grandma's. I went inside and pulled out the watch to wind it and noticed it was one o'clock. I went back out on the porch and sat on the bottom step with my feet on the ground.

I was being ripped apart inside, wanting to reconcile with my father, yet loath to leave the fair damsel Nelda. And that feeling of something undone was drilling into the back of my head. Sawbuck was seated on the ground between my legs, and I was rubbing and scratching his head and ears. He looked at me through hooded eyes that said, "You'll have to stop this by supper time."

"Time is short. Follow the tracks," Gideon said from behind me.

I leaped up and whipped around. He was sitting in his usual pose, staring at nothing. I couldn't take it anymore. I was suddenly pissed off.

"What? What in the hell are you talking about, Gideon? I'm sick and tired of this bullshit. If you got something to say to me, then say it, damn it!"

His dull green eyes slowly cleared, like still water as the mud settles to the bottom.

"The time has come to follow the tracks," he said as he looked straight at me.

"What tracks? The footprints at Whitewater Bridge?"

"Yes, but the time is short."

"What do you mean time is short? What will I find?"

"Follow the tracks. Go right now."

And then, he was gone; his eyes clouded again like someone had stirred up the sediment with a stick. I felt like I had just met the real Gideon, even if it was only for a moment. I stood there in the yard and realized that this was the unfinished business that I needed to attend to. I jumped on my bike and pumped hard for Whitewater Bridge. Chills of anticipation were drag racing up and down my spinal column as I rode.

Where will those footprints lead? Would I finally have some answers? Or was this a wild poltergoose chase?

~

When I got to the bridge, I stashed the bike and slipped and slid, mostly on my behind, down to the creek. I knew it went out behind Wallace and Velma's to the right and to points unknown to the left. I headed left. I hadn't gone five steps when I saw a gum wrapper on the ground. Then, multiple footprints, all similar to the ones behind the Summers' house. With Sawbuck riding point, I followed them along the edge of the water as it turned to the right, and then another bend back to the left. My heartbeat was drowning out the song of the sparrow and the happy little barks of the chipmunks. I followed the twists and turns of the creek for about a quarter of a mile when Sawbuck suddenly ran up the bank to my left and out of sight.

Once I came to the spot where he went up, I could see that this was a fairly well used trail. All the footprints went up here. I couldn't see any beyond that point. I figured that this must be the place, so I made my way up the slight incline. When I came up on level ground, I could see the back of an outhouse, but from this angle, I had no idea where I was. Then, the main house came into view. Even from the rear, I recognized the place. I had been here before. The back screen door opened, and a figure stepped out on the tiny porch.

Chapter Twenty-One

The Coin Flip

"Hello, Scorpion."

It was Cooper Logan. He had a look on his face that made me think that he had been expecting me.

"I been waitin' on you. Come on in." He turned and went back inside. I stood staring at a washtub hanging on a nail beside the door with a rusted-out hole in the bottom big enough to throw a cat through. I wondered why he was keeping it. I also wondered what the hell was going on.

"I ain't gonna hurt you none," he said, sticking his head back out. "I got lots to tell you. Come on in the house."

I had no reason to be frightened of Coop, and he couldn't know why I was there, could he? I had a sudden desire to be somewhere else.

"Please, come in," he called from inside. "I been waiting on you all day. I got some things to tell you that you need to know, Lonnie."

That was the first time he had ever called me Lonnie. It caused a small wave of the Heebie J. Creeps. I drew in a deep breath and took a step. I somehow knew that through that door lay the answers I had been seeking, but at that moment, I didn't know if I wanted to find them. I fought the fear, opened the screen door, and eased into the tiny room that served as both kitchen and living area. Cooper was standing by a paint-splattered little table at the other end of the room with a shot glass in one hand and a fifth of whiskey in the other.

"Have a seat, son. Make yourself comfortable," he said as he poured and downed a shot.

I sat on a stool with a cracked, baby-shit yellow plastic seat near the back door. No sense taking any chances. Again, he threw back a shot. I looked at the stuffed carcass that had once been his pet raccoon, Rastus, sitting on the only shelf in the room. He looked worse than the last time I saw him, if that was possible.

"Sure is a hot one, ain't it?" he asked, not expecting an answer. I didn't answer. He took another shot. I was concerned that he would get plastered before he could tell me anything.

"Lord a'mighty, Scorpion. I don't rightly know where to start. I just …" his voice trailed off as he filled and killed another shot glass.

"Why don't you start by telling me what you mean by the statement that you were waiting for me?"

He put the cap on the whiskey bottle, placed it on the table in front of him, and sat down in a wobbly, metal chair. He stared at the floor, but his eyes were seeing something else.

"Gideon come over here early this morning," he began.

So, that's where he went. But why here?

"Woke me up. I don't never get up that early no more. Ain't really nothin' much to get up for. It kinda scared me to see Gideon at my front door like that. I cain't remember the last time he come out here. And I swear to you, Scorpion … he was just like the old Gideon. It was like all the years and all the troubles had fell off of him, and he was clearheaded and talkin' like he did when we was both young and fulla piss and vinegar."

A look of bewilderment fluttered in his eyes, like he had just witnessed something that defied the laws of nature. He fortified himself with another healthy shot.

"It's an awful thing to get old, Scorpion. A helluva thing. Anyways, Gideon told me you was comin' today. He weren't sure what time, but that whenever you got here, he said for me to be damn sure that I tell you everything. All of it."

"I don't understand," I said. "Why would Gideon come over here to get *you* to tell *me* something? Why couldn't he just tell me himself?"

"Cause you need to hear it from me."

"What are you talking about, Coop? You're not making sense."

"I'm the only one who knows the whole story. Things are not how you're seein' it right now."

I didn't know how I was seeing things at the moment. I decided to be straightforward.

"Coop, are you the Booger?"

He poured himself another shot.

"Looks like you caught me, Scorpion. Ain't no use denyin' it. But I'll get to that in a minute. Gideon also said to tell you what I know about your grandpaw, Tom Spates. I know you been askin' folks about him."

At this point, he leaped up and began pacing the worn wooden floor. Again, he grabbed the whiskey and took a slug straight from the bottle. He was sweating from more than just the late afternoon heat.

"Settle down, Coop. It's all right," I said, trying to sound reassuring while covering the fact that I wasn't sure of anything. "What can you tell me about him?"

"Well … I guess there ain't no other way to tell you but to tell you. Wait right here. I'll be right back."

He turned on his heel and went into the bedroom. I was getting highly agitated with the delays, yet for some reason was dreading what he had been ordered to reveal to me. I glanced at the back door and for a split second considered flying out of there like a half-drowned cat out of a well. He was back in a moment with what looked like a postcard-size piece of paper. He reached for the whiskey and then seemed to think better of it.

"Let's see," he said with the sigh of a man about to bare his soul. "Gideon said to show you this, so you would believe that what I'm gonna tell you is the God's honest truth."

He handed me the piece of paper he had retrieved, which turned out to be an old photograph of three men standing in front of the depot. I studied the picture for a minute. It had obviously been taken during Rocky Branch's glory days.

I was about to ask the identity of the men when I suddenly recognized the man in the middle. It was the man who gave me directions at Whitewater Creek when I was lost in the woods, the one who directed me out to the bridge and then seemed to vanish. I was sure of it. He was dressed in the same stiff khakis in the picture as he was that day.

"That's a pitcher of me and Gideon and your grandpaw. That's Tom Spates in the middle. That was took a week before the train blew up."

I felt disembodied. Nothing could have prepared me for this.

"I … I don't understand. I saw this man in the woods the other day. How can this be? He can't be alive."

"No, Scorpion," he said, soberly shaking his head as he took the picture back and sat down. "He ain't alive like you and me, but he's sure alive in another kinda way. Gideon said he talked to him."

"Talked to him?"

"I know that sounds crazy, but Gideon was his old self again. He was so sure that he spoke with Tom that I believe him. And Tom told him that he wants for you to know what happened."

I didn't know whether to "shit or go blind," as Grandma Birdie would say. I wanted to ask for a splash from Coop's bottle myself, if for no other reason than to drown the imps who were at that moment poking me in the nerve center with white-hot knitting needles. I felt as if the little house we were sitting in had been ripped from the earth and flung into the air, and at any moment, we would come crashing down on the wicked witch that was behind all this.

"See, me and your grandpaw and Gideon Woods growed up together. I reckon you could say we was best friends. We hunted every inch of the woods and fished every creek and waterhole in these parts."

He paused in the narrative to fish out a cigarette from a half empty pack in his pocket. He flipped open the top of a battered lighter, sparked a flame, lit the tip, snapped it shut, and blew out a cloud of smoke. His hands trembled slightly, and his eyes now had the look of a condemned man facing his fate.

"We went to school together and even got jobs with Rock Island at the same time. Boy, we thought we was somethin' else. We had money in our pockets and plenty of sweet, young things to spend it on. We was out cattin' around and gettin' in trouble 'bout ever' Saturday night. I reckon you could say that Tom was the ringleader. He was smart as a whip and funny as hell. Lord a'mighty, he could make us laugh. And talk, man he was a smooth talker. He was the one who could just walk right up to a girl and charm her britches plum off. It was a pure dee joy to behold."

A smile twisted his lips as he relived those footloose Arkansas nights of his youth. The memories seemed to relax him. Or the whiskey was finally kicking in.

"Then, the war come along," he said as his countenance darkened. "The Great War we called it 'cause how the hell was we to know there'd be more comin'. That was s'posed to be the war to end *all* wars. Weren't a damn thing *great* about it, either. Anyway, Tom and Gideon both joined the army right off after the United States got in the fight. They took Tom even though he had a finger missin', but they wouldn't take me 'cause I'm near deaf in my right ear from my daddy slappin' me upside my head when I was a young'un."

He reached up and gently tugged his ear.

"Gideon ended up spendin' his whole tour of duty in the States, but Tom was shipped overseas. He spent a year fightin' in the trenches over in France somewhere. He never would talk about it much. Almost snapped my head off one time when I asked him whether he ever got trench foot. He come on back to work on the railroad when he got home, but there was somethin' different about him. But hell, livin' through that kinda thing would change anybody, you know. So, I didn't pay it much mind."

He sat smoking for a few minutes, as if contemplating how to proceed. I could hear the wind-up alarm clock ticking away the seconds. Outside the grime-smeared window, the day was rapidly coming to a close.

"Then, Tom married your grandmaw Birdie, and 'fore long, your mama was born. Me and Gideon never got married, and we quit hangin' around with Tom as much. We mostly just saw him at work. He didn't joke as much as he used to and had a kinda whupped-dog look all the time, so one day I asked him if somethin' was wrong. He just said, 'Naw.' Then, I asked him if he was happy, and he said somethin' that I found awful strange, he said, 'I'm as happy as I got a right to be.' At the time, I didn't know what he was talkin' about. And I'm tellin' you, Scorpion, I wisht I had never found out."

He poured another shot.

"Please, don't get drunk, Coop," I pleaded. "You still have a lot to explain."

"Oh, don't worry 'bout that!" he boomed, holding up his hand like a cop stopping traffic. "I'm feelin' better'n I've felt in years. I been bearin' this cross for too long and getting rid of it is a pure *relief*. Like takin' that first piss in the mornin' then goin' back to bed and makin' love to your woman. 'Course you wouldn't know nothin' about that would ya, Scorpion."

He forced a weak, little laugh. I saw nothing funny. I didn't give a crap if he was getting his rocks off while relating the tale; I just wanted him to get on with it.

"Some of the things I'm gonna tell you will be awful hard to swaller, but you gotta understand that your s'posed to know everything."

"Look," I said, feeling a bit frustrated, "if I didn't *choke* when you told me my dead grandfather had been talking to Gideon, then I think I can *swaller* just about anything."

The tears that sprang to his gold-flaked, gray eyes gave him the look of a sad, old wolf. His long, white hair was going in every direction, which gave him the look of a sad, old wolf that had just gotten out of bed.

"I loved Tom Spates like a brother. Hell, I was closer to him than my real brothers. And Gideon, too. We was like the three musket-teers. I know'd all a Tom's ways, and I still loved him. I know'd he liked his likker, but shit fire, we all did. And I know'd he liked his women, and so did we, but we didn't get as many women as Tom did. But after he married Birdie, he kinda settled down. He didn't run around like he used to. And without him, me and Gideon was havin' a helluva rough time in the female department 'cause we didn't have Tom's leftovers."

The portrait that he was painting of my grandfather appeared to be flawed, but I wanted to see it complete, genital warts and all.

"Here comes the hard part," he said while pouring yet another shot. He threw it down his throat and continued.

"On the very night that Tom was killed, me and Gideon had just got back from workin' twelve hours on the tracks up near Fordyce. Gideon went on to his mama's house, and since I was off the next day, I bought a jug of moonshine from your Uncle Willie. I was walkin' up the road over by where Suzy's ol' diner used to be, and I run into Tom on his way to supper. He seemed all jumpy-like, so I offered him a pull on the jug a shine, just to help him settle his nerves. Well, one pull led to a nuthern, and then a nuthern. 'Fore long, Tom said, 'Let's walk into the woods a piece, so nobody can see us havin' a drink.' Tom started hittin' the jug pretty hard, and I told him to take it easy 'cause he had to go back to work. Then, he said, 'Aw hell, Coop, I could drink that jug dry and then jump on old 1550 and highball it to hell and back without blinkin' an eye' … Lord, this is hard for me, Scorpion."

"Go on, Coop," I encouraged. "Remember, you're supposed to tell me everything."

"Well … it weren't long 'til Tom was pretty looped and started in tellin' me stuff I didn't need to know about. Said he wanted me to know why he had changed so much. And if you'll allow me to take another small taste of Mr. Daniels here, I'll tell you what he told me that night."

"Sure, go ahead," I said. What could I say, "Absolutely not! One more drop, sir, and I will stomp out of here in a huff!" Or in a minute and a huff, as Groucho once quipped. I no longer dreaded hearing what he had to say, instead I had a quiet sense that it was indeed my *right* to know the truth. It was meant to be.

"Tom told me that before the war, and long before he married your grandmaw, he had fell head-over-asshole in love. Pardon my language, but that's the way he put it. Problem was the girl he was in love with was engaged to another man, and her daddy hated Tom for some reason. But a little thing like that never stopped ol' Tom Spates. He got to seein' her on the sly, sneakin' around, meetin' her in the woods, and keepin' it a secret.

Hell, me and Gideon was his best friends, and we didn't know a thing about it. Then, he told me that right before he left for boot trainin', she had come to him cryin' and all tore up and told him she was gonna have his baby."

He paused and looked me in the eye for a moment, like he was trying to gauge the effect of this revelation. I could only sit stupefied.

"He said he told her that he loved her, and that this was the greatest thing that ever happened to him. Now, they could tell everybody about their love. They wouldn't have to slip around no more. But she wouldn't have none of it. She cried and carried on about how this would just shame her to death. But then she said that didn't much matter anyway 'cause her daddy would kill 'em both. Tom tried to talk some sense to her, told her he would take care of her and their baby, and if she loved him like he loved her, they could work it out. She said she loved him, too, but just couldn't let folks know her sin. She told him if he said anything to anybody, she would kill herself. He never told anybody before he left for the Army, and he wrote her a letter every day he was gone, but she never answered nary a one of 'em."

He lit another cigarette, still visibly angry with this woman.

"When Tom told me who she was, I was plum speechless. I tell you what, Scorpion, she was a pretty thing. Hell, she was probably the prettiest woman in the whole damn state. She was way yonder too good-lookin' for any of us hard-leg, farm boys, except for Tom. Tom always got any woman he went after."

He poured himself another drink, and I could see that the slight shaking had returned to his large, heavily veined hands. I knew it was wrong, but I was feeling a tweak of pride in my grandfather's alleged prowess.

"Once't he told me who the girl was, I remembered how she had left town right after Tom did. Her daddy said she was goin' to visit an aunt of hers up in St. Louis. She was gone quite a spell, and I remember when she come back home, but she didn't have no baby with her. In fact, she got married right after she got back, and her and her husband never had nary a child together."

It was getting late. I knew my mother would start to worry about me soon, but you couldn't have dragged me out of that little shack with a diesel locomotive.

"Then, when Tom first got back from his hitch in the army, before he ever dated Birdie, he said he went to see this woman. She wouldn't even hardly talk to him, he said. He asked her about the baby, and she slammed the door right in his face. He yelled at her and said he was gonna tell her husband all about it, and she opened the door and said, 'If you tell a soul, you'll never know what happened.' She said she would tell him everything when the time was right, but not if he breathed a word of it. Then, slammed the door in his face agin."

Sawbuck was sitting at the screen door casting covetous eyes on the remains of poor, old Rastus.

"Well, Tom just didn't know what to do. He just kinda slunk through life for a while. Then, he said somethin' happened in his head, and he kinda snapped. He got to thinkin' about his child; hell, he didn't know if it was a girl or boy and didn't give a damn which it was. He wondered where in the world it could be, and since it was just a few days before Christmas, he wondered what kind of Christmas his baby was gonna have. He said it was the thoughts of one day sittin' under a Christmas tree with his child, openin' presents, and drinkin' eggnog that got him through all them cold, muddy nights overseas, when he didn't know if he'd ever see Moro again. He made it back in one piece, but he said it felt like a big hole had been gouged out of his heart. That's when he started hatin' Christmas music. Said it reminded him of what he didn't have."

Just how many versions of "Silent Night" can one tolerate anyway?

"Then, Tom told me that on that very Christmas night when he got off work at midnight it was colder 'n hell, and he started in to drinkin'."

I suddenly knew where he was going with the story. My joints were jumping, and I felt short of breath.

"He said the drunker he got, the madder he got, and the sorrier he felt for hisself. She had stole his own flesh and blood from him, he said.

What kinda woman would do such a thing? She had no right, he said. He figgered her husband ought to know all about it, so he headed through the patch a woods to her house. When he got there, he said he just couldn't face her 'cause he was a'feared he might kill her. He tried to look in the windows, but he couldn't make out anything. Then, he said it felt like if he didn't do *somethin'* he would just bust to pieces. Before he knowed what was happenin', he was beatin' on the walls of that house with all his might."

Cooper stood at this point and paced the floor as if to stretch cramped muscles. He lifted the whiskey bottle and swallowed as the Adam's apple in his neck moved up and down. Deep inside me somewhere a plug had been pulled, and everything I thought was real was gurgling down the drain.

"I reckon you done figgered it out by now, Scorpion. It was Wallace and Velmer Summers' house. It was her that he had loved, and it was her that mistreated him so bad. It was her daddy, Elmer Thompson, that hated him. But then not everybody loved Tom the way I did. He said that he only did it that night 'cause he was drunker'n a wild Injun and never had any idears about doing it again. But when he saw how upset it made Velmer and the way everybody talked about it and called it the Booger and all and even getting wrote up in the paper, he just kep' at it. Even after he married your Grandmaw Birdie. He said he got plum hooked on it. And he said if I didn't tell anybody, he was gonna keep on doin' it."

He paused and rubbed his temples.

"Well, I didn't know what to say. I'd never in my dreams thought that Tom Spates was the Booger. I swore to him that I wouldn't say anything, and that he ort to come have somethin' to eat before he went back to work. I felt real guilty about lettin' him get so drunk. But he said naw; he was already late gettin' back, and he had to put the engine to bed. I walked with him 'til we could see the train. Then, we saw a man get out of the cab and run off. But we knew the man and didn't think much of it."

"Was it Richard Hannegan?" I asked.

"No, Scorpion. It weren't Hannegan."

"Well," I said after a long pause, "who was it?"

He drank another shot.

"It was ... your grandfather, James Callaway."

"Papa? You're saying that you saw *Papa* getting off the train that night? Are you absolutely positive about that?"

"It was him all right. Tom even said he wondered what that old bastard was doin'. They didn't like each other very much. So, he went back to the depot, and I went over to Suzy's to get a bite to eat. I had just set down at the table when Ross Newton come in lookin' for Tom. I weren't about to say nothin', but I didn't have a chance to anyways 'cause that's when we heard the explosion. It shook that building and broke the windows like a German bomb had been dropped right outside."

I could almost feel the concussion from the blast hit me in the chest as I sat there.

"Gideon come runnin' up from his mama's house which wasn't far away, and it was me 'n him that found Tom's body," he said as buckshot-sized tears rolled through the gray stubble on his cheeks. "Lord a'mighty, Scorpion, it was a turrible sight to see. I just broke down and cried like a baby. His head was taken clean off, and we couldn't find it. It was just turrible. I just knowed it was all my fault for lettin' him get drunk like I did. If I hadn't asked him to take a drink with me, this would never have happened."

I felt like an exposed nerve. "Was Papa there while they searched for the body?"

"I seen him and Hannegan later, after we found Tom."

"Why didn't you say anything about seeing Papa on the train?"

"'Cause I didn't want to tell anybody about me and Tom drinkin' while he was on duty. And I knew it would just kill Miss Birdie if she thought her own daddy might have somethin' to do with her husband's death. I just couldn't do it."

"Do you think Papa had something to do with the explosion?"

"I don't know what he could have done to rig it so's it would blow. I really don't think he did anything, but I guess it's possible."

He pulled a dirty handkerchief out of his hip pocket, blew his nose, and after a quick inspection of what had been expelled, crammed it back where he got it. Obviously, it was his crusty handkerchief I had found that day on the creek behind Wallace and Velma's.

"After the funeral, me and Gideon was talkin', and I told him everything that Tom had told me. He was just as surprised as I was. Well, me and Gideon had thought the world a Tom, and we both agreed that we had to do somethin' about the situation. We sure couldn't tell Miss Birdie or anybody about what he had told me, about him bein' the Booger an' all, or about him and Velmer. But when Tom died, Birdie already had your mama, and they needed takin' care of. *And*, we was afraid that if the Booger quit comin' around after Tom was killed, that folks might figger out that it was him by puttin' two and three together."

Obviously, Coop wasn't very familiar with math or clichés.

"So, we agreed to flip a coin. The winner would court Tom's widow, Miss Birdie, who was a right handsome woman her own self, after the proper time of mournin' had passed of course, and the loser would be the Booger, at least one time. I lost."

Everything around me had blurred as if I was looking through frosted glass.

"Tom was buried on Christmas Eve, and late that night, I slipped out to the Summers' place and commenced to beatin' on that house 'til my fists was sore. The next day I felt real good when I heard people talkin' 'bout the Booger comin' back. I knowed that nobody would ever suspect Tom now. But I kinda knew what Tom meant about getting hooked on it. It really got my blood up while I was doin' it. So, I thought that maybe, since it gave everybody pleasure to speculate on it, I ort to do it agin. So, I did. Many times."

He paused to drain the last of the booze.

"In the meantime," he said, starting to slur a little, "two years later by this time, Gideon had finally won over Miss Birdie, and they got hitched. Since I didn't have no wife nor children, I'd give Gideon a little money every time I seen him to help out. Then, one day, Gideon asked me if he could be the Booger one time. I said, hell, knock yourself out, and he did it. After that, we took turns whenever the notion struck us. We even got drunk one night and went together. That way we could work both sides of the house at the same time. We knowed that would really scare the stuffin' out of 'em. We still felt like Velmer deserved it for what she done to Tom."

"How did you keep from leaving tracks?" I asked. "The ground all around the house is real soft."

"We wrapped our feet in tater sacks, so we wouldn't leave no footprints. We knowed Wallace was too scared to come out of the house, but he did shoot through the front door one night that just missed me. After that, I always stood to the side of the door. And we always knowed when he was settin' a trap. Hell, sometimes I'd go in the store, and he would tell me about it *hisself.* We took turns doin' it right up 'til Gideon got kicked by that damn mule. Since then, I been doin' it by myself. I didn't think he even remembered anything about it. That is 'til he showed up this mornin'."

"Why do you keep it up, Coop? Nobody would ever link Tom Spates to the Booger after all this time. Nobody even much cares anymore."

"I don't know, Scorpion. I guess it kinda made me feel close to Tom. That somehow he 'preciated me doin' it for him. I know it don't make no sense. I reckon I'm as crazy as Gideon. Maybe crazier."

I became aware that my butt was numb from sitting on the hard stool. I stood up, and the room spun in slow motion. I braced myself with a hand on the wood-stove as I tried to absorb the fact that Papa may have killed my grandfather, who had an illegitimate child, was the original Booger, and might have even returned from the grave to tell me about it … and that with a simple toss of a coin, Cooper Logan could have been my step-grandfather.

"I'm sorry to have to tell you all this, Scorpion, but like I said, you was s'posed to know. I hope you won't tell nobody else, but that's all up to you now. I ain't never gonna do it again, that's for sure." He sighed heavily as the energy seemed to leave him. "I'd like to talk with you some more, but Gideon got me up awful early this mornin', and I'm pretty tired. And that whiskey is startin' to boot me in the seat of the britches, so I better get on to bed."

I nodded my head like an idiot. I turned and walked out the back door.

"I'll see ya later, Scorpion," he said as the screen door closed behind me.

"Yeah," was all I could manage. I stood in the overgrown backyard as the crickets and peeper frogs warmed up for their nightly concert. My whole world had changed in a matter of minutes. I knew I would never be the same. That's when I heard the back door close solidly and the bolt slide into place. Then, I heard the front door being closed and locked. The sound echoed in the dusky air and gave me a jab of concern.

I remembered the picture he showed me and decided to ask if I could borrow it. I wanted to study it to see if that was truly my grandfather I had seen in the woods that day. I saw the smoke curling from under the door at the same instant the smell reached my nostrils. No, no, no, I screamed inside my head. I ran over and started pounding on the back door.

"Coop! I ain't gonna tell anybody, Coop! Open the door! Come on, Coop! I swear I won't tell anybody, Coop! Cooper!"

Then, I heard the gunshot. I ran around to the window and tried to rub a clean spot so I could look inside. I pressed my face to the glass, but all I could see were yellow flames licking the walls and growing taller by the second. He must have doused everything with kerosene from the lamp. I backed up and stood there watching in a trance as the fire grew and stretched and became a living thing.

Chapter Twenty-Two

Your Grandfather's Daughter

Sawbuck was barking and jumping on me when I came to myself. The shack was totally engulfed by the fire and a column of dense, gray smoke was twisting up over the trees. I turned and ran blindly down to the creek and followed it, falling often as I scrambled as fast as I could back to the Fordyce road where I had hidden my bike. I jumped on it and pedaled 'til my lungs screamed. Over my shoulder, I could see the sky lit up from the blaze. Damn, damn, damn. What in the hell was going on? Why did Coop do that?

My fuses were about to blow, but I knew I had to get control of myself. Did anyone see me at Coop's? Would they know he killed himself? What the hell was he thinking? It wasn't fair, damn it. I still had questions I wanted to ask him, and now it was too late. I had no idea he would do something so drastic. I was trembling to the bone.

When I got to Grandma Birdie's, I propped the bike against the porch, caught my breath, dusted my clothes off, and went inside. It was after dark so Gideon had already gone to bed.

"Where have you been, Lonnie?" my mom asked when I walked in the kitchen. "Are you all right? You look like you seen a ghost."

"I'm okay, mama. Just lost track of the time. I really need a watch," I said, trying to look nonchalant.

"Well, I reckon we'll just have to get you a watch next time we go shoppin'," grandma said. "Now, set down and eat you some supper, Lonnie."

I sat and ate without appetite as I tried to keep the volcano inside me from erupting. Then, the distant sound of sirens reached us.

"Lord, I wonder what's happened?" grandma said as she rose and walked out on the back porch. My mother and I joined her.

"Looks like something's burning," she said as she pointed to the glow lighting up the horizon to the north. "I wonder whose place it is?"

She started naming everybody who lived in that direction, including Cooper Logan. I felt like an accomplice to murder. We went back inside after several minutes, and I somehow managed to finish eating. Then, I said I was really tired and wanted to go to bed. Though my mother looked at me funny, she just said goodnight and kissed my cheek.

I lay in bed for hours thinking about what had happened and what I had learned that day. I thought of Coop, probably burned beyond recognition at this point. I felt guilty, but I knew I hadn't done anything to bring this to pass. Had I? What could I have done? Maybe if I hadn't been so determined to find the truth, Coop would still be alive. Did Papa really do something that contributed to my grandfather's death, or was he so smashed he didn't know what he was doing when he sent the cold water into that hot, dry boiler? Was it sabotage, or just another victim claimed by a broken heart and John Barleycorn?

But had he *really* come back from the dead to make sure I knew the truth, to clear his conscience because he never really stopped loving Velma? Or had Coop and Gideon gotten together and cooked the whole story up to clear *their* consciences? That didn't explain the man at the creek who looked like my long dead grandfather in the picture Coop had shown me, but I had been so distraught and disoriented that day that I couldn't be sure of anything I saw.

I determined in my heart that the next day I would force Gideon to talk to me, one way or the other. Maybe I could hold his Prince Albert hostage. The last thing I remember before I fell asleep that night was the smell of the smoke that had clutched Coop's house in its dirty-gray fingers.

~

I was awakened the following morning by heavy steps and low male voices in the house. I dressed with a sense of unease. But then, after what I had been through, I was lucky to have any sense at all. I went into the living room and found two strange men in dark suits standing by the sofa. My mother was sitting with her arm draped around grandma's hunched shoulders. Neither one was crying, but both seemed on the verge.

Oh, God. Did someone see me at Coop's yesterday? Were they here to take me to jail for killing him and burning down his house? How could I prove that I had nothing to do with it? I remember thinking that I would rather have gone to prison for bashing in Waylon Roark's head than for something I didn't do. I felt like throwing up, and my mind was racing faster than Sawbuck after a rabbit.

"Lonnie," my mother said, "Gideon passed away last night."

A mixture of relief and shock roared through me like a locomotive. And the guilty feeling about being glad that these men weren't here for *me* was riding in the caboose.

"He died in his sleep. He didn't suffer none. It was real peaceful."

What was happening here? Coop *and* Gideon dead? I walked out through the screen door like a zombie, across the porch and down the steps, and stood in the yard with Sawbuck sitting quietly by my side as if he understood the seriousness of the situation. We watched as the men wrestled the gurney with Gideon's sheet-covered body down the steps and into the rear of the hearse. Obviously, there had been no need for an ambulance.

I was at a loss. Gideon had been a complete stranger to me all my life, but I had come to see him in a different light these last few weeks. He had guided me, either through his "spirits" or by conspiracy with Coop, to find some of the truth about my family. But now they had both bought the farm, and I was left with unanswered questions and no one to talk to.

I couldn't say anything to my mother or grandma. "Hey, y'all. Did you know that Papa might have been a murderer, and grandpa has a bastard child running around here somewhere … and, uh, oh yeah, he was the Booger, and I know all this because him and Gideon went over to Cooper Logan's house to discuss it with me just before they torched the place?"

I was feeling that if I wasn't insane already, I soon would be from the thought of never being able to close the book on this case. Then, I remembered that there was one remaining actor in this little drama. The one person left who could provide some answers. I jumped on my bike and headed for Wallace and Velma's place.

I rode by the store to make sure Wallace's car was there because I wanted to talk to Velma alone. There was no guarantee that she would be home, but I was willing to take the chance. I did not want to do this, but with Coop and Gideon both dead, I had no choice. I didn't even notice the bone-jarring bumps when crossing the railroad tracks because I was concentrating on what I would say to her. Though I had seen her many times, I had never spoken a word to her in my life.

I turned off the main gravel road onto the little dirt path of a driveway and pedaled up to the front of the house. In my mind's eye, I saw my grandfather and Coop and Gideon running around the yard in the moonlight, stopping every few feet to hoist a jug of moonshine to their lips. I shook my head like a wet dog in an attempt to clear those images and propped my bike against the fence. I went through the gate and up on the porch, soaked in sweat, and my mouth dry as a barren womb.

I saw the bullet hole in the door just like Coop had said. I was trembling all over and knocked weakly. There was no answer right away, and I gave earnest thought to getting the hell out of there. But summoning what courage I had left, I knocked again.

"Who is it?" a voice called from inside.

"Uh, it's Lonnie Tobin, Miss Velma."

"Just a minute."

A moment later, I heard her unlock the door. She swung it open and stood behind the screen.

"I'm sorry, who did you say you were?" she asked.

Though I was looking at her through the filter of the screen, I could see traces of the great beauty she had once possessed, hidden now behind the snowy hair and wrinkles. She had a haunted look in her blue eyes.

"I'm Lonnie Tobin, Miss Velma. Ruby Jo Spates' boy."

I thought I saw a flash of alarm.

"Yes, Lonnie. I know your family. What can I do for you?"

"I was wondering if I could come in and talk to you a minute."

"Well," she said with a look of having something important to do and being unable to remember what it was, "maybe we should talk right here. I have to be gettin' on up to the store soon."

"Could I have a glass of water, please?" I asked, trying to keep my parched tongue from cleaving to the roof of my mouth.

"I've got lots to do, Lonnie, so if you'll just tell me what it is that you came for, I would appreciate it," she snapped.

Her attitude surprised me and at the same time made me a little angry. I swallowed a few times trying to work up enough saliva to allow me to speak.

"Are you gonna say anything or not?" she said as I stood mute as a mime.

"Well," I finally choked out, "I wanted to ask you about a baby you had once." I was definitely no Sherlock Holmes.

She stared at me for what seemed like minutes as something dark, like the shadow of a large predatory bird, passed over her face.

"Get the hell off my property!" she yelled. Then, she slammed the door in my face. Just as she had done to my grandfather all those years ago. I stood there in the heat as huge, red wasps flew to and from a nest the size of a dinner plate at the corner of the porch. Then, the door opened. Velma stepped up to the screen; her face was a mask of pure evil.

"Boy, I don't know what you're tryin' to do, but I got a phone in here and if you don't leave right now, I'm gonna call the sheriff, and you can explain it to him."

"Miss Velma, I know all about it. I know my grandfather loved you, and you had a child by him. I'm not going to tell anybody about it; I just want to know what happened to it."

"Get out of here, you little son of a bitch!" she screamed. Not what I expected to hear from a Sunday school teacher. "Do you hear me? I said get the hell off my property! Now!"

She slammed the door so hard it shook the wasps loose from the nest. Well, I thought, my work here is done.

I pedaled my bike back down the road with emotions I didn't know I had riding on the handlebars. How stupid it was for me to expect that she would own up to everything. That after all those years of living a lie and worrying herself sick that somebody might find out, she would suddenly open up to some little piss-ant that just showed up at her door one day and said, "Duh, tell me about the baby you had once." Even Dr. Watson would have viewed me with disdain.

When I got to grandma's, the comforters had already started arriving, bearing the meatloaf and Bundt cakes. The yard looked like a used car lot.

"Where've you been, Lonnie?" my mother asked. "I was getting worried."

"Just out riding my bike, mama. I had to get away from here for a while."

"I know. I wish I could get away myself, but I gotta help mama."

Grandma Birdie seemed to be taking it well. I still didn't know if she ever had any feelings for Gideon or not.

"Lonnie, I wanted to let you know that Cooper Logan was burned to death last night. His house caught fire somehow, and he couldn't get out. I'm sorry to have to tell you. I know you liked him."

I tried to look surprised. "Do they know how the fire started?"

"No, everything was burned so bad ... oh, Lonnie ... they only found some of Cooper's bones," she said as a chill punched me in the gut.

"It's just so sad," she continued. "I remember him comin' around a lot when I was growing up. I knew him and my daddy had been friends. I especially remember one time, after I got married and you was just a baby, Coop came by and was holding you in his arms, and you reached up and grabbed on to his long hair and snatched a handful right out of his scalp. He yelled and said that it hurt like a scorpion sting."

"So, that's why he called me Scorpion."

"Yeah, I guess so. He always seemed to be partial to you. It's strange how him and Gideon died at almost the same time."

Nothing was strange to me anymore.

"Since this house is so small," she said, "they're gonna wake the body at Big Mama's."

Where else, I thought. It hasn't had any dead people in it for some time now.

"They're gonna bury Gideon and Coop at the same time, day after tomorrow."

They sure wouldn't be waking Coop anywhere. Maybe they ought to spread his ashes around Big Mama's house. It couldn't make what had happened any creepier to me.

"Your father will be out of the hospital in time for the funeral. Are you sure you're all right, Lonnie? You look a little flushed."

"Yeah, I'm fine, mama. Just shook up about Gideon, I guess."

"Well, it was a shock. But it ain't like he was your real grandfather. I reckon we can be thankful for that."

"I guess so, mama."

I spent the rest of that day in a fog. I ate without tasting my food, and I don't remember if I even went to the bathroom. I wanted to call Nelda and tell her everything, but I just couldn't do it. It was all too unbelievable.

That evening we went to Big Mama's where I met Gideon's relatives, who had quit visiting him while he was alive after he no longer acknowledged their presence. The funeral home had removed the bed, where Nelda and I had frolicked, along with the rest of the furniture from the parlor and placed the coffin by the bay windows. What better place was there? That didn't bother me this time though because the only way I would ever lay my head down in this room again would be on the silk pillow of my own casket.

They had Gideon decked out in a dark blue suit with a white shirt and a bright red tie. He could have been an insurance salesman. I sat in a chair while people around me were commenting on how good he looked. I wanted to scream, "How good could he look! He's dead, damn it!"

I didn't stay long and walked back to grandma's in the dark by myself. Maybe I was growing up and losing some of those childhood fears. But then, I *had* to get rid of them to make room for the grown-up fears that were elbowing their way in. I went to bed fully aware that a man had died in the next room. The attraction this town had held for me was dimming by the day.

I was physically exhausted, but even the hypnotic squeak of the window fan couldn't help me drift off to sleep. I lay there late into the night trying to sort out and make sense of all the events that had occurred. Unanswered questions still tormented me. Did Velma ever really love my grandfather? What had happened to their child? Cooper had said she went to St. Louis to visit an aunt. She could have given it up for adoption there. She might even have visited some unsanitary and unethical doctor who simply terminated the pregnancy. All she had cared about was her own reputation. Was there a way that I could discover the truth? The frustration was killing me, but I knew that if the old bitch wouldn't tell me, there was no way to know for sure.

One thing I *was* sure of, however, was that Coop and Gideon must have loved my grandfather. They saw that grandma and her child had their needs met, and they actually *became* the Booger, risking capture, jail, or even being shot to death so that nobody would suspect Tom Spates of being the culprit. They did it to protect my grandfather's memory. And now *they* were just a memory.

At that moment, I knew exactly what I had to do. I now understood what Gideon had meant when he said that I was here for a reason. It all made perfect sense. I jumped out of bed and got dressed. I tied Sawbuck up and told him to wait for me, hopped on my bike, and rode through the dark stillness. Within the hour, I was beating on the walls of Wallace and Velma's house. I would do it just one time. Just so people wouldn't put "two and three" together. Besides, it would give everybody something to talk about after the funeral.

~

The next morning the phone awakened me. I heard my mother pick it up.

"Hello … well, hello, Nelda. How are you? … Oh, I'm sorry to hear that you're not feeling well. I hope you get better soon … Hold on. I'll get him."

I was already at her side. She handed me the phone and went back in the kitchen.

"Hi, Nelda."

"Oh, my God, Lonnie. You are not going to believe this. Oh, my God."

"Calm down, Nelda. What's the matter?"

"You have to come over here right now!"

"What's wrong?"

"Just get your behind over here as soon as you can!"

"Okay, calm down. I'll be there in a few minutes."

We hung up, and I dressed quickly and went into the kitchen.

"Good mornin', Lonnie. Breakfast is ready. Sit down and eat," grandma said.

"Good mornin'. I can't eat right now. I'm going over to Nelda's."

"What's the hurry?" my mother asked.

"I don't know, but she insisted that I come right now."

"Well, just eat you a biscuit before you go," grandma said. "With some of that good ham and striped gravy."

She talked me into it. I sat down at the table as my mother poured me a mug of coffee.

"Miss Martha Davis stopped by early this mornin'," she said, "and she told us that the Booger came back last night."

I nearly dropped my cup at her pronouncement as emotions impossible to describe surged through me. I hoped the way I felt wasn't showing on my face.

"Lonnie, are you all right? You look pale."

"I'm okay, mama." I said after finally swallowing the bit of biscuit that had lodged in my throat. "Did Miss Martha say anything else about the Booger?"

"No, just that it came back. I know you have an interest in that. You've asked just about everybody in town about it. Did you ever talk to Wallace?"

"Uh … no, I haven't."

"He'd be the guy to talk to, don't you think?

"Yeah … I guess."

When I realized that no one suspected me, I was engulfed by a sense of peace. I felt like I had completed my mission. I had insured that the identity of the Booger was protected and, at the same time, felt close to the grandfather I never knew.

"Here's a couple of eggs, cooked just the way you like 'em," grandma said as she set a plate in front of me.

"I really don't have time, grandma," I said as I dug in.

"Ain't nothin' more important than a good breakfast," she laughed.

I was working on my fourth biscuit when the phone rang.

"Hello?" I said after taking the receiver from grandma.

"Why are you still there? Come over here *right now*!"

"What's going on, Nelda? Why do I have to be in a hurry?"

"You'll find out when you get here. Now, get over here, Lonnie!"

I assured her I was on my way and hung up. I yelled goodbye and went out the front door. Gideon's empty chair sat in the exact spot he had left it. Even with the many visitors who had stopped by, the chair had not been moved. Everyone seemed afraid to touch it. I felt the urge to sit in it, thinking that maybe I might see the world the way he saw it. But I would first have to be kicked in the head.

I jumped on my bike and took off with Sawbuck leading the way like he knew where we were going. He hadn't even commented on the fact that I had not fed him breakfast. It was a warm, summer morning with silver-winged dragonflies dancing in midair and a pair of buzzards circling high off to my left. The smell of honeysuckle drifted on the wind, and the trees were alive with bird songs. But my mind was cluttered with thoughts of the incredible events of the last few days, and I couldn't appreciate the beauty around me.

Nelda was standing in the front yard when I rode up. She had been crying.

"What's wrong, Nelda? What happened?"

"Everything's okay. Let's go inside."

"Why? What in the world is going on?"

"All of your questions will be answered, Lonnie. I promise."

She turned and walked to the back door and motioned for me to come. I followed her into the sunlit kitchen where her mother, Miss Debbie, and Velma Summers were seated at the table. Both of them had also been crying. I stopped just inside the door and stared.

"Hello, Lonnie," Miss Debbie said with a weak smile. "Thanks for coming so quickly. You know Velma here, don't you?"

All I could do was nod my head.

"Hello, Lonnie," Velma said. "Please come in and sit down. I want to talk to you."

The room spun a few times as I made my way to one of the oak chairs and sat down.

"Would you like something to drink, Lonnie? Coffee, orange juice?" Nelda asked.

I wondered if they had any whiskey. "A cup of coffee, please."

She set about pouring a cup while I looked at Miss Debbie and Velma. It was obvious that they had been weeping but didn't appear to be sad.

"Lonnie," Velma said, "you asked me a question yesterday, and I want to answer it."

She reached over and patted Miss Debbie's arm. "This is what happened to my baby. This is your grandfather's daughter."

It was like someone had knocked the wind out of me. I glanced up at Nelda as she set the cup in front of me. She looked as stunned as I felt. Our eyes met and a world of communications passed between us in that instant.

"I know this comes as a shock, Lonnie," Velma continued, "but I must tell you what happened. All I've revealed so far is that Debbie is my daughter because I want all of you to hear what I'm gonna tell, and I only want to tell it once. I have been under a curse all these years for keepin' this secret." She dabbed her eyes with a napkin. "But before I tell you, I must ask you a question, Lonnie. How in the world did you know about me and your grandfather?"

I felt the panic rising into my chest. How could I answer her? I was frantically searching my mind for a response when she let me off the hook.

"Oh, I guess it don't matter how you know," she said. "I gotta tell you the truth anyway … all of it. I have not had a minute's peace in all these years."

She was overcome with emotion, and Miss Debbie moved her chair closer and put an arm around her. Nelda sat down in the chair across from me and avoided eye contact.

"Your grandfather," Velma said after regaining her composure, "was the love of my life. And I know that he loved me. I wanted to spend my life with him. I wanted to have his children. But my father hated him and wouldn't allow me to see him. I had to sneak around to be with him."

"Why did your father hate him?" Miss Debbie asked.

"Because he said Tom was wild and dangerous and ran around with married women, and there was no way he was goin' to let me ruin my life. And it didn't help that Tom never made a secret of the fact that he couldn't stand my father either."

"How did your mother feel?" Miss Debbie asked as she rubbed Velma's back.

"Mama died when I was six. I barely remember her. My father raised me, and I felt like I had to do whatever he asked me to. I tried real hard to get him to let me see Tom, but he refused to even let me talk to him. And then, when I found out I was … gonna have a baby … I nearly lost my mind. I didn't know what to do. I thought about just killin' myself and be done with it, but I was scared I would go straight to hell. When I told Tom about it, he wanted us to get married right then. He said we could work things out with my father. But I knew that couldn't happen," she pressed two fingers to her lips and was silent for a long moment. "I'm sorry, may I have some more coffee?"

Miss Debbie got up and refilled the cup. "Did you tell your father about the baby?"

"I had to. Either that or run off somewhere by myself. I was shamed and humiliated. And not just for me, but Tom, too. I knew what people would say about him. He already had a … reputation … around town. I was goin' insane and didn't know which end was up, and it only got worse when I told my father. He went crazy, and I thought he was gonna have a stroke. Lord, I will never forget that day." Velma bowed her head as sobs shook through her.

The lump in my throat wouldn't allow me to swallow. A clock chimed somewhere in the house. This was not the same woman who had glared at me with such evil as she slammed the door in my face. She was now broken and contrite, and her tears of suffering washed out any anger I had felt toward her.

"Why didn't you marry Tom in spite of your father? What could he have done? At least no one would have known anything," Miss Debbie asked.

"That's what I wanted to do, but my father would have none of it. He said he would rather see me … dead. I realized his hatred for Tom was so deep that he'd never give in. Besides, I was so far along that when the math was done, everybody would know that I was pregnant when we married. I know it sounds foolish, but back then I thought there was no greater shame than to be with child out of wedlock. It broke my heart. What was I to do? I didn't want to humiliate myself, *and* my father, *and* Tom. I felt so guilty I couldn't stand it. The whole thing was my fault. So, I did what daddy told me to do."

She blew her nose quietly and took a deep breath.

"He sent me to Camden and put me up in a hotel under a fake name. He told everybody that I had gone to St. Louis to visit an aunt that didn't exist. He set up the adoption for the baby and everything, so after I give birth, she was taken from me. I just cain't tell you how I felt. I had carried that child for nine months … and I didn't even get to see her face." She reached over and stroked Miss Debbie's hair. "I've missed so much."

"How did you find out what happened to me?" Miss Debbie asked.

"I didn't find out for a long time," she sighed deeply, "and this is the part of the story … that is the hardest. When I got home, my father had already arranged for me to marry Wallace, who was a good man but … I didn't love him. We had a horrible argument, and he called me such vile names … and said it was my fault, and that I was just a common whore … so … I finally gave in and married Wallace. Tom was still overseas, and I was so miserable I wanted to die."

She again broke down, and Miss Debbie hugged her close and encouraged her to continue.

"And then, Tom came home," she said as tears spilled silently down her cheeks. "The first time I saw him going into Willie's I thought I would die. I loved him so much … but I was now married. What could I do? I stayed home all the time, so I wouldn't risk running into him. Then, one day he showed up at my door. Oh, how my heart was breakin' … I just cain't put it in words. But I had to be strong. I had to be hard with him. I couldn't let him get to me. He wanted to know what happened to the child. But at the time, I didn't know. But I let him think I did and swore that I would never tell him if he said a word about it to anybody. It was the only thing I could think of to get him to keep it a secret. But if *you* know about it, Lonnie, then he must have told *somebody*."

She stared at me for a few moments as if seeking some kind of answer then looked away.

"Then came that *messenger of Satan*," she said with a slight tremor in her voice, "beatin' on the walls of my house. I hate to tell you this, Lonnie, but at first I was sure it was your grandfather that was doin' it. I was more upset than scared. Then, he … was killed … and it came back … and I was so scared that I couldn't breathe. And it went on … year after year after year. And then … this is gonna be the hardest part to tell … then my father got real sick, and he told me somethin' just before he died …"

She was breathing deeply as she struggled with the demons that had been tormenting her. I sipped the now tepid coffee and looked over at Nelda. She had been watching me but turned to Velma as soon as our eyes met.

"What did your father tell you, Miss Velma?" Nelda asked.

"Well, the first thing he said was that he had to get some things off his chest. He said … he had got all the letters that Tom had sent me while he was overseas and burned them. All the words that Tom had wrote to me … words that I never got to read. I was mad as a wet hen. He had no right to do that. No right at all. Then, he told me … he said … that he …"

Again, she broke down. Miss Debbie held her close and murmured "it's all right" over and over. "Just take your time, Miss Velma. We've got plenty of time."

"Oh my, this is hard," she finally said. "I'm just gonna tell it like it happened. He called me close and said … that he was the one who killed Tom."

"What?" I blurted. "Your father, Elmer Thompson, killed my grandfather?"

"That's what he told me. He said, 'It was me that caused the death of Tom Spates. I killed him, and I have lived with that all these years. I was afraid he was gonna hurt and shame you, so I had to do it. I wanted to tell you before I died.' That was his exact words."

"Did he say if anybody helped him?" I asked.

"No, that was his only statement. He was dead ten minutes later. And I've had to live with *that* all these years."

"Bless your heart. What a heavy load," Miss Debbie said.

"Why didn't you go to the police?" I asked.

"For what? It had happened years before. And now both of them were dead. What good would it have done anybody? And I was afraid that if I told the police, my secret would be exposed. In fact, knowin' that my father was a murderer made me more determined to keep the whole thing to myself."

"When did you find out about me?" Miss Debbie asked.

"My father left me ten thousand dollars in his will that Wallace didn't know about. I used that money to bribe … uh … somebody … to give me the name of the people that had adopted you. I found out as much as I could about you, and I've tried to keep up with you through the years. I was tickled pink when y'all took this church. I got to see you every Sunday and Wednesday night. But it was hard to keep from tellin' you who I was."

"What made you come forward now?" Nelda asked.

"Well, after Lonnie's visit, I was pretty shook up. After all those years, I was sure that nobody knew anything about my baby. But here comes this kid and tells me he knows all about it. I couldn't stop thinkin' about it. Then, last night, that hellish poundin' started again, and I suddenly realized that … if I would just tell the truth about what happened, maybe all this torment would stop. So, I made up my mind to come over here first thing this mornin' and tell y'all everything. And at that moment, the bangin' stopped … and I somehow feel in my heart that it won't never come back."

We sat quiet for a while and absorbed all this information. Velma looked completely drained as she took a nibble of buttered toast.

"Lonnie, I want to tell Ruby Jo and Miss Birdie about this," she said. "Whatever happens, I want them to know. Will you ask them if I can come over this afternoon?"

"Sure."

"Thank you. Just call me and let me know what time. I have to go home now and tell Wallace. I wanted y'all to be the first to know."

"How do you think he'll take the news?" Miss Debbie asked.

"I don't know. I haven't been much of a wife to him. He's suffered because of this, too. I deserve whatever I get. Do y'all have any more questions?"

We all looked at each other and shrugged.

"Well, if you think of anything, just let me know. Thank you for your hospitality, Debbie."

"You're welcome, Miss Velma."

"Oh, honey. I know you cain't just call me mama, but could you try *Mama Velma*?"

"Well, sure, we could try that … Mama Velma," Miss Debbie said as she hugged her.

We followed Velma out to her car and watched as she drove away. Miss Debbie went back inside, leaving Nelda and I alone.

"Wow," I said. "I feel numb."

"Me too. Remember when I said that I felt like our relationship would change?"

"Boy, were you right. It sure enough changed. I'm uh … glad that we, uh … didn't do anything that …"

"Yeah, me too."

We stood there in the awkward silence for a few moments.

"Well," I said, "I guess I better go prepare my mother and grandma for this bombshell."

She stuck out her hand. "Since we're no longer kissin' cousins, I guess we'll have to shake hands."

I took her hand in mine and wondered if she was experiencing the same squeamish feeling in the pit of her stomach that I was. "At least we'll see each other at family reunions."

"Yeah, I guess that's something to look forward to. I need to go in. I'll see you later, Lonnie."

"Okay, see ya."

I took off on my bike still feeling a little dizzy. Even Rod Serling couldn't have crafted such a strange tale. I aim a rifle at my father one day, and the next thing I know I've stepped through into another dimension, where a few dozen words from a brain-damaged old man leads me on a journey, both physical and spiritual, to the solution of a decades-old mystery. And, at the same time, discover brand new relatives. I felt honored to have been chosen by whatever powers were involved, but I knew that nobody would ever believe me. I looked over my shoulder and saw Nelda walking to the house. I wondered if Annette would take me back.

THE END